D1002637

Anna At Last

A Present / Past Saga

by

Cherisse M Havlicek

DEDICATION

I have been very lucky to have loved and been loved my whole life. I dedicate this love story to all those that showed me it was possible.

First my parents, Andrew and Doris Basile, they gave me nonstop love as they shaped me into the woman that I have become. I miss my father terribly, since his passing, but I will always be his Sugar-babe and he will always be my Filet of Fishes. My mother is still my best friend and I talk with her daily, even though she lives in Miami. I do not know what I would do without her.

Then, I fell in love in 1980 to a Chicago version of a Miami Vice guy, named Allan Havlicek. He was a Chicago Police Officer. I have been lucky enough to be loved and supported by him since the day I met him.

Thanks to my wonderful patient husband, we are blessed with two children through fertility treatments. Arthur and Alisse, now grown, are both blessings from above when they aren't giving me gray hairs. I dedicate this, also, to them so that they know that if you have a dream, even if it is sleeping for over 40 years, it can be done!

ACKNOWLEDGMENTS

I must thank, first and foremost, the Good Lord, for leading me down this path. His guidance led me to find the towns of EL Dorado and Lawrence in Kansas that have become so important to my life. I truly believe that he has picked me up and given me this passion for something when other things in my life screamed – give up!

I should thank my family. They have had to hear many parts of this novel a hundred times and I am sure they would have liked to have said 'enough!' Thank you, husband Allan and my children Arthur and Alisse, and my mother Doris.

I want to thank my co-workers at the antique store for reading and encouraging me to continue. Thank you Susan B., Sherry H., Mary Ruth B., Jan and her Mike J., Cyndy W., and Rebecca C. who led me to a writer's group, which led me to my now friend and editor, Marnie Heyn.

I need to thank all my first readers prior to publication. Carol Diane J., Leslie T., Lori L., Lisa C., Dorothy Jean R., Renate K., Sue A., Doreen G., Judy B., Evelina V., Julia V., Julie H., Aunt Anna Marie M., Aunt Marilyn P.,

I need to thank the EL Dorado Historical Society for their help in locating business and street names from 1935, and letting me read a year's worth of 1935 newspapers during my two-day visit. I'd like thank the Lawrence Visitors Center, I talked to a wonderful gal, Susie N., who showed me a part of Lawrence's history that became the fodder for my next book in the series, *A Lewis Legacy*.

Thank you one and all. If I have forgotten to name someone, please charge it to my head and not my heart. I am still thankful for you, nonetheless.

.....

ONE

The First Tuesday of September, 1935
At the Johnson Family Farms Tomato Field
In EL Dorado, Kansas.

"Keep it moving! You, fill that bushel. I want tomatoes to the top. Don't break off the stems with the tomatoes! Don't stare at me. Ain't no breaks here. Women! Not worth the money to keep them," gripes the middle-aged foreman with his hands on his hips and shaking his head. "At least, you young ones are worth somethin'." He moves down the row and gives a little slap to a young woman's bottom. She ignores him.

"A course, ya can't tell much by those pants you're a-wearin'. Ain't you got nuthin' tighter?" He reaches down to feel Melinda's shape through her work pants. He moves his hand from the fullness of her seat, down to her thighs, then back up toward her inner thigh.

"It'd be nice to see a little leg while I'm watching the work," Croner sneers. Melinda straightens up to her full height of five foot two inches. His hand drops to his side. She turns towards him with an evil smile on her lips, as a trail of sweat trickles down between her ample breasts.

She whispers, "Come closer," her bright blue eyes twinkling. He moves toward her eagerly. He'd heard she's not as naïve as her years. He'd also heard she traded favor for favor. Maybe this is his lucky day! The idea brings a twitch to his sweaty brow.

He's in position to hear anything she might whisper. She raises her arm as if to hug him. He sees it coming but can't move fast enough. She slaps his face with a juicy over-ripe tomato. As seeds and juice are dripping down his face, she leans in and whispers, "You keep your grimy hands to yourself, you old bastard. If I want OR need anything from you, I'll let you know. I'll make the first move, got it?" She pounds her pointed finger into his chest.

The other workers can't hear her words with the hot wind blowing, but they see her hit him and they start to snicker. They've all wanted to do that to one foreman or another. Only Melinda would dare!

His hand raises to slap her but her smile stops him. Maybe she'll let him know when she wants to do some business. Dirty Business. So, he takes a soiled handkerchief out of his pocket and wipes his face. "I'll get back to you . . . later." He warns as he moves through the rows of plants.

"You do that." Melinda calls after him. The other workers start to clap. Melinda grabs her baggy pants at the thighs and does a quick courtesy to her rows of admirers.

1

Taking off the scarf that holds up her long brown hair, she runs her fingers through it once or twice facing the wind so that it blows her hair back, then she ties the thick straight strands back into it. She looks down at her outfit, oversized work pants and a sweaty print blouse that are faded and dirty.

One day I'll have beautiful clothes. Melinda's thoughts wander. She won't pick someone else's rotted crops or associate with scum. The foreman moves on to his next victim, yelling. Melinda squints for clearer vision. She realizes that the girl in the large sunhat is her sister Anna, but Pa is there. *He won't let anyone pick on Anna. Anna can't take care of herself. She's always leaning on someone. That isn't for me.* Melinda thinks*. I can take care of myself. Anna has always been the favorite, the spoiled daughter. Perfect Anna never gets into trouble. She's very shy and naïve.* Melinda watches her father try to shield his eldest daughter from the verbal abuse.

"Put your back to it, girl. Let those small ones be. Just pick the big red ones, ya idiot! Ain't you never picked tomatoes b'fore?" Moving down the row, he continues to berate all those hunched over. "I've had 'nuf of you ig'rant workers."

"Don't listen, child. We won't be doing this long." The old man next to Anna comforts her. "We'll have our own farm again, real soon. So, don't fret now." He smiles nervously as lines force their way through his tanned cheeks.

"I know, Pa, I'm not worried. Croner doesn't bother me. You sent us to school back up in Hope, while we had the farm. I don't mind helping when you need me. Someday, we'll get it all back." Anna squeezes his hand.

He notices how scratched and dirty her fingers and palms are. They were so beautiful once. They were made for fine silk gloves or caressing a beau, he thought. Anna is fair and needs to protect her skin from the sun. She has light wavy brown hair with red highlights, but dark brown eyes. He was still holding her hand as Melinda walks by, balancing her full bushel on her hips. *Now there's another real beauty wasted.* Melinda has dark brown hair and olive coloring with light blue eyes. He doesn't know how he could have made someone so beautiful, but he's made two of them, and they're such opposites. *Both daughters are prettier than anyone out here in the field. But look where he's got them. Nowhere, windswept Kansas.*

"You never hold my hands, Pa," Melinda retorts as she walks to the end of the field. She doesn't wait for a reply. Once her bushel gets weighed and her card punched, she'll take a break.

Standing in line at the weigh counter, Melinda's mind complains that tomatoes are the worse crop to pick. All the bending to pick these damn dirty plants, and those disgusting bugs! She can't stand this hot wind and heat, either! The wind bites your skin while the sun bakes the grime into it. She can fill one more bushel before quitting time. *But I've got to take a break!*

A short, scruffy old man with very little hair but a full white beard stands behind the weigh counter. He looks at the large dial. "Why, Melinda, you only got fifty cents worth here. You picked better this morning. Slowing down, huh?" He wipes the sweat off his head with the back of his hand and dries it on his overalls.

"Let me see that, you old coot!" She says as she tries to step behind the counter. Before she can look at the dial, the old man tips the scale so her tomatoes join the others. He smiles, showing some missing teeth.

"Sorry, Chile, rules are rules. You ain't supposed to see. Now, do you want your card stamped for that fifty cents or do you want to forget you ever picked that bushel?"

She holds out her card. *That always happens*. She thinks. *Well, we aren't going to stand for this much longer. Pa knows that they're cheating us blind, but the crop is nearly done. We'll move on soon. We always move on soon.* She grabs her stamped card and heads over to the grassy area to lay in the shade.

Even through her work pants, Melinda could feel the coolness of the bladed grass, which was long and uncut. When the hot breeze passes through it, it immediately cools. She lies on her back in the long grass and tilts her head back to relax.

"Feels good, doesn't it?" She's not surprised by the strong male voice behind her. She moves onto her stomach. She knows who it's and shows no surprise. She eyes him affectionately.

"I know a lot of things that feel better. But out here in the field, this is as good as it gets. Don't you agree, Henry?" She rolls the question off her tongue as carefully as she can. Henry takes his work hat off and runs his hands through his long hair. His hat gets caught by the hot wind and flies to Melinda who catches it. Henry smiles as he reaches for it. As she hands it back, their hands touch. Both pause before moving. Their eyes lock into place as smiles slowly reach their lips. They need no words between them.

Melinda is strongly attracted to Henry. His virile form sends messages she doesn't want to ignore. He's much taller than she, and his smoldering gray eyes and silky deep voice drive her wild. She tried very hard to get his attention, as soon as their families were reunited, and she finally caught his eye. Growing up, it was always Anna and Henry. She'd been the annoying tag-a-long little sister. But things are different now. Henry looks at her as a woman. A woman he wants.

Melinda gets to her feet. She must get that last bushel in before quitting time.

"Melinda," Henry calls, getting to his feet. Standing next to her, he towers over her. "Meet me tonight? Can you get away?" He runs his fingers in his hair again, before replacing his hat.

Melinda simply nods.

"Good, meet me by the General store around ten. We can discuss old times?" Laughing, his gray eyes twinkled.

She silently nods again, and walks toward the rows. *Old times? There aren't any old times to discuss.* Henry was always with Anna, never with me, she thought. Grabbing an empty bushel, she goes back to picking.

"Pa, my bushel is full. I think I'll go get it weighed." Anna says as she picks up the bushel of tomatoes. She's taller than her younger sister by five inches. She has very pronounced cheekbones with small but plump lips.

"Okay, honey. I'll be along in a while."

Anna walks over to the line. It's long now, because everyone is anxious to get home. Anna shifts the heavy tomatoes to her other hip, then decides to put the bushel down between her feet. She takes her handkerchief out of her work pants, removes her hat to wipe her forehead and the back of her neck, while she shuffles forward pushing the bushel between her feet as she goes.

I swear, this work gets harder, instead of easier. Well, it could be worse, she thought. *The Lord has always provided. What was the quote from Job? The Lord giveth and the Lord taketh away? We know about things taken away.*

Anna sees Melinda in another line. *She works hard.* Anna thinks, as she struggles against the wind to put her hat back on. *She brings in about as much as Pa. Anna wishes she could help as much. As hard as she works, Melinda still brings in more than her. She wishes she could be as strong as her little sister. The 'Small but Mighty One' is what she called her when they were young. She still is. She doesn't need anyone to help her do anything. She's going to make it in this world, and she'll do it by herself. She's grown up faster than any of us. It seems so long ago that we were so happy on our farm. Has it been only four years since they took it?*

She gets her bushel weighed, card stamped, then goes over to the paymaster. He gives Anna her daily pay plus her monies due from her stamped card. She goes to the waiting area for the ride back to Camp.

She sees her baby brother coming toward her. She notices how tall he's getting. Suddenly, he steps in front of the setting sun, making Anna squint to keep track of him. She waves her sunhat to get his attention.

"Hi, Anna, finally getting' cool, isn't it? Thank goodness for sun downs, right?" Matthew jokes as they move forward in line. "It's great how a September day can cool off fast as the sun sets."

"How was your day, Matthew? Work hard?" Anna asks as she

ruffs up his dark brown wavy hair. He's already taller than her, but still looks like a puppy with big paws. You can tell he has more growing to do.

"Ya sure did. This heat didn't help. At least we didn't have an unreasonably strong wind today, just a hot one. How about you?" He asks as he runs his hands through his hair to finger comb the mess Anna has made of it.

"Not too bad. Look, here comes Pa and Melinda." Anna and Matthew step aside so they all can board together. The truck has a full canopy over it, and has two benches inside. They're lucky and all get seats.

"I wonder what Ma's making for supper," Matthew questions, rubbing his stomach. "I'm starved." As a teenager, he has no bottom to his stomach. Like Melinda, he has naturally dark tanned skin and very light blue eyes.

"I don't know but I hope she made a lot because I invited Henry and Frank for dinner," answers their father Judd, who has the original set of pale blue eyes.

"Mr. Harrick and you go a back a long way, don't you, Pa? I remember his farm back home in Hope wasn't far from ours. He lost his, too, right?" questions the fifteen-year-old Matthew.

"Yes, Matthew, he lost it, too. With his wife gone, he didn't care about the place. But the drought and dust storms did both our wheat crops in. We lasted a year longer. Frank and I grew up not far from each other and went through school together. He was my Best Man and I was his. So, yup, we go back a long way," Judd says as he leans back and loses himself in thought.

The truck driver puts the tail up on the truck. He gets behind the wheel and starts the engine. It coughs and chokes. He finally gets it into gear, and they start off with a jolt. The benches in the truck are loaded. There are, also, a dozen or more people standing in the center. As the truck gets underway, those standing get jostled and thrown around. They don't complain. They just grab whatever or whoever they can to keep from falling.

The truck makes its way down the long dirt roads until it finally stops at the farm camp store. Surprisingly, this camp is the best place Judd and his family have stayed at since losing their farm. It has two dozen or so Quonset huts and a General Store. Four huts share one outhouse, but each hut has a hand pump in the kitchen. A giant leaky old barn serves as their church.

The truck pulls up to the General Store and stops. The driver gets out and lets the gate down. All the workers slowly climb out. They're tired and sore from bending. The men help their womenfolk down. Some go into the store, but most start their last leg of their journey home.

"Does Ma need anything from the store?" asks Matthew as he helps Anna down from the truck. Judd, who has just helped Melinda down, is scratching his head in thought. He's a tall man with sprinkles of black in his already grayed hair. He still looks strong, yet he looks aged and beaten by money problems and the sun.

"Your Ma didn't say anything to me. If she needs something, one of us can come back. Ain't that far," Judd answers.

Matthew leans in closer to Anna. "That means me." Anna nods in agreement. Whenever Ma or Pa say 'one of us', it usually means Matthew. He doesn't mind. He's a good kid, she thinks, as she puts her arm up around his neck, and gives him a peck on the cheek. It's always crowded this time of day at the store. Anna noticed that the young cute store manager likes to take his time when it comes to waiting on Melinda. Maybe if Ma needs something, she'll suggest Melinda go, instead.

TWO

The First Tuesday in September
Legacy Plantation, over 100 Miles Away,
In Lawrence, Kansas, just outside of Topeka

It's late morning and the Colonel is finally dressed and Rosanne is helping him go down the stairs. She had to help him dress, too. He was once a tall robust man, she can tell. His skin now hangs on him like his oversized clothes. He's totally gray at seventy-six. Rosanne has come to love this simple, continuously confused man. When she first came here, she was the one who needed constant attention. She couldn't begin to repay the kindness that she's been shown. Unfortunately, as she has gotten healthier, the Colonel has declined. He was there for her when she was at her lowest point. Now, while Carolyn has many other duties, Carolyn's grandfather, the Colonel, has become Rosanne's.

Rosanne remembers his stories of how he was in the Cavalry in the Kansas' Cheyenne War of 1879 when he was just twenty years old. He must have been a sight on his horse! Back when she was too sick to get out of bed, in too much pain to care if she lived or died, he told her about the love of his life, Julia. They had one child, a boy named Kevin. Kevin and his wife died young in an accident and left their children to be raised by the Colonel and Julia. They're his beloved Carolyn and her adorable brother Joshua. Those stories made her forget about her pain and loss. That man and his stories, saved her life.

Rosanne is making the Colonel, his favorite breakfast. Carolyn is up and out of the house for several hours now, but Colonel William Clyde Lewis keeps his own schedule. So, his breakfast is usually at about eleven o'clock. She's scrambling his eggs with fried bologna. Somedays, he prefers oatmeal, but today it's eggs.

"What are we doing today, Rosanne?"

"I'm not sure, Colonel, what do you want to do?"

"I'd like to go to the Market with Carolyn."

Carolyn is going to the market with her farm foreman with a truckload of tomatoes. She is pleased that the crop has been so abundant. The constant drought of the last few years, has ruined many smaller farms, but Legacy Plantation has very diverse crops, which helps. Carolyn used her engineering degree to design and set up a rotating wand type sprinkler and irrigation system that's kept them from ruin.

"We discussed that, Colonel. Carolyn is going with her foreman Joseph and his assistant Jose. There's no room for you in the truck

7

cab."

"But I'm the one that needs to be at the Market. They'll try to cheat her if the Colonel isn't by her side. She's only a little girl!"

"Colonel, Carolyn is a grown woman. You have taught her very well, and there's no man that will ever cheat Carolyn. She's smarter than most of them and has your 'don't tread on me' attitude. Most men are intimidated by her, if I may say."

"They are? I need to meet this Carolyn that you are talking about. She sounds like someone I'd like." The Colonel has done it again. He follows the train of the conversation just so far. Then the train jumps the tracks and he's confused.

She has made him two eggs with one slice of cut-up fried bologna but as usual, he has left half of it in his bowl. He calls his little dog, who is always waiting for food. He puts the bowl down for the dog to finish the other half.

"Colonel, how many times have we told you to finish your own food and not to feed Robbie. He's overweight as it is, and you need to gain!"

Each month of the last six months, he has lost a few pounds, which makes no sense. He's a cake and ice cream junkie. All his calories, tend to be empty ones. If he's served something healthy, he usually eats only a small portion of it and then reaches for something sweet a few minutes later.

The Colonel gives her a knowing smile and says, "I forgot." He loves to use this excuse when he does something against the rules. He always says it with a smile, so you know he means just the opposite.

"Rosanne, can we go outside for a little while? I'd like to sit in the sun. I don't know why I can't go with Carolyn? They're going to cheat her if I'm not with her, you know."

"I'm almost done in the kitchen. We can go outside after that."

"Okay, I'm going to go in my chair until you call me. I'm tired."

This once vibrant man only sleeps three to four hours at a time but he does this around the clock. Rosanne tried to be awake during his awake hours but that was too much for her already frail and taxed body. *But, now isn't the time to think about that.*

Now, Carolyn has an attendant that works an eleven p.m. to seven a.m. shift so Rosanne can get a few good hours of sleep. At night, the Colonel likes to roam around the six-bedroom home that he'd built for his Julia and pick things up. He walks around with them then puts them down with no memory of touching them. It was very hard, at first, trying to figure out why the dining room table flowers were on the staircase. Or why the milk would be out of the icebox. Sometimes he'd decide something was broke and would take it apart to try to fix it but would go to bed with things left in pieces. The attendant keeps him from doing this.

When Rosanne is done cleaning up, she uses the bathroom right off the kitchen. *It's so nice to have indoor plumbing and this home has five bathrooms*! Two downstairs and three upstairs. She checks herself in the mirror. Her scars are almost invisible now. She cannot believe that Carolyn, a total stranger, paid her medical bills, just like the good Samaritan in the bible. The doctors did an amazing job. She can look in the mirror now and not be sickened by the swelling, the bruises, or the cuts. She loves her new hair style. It looks just like the girls in Hollywood! Her natural waves, go perfectly into the finger waves which are so popular. After the 'accident', the hospital shaved off her long beautiful hair so that they could sew up the many cuts and gashes that were all over her head and body.

She walks through the formal dining room to get to the sitting room and the Colonel was in his chair, wrapped in a blanket to keep warm, and sound asleep. The room is spacious and cozy and has a full wall brick fireplace. The Colonel's chair is to the left of the hearth and a matching chair to the right. A tufted couch sits across from it. She goes to his side and shook him. It's her job to try to keep him awake during the day.

"Colonel, time to take a walk outside. It's still very warm for September. Afterward, let's sit in the sun together," she says as she takes a book out from the wall of books behind the couch. He gets up with a little help from her.

"My bones are aching fierce today." He says as he moves stiffly and slowly.

"I know, Colonel, the sun will help with that."

After they take a walk around the house, they sit on the attached back veranda. Sitting in the rocker, the Colonel lifts his face up to the sun. "I love sitting in the sun now. I hated the hot sun when I worked the fields. Turned my skin to burnt rawhide. Is it time for Joshua to come home from school?"

"Joshua is in the city at Washburn University. We won't see him until he comes home for a weekend. I don't know if that will be this one or the next. You know he never stays away for long."

"College already? They grew up too fast. Don't you do that, Rosanne, okay?"

"I'm already grown." She laughs.

"Are you?" He squints at her. "I guess you are. I never thought of you that way because you needed so much help when you came here." His little dog, Robbie, has jumped up on the rocker with him. He twirls arounds three times before settling down on the Colonel's lap.

"I know, and I can never thank you enough for all that you've done."

"Rosanne, how old are you?" Rosanne is always troubled by this question. *A person should know how old they are. Why don't I?*

"The doctors think I'm about twenty," she says, but thinks, *where was I for those twenty years? My 'accident' cost me the knowledge of those years and I may never get it back.*

"How old is my Joshua? I keep thinking he's a twelve-year-old boy. They don't take twelve year olds in college, do they?

"No, they don't. Joshua is twenty-one now, and just started his senior year."

Rosanne is sitting on a lounge chair in the shade with her new book. She has yet to open it. She's just enjoying sitting in the very warm extended summer day. Her fair skin doesn't tolerate the hot sun. She has very large dark brown eyes. Her light brown hair is naturally wavy and has finally grown out, so she looks like a normal person. It's been a year since her accident, and she has worn scarves on her head whenever in public to hide her shaved head. Right now, she feels good and finally can say, she looks good, too.

They sit on the outside veranda for two hours. Now it's time to make the Colonel some lunch. She brings him inside to his chair in the sitting room and goes in the kitchen to make him a half of a sandwich. The kitchen is very spacious. The large gas stove has six burners. The large two-door refrigerator was to the left of the stove. Across from the stove is a large rectangle white marble counter that has five padded stools around three of the sides. It always reminded Rosanne of a fancy diner. She puts the sandwich on the counter and puts the kettle on for hot tea. Then she goes to him to see if he needs to use the bathroom, before eating.

Rosanne sits and has her half sandwich with him. The Colonel is talking about his Julia again, it's as if she's in the next room. "Wait until you meet her, you'll love her, she's your size and height. She keeps her hair long and uncut but twisted up on her head. When she lets it down for the night, it reaches to her bottom. You've met her, haven't you?"

"No, Colonel, she passed before I came here," Rosanne says. Carolyn's instructions were, to always be honest with her grandfather. If he asks, tell the truth. If he's just talking, let him talk.

"Oh, that's right. I keep forgetting." He doesn't get upset when he hears that she's gone, just a little sad. "How long has it been?" He breaks off a large piece of bread from his sandwich for Robbie. Rosanne ignores the transgression, this time.

"I think Joshua was eleven years old. So, she been gone ten years." Rosanne puts her hand on his. "I'm sorry for your loss."

"That's the only good thing about forgetting things - you forget they're gone. She's still so alive, to me."

"I can see that, Colonel. Tell me how you met her, again."

Rosanne cannot hear this story enough. They were childhood sweethearts, but her family moved away. He'd gone into the Cavalry and met someone else and almost married her. Julia was visiting his mother, and they started writing, he immediately broke up with the other woman, and married his Julia as soon as he saw her again.

Rosanne felt this was a familiar story, not just because he'd told it to her multiple times, but because it felt it was like her story. Ugh! Every time she tries to remember something before her accident, she gets a headache from trying.

She looks up at the kitchen clock, "Carolyn should be getting back soon." She was careful not to mention the market again.

"Time to start our dinner." She starts pulling out the apples and potatoes to cut. She likes doing all the prep work ahead of time so that everything is handy during the actual cooking of the meal.

A short while later, Robbie starts barking. "That must be Carolyn," she says aloud. She can hear Carolyn's other half, Rocco, returning Robbie's bark. He's a large German Shepherd that accompanies her wherever she goes about the Plantation.

This morning, Rosanne baked some special treats for this wonderful dog. She spoils him whenever she can. She wouldn't be alive if not for this intuitive dog finding her.

About a year ago, Rocco was beside Carolyn as she drove through the back acres of the land that they owned. Rocco somehow knew Rosanne lay there hurt. He barked and scratched at the door, as if something was wrong, so Carolyn stopped the car. Rocco jumped out the window on the passenger side.

He ran to the crumpled brown mass that was dumped like the trash. He sniffed, then ran back to Carolyn. She couldn't tell what it was and was hesitant on approaching it. Rocco left her side again and ran back to the naked, broken, barely alive body to lick her face. *My face.* Rosanne doesn't remember any of this. Carolyn told her this part of the story. Her memories start with waking up in the hospital in such pain, that she wanted to die.

Her neck was fractured in two spots and her shoulders were both broken, as well as her nose. They said that her brain was swollen and bleeding on the inside. They didn't know why she survived her injuries. Carolyn was at her bedside, but it took months before she got out of the hospital. Carolyn came and sat and prayed, almost daily.

Rosanne is almost done prepping for dinner, when Rocco bounded through the kitchen door, jumping on Rosanne and giving her several big wet kisses.

Directly behind Rocco is Carolyn. She has her arms loaded with groceries. She's shorter than Rosanne's 5' 7" by two inches. She has reddish brown hair that she wears in a short bob, and her eyes are hazel green. She's flushed from unloading the groceries. She's heavier but still

11

a voluptuous woman with bold features and has a no-nonsense bearing.

Rosanne says, "What's all this? You went to market to sell not buy!"

"I couldn't help it, Rosanne, I love the market this time of year! I bought cabbage, green beans, sunflowers, zucchini and cucumbers."

"Are my green beans and cucumbers different varieties? And why did you buy sunflowers? You have two acres of them *near* ready!"

"Silly girl, they're indeed, different varieties," she says as she points to the bags of veggies, "and because these heads ARE ready!" Carolyn holds up the large sunflower head and is as excited as a school kid; instead of the twenty-three-year-old that she is. "What are we having for dinner?"

"I was going to fry up some pork chops and apples and make my cheesy potatoes with them and a salad."

"Girl, I don't know how you do it!" Carolyn had the same cook in the house since she was a little girl. Josie was over seventy years old and was getting frail, so Rosanne started to help her, then slowly took over the cooking completely, so Josie could retire. Carolyn was amazed that the girl who didn't know her name, could cook for the household and a dozen field hands, without breaking a sweat.

"I think I've always loved to cook. It's like I didn't have to learn it, I knew it."

"We are all forever grateful for it."

"I can cook a thousand meals for you, Carolyn, and my debt wouldn't come near to being paid off. I would have been dead multiple times, if it wasn't for Rocco, you, and the Colonel."

Carolyn is putting the vegetables away and says without emotion, "That's what you always say. I'm so tired of hearing it." Rosanne turns to look at her, surprised.

"Carolyn, you don't think I'm serious?"

"Yes, of course, you are serious. But enough already."

"Carolyn, sweetheart, I think we are having our first real fight." Rosanne gives her a pretend pout. Carolyn starts to laugh and then laughs harder, until her whole belly starts to shake.

"See, this, is why I keep you around. You are so good for me. I was never close to other girls and didn't have a sister." She pauses, and she puts her hand, lightly, on Rosanne's arm then adds, "until now."

Rosanne just responds with her infectious smile.

THREE

The First Tuesday in September, 1935 cont.
Johnson Family Farms Encampment
In EL Dorado, Kansas.

Judy Masters is taking a second loaf of bread out of the oven when her family comes home. Home is a strange word. This Quonset hut isn't their home. The farm was 'home'. Their hut has four rooms; the kitchen, the girl's room, the living room where Matthew sleeps and her parents room. Agreed, it's larger than what they were used to recently, but they can never call it home.

"Hello, Ma." Judd greets her as he walks straight into the kitchen. "Smells good, what's to eat?"

"Stew, again." She answers. She looks up from her slicing. "How did your day go?" Before Judd can answer, Matthew is in the kitchen trying to steal a slice of the freshly baked bread.

"Get your dirty hands out of here, young man," she says as she swats his hands. "Do you want to spoil your supper?"

Matthew has already given up the idea and is pumping for water when she adds, "Wash up and help me get supper on the table. Can't you see your Pa is tired? Judd Andrew Masters…" She looks at him quizzically. "Is there something you need to tell me?"

He nods guiltily. He knows when she uses all his names, he's in trouble. Before he can answer, she says with a smile, "Let me guess, you invited Frank and his boy over for dinner?" She pauses, then explains, "Frank stuck his head in our window, around noon" as she points to the open kitchen window, "and asked what he was getting for dinner tonight. Luckily, I bought extra potatoes at the Camp Store this morning and I baked a second loaf of bread."

By this time, the girls are at the pump washing up. The three siblings set the table in just a few minutes, then they go and change out of their dirty work clothes.

"Is it suppertime, yet?" Asks a face through the kitchen window.

"It's all ready, Frank, come on in," invites Judd.

"I can't this window is too small!" laughs Frank, as he disappears, from view. A few seconds later both he and Henry walk through the door.

"One of these days, Frank," starts Judy, "your gonna try to stick your head in that window but you'll go right through glass instead." Everyone laughs. "You think, I'm kidding. The way you sneak up on me all the time, it'll serve you right."

The handsome older man goes behind her and speaks over her head. "Judd, where is your lovely wife tonight? I hear her but I don't see her." Then he stoops down and puts his arms around her waist and lifts her off the ground. "Why Judy! I didn't see you down there," He acts surprised that she's in his arms. Only after everyone stops laughing, does he put her down. She grabs a wooden spoon off the table and turns around.

"Now look here, Frank, didn't your Mama ever teach you to respect a lady?" She demands as she waves her spoon. "Well, you ain't too big to learn that lesson NOW," she warns as she swings around and starts to hit his bottom sharply with the spoon.

"Judd, call your woman off me." Frank pleads as seriously as he can. Everyone was laughing very hard.

Judd explains, "You know that isn't how it works 'round here, Frank. I try to give her anything that'll give her pleasure. And right now, she's getting' a great deal of pleasure whooping the tar out of you." Then he adds, "And isn't costing me a cent, so that gives me greater pleasure!"

Judy stops and walks over to her husband and stands next to him. "Thank you Frank, that was real nice." She runs her hand over her hair to see if any strands had fallen out from her tight bun.

The children think this is the funniest thing. Even when they were little, their Ma never hit them. She'd just say 'wait 'till your Pa comes home'. She never raised her voice to her husband. The only touching that they did was hold hands, but the children knew they loved each other, deeply.

They all sat down to a quiet meal. Frank jokes continuously. He isn't very tall, both Judd and Henry are taller. Judy is just very short, just under 5 feet. Melinda is just a few inches taller. Judy thanked God her other two children took after their father. Matthew might be taller than his dad, someday.

They all took turns talking to each other, except Henry and Melinda. They talk to everyone else but not to each other. No one seems to notice.

Anna is sitting next to Henry. They have a quiet conversation about the different crops they've had to pick.

"I do think tomatoes are the worse." He says. "And, I don't think women should pick. Especially tomatoes. That hard work and bending will damage your insides. Nope, I wouldn't let any of my womenfolk pick tomatoes."

"It hasn't been too bad. I feel healthy after working hard, all day. Besides, I feel if a woman is in good shape, she should help her man. Now my Ma doesn't and she shouldn't. Her job is to take care of us. But Melinda and me do all right, don't you think?"

"Well, if I had my say, you'd be busy cooking, cleaning, never picking. My wife will never work in the fields."

Anna just looks up at him. They go back a long way, but she doesn't know him anymore. They haven't seen each other for more than four years. He has gotten more intense and much, much taller. His brown wavy hair needs cutting but he has it combed behind his ears, neatly. His voice has deepened and is wonderful to listen to, but she isn't sure she likes to hear what he's saying.

They were best friends before they lost the farms. When Henry's father decided to move, and Henry agreed it was for the best, she felt almost betrayed. She felt that her best friend was leaving her because he wanted to find a better life somewhere else. She thought they should stay and stick it out together.

She knows better now. Poor Mr. Harrick and his wife never got along. They argued in front of everyone. Henry got very upset about it. He noticed the difference between the families and it hurt. It was shortly after that, that Mrs. Harrick left. She left a beautiful note for her son. Henry had showed it to her a few weeks later.

His Da (that's what Henry always called him) never got over her leaving. He got so sick that Anna's Ma had to go over and take care of him. It was his heart. Anna's young mind thought Frank Harrick had an actual broken heart. One thing she couldn't understand was how can you love someone you always fought with?

It only took about six months before they gave up trying to work the farm alone. They had no one to cook or do the house chores, and the drought was devastating. Also, they missed her so much and the farm had too many memories for them.

It was a coincidence, meeting the Harrick's here. Mr. Harrick only works a half a day. He goes home to cook, clean and rest, as he still gets chest pains. Henry makes as much money as her whole family combined.

"Anna, did you hear me?" Henry asks.

"I'm sorry Henry. I didn't mean to be rude, but I was just remembering the way we were. We've had to change so much, with the droughts and the Depression, I guess. If we could only go back."

"I don't want to go back. I like it fine now," he says with quiet authority. "Besides, even if we have all changed, I don't think you have. You're still caring, sweet, pure and very naïve. You need protection from the world."

"Why?" Her curiosity peaked. "Is the world out to get me?" She laughs but doesn't understand him anymore. He seems so bitter. What could have changed him so dramatically?

Henry just shrugs off the question. Anna didn't understand. She hasn't seen the ugly things that he has. He doubts that it would change her if she did. *That could get on my nerves after a while,* he thought.

When everyone is finished eating, the women begin to clear the table. Frank suggests that he and Judd step outside for a cigar. Judd jumps at the offer. He hasn't had a cigar in ages. They excuse themselves and leave. Matthew gets out the old checker board for Henry to play.

Once outside, Frank begins, "Judd, it's really good to be with you again. I can't believe that we met here of all places."

"A mighty step down from our little farms, ain't it? Well, I'm saving to buy mine back, you know?"

"No, I didn't know that," Frank says in a cloud of smoke.

"Yep, with what the kids bring in, we're doing alright. Besides, the stupid Depression can't last forever, can it?"

"Nope, nothing lasts forever." Frank comments. Both men think about it a minute and agree.

"Your family has sure changed. The kids are already adults. It's truly a miracle."

"I think you're rushing my Matthew a bit, but you are right. I thank God every day because they're strong, healthy and bright. Your Henry surprised me. He was so short, when you left. Last time I saw him, he was shorter than Anna and I don't think he was shaving, yet."

"No, he was shaving before we left, but it was just peach fuzz. He did shoot up overnight, a foot in less than six months! He's slowed down some, but I think he's still growing. Oh, but he's a wild boy, Judd. Guess that's because he's been motherless all these years. My poor Henry."

"You can't go blaming yourself again. You did your best by her. Nobody will ever be loved as much as you loved Ellen. It was just one of those things."

"I try not to blame myself. I don't want to leave this earth until I know my Henry is taken care of. I worry about him so much"

"Frank, I don't like the way you're talking. Is it your heart, still?"

Frank just nods. "Listen, Judd, don't mention this to anyone. I could have years yet or I could go tomorrow. My only thoughts are about Henry. I want certain things for him. And that's what I want to talk to you about."

"Why me?" Asks the thoroughly puzzled Judd.

"Henry needs to settle down. He needs a good woman behind him. Do you know what I'm getting at?"

"Anna?" Judd asks.

"She's perfect for him. They were inseparable when they were young'un's. She won't argue when he says 'jump' but I don't think she'll let him say it too often. She's too much like Judy." He sighs, then continues. "They've always gotten along, well. Remember how close they were? I think they'll love each other eventually, if they don't already."

Judd interrupts. "But Frank, I've no dowry for her. All's I have is my farm savings. And that don't add up to much."

Frank stops walking and turns to his old friend. He reaches out to put his arm around Judd's shoulder. "Judd, my dear old friend, the way I see it Anna will be bringing more into this marriage than Henry. I should be paying you, or Anna herself, to put up with him."

They walk silently puffing on Frank's cigars. After a few moments, Judd breaks the awkward silence. "I think this calls for a celebration." He announces. "My Anna is getting married!"

FOUR

First Tuesday of September cont'd
In Lawrence, Kansas

Rosanne cooked another wonderful meal, and serves it in the formal dining room. The Colonel only eats half of one pork chop, complaining he cannot swallow the meat. He has a few of the cheesy potatoes but has plenty of the fried apples to make up for it. It goes without saying that he eats none of the delicious salad.

Carolyn thinks it seems so quiet without Joshua. He has a vibrant personality and he cannot let of moment of silence go unpunished. Before they can remove their napkins from their laps, the phone rings and Joshua, as if sensing Carolyn was thinking about him is on the line. He's all excited and wants to talk with Rosanne, Carolyn holds out the phone to her.

Rosanne is uncomfortable using the telephone. She isn't used to it. The handset is very heavy and hurts her newly healed neck and shoulders. She also feels that she must yell into it for the other person to hear her, all those miles away. Carolyn is prepared for the loud voice, but the Colonel is startled when she starts to talk into the phone.

"Joshua, hello, this is Rosanne, how are you? What? A dance at the college? No, Josh, I couldn't. I don't think I know how and I'm still weak from . . . You'll come get me? But that's a very long drive just to drive me back here. Joshua, I think you should ask a . . . I'm just saying that it's so much trouble . . . I don't think it's a good idea. But Josh . . . why won't you listen to me? I'm saying that you should ask . . . Honestly, Joshua Morgan Lewis, if you'd let me say a complete sentence, I'd appreciate it. You need to ask a college girl, not the girl with no memory. No, I don't think I'm being unfair. Okay, hang on, I'll put her back on the phone. Have a good night, Joshua!" She puts the receiver down on the sideboard and calls Carolyn back to the phone.

Carolyn picks it up, "I'm here, Joshua . . . I understand but if she doesn't want to . . . I'm being reasonable. Look at all she has gone through . . . Come on home, if you think you can talk her into it, in person. I'll take any excuse to see my little brother. Okay, I'll see you Saturday morning . . . Oh, okay, I'll tell him. Bye."

She hangs up the phone and walks to the Colonel. He's dozing at the dinner table. She puts her hand on his shoulder and he awakens and looks up at his granddaughter. "Yes dear, did you need something?"

She holds out her hand for a handshake, but the Colonel doesn't understand until she says, "Joshua wanted me to tell you that he misses you and he wants to give you a shake." The Colonel takes Carolyn's hand as a stand-in for his grandson's, and shakes the hell out of it.

"He's a good boy, isn't he?" The Colonel is smiling.

"Yes, Colonel, he is." Carolyn and Rosanne say at the same time.

Rosanne begins clearing the table. Carolyn takes the Colonel to the sitting room. This is their time, together. Carolyn always reads to her grandfather after dinner. He can only stay awake for about one chapter so when he falls asleep, Carolyn silently, continues to read. She feels guilty but after years of this practice, she knows that if she only reads when he's awake, he can't follow the story, anyway.

When Rosanne is done cleaning, she peeks into the sitting room. "Carolyn, did you want a cup of coffee or tea? A sweet treat, maybe?" She whispers the last part so the Colonel doesn't wake.

"No, dear, I'm fine, come join me?"

"I will in just a few, I have to find my book, I think I left it out on the veranda."

She's gone but a minute and then comes in the sitting room and sits on the matching chair opposite the Colonel.

"So what is this dance, Joshua wants you to go to? Don't you think you'll have a good time?"

"Carolyn, how can you be serious? There are many reasons not to go and none to go. I don't think I know how to dance. I tire from being upright for too long. I can't imagine how I'd feel after dancing. Joshua needs to forget about me and going to a dance wouldn't accomplish this."

"If you are still tired from being upright, why have you taken over the cooking duties? You also said that you don't need physical therapy anymore. I should hire Walter back. It would be good for him to work on the Colonel as well as you."

"Carolyn, why go through all that expense? I can never repay you for all the money you spent on my hospital stays or any of the home care. Why have you been so generous to me, when I was a stranger?"

"You weren't just a stranger. You were on my land. I take care of everything on my land. If you were one of my cattle, stranded far from the herd, I would have done, no less."

"Big Fat Liar!" Rosanne is smiling. "Carolyn Diane Lewis, you'd never put cattle in an upstairs bedroom, not in a million years!" They both laugh.

"Rosanne? Are you happy here?"

"I love being here with you and the Colonel. I don't know where else I can go. You did everything you could to find out who I was. That detective agency couldn't have come cheap."

"Yes, but maybe we should try another one. I feel so bad, you had a life somewhere, someone must be missing you." Carolyn can see that she has gone too far. Rosanne's eyes are looking at her book but quickly filling with tears. "Especially, if you cooked for them. They're probably starved half to death without you." Rosanne looks up, with half of a smile, at the compliment. She wipes her eyes.

"I do wish, I could be more helpful around here. You oversee so much, and with Joshua back at school, not sharing your load, I feel very guilty, sitting around all day."

"Do you take care of my grandfather? The Colonel's care is very important to me."

"Well, maybe I can help with some of the bookwork? Or housework?"

"You aren't physically strong enough for house cleaning. I like the job Molly and her crew does, they come in to clean, daily. Do you want me to fire them, also?"

"I didn't want you to fire anyone. I just didn't want you to spend money on something I can do for you."

"I know, Rosanne. You worry so much about my money. That's a clue, I think, that you didn't have much before your accident. I know you didn't have an indoor toilet or a phone. What your life must have been like!"

Rosanne counters, "I think, you're the exception, Carolyn. I think, most 'country' households lack those things that you think are standard. Ask anyone picking in your fields." Rosanne stops for a second as a fleeting image comes to mind of squatting down in a tomato field row, picking alongside dozens of people. She shakes away the nuisance image. "I know this might sound silly, but did you check to see if I ever worked your fields? I seem to remember picking tomatoes."

"That's the first thing I did. I went to our encampment and held a meeting to see if anyone knew if someone was missing. Now, what about this dance, don't you want to meet people your own age? You'd have a good time, with Joshua by your side."

"Carolyn, you know I like Joshua, but he deserves someone who knows their past."

"He deserves someone who'll give him a good future."

"What if I was married, Carolyn? You both keep forgetting about that."

"The doctors were sure you were raped, Rosanne."

"But that doesn't mean, I wasn't married or even a virgin before the accident." Rosanne blushes, she isn't comfortable talking about it but refuses to let her comfort level lead them to thinking she wasn't damaged goods.

"Joshua is crazy about you, Rosanne. I don't think he thinks about that."

"That's my point, I'm not good enough for him. I'm damaged goods in many ways. Don't try to object. You have put me back together better than I deserve but this Humpty Dumpty is still cracked all over. He deserves a whole educated beautiful woman. I'm none of those things." She thinks to herself, *I might have been once, but not anymore*.

"Rosanne, you must stop feeling sorry for yourself. You still see the scars. We see you, the beautiful you."

"Big fat liar." She smiles again. "I don't want to talk about it anymore. It's time to get the Colonel ready for bed.

FIVE

The First Tuesday in September, 1935, cont'd
In EL Dorado, Kansas

The dishes are done and the kitchen is sparkling clean. Henry and Matthew are on their second game of checkers. Anna and Judy are mending socks and Melinda is flipping through a Sears and Roebuck catalog without looking at the pictures. She's staring at Henry. How long must sit here in the same room with him and not be able to go to him?

The two fathers walk back in, smiling so wide that everyone stops what they're doing to look at them.

Judy says, "What are you two doing with grins from ear to ear? Do you know how silly you both look?"

Judd crosses over to his wife and pulls her out of her seat, mending still in her hand. "We've got great news to share with everyone." Judd starts.

Frank walks over his son. "It's the best decision we've ever made. It's like it was meant to be." He stands behind Henry and puts his hand on his shoulder. "Henry stand up, please."

Judd pulls Judy to Anna and says, "Anna, we need you to stand up, too." Anna listens to her Pa and puts down the sewing and slowly rises. "Hurry up, Anna honey, I'm about to bust at the seams, here."

Anna and Henry are both up, but so are Matthew and Melinda. Everyone was trying to figure out what was happening. Frank leads Henry past Melinda and makes him stand next to Anna.

"There", Frank says. "Judd, you tell them."

"It was your idea, you tell them." Judd returns.

Anna, Henry and Judy say at once. "Just tell us!"

Judd says "It's official, we've decided that you two are getting married. Isn't that great?"

Anna turns white and slowly sinks back to her seat. Henry on the other hand gets bright red, as does Melinda, but all eyes are on Henry. "How could you?" He asks. "Am I not an adult, who can make my own decisions here?" He pushes past his father and heads for the door.

Frank yells, "HENRY, STOP RIGHT THERE!" Surprisingly, Henry freezes with his hand on the door knob. He turns slowly around. He's very mad but hears the dead serious tone of his father's voice.

"Henry, we need to discuss this. It isn't gentlemanly to walk out on your fiancé and her family. I've my reasons for this . . ." He begins to gasp for air. "Just listen to . . . Me." Frank is having a hard time finishing up his sentence and is suddenly breathing hard. Though the night is cool and a strong breeze is blowing through the open window, he's suddenly drenched in sweat.

Judy sees his discomfort and leads him to a chair and tells Matthew to draw him some water.

"Henry . . ." Frank tries again. "I'm not very healthy . . . the fact of the matter is that . . . I'm dying." His breathing is getting very labored. Judy goes into the kitchen for a damp cloth and a paper bag for him to breathe into to slow his breath down.

Judd tries to take over the explanation so that Frank can breathe into the bag. "It's that he's worried about you, Henry. He doesn't want to see you alone, after he's gone. He'd like to see you happy first. He'd like to bounce your son or daughter on his lap, if there's time."

Henry softens as he sees his father struggling for air. He takes the damp towel from Judy and wipes his Da's brow, then he kneels at his feet. "Da, I'm not ready for any of that. I'm not ready for a wife or a child. I'm, certainly, not ready for you to leave me. Can you promise me that you'll give me time to get used to all these changes you want? I tell you, I'm not ready." He puts his head in his Da's lap and Frank reaches down and gently touches his face with the back of his hand. "You looked so much like your mother just now. I'm not going to leave you, yet. But do consider what we've discussed. It really is best for both of you."

Anna is still white in the chair as this is happening. Melinda thinks she'll explode if she must stand and witness this. She says in a voice, a little too loud. "We haven't heard from Anna yet." All eyes turn to Anna. A slow blush starts to rise-up her fair skin. She stands up and walks to her father. "You really think that I should marry Henry?"

"Of course, why not? You've known him your whole life and were always 'frick-and-frack' together. Don't you love him just a little?"

Anna turns to Henry before speaking. "Well, I don't know. I haven't had time to think about it. I haven't seen him for four years and this is happening so fast." Tears start to well up in her dark eyes. She turns to her Pa. "I just thought that a man would ask me - not my father tell me to get married. I would have liked a little romance involved." She's calm but her tears give her sadness away. "I know times are bad now but don't I deserve those things?"

Her father softens. "Oh, Anna honey, I didn't want to rob you of those things. But I want what's best for you. Henry is a good man and he comes from good stock." He says nodding toward Mr. Harrick. "Don't you think that you could be happy with Henry?"

"I don't know, Pa, I just don't know." She turns back to Henry. "I certainly don't want to be with someone who doesn't want to be with me." She searches his face for a hint of feeling. She did love the Henry of her childhood. This man in front of her is a stranger. She can tell that he feels the same way. "We don't know each other anymore. Can't we get to know each other before it's decided, one way or the other?"

Frank stands up and goes to Anna. "Darling, forgive an old man for not considering your feelings. I just want the best for my boy and I look at you and see that for him. How could he not love a beautiful sweet girl like you. I mean, if he doesn't yet, he will." He bends and gives her a light kiss on her cheek. "Maybe you and Henry need some time to get reacquainted. There's no rush, really. I just like the notion that someone will look out for him when I'm gone. Do you think you can consider it?" He searches both their faces.

Henry smiles at his father and says, "we must get to know each other again, Da. I won't be engaged to a stranger and Anna deserves that, too. Can we just say that we're . . .? I don't know . . . pre-engaged?" Now he was smiling at Anna. It was the 'young Henry' from the farm smiling through the man in front of her. It warms her and makes her stomach flutter at the same time. She smiles back. She reaches up and tucks a stray strand of hair that had fallen forward from behind his ear. That simple delicate, intimate act made his stomach flutter, too. She was so simple and sweet and if someone can make him happy, she's as likely a candidate as any.

Before Anna could respond, a throat clears, loudly. "Um, is it getting hot in here or what? I need some air."

Melinda starts for the door but pauses when her mother says, "Don't forget to take a wrap, dear." Melinda takes her mother's shawl off the hook by the door, puts it around her shoulders making a point to fling her long dark hair before she storms out and slams the door behind her. Everyone just stares at the closed door.

Then Frank breaks the silence, "Well, my dear, do you agree with Henry to be . . . how did you put it, Henry? Pre-engaged?" He winks at her.

Judy butts in, "I think that enough has been said and we should all call it a night. I never heard of such a thing as 'pre-engaged'! Absurd, my daughter can be courted by Henry but will only be engaged when the young man asks her to be his wife, and not before. Foolish old men! They think that they can rule the world!" She put her arm around Anna's waist, then adds, "Say good night to Mr. Harrick and Henry, Anna. They're leaving."

"G-g-good night, I had a wonderful evening." She says by rote. Then she laughs, "I mean it's been an interesting evening, gentlemen." With that, Judy leads Anna to the girl's room, and goes in with her. She closes the door behind her.

Matthew is putting away the checker set. "I think you owe me a rematch, Henry. My sister is right, though, it's been an interesting evening."

Judd pats his old friend on the back. "I didn't think that it would have gone this way but . . . Slow and steady seems to be the agreed route here. Frank, take it easy. Henry, until you come a-courting, goodnight."

Frank was about to reply when Henry says, "Mr. Masters, I hope I didn't cause Anna any heartache with my reaction to your announcement. That was not my intention, at all."

"Understood, son. I think it ended on a good note, don't you?"

"Yes, sir. Maybe I could take Anna to town for dinner, on Saturday night? I'll ask her in the field tomorrow. Good night, sir. Let's go, Da, we are standing in Matthew's bedroom and the young man needs his sleep. As do we."

After Judd closes the door behind Henry and Frank, he goes to the girl's bedroom and softly knocks on the door. His wife says to come in. As he opens the door, he sees that Anna has taken her mother's hair down and is brushing it. It appears that Judy has already done this for Anna. Judy has a sprinkling of gray in her light brown long hair. He never realized how much Anna looked just like her mother. Same fair coloring, same dark eyes, same light brown wavy locks, same mouth that smiles so easily. God help him, he loved his women. "Judy, time for bed?" He asks hesitantly.

"Yes dear, I'll be right along." With that, Judd turns and walks into their bedroom. Judy moves toward the door but turns to Anna. "I should wait up for Melinda, she shouldn't be out this late."

Don't worry, Ma. I'll wait up. I'm not the least bit tired after all the excitement. You and Pa go on to bed."

"Okay, sweetheart. Let us know if she isn't back in a little while. Your Pa can go see where she's gotten to." Judy walks back over to Anna to give her a little kiss. "Such a good daughter. What a blessing you are."

"Hmmp!" Replies Melinda who is now standing at the bedroom door, looking impatient.

Her mother doesn't notice but says, "Oh, good, Melinda, you're back. Now, we can all get a good night's sleep. Good night, Girls." She kisses Melinda's cheek as she leaves the room and closes the door behind her.

Melinda is in inner turmoil. She wants Henry. She wants to know what those long arms feel like around her. She wants to hear his low loving voice whisper sweet nothings in her ear. It was apparent that Henry wants those things, also . . . until their fathers meddled in their affairs. What is she to do now?

Anna is at the dresser, looking at herself without emotion as she's brushing out her long locks, again. She forgot that Melinda is even there. Melinda walks over to Anna and takes the brush from her hands and says, "Last I heard, you were pre-engaged? How does that work?"

"I don't know. I've never heard of that before, either. I guess he's going to be courting me. What do you think?"

"Well, I didn't think that you were attracted to him anymore." Melinda starts brushing Anna's hair. "It's been a lot of years since you were close." Melinda stops and takes the clips out holding her hair away from her face. She starts to brush through the long strands. "You'll go slow with this, right? I cannot see you married to Henry, right now."

"I thought about it when we were both on the farms. But that was just a child's fancy. I don't feel right about getting married and leaving the family while we are in such a bad situation."

"I can. Just say the magic word and I'm out of here. Ma and Pa think we are little and still need them. I can make my own way without them."

"I guess I could too, but why would I want to? I can't imagine not being able to talk with Ma about everything. What if Henry wants to move away? I must go where my husband takes me."

Melinda thinks about this. "I imagine a relationship where a husband wouldn't want to cause that pain of separation. A man that would be considerate in all things."

Anna chuckles. "Like Pa, you mean?"

"Yes, I guess so, but with looks like Errol Flynn, is that too much to ask?" Melinda puts down the brush and turns to Anna. "You deserve better than this, Anna. Truly, you do." Melinda says and is surprised at how much she means every single word.

SIX

The First Wednesday in September, 1935
In EL Dorado, Kansas

Melinda tosses and turns on her cot. It isn't the bedding that keeps her restless but thoughts of Henry courting her sister.

Why doesn't he just admit he's attracted to me, the younger sister. I'm not a child. I'll be eighteen in a few months. Henry is twenty, and a man in every way that counts. He has those strong muscular arms that I wants around me. Just the sound of his voice makes me feel warm inside, she thinks. They hadn't time to talk after he left with his Da. She was just outside as they passed by and he caught her eye and just shook his head no and kept going. He had to get his father to bed but they need to talk. He wanted to be with her before this whole engagement thing, *but what about now?*

Melinda looks over to Anna. As far as she can tell she's sleeping soundly. *Sure, without trying, she gets Henry and doesn't have a worry in the world. God, I cannot sleep. Maybe a walk around the camp, will help.*

She gets out of bed and dresses as quietly as a mouse. She carefully opens the bedroom door and walks past Matthew sleeping. He's muttering in his sleep. Poor kid, no wonder, he's too big for the couch that he sleeps on. He'd never complain, though. *He's a go-along-er like Anna.* She eases herself out of the hut and crosses across the open area.

"Can't sleep?" Henry says softly. He's leaning his tall frame on the side of the grocery store. Has he been waiting for her? "I wondered if you would come after all that's happened tonight." He says, as a matter of fact. *How can he be so calm?*

"I didn't realize our 'date' was still on since you didn't leave my hut until almost eleven p.m." Then she adds. "And you are now engaged to my sister."

"Yea, that seems to be the consensus." He straightens up. "I had no idea or even a hint that this was coming, you know." He saunters up to her and takes her hands.

"Henry, what are you doing?" She asks. "Are you engaged to my sister? Or . . . ?" She trails off.

"I'm not engaged. I'm standing here with you. There's no other place that I'd like to be right now."

"Yes, but . . . " He stops her in midsentence by putting his finger to her mouth to silence her. "Shhh, things will work out." His finger slides down as he cups her face and lifts it up to him. "I've wanted to kiss you since the first time I saw you in this camp." He slowly bends to her mouth and lightly meets her lips with his. She's surprised but accepting of his mouth and eagerly stands on her tippy toes to meet him more than halfway. He draws her to him so that he can feel her breasts against him.

He breaks away suddenly, then takes her by the hand to the side of the store, where he was just standing in the shadows. There's a milk crate on the ground and he lifts her up to stand on it. She's amused at the thought that she needs a leg up to kiss him but his mouth was on hers again so fast that she didn't have time to even laugh. Warm and inviting, his tongue finds its way to hers. His hands are finding their way also. They're under her blouse caressing her bare breasts and she's amazed how quickly she's ready for more. Her hand slides down his waist, past his belt.

"Melinda, you are driving me crazy, I want you, so bad." She has been longing to hear that from him.

"I want you, too."

He pulls away from her and looks in her eyes. "Do you mean it? I don't want to push you into something that . . . well you aren't ready for."

"Henry, when you look at me, I quiver inside. I want you so bad. I've been saving myself for the right moment, for the right guy. You are that guy." She unbuttons her blouse as if to prove her willingness. He kisses her on the lips but his kisses slowly move south. She moans at the deliciousness of the feeling. His mouth is hungry on her. She cannot believe how wonderful this feels.

"We must go somewhere else. We can't do this here." She manages to say between moans. "Henry, oh Henry, take me someplace, please."

He struggles to let go. He buttons her blouse a button or two but his mouth is on hers again. "I've an idea." He leads her to the back of the store where the camp truck is parked. He puts down the gate and hoists her up. He lifts the gate back up, as quietly as possible, then swings himself up and in. She's sitting on the long bench waiting for him. There's very little light from the camp store coming through the canopy, but there's just enough to create a romantic atmosphere. He sits next to her and he touches her face. He looks in her eyes as he says. "You won't believe me but this is my first, too. I mean, um, I've kissed several girls but . . . I don't know, it didn't seem right to go further. I guess, I've been saving myself, too."

She reaches up for his face and kisses his forehead, then lips. "Henry, your voice is so sexy, say my name. Say you want me. Say you'll <u>die</u> if you don't have me."

SEVEN

The First Wednesday in September
In Lawrence Kansas

The Colonel didn't have a good night. He only slept two hours at most. When he got out of bed each time, he was looking for his wife, Julia. Andrew, the attendant, last night, couldn't get him to settle back down and had to get Rosanne at three in the morning. She got him to sit down and tell her the story of how he met Julia. This always calms him down. The Colonel always tells it a little different. This time, he started as a young boy and called himself 'Young Willie'. Sometimes he starts when he is in the Cavalry and he calls himself Young Will. It doesn't matter how he starts it, if he makes it to the end, he finishes it with 'and they lived happily ever after.' Last night, he didn't make it to the end. He fell asleep in his chair in the sitting room with a warm blanket surrounding him. Once he was asleep, Rosanne left him in the hands of Andrew and went back to bed. Andrew will wake her again, when his shift is over.

History proves that a bad day always follows a bad night for the Colonel and Rosanne. He was back in his bed, when Andrew woke her but he didn't stay there for long. Rosanne usually does her baking in the morning while he sleeps and before the heat of the day becomes overwhelming. The Colonel was ringing his bell before nine. She'd just put the bread to rise in the pre-warmed but turned off oven. She double checked the time to make sure that she comes back to it in time to knead it.

She gets upstairs just in time to catch him bending to the floor, rubbing the wood with his hand. She stands there watching him. "Colonel, what are you doing? Can I help you?"

"Yes, don't you see, Robbie peed here. Damn dog! I don't know why he'd do that! I feed him all day long and this is how he pays me back? Damn dog!" He says again.

The normally calm Colonel is very agitated. He's still rubbing the wood, which seems dry. Rosanne bends down for a closer look. It's dry, with no trace of a pet stain. It's no use arguing with him, time to distract.

"Colonel, let's go wash your hands, I'll clean this up, don't you worry. The floor isn't damaged and I'll keep Robbie in the kitchen at night where he belongs."

She leads him to the bathroom, rubs his hands under water, then soaps them, and rinses them. He starts to squirm, which means he needs to go. "Do you need to use the toilet, Colonel? I'll help you or step out which ever you prefer." Somedays he doesn't mind and other days he does, so she always asks.

"I don't need go. You always want me to go. I don't think I like you or that dog Robbie!" He's drying his hands on the towel. Then turns toward the commode and lets out a small 'uggghhh!' "Rosanne, now you made me have an accident."

"It's okay, Colonel, just have a seat on the commode, and I'll get you fresh pants." *This isn't going to be a good day*, she thinks, as she goes to his dresser for fresh bottoms.

After she changes his clothing, she suggests that he lay down for a nap. He refuses and says he wants to go sit in his chair. *Well, good, at least he'll be on the same floor as the kitchen, so I can get back to making the bread.*

Once downstairs and in his chair. She asks, "Did you want to have breakfast?"

The Colonel shakes his head no. "Can you just bring me a couple cookies and a cup of hot tea, in the sitting room, please. I'll have breakfast later."

"Whatever you want, Colonel. I'll just be a minute." She heads to the kitchen and peeks at her bread. It's not quite there yet. She puts the tea kettle on the stove and gets a plate for the cookies she made yesterday morning. As she plates them, she thinks aloud, "So what is this, his pre-breakfast?" He keeps her very busy on days like today. *At least, Carolyn doesn't have the additional worry of taking care of him, herself. She'd run the farm right to the ground if she'd to deal with him like this.*

Rosanne brings him his 'pre-breakfast' into the sitting room, where he's asleep, wrapped in his blanket, once again. Rosanne puts down the plate and cup and tries to wake him. She hates to do that but he doesn't like cold tea and in his current mood, she doesn't want to give him any more to complain about. *What a difference from yesterday! Even though he was confused yesterday, he was very pleasant to help.*

"Your hot tea, sir, and your cookies. I need to knead my dough. Can I leave you for a few moments? I'll come sit with you, as soon as the bread is in the oven."

"Sure, leave me alone. I don't want your company today. You made me have an accident. And don't let that dog, near me either."

Rosanne thinks, *yup, this day is starting out just great!* She's back in the kitchen kneading the dough. This job is the one that's been the hardest to resume after the accident. Her fractured neck and broken shoulders took months to mend. It was lucky that she was in a coma during that time. She'd have been in pain, tied to the bed in traction, otherwise. Kneading the dough, though, makes her think she can feel all the repaired cracks in her bones. Luckily, she only makes bread three times a week.

The phone rings when Rosanne's hands are deep in the dough. "One minute!" She calls to the phone. She towels off the dough as best she can and runs to the dining room where the downstairs phone is kept.

"Hello, Lewis Residence, this is Rosanne. How can I help you?" She says loudly into the phone.

"Rosanne, this is Joshua. I was hoping to get you to change your mind about the dance. It looks like the whole campus will be going. It's going to be huge. I've wanted to bring you up to the University, for some time, anyway. Won't you come with me?"

"No Joshua, Carolyn and I talked about it last night. I'm not up to a 'dance'. I want you to find a college girl to take. The University is filled with them, I hear."

"They're not you, Rosanne."

"You say that like it's a bad thing."

"Rosanne, I thought you liked me. We got along so great this summer. I miss you, terribly."

"We did, Josh. I like you enough to want this for you. Please date someone from school and stop trying to court me. I'm not available."

"Rosanne, stop feeling like you aren't worth courting."

She pauses, thinking what to say to this caring, funny great young man that she has come to know and love. How about the truth? "Joshua, you know that I love you and Carolyn."

"Me and Carolyn? You love me like you love Carolyn, is that what you are saying?"

"Well, yes, I love you like a brother. A BIG annoying brother." She doesn't like hurting him like this and her brown eyes are filling with tears, again. "Joshua, we had this talk before you left for school. I thought you understood how I felt."

"I thought absence would make the heart grow fonder."

"You haven't been gone long enough, obviously." She's trying to joke. "Joshua, your grandfather had a bad night and is having a bad morning and my hands are covered with dough. I've to go so that I can get that bread in the oven, before his nap is over and my hands are full again."

"Rosanne, I decided that I'm going to tell you that I love you and I won't stop until you believe me.

"Joshua, I do believe that you *think* you love me, romantically. I'm telling you to stop it."

"I won't stop, good-bye, Rosanne. I love you." He hangs up and Rosanne puts the receiver back on its cradle. *Boy that's heavy*, she thinks. She takes three steps and the phone rings again. She turns back to the phone.

"Hello, Lewis Residence, Rosanne speaking."

"I just thought of something. I'm coming home on Saturday and taking you out on a date. I'm not taking no for an answer." He hangs up, before she can say anything. She stares at the handset. *That boy is crazy*, she thinks. *Oh, my dough*! She runs back to the kitchen. The dough has risen again so she must knead it a second time. *This bread isn't going to turn out any better than this day has*, she thinks as she reworks it.

Rosanne thinks about Joshua's insistence on being in love with her. *Complete and utter nonsense. I must get him to understand. I'm not going to put up with his behavior. I must get him to stop thinking this way, even if I make him hate me, instead. I'll go so far as to leave here if he insists, even though this is the only home that I know*, she thinks as her eyes tear up again.

EIGHT

The First Wednesday in September, 1935
In EL Dorado, Kansas

Anna woke up feeling funny. Somehow, she feels lighter and happier. *Did almost get engaged last night*? Henry was very upset at first but so was she. She saw glimpses of the Old Henry. *She could marry that Henry*. She was taller than him when they parted, but four years later and a foot taller or more, he's a very different person. But she has a beau. *What a weird feeling*.

She looks over to Melinda. Melinda is sleeping on her stomach. That's odd, Anna thought Melinda was wearing a nightgown when they went to bed last night, wasn't she? But here she's wearing the outfit that she wore at dinnertime.

"Melinda, darling, it's time to get up. I smell Ma's coffee. That means we must get a move on, if we are going to make the Camp truck for its first run to the field." Melinda doesn't move. Anna gets out of bed and crosses over to her to shake her.

"Come on sleepy head. Time to get up. Rise and shine." Melinda is groaning, but not moving. "Melinda, come on sis, this isn't like you to not get up, when called. Did you have a bad night?"

"Bad night, no – a GOOD night." She says, as she rolls over to her back. Anna thinks she's talking in her sleep, because there's a smile on her face but her eyes are not open. "Melinda, Ma will be here in a minute and you don't want to see her mad because you won't get up."

"Anna, please, I'm having the best dream, leave me be."

"GIRLS, get up lazy heads. Breakfast is almost ready." Judy burst into the room. A coffee cup in each hand. "I brought you each, a cup of inspiration. Anna Rose Masters, what's wrong with your sister? Didn't she get undressed for bed, last night?"

Anna shrugs. "I thought she did but, I guess not. This isn't like her, though. Melinda, come on." She gives her another shake.

"Alright then, everyone. I'll get up. Coffee, I smell coffee." Her eyes still aren't open, but she starts to sit up. She holds out her hand. "Give me my cup, dear sister, please." Anna does as she requests.

Melinda sniffs the cup's warm aroma. Her eyes open as she sips the strong brew. "Ummm, this is good, Momma, I needed this, this morning." She takes a few more sips, then opens her eyes and looks up as Judy and Anna were both looking at her and says, "What? Do I've two heads or something?" They all laugh.

Judy, pats her head. "No darling, you just wouldn't get up. Come on, I've to go, breakfast might be burning." She rushes out of the room as quickly as she rushed in.

Anna is dressing for the day. She's pulling her hair into a bun. "I think it's going to be another hot one today." She says.

Melinda answers, smiling. I'll agree with you on that."

The first camp truck run to the field is at seven a.m. sharp. The earliness of the hour doesn't keep it from being overfilled. Everyone wants an early start to the day. The tomato plants are starting to die off and the ripe fruits were getting fewer by the day. Soon the season for tomatoes will be over. A few workers will be kept on to pull the dead plants and till under the field for the cover crop. Most of the migrant workers will move on to pick another crop.

Judd and his family are on that first run. They're the last to get on and the driver can hardly close the gate without jostling them. They hang on for dear life as the jalopy seems to hit every hole in the dirt road. Both the girls are in good moods, a rare thing. Judd thinks it was odd and, as if reading his thoughts, Matthew says in his ear, "Why are they both smiling this morning? Geesh! It's too warm, windy and crowded on this bus for smiling!"

"I don't know, son, but enjoy it. It's better and rarer than a blue moon." Judd chuckles and elbows Matthew.

When they arrive at the field, Matthew is the first one down and starts helping the others. It's an orderly movement. First you go to the paymaster and get your crop card and a bushel, then out to the rows. The Masters family are all picking before the truck heads back down the road for the next load of workers.

Melinda wants to distance herself from her family so that she can meet up with Henry. She couldn't wait to see him again. She didn't want their first meeting in front of Anna or her Pa, though. She uses the excuse of going to the outhouse to get some separation between them.

Anna is apprehensive of seeing Henry today, too. There's so much to be said. How can they expect her to get married to him so soon after their reuniting? She thinks that there's more going on behind those cool gray eyes than he's willing to share with her. *He seems so cynical, now. Was it his mom's leaving? His dad's long illnesses? Did something else happen to them that she doesn't know about?*

She's lost in thought, when her father repeats his question to her. "Are you mad at your interfering Pa? I really have your happiness in mind, first and foremost, you know?" He's trying to look in her dark eyes for a twinkle of happiness. What he sees is indecision. "Anna Rose, did you hear me?"

"I heard you Pa. I know you are worried about me. I'm fine, I'm not mad. I'm just not sure that Henry and I are suited for each other anymore." Anna explains.

"Henry apologized to me, he was worried that he hurt your feelings with his reaction to our announcement. I was impressed by that. You'll give him a chance, then?" As Judd says this, he sees the truck pull back around and watches to see if Henry and Frank are on it.

Croner walks past him. "What are ya sight-seeing? Craning to see the Queen, are ya? TOMATOES, people, all your concentration should be on pickin' tomatoes!!" He roughly brushes past Judd. "Lazy asses. Can't get the first bushel out of them without their taking a break." He says out loud. Judd, just puts his head down and grabs more tomatoes that he can hold. One drops and rolls to Anna. She puts it into his bushel, careful not to look at her Pa. *Why does Croner feel the need to yell at everyone?*

Croner is onto the next person. Yelling as he went. *If he'd a whip, he'd be cracking it*, Anna thinks. *He doesn't need be this way.* "Thank God, this crop is just about over." She says out loud. She looks up her Pa. He just nods and continues to pick.

Melinda comes out of the outhouse when she hears the camp truck come into the fields. She sees Henry climb down off the truck. He's alone and looking around. He sees Melinda and nods toward the Paymaster's line. She gets in line next to him so that his height will hide her. "Your Da not well today, Henry?" She asks hesitantly.

"He had a bad night. He woke up before I got home and was upset that I was out. He panics when alone. I only go out when he's asleep, because of it." Henry explains. He bends down to whisper in her ear. "It was worth it. Can we do a repeat?"

Melinda shakes her head no. "Are you going to tell your father or mine that Anna isn't the one you are interested in?"

"I don't think I can do that just yet. I promised to give it a chance. My dad will be crushed if I'm not interested in your sister." The hot wind blows his long hair into his eyes. Henry runs his fingers through it, pushing the long strands back behind his ears. He takes his work hat out of his pants pocket and puts it on. "You must give it some time, Melinda. I must show that I'm trying. In fact, I have to find her and ask if I can take her to town on Saturday for dinner."

"Well, don't be looking for me at the General Store, then." She starts to walk away, but changes her mind. She enjoyed last night, and doesn't want to wait. "Meet me, later? We can 'talk' about what we did last night." She feels herself blush and hopes he doesn't notice.

Henry nods, "I'll find you later. I've to pick for two, today." By now, he's next in line to get his pay card and bushel. He wants to get picking but he didn't want to leave Melinda just yet. He has never felt so drawn to someone. *I could never feel this way toward Anna,* he thinks. *Or at least, I don't think so!*

It was later in the morning that Matthew sees Henry and makes his way over to him. "Hey Henry." He says simply.

"How are you today, Matthew?" Henry says with a smile. Matthew was always the little brother he never had. Little isn't going to describe him for long, they're almost eye to eye.

"Do you think we'll have any cool weather before this crop is over?" Matthew asks. "This is just too hot to work." He complains as he bends down to start picking.

Henry stops to stand and straighten out his bent back. "I don't think so, Matthew. I would love it if the wind would just give us a break or at least cool off. It feels like it's been blowing for 4 years!"

Matthew nods in agreement. After a few more minutes of picking, side by side, Matthew says hesitantly, "Um, I think I noticed something about you, yesterday." He looks up to see Henry's reaction. Henry just keeps picking and waits to see where this conversation is going. "I don't think playing checkers is your thing. You seemed to have your mind somewhere else, yet you still beat me."

Henry laughs with relief. "I'm more a card player, or better yet, a good game of craps, but don't tell our fathers, OR your sisters!" He pats Matthew on his back.

Matthew looks up eagerly. "Do you think you could teach me? I'd love to play craps. Where do you find a crap game?"

Henry shushes Matthew. "Quiet Matthew. You are a little young for such late-night activities. I don't mind teaching you how to play, the game is very exciting."

"Hey, I'm going to be sixteen in a little more than a month! Everyone treats me like a kid. I'm not a kid. I can drive a car. I'm taller then everyone in my family except Pa. I'm not a child." Matthew is very adamant and upset.

"Take it easy, Matthew. Listen, I promise that I'll teach you the rules and I'll be the one to take you to your first official game. But please, realize that the people I play with aren't good losers. You need to be very careful around them. I won't treat you like a child but you must show me an adult in playing the game or you won't be going with me." He likes Matthew. He wants to be someone Matthew looks up to, and he isn't referring to their height. Henry begins, "For Craps, first you need a pair of dice . . ."

***

It's late morning, when Henry brings another bushel to be weighed that he sees Anna. He didn't know what to do about the engagement. He can remember how close they were growing up and she hasn't changed. *That's the problem, she hasn't changed. After all these years, apart, she just seems so young! How is it that her younger sister is so much . . . what is the word to describe Melinda? More . . . she's so much more.* Again, the memory of Melinda last night takes over. He can remember the smell of her skin, as well as the softness of her caresses. *How can I talk to Anna with Melinda possessing my thoughts?* Anna waves at him and he has no choice but walk over to her.

"Good morning, Anna." Henry couldn't think of anything else to say. "I've been with Matthew most of the morning. He has a grown into a great young man."

She's just finishing filling up her bushel and stands and stretches. "Grown is the word to describe him. I think that he will be taller than Pa, soon. Don't you?" She says. She also doesn't know what to say to the stranger in front of her. She fidgets slightly, taking off her sunhat and fans herself with it. She reaches for her handkerchief and wipes her brow. "This is a very warm day, again, isn't it?" *The weather is about the safest topic right now*, she thinks. "Melinda says your Da had a bad night and didn't come to the fields today. I hope he . . . we . . . weren't the case of his . . . latest setback." She says with sincere regret.

"Anna, you are so sweet. Our fathers spring this ridiculous engagement on us and you hope WE didn't cause his condition?" He asks but doesn't wait for an answer. "What are you doing Saturday night? Want to have dinner with me in town?" Henry rushes the question out so that he doesn't have to think about it anymore.

Anna's kerchief has caused a few hairs to loosen so she smooths them back up into the bun. "I don't know Henry. I have to ask Pa."

"I've already asked him if I could take you. So, I just need your permission." Henry says. *I cannot believe that she's so childlike. She's nineteen but feels she needs to ask for permission to go on a date with her fiancé. Well, almost fiancé.* He shakes his head as if trying to get rid of these bad thoughts "Well, Anna? Meatloaf at the diner, sound good? I'll get you home early, unless you want to go to a moving picture show in town. I don't know what is playing at either theater but we could go there, also . . . if, you want."

"Oh, I love moving pictures! Are you sure you can afford that? I haven't seen a picture in ages." She forgets that she is hesitant about being with Henry. "Yes, I would like that so very much!"

She is smiling with excitement. *When she's not being a meek little mouse, she's quite remarkable,* Henry thinks. He likes this Anna. Her heart shaped face was framed beautifully by all the wavy tendrils that escaped that bun. He suddenly imagines pulling at the ribbon that was struggling to hold her hair in place and watching her full waves come tumbling down. He imagined running his hands through her hair, feeling its softness as he leans in for a kiss. *What was happening? How can I have such thoughts about Anna when I wanted Melinda so bad, just moments ago?*

"Um . . . well, I'll find out what is playing at the ERIS Theatre and the Hotel EL Dorado Theater. We will decide which movie to see. We need to know what time to have our meatloaf, so we aren't late for the movie." He struggles to get his mind to make plans that didn't involve kissing one sister or the other. He sees Albert Croner coming up behind Anna and warns, "better get that bushel weighed. That asshole Croner is coming this way."

Anna is shocked at his language, almost to the point of not moving. Henry gives her a nod in the direction of the scales and it gets her going. She thinks to herself. *I don't know anyone who uses such words in front of a lady! Henry was not raised like that.* She walks quickly, though, because she didn't want Croner to start yelling at her. *Wasn't this work hard enough without Croner's abuse? He really was <u>a-hole</u>! Oh, my goodness, I just thought the very word Henry used!* She giggles to herself. *If the shoe fits . . .*

NINE

The First Saturday in September
In Lawrence, Kansas

True to his word, Joshua comes home to court Rosanne. Carolyn is up at her normal time, six-thirty in the morning, to find that her brother drove down during the night. The Colonel's night attendant, Andrew, let him in and he slept in his bed until Carolyn found out that he was home.

She bursts into his room, yelling, "Rise and Shine, little brother!"

"Carolyn, always the morning person, aren't you? Let a man sleep, will you?" He groans.

"Rosanne told me about your phone call on Wednesday morning. Don't you think you are wasting your time? She says she doesn't love you that way. She's very insistent. What are you going to do?" She sits down on the foot of his bed.

"Well, take her out to dinner and a movie, I suppose. I don't know. Dazzle her with my charms?"

"You've tried that, unless you learned some new tricks during the month you've been back at college."

"Well, I feel my persistence will wear down her resistance, I'm sure of it."

"She has a good point, you know, since we don't know her past, she might be married. You are taking a big chance, not knowing. Maybe we ought to hire another private investigator so we can find out who she is, once and for all.

"If we find out she's married, then I've no chance."

"Joshua, you would be so selfish, as to keep her from finding her family if it means losing her? Then Rosanne had it wrong. You don't deserve HER!"

"I'm kidding. We should keep looking for her family. That doesn't mean that I cannot take her to a dance, in the meantime. How has the Colonel been?"

"Getting hard to handle. He's had two bad days this week. I may must hire another person for the day. He taxes all of Rosanne's strength, on those days. Speaking of Rosanne, she's awake and the coffee is ready from the smell of it. Are you getting out of bed?"

"I guess I'm awake, now. So, why not. I do have some homework to do this weekend but I can do it tomorrow. Is there anything you'd like me to handle for the farm, while I'm here? I could ride out to the tomato field to see how things are going for you. I know how you hate going there, and I don't think you should just leave it in the hands of your foremen. Sometime those old coots get drunk with power, I hear."

"I cannot wait until you graduate and come back to run this place so I can work on my inventions. Did you know that three farms have offered me a fortune to go set up my irrigation system for them? I've other ideas that I want to get started on. I cannot wait."

"Well, wait you must, sis, for just eight more months, at least."

"The smell of that coffee is driving me crazy, I have to have some!

They both dress and head down the stairs where Rosanne is making their breakfast. They both stop at the doorway and watch Rosanne. She's humming the Fred Astaire song, _Day and Night_, while whirling around from stove to counter. Not just cooking but dancing between the food prep, the stove, fry pans and plates. They haven't seen her do anything like this, before. Of course, she has just gotten her full strength back, obviously. Joshua leans in to Carolyn. "She said she can't dance!"

During one of the whirls, she spots them watching her. For some reason, she isn't embarrassed, "Good morning, it's a wonderful day, isn't it?"

"Good morning to you, too." Carolyn goes to her, "It's so good to see you like this. You are just glowing. You must have slept good, did you?"

"Yes, I dreamt something last night. It was a memory. I'm sure of it. But you know how hard it's to grasp dreams in the daylight. It just got away, oh, but it was a good one." She swirls one last time for good luck.

"Is there any part of it, you can remember?" Joshua asks.

"It's hard to explain, wait, I must turn the bacon." She turns to the stove and does her magic then turns back to them. "It was like I was in very small kitchen humming that song, then others joined in with the words. We were all so happy. I didn't see faces but they were my family, I know it. They're out there."

"Joshua and I were just talking about this. We are going to hire new private detectives. We have more clues now. Your partial memories, the things we've noticed about what you can do and things you didn't have."

Rosanne laughs, "Lots of people can cook, and didn't have phones or bathrooms. Not exactly a rare thing, those."

"We now know that you had a small kitchen. See, we are half way there." Joshua adds to keep it light.

"Dreams aside, where's my coffee?" Carolyn says impatiently.

After breakfast, Carolyn heads to the Farm Office. Joshua plans to go to the tomato field to check on the workers. Saturday is only a half day for them, so he knows he'd better hurry. He asks Rosanne to join him. She laughs and says, "I've seen tomato fields. Had I known in advance, though, I would have gotten an attendant for the Colonel."

Well, be ready when I get back. I want to take you to dinner and a movie, tonight. Don't argue or make excuses. You deserve an evening off and away from the Colonel. You need to care for yourself, first.

"Did you read that in a book at school?"

"No, I just know how difficult it is to take care of the Colonel for a short time. You have done it, day in and day out for a long time. You remember what happened last March? You worked around the clock taking care of him and made yourself sick.

"That was an unusual circumstance. That couldn't happen again."

"Well, something like it could."

"You don't know do you?" She looked up at him. *Carolyn didn't tell him*, the thought surprised her.

"I don't know what you mean. Look, we will talk about this later. I've to get to those fields." With that he grabs his hat and leaves.

The Colonel is being very pleasant today. While she was dressing him, Rosanne told him that Joshua was here. He said he's very excited about seeing his little grandson.

"He's a grown man, Colonel."

"I can't wait to see the grown Joshua, then. What's he like?"

"He's tall and built with wide shoulders. He has dark blonde hair and light brown eyes. They have Carolyn's hazel flecks in them. He's very quick to make a joke."

"He likes to hear you laugh, I suspect."

"Why do you say that?"

"That's how I got my Julia. I made her laugh. It's not like I was a pretty boy, so I had to rely on something."

"I think you did more than just make her laugh."

"That and I made her feel loved. Every chance I had, I told her. I know she went to her grave without a doubt of my total devotion to her. She knew she was my everything."

"Wow, Colonel, you were so lucky to have had that."

"There wasn't a day that went by that I didn't believe that I was the luckiest man alive. I still am the luckiest man, alive."

"Why do you say that Colonel?" Rosanne is combing his hair when he stops her hand in motion and lowers it to his heart.

"I'm lucky because she never had to see me like this. I'm the shell of the man, I once was. It would have broken her heart to see me how I'm now."

"Aww, Colonel." Rosanne is touched by his sadness. "I love the man you are now."

"I don't mean she'd have stopped loving me. It's just that, it would have changed if she had to become my caretaker, don't you think? I'm sorry that she's gone but so lucky that she missed this long slow good-bye journey that I'm on."

Rosanne cannot look at him. She understands, completely. He's forgetting the here and now, more and more. He still remembers the past, vividly. He's Rosanne's opposite. She cannot remember her past and is stuck in a here and now, that isn't hers. *What a pair they make!* She starts to cry, again. *I can't show him tears,* she thinks. *That will make him uncomfortable.* She blinks and wipes her tears before she turns to him.

The Colonel has his own tears running down his cheek. Rosanne thinks, *he must have been a gentle giant in his day. Very easy for Julia to love every day of her life.*

"So Rosanne, I think I want oatmeal, today, if that's all right." He stands up as if this conversation never took place. He holds out his hand for her. She gladly takes it and they go down the stairs.

Once he's breakfasted and back asleep in his chair, Rosanne goes upstairs to straighten the Colonel's bedroom and her own. Then she starts to look at her limited choice of clothing to go out with Joshua tonight. She loves the thought of going to a movie. She doesn't remember going to one, but she knows that she loves them. Just like cooking. She doesn't remember ever doing it before but she knows how. How weird and awesome the brain must be to compartmentalize like that, she thinks.

She hears the kitchen door and Rocco barking at Robbie. So, Carolyn is home. Soon, Joshua will be here. Maybe she can talk him into staying home for dinner, but still see the movie. This way she can cook for Carolyn and the Colonel and not leave Carolyn stuck with it.

She hears Carolyn on the staircase. "Can I come in? She asks a moment later.

"Yes, of course. Please, I was just looking at what I can wear, this evening."

"About that, I bought you a little something." She goes back to the doorway where she left a package. "It's for tonight, if you like or maybe tomorrow for church service. I just thought you'd like a dress to wear. When you had to wear those damn shoulder braces, the only thing that fit you was the Colonel's shirts. You haven't had the braces for a long time but you never changed your look. It's time to be a girl, girl!"

Rosanne opens the box. It has a very simple dress. It buttons in the back and is very sheer. It's spaghetti straps and is a pretty soft flower print. "I love it, Carolyn but you shouldn't have done it. I should go shopping sometime. I do need a clothing pick me up. Will you take me sometime?"

"I'd love to, maybe next week. Do we need to shop for a dancing dress?"

"Absolutely, not. I refuse to go. I'm not going to the dance and that's that."

"Will you wear this one, tonight at least?"

"Absolutely will, it's beautiful. Can I ask you something?"

"Sure, what is it?"

"Can I cook you something, before I leave?"

"On your dinner date? You are too much! Please! I can handle a meal with my grandfather, Rosanne. You mustn't worry about it. I won't poison us, I promise."

"That's exactly what I was worried about, you got me."

"Okay, sister, get ready. I hear Joshua with the Colonel. I'm going down to be with them. We don't get much alone time together now that Joshua is away."

"Even more reason for me to cook dinner before we go see a movie!"

"Tempting, girl, but get ready and get out of here. That's an order."

The dress fits Rosanne perfectly. She's so glad that Carolyn looks out for her the way she does. How can one ever say thank you enough? She looks in the small mirror on her dresser. Her new hair style looks so good and her dress is pretty. Rosanne pinches her cheeks for color and hopes for the best before she heads downstairs.

When she walks into the sitting room, all heads turn her way. They all smile. Joshua is the first to speak. "You look beautiful, Rosanne. Nice dress, is it new?" He smiles at Carolyn, and she winks at him.

"You too are in co-hoots with each other! What's going on?"

"We just thought you deserve a nice night out, is all." Joshua explains.

"Where are we going, Joshua? I'm starved, what movie is playing?"

"I'd like to keep the restaurant a surprise but do you want to see the musical Show Boat with Irene Dunne? I read in the Topeka Times that it's very good."

"Oh yes, please. I'd love to see a musical." She's very excited and suddenly can't wait to leave.

Joshua takes her to a restaurant that he thinks the food is something that she has never seen or knows how to make. He takes her to an Italian Restaurant for Pizza. She thinks a pizza pie is very odd, but she loves its taste. She's so happy, and she shows it. Joshua thinks, *God, I love her. Why can't she feel the same for me? She's holding herself back with me but she doesn't need to, I just want to be with her.*

The movie was terrific. She's sitting in the car, afterward, humming 'Old Man River'. She cried at the end, of course. All the girls cried. *Perfect date movie!*

On the way home, he asks her, "Did you have a good time tonight?"

"The best, thank you, Joshua, you've been a perfect date."

"Did you want to stop for ice cream?" He doesn't want the date to end. He loves making her happy.

"You know we have some in the icebox at home? Why don't we go there? I like to see the Colonel before he goes to bed."

"Come on, Rosanne, let's stay out a little longer. I love being alone, with you."

"Joshua, take me home, you said the bad word."

"I didn't curse, I said 'I love being alone with you'. What did you hear?"

"Exactly that, Joshua, the bad word is 'love'. I'm going to call you brother, so that you stop thinking of me as anything more than a sister. I'm not the one for you."

"What makes you so sure about that?"

"Joshua, can you pull over someplace, I want to talk to you while you aren't driving." He's very surprised at this but does as he's asked.

"I'll repeat my question, what makes you so sure you're not the one?"

"Do you remember the time, last March, that I got so ill, taking care of the Colonel at all hours? You mentioned it, earlier."

"What about it, Rosanne?"

"I wasn't just worn out, Joshua, I lost a baby. The doctors who put me back together after the accident, said there was evidence of rape when I was discovered. After I got out of the hospital, I was in that big chest / shoulder brace thing. I knew that my cycles didn't come and that I had all the symptoms of being with child. They figured, I was about five months, along."

"Rosanne, I'm so sorry. I didn't know."

"That's my point, Joshua, you don't know if the baby was my attackers or if I was married before the attack? What if I was a loose woman and slept around? Either way, I'm not a virgin and have a 'history' even if WE don't know it. I'm damaged used goods and you deserve better than used goods. I want you to ask someone at school to that dance and forget your feelings about me. Or when you come home at the end of the school term, I won't be here. I swear it. I don't want to leave Carolyn or the Colonel or you, but I'll leave and never come back unless you stop this nonsense. We don't have a future, can I be any clearer than that, brother?

"Perfectly clear, you don't love me, say no more." He starts the engine but before he can find the gear, Rosanne puts her hand on his arm. He looks in those soft moist beautiful brown eyes that he can get lost in.

"I do love you, Joshua, but as my brother and my best friend. Don't ask any more of me, please." She starts to cry. "I don't want to lose you, or Carolyn or the Colonel!" He melts as he sees the tears fall from her loving eyes.

TEN

The First Saturday in September, 1935
In EL Dorado, Kansas

They had two more very hot windy days in the field followed by cool evenings at the farm camp. They spent the morning in the fields because Saturdays are half days. Anna was very excited and nervous for her first date with Henry. She saw him a few times in the fields over the last two days, but he spent most of his time with Matthew. The thought of Henry spending so much time with her baby brother makes Anna think more kindly toward Henry. Matthew and Henry were joking and had their heads together in some sort of secret discussion every time Anna looked their way. Each night, Matthew would say "Henry said . . ." or "Did you know that Henry . . ." several times. Anna almost started to feel jealous of their closeness.

Melinda has been enjoying the cool breezy evenings sneaking out to meet Henry. She knew that it was wrong but somehow that made it so *RIGHT!* She thought she could make him forget this foolishness of being engaged to her sister. She knew that she was being a harlot, and that she should feel bad but having Henry *want* her meant everything to her. She didn't care about anything else.

Anna is nervously getting ready for her date. She bought new stockings and is having trouble getting the seams straight. Judy is helping her curl up her hair high on her head. Judy asks, "Do you know what picture you will see with Henry?"

"I think it will be the new Shirley Temple movie, *The Little Colonel.* I just adore that little girl! How does she learn all those dances?" Anna asks curiously.

Melinda is being very moody. When Judy asks her to help clean up after lunch, Melinda says, "Why don't you ask your favorite daughter?" Judy thought that it is simple jealousy of Anna dating. Matthew tries to get her to play checkers but she doesn't want to do that, either. Finally, Melinda announces, "I am going to go see a friend on the other side of the camp. I'll be back to help with supper." She leaves with a slam of the door.

Henry and his father drive up in their old truck. They both have flowers. Frank asks Judd if he could give the bouquet of gladiolas to Judy as a thank you for sharing a meal with him, yet again. Henry bought a small wrist corsage for Anna. She loves the little roses and baby's breath. She has never seen flowers for the wrist. She is so taken by them, that she gives Henry a kiss on the cheek then blushes at her own boldness. All eyes are on the couple as Henry walks Anna to the truck and holds the door open for her to get in.

As the truck drives away, Melinda comes back to the hut. Her mood hasn't improved with her outing. She's barely polite to Mr. Harrick and is quiet all during dinner.

Anna feels very shy with Henry and doesn't know why. She's known him all her life. She doesn't know how to start a conversation with him. She notices that he found the time to get a haircut. His hair was always breaking free from behind his ears when it was longer but now the light brown waves are tamed and cut over his ears and slicked down with a nice smelling pomade. "I like your haircut." She says just barely loud enough to be heard over the sound of the old engine of the truck.

"Da made me get it cut. I like it long, but with the intense heat of late, this will be much cooler. I went to Crystal Barber across from the EL Dorado Blooming Place where we bought the flowers." He says without taking his eyes off the road. "Your hair is very pretty, up like that. It brings out the beautiful heart shape of your face."

"Heart shaped face?" Anna asks. She has never thought of her face's shape in those words or in any words for that matter.

"Yes, well, large eyes and cheekbones, widow's peak in your high forehead and your tiny mouth and chin. Perfect heart. That describes you, and I am not talking about your face, anymore." Henry smiles as he sneaks a peek at her while driving.

Anna is blushing. She doesn't know what to say. Compliments make her feel uncomfortable. She cannot believe that he noticed her face at all. This new Henry is surprising her again and again.

Sally's Diner is two doors down from the ERIS Theatre. From the outside, the restaurant seems small but looks much larger once inside. Anna is impressed with how clean it looked. They have a black and white tile floor and white tables with black chairs. The white counter has a black border and ten black cushioned stools. There are six booths that have black and white checkered cushions. Henry tells her that his favorite meal there is the meatloaf. Meatloaf is her favorite meal too, but she doesn't think someone can make it better than her mother, so she orders the fried chicken. The waitress says that it takes an extra twenty minutes to fry the chicken, which would make them late for the movie. Anna orders the pork chops, instead.

Henry is being the perfect gentleman. He opened the truck door for her to get out, opened the door of the diner and pulled out her chair to sit down, once inside. Anna is feeling very conflicted. He is talking about going to Wichita or Kansas City to get a job in a factory, explaining that the pay would be so much better. She cannot imagine living in a crowded city, no matter what the pay. She loves small towns and the farmland.

"Henry, don't you want your own farm, someday?" Anna asks. "I cannot imagine living somewhere I cannot grow things, like the golden wheat fields our fathers grew. Do you remember the herb and flower garden my Mother had in the side yard? She misses that garden and I would love to have my own someday."

"Anna, there is no money in it, anymore. The small farmer cannot compete with these huge places that can hire day workers, like the Johnson Family Farms. I've had enough of the quiet life. I'm looking for adventure and a better chance of earning." Henry explains. He thinks, *she'll never understand this need. Melinda does and as a need for adventure greater than his own. How is this going to work? I have so much more in common with Anna's sister. Melinda doesn't want to be tied down to a farm or marriage any more than I do.* As old fashioned as it sounds Henry cannot help thinking, *when it comes time to start a family, though, Anna would be the one I'd want to have my children and keep my house.*

They finish eating in uneasy silence. Neither understanding the other and each lost in thought. Henry pays the bill. With tip the meal cost $1.25! Anna was about to say they should have stayed home to eat with the families to save money but somehow she knew that Henry wouldn't like that.

They walk down the street to the ERIS Theatre for the moving picture show. Shirley Temple's movie cost 15¢ each. Anna liked how her character made everyone fall in love with her, even her grumpy old Grandfather.

Anna asks Henry if he liked the movie and he says, "Waste of money. I don't know why they don't have anything more adult to play. I mean, the little girl is very talented but the plot lines are always the same in her movies." He complains. "Do you want to get an ice cream cone, or shake or something before we head home?" Henry changes the subject. He feels that he must try to turn this date around. They aren't seeing eye to eye on much.

"I would love an ice cream . . . is it a lot of money?" Anna asks without thinking.

"Anna, if I thought I couldn't afford it, I wouldn't have asked. Geez!!" They walk back to the truck. Central Avenue Soda Shop and Ice Cream Parlor is on the other side of downtown. When they get to the truck, before he opens the door for her, Henry says, "I'm sorry Anna, I didn't mean to snap at you. There just is so much pressure on us for this to work out. Can you feel it, too?" She stands for a moment, thinking and then slowly nods yes.

"I think that it's worse for you, since this was Da's idea. Ma said that I don't need to make any decisions until I am ready. Pa hasn't said anything to me since that night. Well, he has talked to me but not about this." She continues. "I think we should just take our time. If it isn't right, it isn't right. I'm sure that your dad wants you to be happy. I might not be the right girl for you." She pauses a moment. "I would like to be, but that doesn't make it so."

Henry bends down and gives her a chaste kiss on her cheek. "You are so very sweet, Anna. 'Pure Heart', like I said on the way here." She is caught by surprise with his sudden kiss. Though her stomach is a twitter, she's brave enough to tippy toe up and give him a return kiss on his cheek.

They ride to the ice cream parlor in silence. It takes only a few minutes. After a moment of looking over the flavors they both say at the same time, "Butter Pecan" and laugh. There it is the old Henry and Anna together. The counter girl looks at them both and says, "Well, cone or bowl?" Now they look at each other again and both say "Bowl". With bowls in hand, they go sit in a corner booth to enjoy it.

Anna asks, "What have you and Matthew been cooking up? There is something going on there, I know it."

"Matthew is a great kid. He's a very quick learner, too. Very bright young man. He was asking me about playing craps. I've been on a winning streak and he's intrigued by it. I've been explaining the rules to him."

"You are teaching my baby brother to GAMBLE? Why?" Anna asked, incredulously, sitting back in her chair in disbelief. "What are you thinking!!"

"Calm down, Anna, there's no harm in knowing how to play an innocent game of fun. Like I said, I've been very lucky lately. You should go with me sometime. It's fun."

"I don't approve of gambling." She says abruptly. "I don't want you showing Matthew. Does your Da know that you gamble?"

"Well, he knows I go out at night to let off steam. He's noticed when I've had a drink or two and doesn't like it, with this being a dry state and all. I don't think that he knows about my crap games. I'm a grown man. He cannot stop me from having a little fun after all the hard work I put in every day."

"But Matthew isn't a grown man and you are being a bad influence on him." She says hesitantly. "I don't want you hanging around him. I am not sure if I want you to hang around me, either. We are so different, now." She shakes her head and looks down into her empty ice cream bowl. She is so disappointed that this isn't working. A single tear starts to fall from her large dark eyes. "I think I want you to take me home, now." She says very quietly.

"Anna, you are putting too much into this. I'm just having some innocent fun. I'll take you home but I cannot believe that you are cutting me off like this. Can we talk more about it?" Henry stands up and offers Anna his arm to lead her to the truck.

"I am not sure what else there is to say." Anna says sadly. She stands up and takes his arm and they walk out of the ice cream shop in silence. Henry opens the truck door for her and she slowly gets into it. She looks down in her lap and sees the wrist corsage, again. *How can he be so romantic and thoughtful in some ways but reckless in others?* She thinks to herself.

Henry gets in the driver's side of the vehicle but before he puts the key into the ignition, he turns to Anna. "Look, I promise not to teach Matthew about the games, anymore, but will you come out with me, just once more to see how innocent these games are? You are very naïve and you are jumping to conclusions. Please Anna?"

His voice says her name just barely above a whisper and the deep silkiness of it sends her insides to quiver, again. *It's like he has a special power like the heroes in the comic books that Matthew used to read. Why does my body respond to him even though my head isn't sure about him, right now?* She thinks.

"Henry, I would like to go out with you again, but I don't want to see a crap game." She thinks of an alternative. "Henry, will you come to Sunday Worship with me tomorrow? I mean, come pick me up and we can walk together to Service? I would like that very much. What do you think?"

"I think, you think that I need God in my life, right now." He chuckles. "Will he set me on the right path, ya think?"

"We all need God in our lives, Henry. There is going to a Social in the Barn after the Service. Ma is planning to fry up her chicken. I hear that a few of the fellas will bring some musical instruments and play some dancing music. Doesn't that sound like fun?

Henry starts the truck. As he's revving the engine, he gives an answer in the manner of a 'hmmm!' He thinks that the engine noise will drown it out but Anna hears it. He looks over to her and she repeats, "Oh, 'hmmm' is it? Not sure that you can have real innocent fun at a church social?" Her eyes are twinkling as if to dare him NOT to have fun. He cannot help but admire her optimism, even if it's based on her ignorance of the world.

"All right, fine. I can pick you up and walk you to Service and we can stay for the Social afterward." He sighs.

"Yippee!" She says enthusiastically. "And thank you." She adds.

"For saying yes?" He asks confused.

"No, silly, for dinner, the moving picture show and the ice cream." Anna explains. "It was very generous of you to spend so much on me in one night, but I did enjoy myself."

As it is going on eleven p.m., Henry decides to leave his loud truck in the lot at the front entrance of the camp and he will walk Anna to her hut. Henry doesn't know if his Da will still be there or if he went home earlier. About halfway to the hut, Henry stops and turns to Anna. "I don't want an embarrassing moment at the door, especially if Da is there. Can I kiss you good-night, now?"

This catches Anna off guard. "Well, I don't want to do it with family around, either." Henry leans in and just as his lips are to touch hers, she turns her head so he places the kiss on her cheek, instead.

"So, not even a real kiss, then? Was I that bad of a date?"

"No, of course not, but Ma says a *good girl* never kisses on the lips on the first date."

"And you always do what your Ma says?"

"Always." She says smiling.

"Does she have a second date rule?" He asks.

"Not that I know of, but I'll ask her before you pick me up for Service. I'll let you know what to expect."

"But, if you don't ask her, can I kiss you, tomorrow?"

"Well, if I don't ask her, I might have to assume that a good girl doesn't kiss on a second date, either." She says with a twinkle in her eye. "I do want to make sure that I am a good girl, first and foremost."

"Lucky, me." Henry says dejectedly. She laughs at that.

They are soon at the door of the hut and the lights are off except for a small table lamp next to the couch where Matthew sleeps. Before going inside, Anna turns to Henry. She says in a whisper, "I will see you on the morrow, then, kind sir?"

"Yes, you will, milady." Henry bows like a lord before his queen. "And sweet dreams to you. I will see you at ten a.m. then."

"You are correct, Sir Henry. Please, you may stand now, my most nobleman." *What fun!* Anna thinks.

As Henry straightens up, he takes Anna's hand and gives it a brushing of his lips. "Until the morrow, Milady." He turns and walks into the darkness of the camp.

The house is silent as Anna lets herself in. She shuts off the small light. Matthew rolls over on the couch but does not wake. Anna tiptoes to the bedroom. The door is ajar and the room has moonlight flooding in from the window above Melinda's bed. Anna is thankful for it so that she can undress, take down her hair and get ready for bed. Melinda seems sound asleep as Anna goes to the kitchen to pump water to wash her face and brush her teeth. When she gets back to the room, Melinda is sitting up on her bed with her arms around her drawn up knees. Melinda asks, "How did it go? Did you kiss him? What movie did you see? What did you have for dinner? Did you kiss him?"

"Whoa, Melinda – you asked if I kissed him, twice! He gave me a kiss on the cheek. We saw a Shirley Temple movie. I had pork chops for dinner. Did I answer them all?" Anna asks as she is climbing into bed.

"Well, I've got to go to the outhouse. I'm glad you had a good time. Don't wait up for me." Melinda says as she puts on overalls to go outside. She slips out of the bedroom before Anna can say that she didn't know if she had a good time.

Anna is smiling as she lays her head down thinking about the Social tomorrow. She doesn't think for long. She is sound asleep in just a few moments.

Melinda doesn't know if Henry is going to be at the camp truck, but she will be waiting for him if he isn't. She's taking her time, walking very slowly. She isn't sure what to do. She knows that she wants Henry's arms around her. She doesn't care if he feeds Anna or that they saw a movie together. She knew that Anna would leave him wanting.

Henry is at his usual spot, on the side of the store. Melinda walks up to him. She stands next to him and waits a moment before she raises an eyebrow with the unspoken question of 'how was it?'

Henry holds out his hand to her. She takes it and he pulls her to him with his arm around her. He bends down to snuggle against Melinda's neck. "So good." He simply says.

"What is?" She murmurs.

"All of you. You drive me wild." He speaks low and slow on purpose. He knows that his deep voice makes Melinda crazy. He's delivering small kisses behind her ear. She starts purring. She breaks away from him and heads to the camp truck. He follows very closely behind her. No words are needed. She climbs up and in herself. She is sitting on the bench unbuttoning her top as he slides in next to her. He feels uneasy about being with Melinda so soon after being with Anna, but he wants Melinda so bad! They don't stop to talk. Each knows what the other wants and they give everything they have.

After they are spent, they dress slowly. Henry doesn't know what Melinda wants to hear so he asks. "What do you want to know?"

"I want to know that we can keep doing this. I want to be the one you want always!"

"You are deep under my skin. You and I are so much alike. I'm going through the motions with Anna but what we have is powerful. You are like a drug that I don't want to stop taking."

Melinda smiles at this. She likes being described this way. "Matthew was telling me about your crap games. I would love to go."

"How are you and Anna even related?" He chuckles a little. "She was adamant that she'll not have me going to play craps, and warned me to stay away from Matthew. She wants to bring me to God tomorrow and the Church Social afterward. Of course, I had to say yes. Will you be going?"

"Yes, John Walker asked me to go with him and I said I would. You know John, don't you? He says he knows you."

"John is one of the guys that I play craps with, actually. We are going to play tomorrow night. You should tell your parents that John wants to take you out and bring Matthew as your chaperone. This way I can keep both my promises. I promised Matthew to take him to his first crap game and I promised Anna that I would stay away from Matthew.

God, I feel like I am leading three lives all at once."

"I know the feeling but I like the thrill of all the secrecy. The risk of getting caught makes everything we do more exciting. I'll tell my folks at the Social that John will take Matthew and I for ice cream or something and we will meet you there. I better get back to the hut before someone notices that I am gone."

ELEVEN

The Second Sunday in September
In Lawrence, Kansas

The Colonel didn't like Carolyn putting him to bed last night. He likes Rosanne to do it for him. He kept getting up to look for Rosanne or his Julia. One of them needs to be here for him. Why can't he find them?

When Joshua and Rosanne come home, Carolyn is at her wits end. "I don't know how you do it Rosanne, but he won't settle down without you." As she rushes these words out, she notices that Rosanne's beautiful brown eyes are red from crying and her cheeks are tear streaked. She looks to Joshua, who doesn't look his happy self, either. "What's happened?"

"She threatened to leave us if I don't stop loving her. She's being unreasonable. She can't leave us; she needs us as much as we need her!" Joshua is saying this as he's helping her off with her wrap. "You must talk her out of this."

"Stop talking about me as if I'm not here. I hate that! I'm going up to the Colonel. At least, he has some sense about him!" She goes up the stairs, stomping her feet with a purpose, leaving Carolyn and Joshua just staring up at her.

"What have you done, Joshua? I told you not to push her. Poor thing is walking a tight rope of emotions, every day."

"We were having a great date, and I told her that I loved being with her and she cut me short. She said that she's going to call me brother until I accept the fact, that's how she feels for me. If I can't do it she says, she'll leave."

"We have the ultimate battle of the wills! Go back up to school, Joshua, date other girls, try and forget Rosanne. I think that's best for all concerned."

"You can't begin to know how I feel for her. I want to take her in my arms, every time she smiles or cries. I do love her, Carolyn, this isn't just a crush."

"I believe you, brother. I love her, also. I've wanted to hold her and care for her and protect her since the moment I saw her beaten and bloody in the dirt. It's like she's my long-lost child or something. My heart breaks with every one of her tears and it's light as a feather with every smile. It goes beyond logic, that I should feel this strongly about someone, that I don't even know, who doesn't know herself, who was barely alive; but I did and still do. You are hurting her with your talk of love. You must stop it and distance yourself, emotionally and physically."

It was decided, then. Joshua will stay the night and leave after Service to go back to the University. He'd his homework to do, and he needed the library, anyway.

Joshua's mind isn't on the Service at all. He's sitting between Carolyn and the Colonel and Rosanne is on the Colonel's other side. Rosanne hasn't said a word to him all morning. She made everyone breakfast, got herself and the Colonel ready to leave, but was as silent the walls. She must still be mad at him. He can't go back to school with her mad. It will eat him up inside.

Rosanne is holding hands with the Colonel during Service and looks up at him so sweetly. She does love the old man, with all her heart. She's had it so hard, this last year, with her injuries, the miscarriage, trying to remember who she is. *Yet she has room in her heart to love the Colonel, Carolyn and myself. Probably in that order,* Joshua thinks. She doesn't need the unwelcomed advances of a suiter, right now. His head knows this, but his heart won't listen. It just aches for her.

After Service, they head back home. Joshua will leave immediately. The day attendant, Harry, is there to take care of the Colonel. Carolyn makes sure that Rosanne has Sunday off to rest or go out, if she wants. Rosanne still hasn't said a word to Joshua, but she's talking to Carolyn about going shopping, today. "I know that a few of the stores are open in Lawrence today. Do you think you can take me?"

Carolyn is very surprised by this. "Of course, Rosanne. Harry is here for the Colonel. Why don't we go out for the day, and just have fun, sister?" She adds that part for Joshua, who was looking so rejected. He must get used to the idea that Rosanne is their sister. Nothing beyond that.

Joshua says, "I'll leave my girls to it then." He walks to the Colonel in his chair. "Colonel, please stay healthy until I come home, again. I'll miss you, sir." He gives the Colonel a little salute then bends down and kisses his cheek. "Okay, my sisters," he says with an emphasis on the word 'sisters', "who is going to walk me to my car?"

Carolyn and Rosanne look at each other, "We both will." They say together. They're arm in arm and they each give him a kiss on the cheek and a wave good-bye as he drives away.

Rosanne turns to Carolyn. "Can we go right away? Or do you want me to make us lunch first?" Carolyn can hear the excitement in her voice and it's contagious.

"Let's leave right away. We can have lunch in the diner, downtown. Harry can feed the Colonel. I've wanted to show you this one shop that has all the newest fashions for the longest time. You have the most adorable figure for everything there. They have some things for my size, too. I haven't had anything new in a while."

They're in Carolyn's car, not her work truck, to go to downtown. It's a 1934 green Hudson convertible. The top is down and Carolyn looks over at Rosanne smiling in the passenger seat. "I'm glad you aren't upset with Joshua."

"How could anyone stay mad at the goofy kid? I just hope that he asks someone to the dance. It's the only way we can stay together as a family."

"I understand, sister, I think he got that message loud and clear."

Once in the first store, Rosanne is trying to decide between a blue dress or a peach colored one. They're both similar styles and both look great on her. She asks Carolyn for advice.

"That color blue is great for your fair skin. I think the peach is a little too bland."

"Bland is what I need for when Joshua is visiting!" She says with a smile. "They're priced little more than I feel comfortable spending and I want to go to more places. I'll just get the blue one, for now." Carolyn has tried on a few things but nothing looks good on her. Is *that because I'm shopping with her perfect size six, sister?* She wonders.

Rosanne pays for the dress and they head to the car. She stops Carolyn a few feet from the Hudson. Carolyn asks, "What's wrong?"

"Can I drive?" Rosanne asks.

"I don't know, can you? Do you remember driving?"

"Something about lessons, yes. I won't know until I'm behind the wheel. Do you mind?" Her brown eyes plead.

"Take the keys, I'll live dangerously. Let me know if you are uncomfortable, at any time."

Rosanne takes the keys and starts the engine perfectly. She starts to back out of the spot with her arm behind the passenger seat. She puts the car into drive and eases it forward. As she's leaving the parking space, she checks all her mirrors, multiple times as if worried about something. She suddenly starts trembling as she stops the car, puts it in park, and abandons the car right in the middle of Massachusetts Ave! Rosanne is pacing up and down shaking her arms all about as if trying to shake away a bad feeling. She says out loud to herself, "I don't like this; this is a bad idea." Carolyn is out of the car, instantly. She can tell, this is a memory, and not a good one like yesterday's.

"It's okay, Rosanne. You are safe. Nothing else bad is going to happen to you." She puts her arms around her. "Rosanne look at me. I won't let you get hurt again. Do you want to walk for a bit? Let me just park the car. You stay here and I'll be right back with you." Carolyn puts the car in the nearest open space and is next to Rosanne in a jiffy. "Okay, let's walk across the street. There's a park there. We can sit on a bench if you like." Rosanne just nods, still trembling.

Carolyn has her arm around this fragile woman's waist. *How could anyone have done those unspeakable things to her?* She asks herself that, all the time. *He must have been a monster.* She just prays that it was a stranger and not someone Rosanne knew. That would make it even harder for her to remember or go back home.

They're on the bench and the little walk helps calm her down, but she's still trembling, just a little. Carolyn is holding her hand, waiting to see what she needs. Quiet time to absorb this new memory, or saying it out loud to get it out in the open and off her chest. Quiet time wins out for at least ten minutes.

"Carolyn, it was bad, that was the worst feeling I've had."

"I can tell, but you are safe now." She reassures her.

"I was driving when it happened. I was behind the wheel, driving and I was afraid for my life. I don't remember why or how but I was alone behind the wheel when it started."

"This is where Joshua would say, if you were behind the wheel, we'd all be afraid for our lives." Rosanne just smiles at this.

"That's Joshua. Thank you, Carolyn. I'm much better, and starving! Spending half a week's pay on one dress can really make you hungry!"

"Yup, you're better. Let's walk to the diner. The car is safe where it's, for now."

TWELVE

The Second Sunday in September, 1935
In EL Dorado, Kansas

At ten a.m., sharp, Henry is at the Masters' hut. Anna is just as nervous as she was the day before. She's wearing a flowered sundress with a large matching flowered hat that's very fashionable. Henry is in awe of her simple beauty. Melinda is in the background, waiting for her date. She's wearing a pastel pink dress that highlights her dark skin and long dark hair that she has in a very simple side braid. It amazes Henry that the sisters are such opposites. Anna's fair with dark eyes. Melinda's dark with light blue eyes. Anna is tall. Melinda is short. Anna is very slender. Melinda has ample curves and loves to flaunt them, while Anna is very shy. Melinda loves adventure while Anna loves to be a homebody.

John Walker arrives shortly after Henry and the couples start out for the old barn where the Services are held. Matthew tags along. Judd and Judy were already at the earlier Service. Judy is now very busy making her delicious fried chicken that they're going to bring to the Social afterward. Anna asks her mother if she wanted help, but Judy just waves her hand at her as a signal to go.

The new preacher is from the big city – Topeka. He's very intense, and it seems like he's trying to bring fire and brimstone to the Camp. Even Anna is glad when the Service is over. She likes the young Minister that normally preaches. She tells Henry that she's dragged him to Service on the wrong day.

"Pastor Tyler is very sweet and makes you feel that our Lord is a loving god. Today's Preacher makes it seem as if we have no way of recovery. We are doomed before we start. I hope that Pastor Tyler will be back next Sunday. You'll like him so much better." Anna says as though it was decided that he'll accompany her again.

Melinda adds her two cents. "I wish we could find out beforehand. I'll skip Service, altogether, if I must listen to this Preacher again. Ma didn't mention that Pastor Tyler was absent today."

"Ma was preoccupied with frying the chicken. It's possible that Pastor Tyler did the early Service and is busy with the last-minute details of the Social." Offers Anna.

They all agree that it's possible and they start helping change the barn from a church to a dance hall. The chairs are moved from the center to the outer walls. Tables are being set up for eating and where the Preacher gives his sermon, the band will set up. Judd and Judy come in with two big baskets of fried chicken. Other families are coming in with big bowls of food, too. Mark Collins, from the Camp Store is there, bringing a punch bowl set and all the fixings for an ice cream punch. Anna thinks that it's so generous of everyone to share like this even though everyone is down on their luck. She helps Mark set up the punch, she mentions that this is Melinda's favorite. He returns, "she mentioned it to me, that's why I brought it." He blushes, through a small nervous smile.

Henry's Da is there, too. He looks more drawn than ever. Anna mentions it to Henry. "He's fine, at least that's what he keeps telling me." Henry says. "There isn't anything I can do, if he won't admit that he's getting worse. He only listens to your mother. She was the one that nursed him back from the first attack."

"I'll tell Ma to look at him. Everyone is loving her chicken. She looks so happy, doesn't she?" She points to her smiling mother. Judy has her hair down for this special occasion and Henry cannot believe that he never noticed how much Anna looks just like her, except Anna is 9 inches taller.

They eat until they can't move but then dance the night away. Anna and Melinda are the Belles of the ball. It seems that every man there asks them to dance. Henry dances with Anna for two songs and tries to dance with her for four more but someone always cuts in. Anna is on top of the world with all the attention so Henry is happy to share her. Melinda also is getting plenty of attention. John Walker, though, DOES seem to mind. At one point, he says to Henry "This is ridiculous, is she my date or not?" Henry laughs, "We just get to pick them up and bring them home. We are pretty lucky to have that."

Matthew does his share of eating and dancing. As Henry watches him, he concludes that the young man is more like Melinda than anyone. He likes attention, he's as smart as a whip and he has a lust for all that life can give him.

Melinda goes through with the plan to tell her parents that John Walker wants to take her and Matthew for ice cream in town since they heard Anna talk about how good it was. Henry walks Anna back to their Hut. Anna is still dancing in her mind, and humming some of the songs. Henry can tell that Anna had the best time and he's glad to be a small part of it. She, really, is as sweet and as wholesome as anyone can be. She is definitely the marrying kind, he thinks. IF, he was in the marrying mood.

THIRTEEN

The Second Sunday in September, 1935
In EL Dorado, Kansas

Henry gives the password so that he can walk into the basement of KC's Smokehouse and Billiards on Central Ave. Melinda and John are getting drinks. He hopes that they aren't getting anything for Matthew. He's a little young after all. The pool hall is crowded and loud. There are poker tables and crap tables set up, and all have people surrounding them. John has his arm around Melinda's waist as a little more than a friendly gesture but she doesn't seem to mind.

Matthew sees Henry and goes straight to him and says excitedly, "I cannot believe you kept your promise to show me my first crap game. That was only a week ago, too!"

Henry says, "More than happy to oblige, Matthew! You are like my own little brother. Except you are too tall to be little. Do you want to get started?"

"Oh, yes! I'm ready. I think I remember all the rules. Just stick with me, okay? I did bring my money to play. I know that it isn't much but I'd like to get a feel for the game before I go broke, at least. Where do we start?"

Henry takes Matthew to the game table where John Walker is playing. John is shooter and Melinda blows on his dice for good luck. *Boy, she looks sexy as all hell, tonight*, Henry thinks. John is having a great run with her by his side. Henry tells Matthew to place his bet. Henry cannot keep his mind on the game. Melinda is flirting with John. *Is she trying to get me jealous?* Henry wonders.

Melinda watches Henry and Matthew as they approach the table. John promised her a cut of his winnings if she stays at his side. *'Easy Money'* she thinks. Melinda told John that the plan is to make Henry jealous but John is starting to believe his own con. John is the type of guy that takes what he wants and he says that he wants her. When he rolls a seven on the dice, they call Matthew to be new shooter. Melinda goes to his side and cheers for him. She looks at John and he doesn't seem to like it very much. Henry catches the side looks between them and understands. He puts a hand on his shoulder and tells him to take it easy, but John just shrugs his shoulders and walks away. Melinda can see the potential problem, too. Meanwhile, Matthew is on a good roll, and is building up some cash right out of the gate. Beginner's luck after all.

They play for two hours or so. Matthew is getting nervous about the time. He doesn't know what he'd tell his parents if they're waiting up.

Melinda doesn't want to leave. She sees several men there that she knows. A few of the them were at the Social and danced with her. When Henry is ready to go, he cannot get Melinda to leave, though. Matthew finally grabs her by the arm, and she reluctantly goes with them.

Matthew drives home since Henry had more than a few drinks and Mathew didn't. Matthew is high on the excitement of the evening, though. He says that he doesn't know how he'll get to sleep tonight. Of course, he wants to know when the next game is to take place. He's disappointed that it won't be until Wednesday.

FOURTEEN

The Second Monday in September, 1935
In EL Dorado, Kansas

The next morning was a real bear for Matthew and Melinda. Anna and her parents were not awake the previous night but they're sure up now!!! They all usually try to get the first Camp truck out to the fields but neither of them could get up and ready early enough. Anna and her Pa go without them.

Judy makes sure the two sleepy heads are on the next Camp truck out. Both Melinda and Matthew are exhausted, from dancing and gambling until late.

Once off the truck, they meet up with Henry, who asks, "How did it go for you once you were in the hut?"

Melinda let Matthew do the talking because she can see he's excited to relive last night's adventures. "Ma and Pa and Anna were all knocked out. We were very lucky. I don't know how many times that we will be able to pull that off." Henry just smiles, knowing that Melinda has been doing it for a week now. Melinda smiles back, knowingly.

Henry is being occupied by Matthew's replay of the evening, but all he wants is to get to Melinda and ask what is going on behind those pale blue eyes of hers. She seemed to enjoy all the attention from other men last night. Does she still want his?

Henry reminds Matthew that Anna wants him to stay away from each other while she's around. He knows that will be hard for Matthew. He won last night and has no one to share his excitement, except Melinda, but she seems to be very distant this morning. Matthew assumes she's hung over.

Melinda was never drunk or even tipsy, last night. Not on the booze, at least. She sees that Henry is watching her from the next row. *Well, let him,* she thinks. *If he can dance the 'Anna-then-Melinda Waltz' for a week then she can do the same.*

She worked her way to her Pa. He's working a little slower this morning. She asks him if he feels okay and he answers, "I 'spect a little rain is coming this way. My bones are aching fierce. I'm glad that you and Matthew got here. You must've come in pretty, late last night to be so tuckered this morn. Did you have a good time, then?"

"I had a wonderful time, Pa. I cannot wait till the next Social." She sees Anna heading back from the scales with an empty basket to fill. Melinda decides to let Anna keep Pa company. She works better on her own. "Anna, I'm going to work a row or two over, you'll stay with Pa? He's not feeling too strong today."

"I usually am the one by his side, aren't I?" Anna answers Melinda's question with a question. "Look at 'Miss-Show-Up-Late-and-be-all-concerned." She adds.

"Where is that coming from sis? Did I say something wrong?" asks Melinda, pretending to be hurt.

Anna looks down at her bushel, immediately regretting her words. "Sorry, I don't think I got enough sleep last night. I'm a bit cranky, again sorry."

Melinda softens. "It's just not like you to be snarky. That's my thing, not yours. Why? Didn't you sleep? You looked asleep when I got home?" she says as a question.

"I don't know, I tossed and turned, I guess. I'm still trying to figure this 'pre-engagement' with Henry. He's being the perfect gentleman with me but it's like he's holding some part of himself back from me. I cannot put my finger on it and it's bothering me." Anna explains. "Does that make sense?"

Suddenly, Judd clears his throat. "Do you ladies want to discuss this without your Ole Pa, to hear, please? I feel guilty about this already."

Melinda and Anna move to the next row, but they stay even with Judd to keep an eye on him. "So, what do you mean he's holding something back?" asks Melinda.

"Well, I don't know, exactly. I feel he should be sharing his hopes and dreams. He seems to be all about today, no concerns or plans for tomorrow. I don't know if it's real or a cover-up for a feeling of hopelessness. Do you get that sense about him?"

"I think he's genuine. He likes his fun after a hard day. You said he admitted that to you. Not everyone is a planner. I didn't think that you were." Melinda had to admit.

"I don't talk about it, but I would love a farm like we had growing up. I would love my own side garden for herbs and flowers like Ma had. That's my dream."

"So not only do you look like Ma, you want to be Ma? Is that all? No big plans? No fame, no fortune? Just a boring farm?" Melinda asks.

"I don't think farming is boring. It's hard work but very satisfying. I'd like a big family. Lots of kids. Lots of dogs. I hated to give up our big dog, Lucy, when we hit the road." Anna says, she wants to cry whenever she thinks of the old girl that they left behind.

"I don't want any of those things. I want to wear fine clothes to nice places. I don't want to plant or harvest another damn thing. I don't want a husband or kids. I want to live!! I'd like to go to California, and meet real Movie Stars, take a train, get on an airplane, maybe. Just live a great Life!!!"

"Now you sound like Henry. Why didn't Pa engage you to him?"

Anna says without meaning it.

"It's not like they asked any of us what we thought?" Melinda tries to sound as a matter-a-fact as possible. It's so complicated. Melinda thinks, *I am more like Henry. Neither of us want attachments, but that doesn't mean that they didn't WANT each other.* Those first nights of sneaking out were amazing. She cannot ask for anything more from Henry, considering they were forced to meet in the camp truck. He's tender, caring and seems to be as satisfied with her as she's with him. Melinda suddenly wonders if any of the others from last night will be as gentle and loving. *How can she be so bad, thinking about these things in broad daylight*?

"Melinda, where are you?" Anna interrupts. "Is the heat getting to you? You are bright red, under that dark skin of yours."

"Yes, I'm too hot." Melinda says simply. "What were you saying that I missed?"

"Nothing, it doesn't matter. Why don't you go get a glass of water from the paymaster?" Anna looks at her with concern.

"I'm fine, I'll take my bushel up to the hill and try to catch a cooler breeze that might blow up there. You'll stay near Pa?" Melinda asks.

"He does look a little slow today. I'll try to convince him to go home on the noon truck with Mr. Harrick. Do you know if Mr. Harrick is here today? He came to the Social, yesterday. I hope it wasn't too much for him." Anna says as she looks around.

"Henry said his Da is sleeping all the time. He thinks it's his new heart medicine that Dr. Johnson prescribed him. I don't think he's here, today. But Pa should go home early, either way." Melinda says.

FIFTEEN

The Second Wednesday in September
In Lawrence, Kansas

Carolyn is working at the Farm Office. She's interviewing private detectives. After Rosanne's scare in town, Carolyn thought she needed to get another one. She's trying to figure out how to tell who'll be worth the money. *What does one look for in a private detective?* She thinks about Dashiell Hammett's Sam Spade novels. She needs someone who'll take the few crazy clues and go find Rosanne's life and identity.

After the third guy left the office, she was about to call the whole thing off. She called her little brother at his dormitory apartment for a pep talk.

"Joshua, I'm at wit's end! What do I do? We must continue the search for Rosanne. On Sunday, she nearly had a melt-down behind the wheel of my car from a horrific flashback. We've got to try to get her some help! If she learns who she's and how it happened. She can face it and get over it. Right now, she's vulnerable to a wonderful memory or terrible flashback without warning! I'm afraid for her."

"Carolyn, let me make a few calls up here in Topeka. I know a Criminology Professor, who might give me some suggestions. I do agree, we need to step up the search for her. I know that means she might leave us, but as much as we love her, someone is back home loving her more and missing her, terribly. Let me call you when I get some idea of what else to do."

"Cheer up, Joshua. We could find out that she isn't married and that she didn't know her attacker but can remember him enough to send him to jail."

"From your lips, to God's ear, sister. Look, I'll call that professor, as soon as we hang up. I'll follow up on any of his suggestions and let you know what I find out. Keep your fingers crossed that he can help."

"Thank you, Joshua, I don't know what I'd do without you."

"Let's hope you never find out."

"Amen to that, brother, do well in school and call me back when you have something for me."

Three hours later, Carolyn is still at her desk in the Farm Office doing the payroll for the permanent farmhands. She's looking at the accounts receivable to move a large amount of cash over to the Paymaster for the day workers of the tomato fields. The tomatoes are producing as large a crop and as long a harvest than even last year's record year. The next duty is to order feed and hay for the cattle. She was exhausted from the private detectives before she even started her real work. She's lost in the circus wrangling of managing the farm when the phone rings and scares the bejesus out of her.

"Carolyn, the professor I called is very interested in Rosanne's case. He'd like to have his class become the private detectives and try to find out who she is. Isn't that wonderful? We'd have about twenty students pursuing the truth! He wants you and Rosanne to come up to the University and sit in on two or more classes so that they can question you and get to know her."

"When would they want to meet her?"

"I think he wants to start as early as next Monday."

"That soon?"

"Yes, and he was even talking about coming down here with the class to see the site where you found her. He was very excited about it. I was telling him about her injuries and he thinks even that's a clue. He says the 'how' she got hurt is a clue to who hurt her, which is a clue to who she is. This guy is amazing!"

"Joshua, they don't want to take Rosanne out there, do they? I won't let her go there! Not the way she's, she needs more good memories, before she can handle any bad ones."

"I agree, Carolyn, I'll tell Professor James that, the next time I talk with him."

SIXTEEN

The Second Wednesday in September, 1935
In EL Dorado, Kansas

The last couple of days were just as unseasonably hot. Judd did go home early on Monday and as their children predicted, Judy's soup and rest did him a world of good. Much to the relief of everyone, he was back on his feet the next day.

Matthew snuck around Anna to talk to Henry about odds for the crap game. He won on Sunday but wants to play faster/riskier bets. Henry is surprised at how quick Matthew is with the numbers. He's a natural and he wouldn't be surprised if Matthew's running a game before he's eighteen!

Henry is going out of his way to be attentive to Anna. On Monday, when she was so worried about her father, Henry accompanied Judd back home. He came back right after to report to Anna that Judd was in the capable hands of Judy. He stayed with Anna the rest of the day, but his mind was preoccupied with Melinda.

To get out on Wednesday night, Melinda tells her parents that she has another date with John Walker and that John has a cousin that he's bringing for Matthew. It's almost the truth because John's younger cousin, Susan, went to the social and Matthew danced with her. She was also at the crap game. Matthew didn't have time to talk with her there, though, because she left early with John when he lost all his money.

Henry is already at the crap game table when Melinda and Matthew arrive with John. The floating crap game was moved to an older large home downtown, at 6th and Taylor Street. Henry can see Melinda is wearing another rather tight top and clingy skirt so that her ample curves were magnified.

When Melinda approaches the table, Henry is the next shooter. His number is six and Matthew puts a few dollars down on the pass line. When Henry shoots a nine on his next roll, Matthew adds two Come bets to the board. Henry calls to Melinda to blow on his dice for luck. She walks to Henry slowly, keeping his eye contact. Henry almost forgets what she came to his side to do. She reaches up, still holding his gaze and takes his hand holding the dice and blows on them slowly. *She's trying to drive me crazy and it's working*, he thinks.

Henry throws several more times before getting his number six. Matthew more than doubles his money with Henry throwing and becomes the next shooter. After he places his bet on the pass line, he looks to see what Henry is going to bet but Henry is gone, and so is

Melinda. Matthew just shrugs his shoulders and throws his first roll. He rolls an Eleven! The rest of the gamblers shout at his luck. He still is the shooter so after he gets his pay, he places a new bet and rolls a nine. He can't believe that Henry is missing this!

Henry leads Melinda to the bar area, and orders two beers. He leans down to her and whispers in her ear. "You know that you are making me crazy. I cannot keep my mind on the game or anything else when you look like this and then look at me that way."

"I know, but I didn't know what I was doing at the time." She says with a smile that contradicts her words. She looks in his gray smoldering eyes again. They seem to touch her deep within her body. She doesn't know what is going on, she thinks as she sips her cold beer.

Henry is leaning into her again. "Can we get out of here?" His silky low voice is more intoxicating than the weak beer.

"What about Matthew?" She asks.

"Let him get his own girl." Henry says.

"Be serious, you started him gambling and now you want to leave him in this den of thieves?" Melinda shakes her head in mock alarm.

"I guess we better stay then. But I want you to stay by my side. No wondering around to see if you can do better than me, got it?" Henry says being totally serious.

"Don't you think that Matthew will notice? He isn't blind, or stupid. We should say something to him, don't you think?" Melinda asks. She cannot believe she's saying that. *How can they explain this to Matthew when they don't know what is going on, themselves?*

"I don't think we should put anything into words unless he asks. He might think that I'm just looking out for you like I am for him. Big Brother-like."

"What I have in mind for later isn't in a 'brother-like' category." She smiles with a seductive lift of her eyebrow.

"Cut that out! We are with Matthew tonight and he will catch on if you keep that up." Henry does a shrug of his shoulders. "Right now, I think we'd better get back to the table to see how he's doing."

When they walk up to the action, they see that Matthew is betting all over the table. Henry thinks that he's spreading himself too thin. Too many bets cancel each other out sometimes. Matthew looks up at Henry like a little kid showing off his finished coloring book. Henry starts to shake his head 'no' to Matthew to tell him not to put down any more money on the table but he's too late. The next roll comes up seven. Matthew loses everything on the table. He looks at Henry like Henry brought him bad luck. He places a bet on the "Don't Pass" line for the next shooter. Unfortunately, the first roll for this shooter was seven. Matthew loses again.

He only has a few dollars left. He places it all on the pass line. The next new roll is a twelve – Craps! Matthew is out of money in less than hour! He walks away very upset. *How did I do so well the time before and so bad tonight?*

Matthew walks quickly to Henry's side and says, "I want to go home, NOW! I did so well on Sunday, I don't understand." Matthew hangs his head. "I want to die." He says half under his breath.

Melinda is standing next to him. She thinks that she misheard him. "What did you just say?"

"I want to die! I borrowed two hundred dollars from Pa's Farm fund. I thought that I could double it so that we could get back the farm sooner. I have to make up the money before Pa finds out it's gone." Matthew is running his hand in his hair. His normally light blue eyes look like a dark sky with storms coming.

They're headed toward the door when a smug John Walker approaches them. "Matthew, if you want to make up that money, I could use you on Saturday night for a little work. Interested?"

"Of course, John, thank you. What do you want me to do?" Matthew looks so relieved.

"We'll talk about it tomorrow in the field, you head home, now, and don't worry about that money." John puts his arm up around Matthew's shoulders, which is hard because the young man is so much taller.

Henry and Melinda just look from John to Matthew. If John needs help and can pay, they're interested, too. As if reading their minds John says, "Sorry guys, just a small job, just for Matthew."

They ride back to the camp in complete silence. Henry is suspect of the type of job John Walker might have. It cannot be one that's purely legit. He doesn't want to say that in front of Melinda. He needs to get Matthew aside and talk to him tomorrow.

Melinda is very upset about the loss of the money. She doesn't know how Matthew is going to keep this from Pa. *He's just a dumb kid who was trying to do a good thing for the family.* She's especially worried about how bad Matthew feels, though. She has never seen him take anything so hard. She has never heard anyone say they want to die.

Matthew's thoughts are all over the place. He cannot believe that he lost so much money in so short a time. *That money equals months of pay for all of them working!* He's praying that Ma and Pa are asleep. He knows that if either of them see him tonight, he'll break down and confess the whole thing. He's praying for that and that he can replace the money before Pa goes to add this week's income to the funds.

They walk from the truck to the hut and Melinda is the first to see that the hut is dark. They're safe for the moment. Matthew shakes Henry's hand and says. "Thanks for your help tonight. I'll let you know what John says tomorrow." With that Matthew slips into the hut.

Melinda hesitates before entering and says to Henry, "I think that I'll turn in, too. I'm very worried about Matthew. What do you think John has for Matthew to do? Do you think it's safe?"

Henry shakes his head. "I don't know but to replace the kind of money that Matthew lost, it cannot be legal. I'm very worried, also. Hopefully, Matthew will let me know what it's so that I can advise him whether he should do it or not."

"I think Matthew will do anything to get that money back. You might have trouble talking him out of it." She leans into him. "I'm glad that he has you to talk to about this." She puts her hand on his chest, and looks in his eyes. "You are like an older brother to him." Henry puts his hand over hers and bends down and places a sweet kiss on her lips.

She tippy toed a return kiss. "We are being very bold. Do you realize we are right outside my bedroom window? Thank goodness it's closed or Anna would have heard everything. I would hate for her to be hurt by us. You need to be more careful." She gave him a mock punch to the jaw. With that, she enters the hut.

Matthew is sitting on his couch with his knees drawn up. He looks up at her, and she sees he's crying. She sits down next to him. She doesn't know what to say, so she just ruffs up his hair. "It will be fine" she says unconvincingly.

"I really thought I was doing something good. I'm such a moron." He sobs.

"Quiet, little bro, don't wake Ma and Pa. Henry says that whatever John wants you to do, might not be safe or legal. You better be very careful. Listen to Henry, okay? He'll look out for you."

"Of course, sis. Henry is like my own brother. I must admit that he isn't right for Anna, though. He's perfect for you. I think Henry knows that too. How do you feel about him? Or is John Walker your guy?"

"Whoa, take it easy. I don't know. I don't want Anna hurt, so please, keep it down. She must see for herself if Henry is the right one for her. If she rejects him, I'll let you know what I think about him, not before."

"I never want Anna hurt either. She must see that Henry isn't her true mate, though. She's not stupid, just naïve." Matthew says.

"Very astute little man. When did you get so smart?"

"After this night, Melinda, I can never claim to be smart, or I wouldn't have done what I did."

"True enough." She says as she gives his thigh a pat. "I've to get some sleep, and you should, too. Try not to worry, okay?" She leaves him sitting there and goes to her room.

SEVENTEEN

The Second Thursday in September, 1935
In EL Dorado, Kansas

The next morning the Masters clan are all on the early truck to the fields, as well as the Harrick's. This is the first day Da has been to the field all week. He and Judd talk the whole ride. None of the others say a word.

They're in the fields when John Walker comes. He didn't even bother getting a pay card or a bushel but goes directly to Matthew and pulls him off the row and over to the side area so that they can talk.

Matthew, though only fifteen, is more than a few inches taller than him. John explains, "I've seen how you carry yourself, Matthew. You are very smart and more mature than your actual age. I could use someone like you. This is a little risky but IF you can earn back all money in one night's work, I think it's worth it, don't you?"

Matthew is now getting nervous. He asks, "What is it I have to do?" Henry must be right about this being illegal, Matthew thinks.

"You can drive, right?" John asks.

"Yes, I can drive anything with wheels. I was raised on a farm." He adds as if that explains it.

"Just checking. We will borrow a car for the job and all you must do is three things. One – drive, two - keep your mouth shut, and three – don't ask no questions. Sound easy?"

"Too easy. When will I know where I'm driving? Sorry, does that question count?" Matthew chuckles as his nerves got the better of him.

"We will tell you where to go when we are all in the car. I'll pick you up in the camp parking lot on Saturday at seven p.m., and take you to meet the guys. Wear something dark. All good?"

"Sure John, so I'll earn back the whole two hundred dollars for this one job? I just want to make sure. I've to replace that money as soon as I can so my Pa won't have a heart attack when he discovers it missing."

"Oh, I understand Matthew, that's why you are perfect for this job. You are desperate, if you don't mind me saying so." John says as a matter of fact.

"No, that about sums it up, John." Matthew turns to go back to the rows to pick.

"Matthew," John calls after him. "Not a word to anyone. Not your sisters, or even Henry. Can you do that?"

"You got it. Not a word." Matthew knows this won't be easy because both Henry and Melinda are staring at him, waiting to hear what the job is. Of course, he cannot tell them since he doesn't know anything.

Matthew goes straight to them and they stop what they're doing to listen to 'the plan'. Matthew says, "All I know is when and where to meet up with John. I don't know anything else and I was told not to tell you anything." They both look as if they were going to interrupt, so, Matthew puts up his hand to silence them. "If I can get Pa's money back for being silent, that's what I'm doing." He says stubbornly and walks off without waiting for further objections.

Melinda and Henry exchange looks. Henry says. "I've a bad feeling about this."

Melinda says. "Same here, but Matthew seems to be handling it better than I could under these circumstances."

"I agree." Henry says, simply.

"What are you agreeing with?" Anna asks as she walks up to them, wiping her forehead with her handkerchief, while balancing her sunhat and full bushel on her hip.

Henry and Melinda look at each other for a second. Melinda smiles and turns to Anna. "That the tomato crop is lasting longer despite this dreadful heat. I on the other hand, am wilting under these circumstances."

Melinda looks just the opposite of wilting, but Anna just nods, puts her hat back on and keeps going to get her bushel weighed.

Henry looks down at Melinda. "Great save."

Melinda watches as Anna makes her way down the row. "It seems everything I say to her is a lie, these days, and I hate it!" She looks up at Henry, and a slow smile comes to her lips. "I blame you," she says without any malice, as she takes her full bushel to be weighed.

Later that morning, Henry catches up with his father and to work beside him until Da's regular quitting time. Frank can sense that Henry is concerned about something and asks, "Son, what's going on with you? Is it something I can help you with?"

Henry looks in his father's eyes and is speechless. He cannot admit to his father that he's attracted to Melinda but feels drawn and obligated to Anna. He cannot tell him that he loves the night life, but has introduced Matthew to it and that's led to bigger problems.

"Da, I know that you worry about me. I'm doing my best to make you proud, but life isn't making it easy."

"Henry, I was proud of you the moment I saw you and all you had done up to that time was bawl your head off. Being proud of you comes automatically with loving you. You don't need do anything but be safe and happy."

"Yah, that's the hard part. It seems that those two streets don't live in the same part of town here in EL Dorado."

Frank Harrick laughs at that. "Son, it sounds like you've learned how living can get in the way of your life. I've been down those roads, myself." He becomes serious now. "I cannot help until you give me specifics."

"I cannot do that yet, Da. They aren't just my secrets to tell. I need to work these things out on my own." Henry was looking down, picking tomatoes with precision. Frank senses that Henry needs time alone so he moves down the row to finish his last bucket before heading home on the noon truck.

EIGHTEEN

The Second Saturday in September, 1935
In EL Dorado, Kansas

Matthew is very silent and works very hard the next day and a half. His troubles are ruling his thoughts. All he can think about is replacing that cash before his father finds out.

His father has an old valise that he keeps in the wardrobe. It's smaller at the bottom and opens from the top. It splits practically in half when the top latch is released and resembles a capital letter Y. Matthew left about fifty dollars of the family farm fund money in it. He put a couple of dime novels at the bottom of the valise when he removed the two hundred so that the money left would be at the right height. His father usually put their wages in at the end of each week. But IF his father wanted to take it out to count it or anything, the loss could be easily discovered. He still cannot believe he was so stupid. Saturday night couldn't come any sooner.

Melinda, on the other hand, was enjoying herself sneaking out to see Henry, and didn't look forward to Saturday night. Henry was going to take Anna out again, but he made an excuse, at the last minute to get out of it so that he could help Matthew out. He didn't know what he could do but he thought that he should be available to help, if needed.

Henry tried to get John Walker to tell him about the job, but the little fat rat wouldn't bulge. Henry warned him that if anything happened to the kid that he'd hold him personally responsible. Not that it helped, John just laughed in his face. Henry wanted to punched him but he knew that Matthew was counting on this job.

Saturday afternoon is very hot and muggy. Matthew is pacing back and forth inside the hut, too nervous to sit still, even after working in the fields all morning. His mom tells him that she needs a few things from the store and since he has so much energy he can go get them one at a time.

When he gets back, he tells his parents that he saw John Walker and that they're going to grab some dinner together in town. Anna looks at Melinda for confirmation, but Melinda just shrugs and says, "He gets along better with him than I do, so why not?"

Anna thinks that Matthew's nervousness is very unusual so she sidles up to him and comes right out and asks. "What is up with you today, little bro? You are as nervous as a long tailed cat in a room full of rocking chairs." She tries to muss up his hair but he stops her by dodging her hand.

Matthew must think fast. He doesn't expect an interrogation

before he even gets out the door.

"Its John's cousin, Susan," he says at last. "I really like her but I don't think she's as attracted to me as I'm to her. I want to ask John for his help. Am I too young to think she could be 'the one'?" He smiles sheepishly. He waits to see if she buys this line.

"You are very young, Matthew, but Ma and Pa were your age when they first started courting. Look at Henry and me, we were best friends all through grade school. And now . . . okay, I don't know what we are now but . . . I don't think the heart knows its age when it comes to love. The heart wants what the heart wants." She pauses for a second. "Do you want to tell me about her? I haven't met her."

Crap, he thinks! She would ask me more questions! He answers slowly. "Well, she's cute. Blonde hair that she wears just above her shoulder but with lots of curls. She looks a little like John but in a very feminine way. She's about as tall as him, too. Or should I say as short as him? I don't know what else to say, Anna, I just like her . . . a lot!" He runs his hand nervously through his hair. "John said he'd a few suggestions, and after we talk, we might pick her up for ice cream again and see how it goes. I must get ready now. Do you think I need to shave?"

Anna chuckles. Matthew has a very heavy shadow on his upper lip but it's the peach fuzz kind of hair. She knows it's important to him to feel older right now; to give validity to his feelings, so she says, "You can use a shave. I can loan you seventy-five cents if you want to go to the barber in town and get a shave, haircut and some tonic water. This way you'll smell as good as you look . . . It can't hurt, can it?"

"Anna, that's the perfect idea! Now I must go, if I want to get that done, too." He bends down and lightly kisses her forehead and grabs a clean dark shirt but doesn't put it on. He says, "I'll put this on after the barber is done with all this hair. Thanks, Anna."

He glances over to Melinda, who had just come in the room from helping her mother with dinner. She just gives him a quick nod and he's out of the hut in a flash.

He's rushing to the front parking lot, but Henry is waiting near the roadway. Matthew can see John Walker waiting in the distance and is worried that Henry is going to get in the way. He looks down and is shaking his head no to Henry. Henry calls out. "Matthew just give me a second." Matthew slows down. Henry takes advantage of the moment and says, "Please be careful, you don't need to do this. I tried to get John to tell me what is going on, but he wouldn't give. We can figure out a different way to get your money back." Henry can tell that he isn't getting through to Matthew and he's still walking toward John, so he pleads. "I'm very sorry for getting you into this situation. Let me take your place and I'll give you all the money earned, I promise."

This stops Matthew in his tracks and he turns to Henry. "I can't let you do that. I took the money, I lost the money, I need to replace the money. It isn't up to you but I'll never forget this offer. You are my true brother from this moment on." He walks to Henry and puts his arms around him. Henry returns the hug and doesn't want to let go. He does love Matthew like a brother. *God, let him be okay*, Henry thinks as he pats Matthew's back and then slowly lets go.

Matthew continues to John without looking back. John is chuckling as he approaches. "What do you call what just happened there?" He points toward Henry. Without turning to look, Matthew just says, "My brother was wishing me luck, tonight. Got a problem with that?"

John loses his smile and says, "Brother, huh? You didn't tell him anything, did you?"

Matthew gives John a stern look. "John, you told him it was a Saturday night job, so he's here. He offered to take my place but still give me the money. He's known me my whole life and is like family. Again, I ask, 'Got a problem with that'?"

"Relax Matt, I was just giving you a hard time. Geesh, can't take a joke?" He walks Matthew over to a 1931 Ford Model A. "Here is your vehicle. She a beauty, ain't she? You can drive her, right?"

"Wow, you bet I can! I've wanted to drive a Model A since Ford came back out with them! Are you serious? Let's go!" Matthew gets behind the wheel and John gets in the passenger side. Matthew turns the key and says, "Where to, Sir?" He thinks that this 'job' might not be too bad, after all.

"Head to town, we must pick up the rest of the crew and a few supplies." John doesn't say anything else beyond that. So, Matthew decides just to enjoy the ride.

"John, she runs smooth. She mustn't have been in Kansas last April for Black Sunday. There isn't a car within 100 miles that didn't get 50 lbs. of dust in the engine. Where were you that day, do you remember?"

After so little rain for years, Kansas has been hit with horrible dust storms. Spring's the worst time for them, because of all the snowless winters. The one in April lasted hours and buried multiple states with dust and dirt. Most folks thought that it was the coming of the end of the world. The Masters were lucky to have been near a small church when the storm rolled in and they ran in for cover to find they were joining forty others praying for tomorrow to come.

John answers, "I was here, in EL Dorado, it's my home town. I was born here, I thought you knew that"

"I just assumed you were roaming the harvests, like us. It makes sense with your cousin Susan here and all. How bad did you get hit here that day?"

"It was bad! You couldn't see either end of the town from the middle of Main St for days. The town lights were on the whole time. My ma thought that the 'End of Times' was here. God rest her soul. She caught the Dust Influenza from that storm, and didn't last a month afterward. I was working at the oil refinery and when I took time off to take care of her, they let me go. The bastards!" John shakes his head. "You were right about this Model A. It came down from New York a month ago. How did you know?"

"I've been helping Pa with engines my whole life. I had to help half the town we were in to get their engines cleared off. Even after we washed them down and re-greased them, they ran rough. I haven't heard anything run this smooth this year!"

When they ride into town, John tells Matthew to turn left and pull in Powell's Hardware store's backlot on the north end of Main St. Two guys came from the alley, each carrying a small dark bag. They climb into the rear of the 'A'. John introduces them. "Pete, Harry, I want you to meet your driver, Matt. Matt meet Pete and Harry. They're friends of mine and we go back a long way. I vouched for you, kid, so are you ready to drive?"

"Nice to meet you guys. Tell me where to take you." Matthew didn't care much for being introduced as Matt but didn't say anything. "So where to?"

***

Matthew thinks, *I can't believe that this is happening, HERE.* John had given him road by road directions instead of just telling him the destination. He figured John did it this way so that he'd not have a chance to change his mind. So, here he's sitting alone in the car waiting for the three of them to come out of the Paymaster's office in the tomato field that they work in, every day. It's dark and deserted out here at night. Matthew is sitting behind the wheel with the engine on but the headlights off, just waiting. He watched the new guys play with the lock of the office door for a minute before they got it open. He assumes that they're robbing the place and he's sitting here letting it happen.

My God, what is taking them so long? He thinks as he sits, impatiently. He's constantly looking around for someone to catch them. *Henry was right all along. This is both illegal and unsafe. Why don't they just hurry? What are they doing in there?*

Finally, John appears and jumps into the front seat. He's holding a dark color linen duffel bag like the soldiers carried in the big war. Two minutes later, Pete came out, also carrying a duffel bag. Another minute goes past before Harry comes out. He carefully shuts the office door before jumping into the last empty seat with his duffel bag. John says to Matthew. "Drive boy, what are you waiting for, a parade?" Matthew puts the 'A' in gear and circles around to head out the way they came in. He doesn't turn on the headlights until they're on the main road back to downtown.

The three men are very quiet, at first, but when they're far enough away from the 'job' they start to congratulate each other and complement each other on how good things went. Matthew drives back to the lot behind the hardware store. All three guys get out of the car and John reaches into his pants pocket and pulls out two hundred dollars in fives and tens all rolled up and tied with a string.

"Here Matt, my boy, thanks for driving. Take the car back to the Camp lot where we found it and go home. Remember not to say anything to anyone. You did good, kid. We might use you again, if you want."

"Thanks John, I think I'd like that. This was nerve-racking but very exciting. And the more money I make, the better my family will be. Thanks for trusting me." With that he drives away, back toward the Camp.

What am I going to tell Henry and Melinda? What can I tell them? I still don't know anything. I drove, they had duffel bags, I drove again. Nothing to tell, at all. But what was in the duffel bags? The paymaster pays everyone in cash but that couldn't be ALL cash. I was part of the crew but I'm completely in the dark. Is that because they don't trust me? If the duffels had all cash in them, why did I just get paid two hundred? Now I'm getting greedy. Matthew's mind is going much faster than the Model A can take him. He parks the car in the farthest spot from the Camp huts as he can, and walks with purpose toward home.

Sitting on the ground in the garden outside of the Masters' family hut, Henry was waiting for Matthew to come home. When he sees the young man approach, he gets to his feet.

"Matthew, I've never been more worried about anyone as I've been about you. Are you okay? Do you have the money? Are you sorry you did this?" Henry's blocking the path to his front door, so Matthew must answer him.

"Listen, Henry, it's not that I don't want to tell you anything, it's that I don't know anything. I've my money. It seemed safe, there were no one witnesses, and no one was hurt. I'm glad it's over and now I can replace the money and forget this ever happened. I'm beat. I appreciate your concern, brother, but everything is fine, now. Will I see you tomorrow for service? Anna is counting on you to be here."

"Yes, Anna . . . well, I don't know what to do about her, either. I'll be here for her as promised. Matthew, you can see that she and I are . . . very different. But, she was right, I should have never taken you to that first crap game. I feel terrible about that."

"Henry, that's nonsense. I learned a great lesson. I'll play craps again, but I'll not play with money that I cannot afford to lose. You aren't to blame, the game isn't to blame, I'm to blame for losing so much in one night. It won't happen again. Anna wouldn't understand any of this. She isn't like Melinda or you or me, she doesn't need the excitement to make her feel alive. She doesn't know how blessed she's. She's too good for us, Henry."

"Wow Matthew, what are you fifteen . . . going on what forty? You have quite a head on your shoulders. I'll let you get some sleep. I'll see you in the morning."

Matthew lets himself in. Melinda's sleeping in his spot on the couch. He considers for a minute going to sleep in her bed but she must have sensed he was there and she opens her eyes.

She whispers. "Your home, thank God, everything okay?"

Matthew whispers back. "Sure is. I've what I needed. You should go to bed. We can talk in the morning, sometime."

"Did you see Henry? He was waiting for you outside. We were both so worried." She asks as she gets off his couch. She's rubbing her eyes. He could tell that she's still half asleep.

"I saw him, we talked. Now go to bed and let me go to 'couch', will ya?" He sits down and grabs his pillow and punches it a few times to erase her head impression. He's exhausted. He takes off his shoes and lays his head down. He's asleep before Melinda reaches her bedroom door. She looks back at him with amazement. Will she ever know what he'd to do to get that money? She doesn't think so.

NINETEEN

The Third Sunday in September, 1935
In EL Dorado, Kansas

Judd and Judy are up at five-thirty as usual. She starts making breakfast for the family. Judd takes care of the coffee and toast and helps set the table. Nothing is said between them. They have the routine down to a practiced dance. Matthew's awake before they come out of the bedroom and watches them through half closed eyes. *God, I love my parents.* He doesn't know what they would think of his gambling, the loss of the farm fund money, or his being driver for the 'job'. He says a silent prayer that they'll never find out.

Anna comes out of the room next. She's still in her nightgown but lends a helping hand to the cooking wordlessly. Melinda comes out too, so now it's his turn to rise. When Melinda sees, him stir, she announces that she's going to relieve herself and grabs the shawl on the hook by the door and heads to the outhouse. Matthew nods good morning to everyone in the kitchen and follows her out. They each use the facilities, and then wait for the other so they can talk.

"What happened last night, Matthew? Can you tell me anything? I'm dying to know why they paid you two hundred dollars for one night's work." She said.

"Well, I got to drive a '31 Model A. It ran very, very smooth. It came from New York so there was no dust in the engine. It was amazing."

"What does that have to do with the 'job'?" She asks confused.

"I was the driver; I drove the 'A'. I know nothing about why I was needed or what the guys 'got'. I just drove, and I'm not telling you where or anything else. Like I told Henry, I was safe, no one saw, no one was harmed. I'm done talking about it."

They go back inside, have breakfast and get ready for Sunday Service. Henry came before ten, as promised and he and Anna walk to the barn for Service, together.

Anna forgot to find out which Preacher is officiating and could have kicked herself. If it's the one from Topeka with the brimstone and fire sermon, she might just get up and leave, herself. Luckily, it's Pastor Tyler, her favorite.

The Pastor starts the service with a reading from the Book of the Prophet Isaiah. "Seek the Lord, while he may be found, call him while he's near" ... is how the passage starts. Anna couldn't have picked a better way to send a message to Henry. The Gospel is from Matthew 20:1-16a. It's Jesus's parable about the laborers in the vineyard. It tells of the Landowner who hires workers at different times throughout the day but pays them all the same daily wage despite the lack of hours worked.

When they exit, Henry jokes that evil landowners were a pain then and are a pain now. Pastor Tyler overhears him and explains that whenever the call to serve the Lord comes – all will be given the same benefits, but the first who serve Christ shall be the last or the 'least' in the eyes of this world.

Henry just says, "That makes sense, those who serve are always looked down upon, aren't they?

"Exactly, see you get it now. Henry, isn't it? Your father and I've had a few conversations about you, young man. He's devoted to you, you know. You look very much like him, too.

"So I've been told. You know Anna Masters, don't you?" Henry doesn't know what else to say to a minister. He has never talked to one before so he let Anna take over the conversation.

"Pastor, last week's social was so much fun. Everyone has been talking about it all week. I wish there was another one scheduled. We have felt more 'at home' here than anywhere since we lost our farm up in Hope. We have been very lucky here in EL Dorado. This great camp, the long harvest, and reuniting with the Harrick's. Our farms were near to each other. I miss home and our little town. Have you ever been to Hope, Pastor? It's a beautiful place. When our money is saved up, we plan on buying back our land from the bank."

As Anna is talking to the Pastor, Henry's thoughts wander. *Can she really, want to go back to that dead-end town? It was great growing up but what's done is done. I mean, there's no going back. Doesn't she know that?*

Henry also notices that Matthew is still in the barn, sitting in the back row, long after everybody else filed out. He excuses himself from Anna and goes back into the barn. Matthew gets up and starts to slowly stack the chairs to put the barn back to its original purpose. He looks lost in thought. Henry doesn't say anything to him but starts to stack alongside him. Matthew nods to him but just keeps working. As they finish up, Henry just says, "Are you doing okay, today?"

Matthew just nods. Then he extends his hand to Henry. When Henry reaches out to shake it, Matthew pulls him close and whispered. "I'm worried. IT was too easy, something's not right."

Henry pats him on the back and whispers in return. "I understand, little brother, I'll watch your back. We must wait and see."

Anna stands at the opening of the barn, watching them. She warned Henry not to have these private conversations. Could it be about gambling, again? She wonders.

"Henry, here you are," she calls out.

"Sorry Anna, I was just helping your brother with the chairs. Talk to you, tomorrow, Matthew. Take it easy." Henry heads toward Anna.

Anna looks at Matthew, strangely and asks, "Matthew, I thought you were going to the barber, yesterday, for a shave and a haircut?"

"Well, John Walker and I took too long talking, and his barber, William Money, closed before we got there. We didn't pick up Susan, after all. John says she's interested in someone else, so we talked for hours at the diner. He told me a few things about her that makes me feel she's not the one after all." Matthew explains.

Henry says, "That's a shame, Matthew. I'm sorry. Well, you are still very tall and handsome, you won't have any problem finding someone." Then he adds, "I can keep an eye out for you, if you like."

"Henry, brother, stop. I can find my own girlfriends." He laughs.

Henry interrupts, "Let's be off, Anna. I would like to go to town, would you like to come with?" He changes the subject and winks at Matthew as he put his arm around Anna's waist and leads her out of the barn.

They spend the afternoon downtown, going from shop to shop, just browsing. They started on the north end of Main St. at Powell's Hardware. Anna wanted to look in the Singer Sewing Store at the new sewing machines. They also went to two Dry Good's Stores and J.C. Penny's. As they look around, Henry is trying to hear any rumblings regarding Matthew's activities of the night before. Anna is in a very light and carefree mood, which makes her so lovely. As she looks around the different stores, she holds things up for him to see and tells him things she'd like to have someday, when she has her own home. They had a light lunch at the Hotel EL Dorado Café and went for ice cream again at the Central Avenue Soda Shoppe and Ice Cream Parlor.

Anna is much more relaxed with him, today. *She's so different from Melinda.* Henry thinks for the hundredth time. *All Anna wants to do is 'set-up' house, just like her mom. How could she be so content to have things the way they were? I want to take her for a long ride to a big city, to show her what can be. Maybe, we can take a day trip up to Wichita. She might feel different if she can feel the excitement of the City. I might be just wasting his time, but it's worth a try, at least.*

TWENTY

The Third Monday in September
At Washburn University, Topeka, Kansas

Carolyn and Joshua are sitting on both sides of Rosanne. They're both holding her hands to give her strength. It took a lot of convincing to get her to come here. It isn't that she didn't want to find out who she is, it was that she might must relive the event that just barely missed killing her.

Rosanne used every excuse to get out of it. The Colonel can't be without her. Carolyn can't afford to miss a day of work. Even this morning, Rosanne tried to fake a migraine.

The ride into the big city, for Rosanne, is nerve racking. She says that she'd never seen so many cars and people! Carolyn jokes, "A Clue!" Rosanne slaps her arm. "Rosanne, I'm driving, do you want us to get into an accident? Wait, don't answer that, you are looking for another excuse, I know. Look, Joshua and I'll be there with you. The Professor has been told that we won't let you get upset, even if it means that he doesn't have enough for the class to start chasing down clues. So just relax and enjoy the urban sprawl, and leave your hands to yourself, sister."

Joshua meets them at the Campus front entrance and takes them through several buildings and outdoor walkways. Rosanne is in awe of the size and complexity of it all. Joshua can see it on her expression. Carolyn is an Alumni of the College, but had no reason to be on this side of the campus, so she's glad that Joshua can lead the way. They're a few minutes ahead of schedule, so the classroom is empty except for Professor James.

Professor Edward James is at his desk but eagerly goes to them, as they come in. He looks very young to be a professor in his early thirties. He has a thin black mustache that accents his thin face and jet black hair. He goes directly to Rosanne and takes both her hands. "My dear girl, I'm so sorry for what you have been through and I'll try to make this as easy on you, yet thorough as possible. You have my promise."

Carolyn is surprised that he didn't need to be told which of them was Rosanne as Joshua says, "Professor James, this is my sister Carolyn and this is the girl we call, Rosanne."

Rosanne's jaw drops. "What did you say?" Her heart starts pounding, wildly. She never thought that Rosanne wasn't her name. When she woke up from the coma, she was confused and obviously had amnesia but they were already calling her Rosanne. She just assumed that was who she was.

Carolyn is turning red. "Darling, you were unconscious for so long. I was by your side praying for your recovery and asked God to give me your name so that I could use it in my prayers. The name Rosanne, immediately, came to mind. When you came out of the coma, several doctors, and the psychiatrists asked you, who you were and you said you didn't know. They were going to call you Jane Doe but I protested and said to call you Rosanne."

The Professor is listening to this exchange as he's moving chairs around so that all three can sit and face the class. When he's finished, he suggests they sit. "It will be a few more minutes, before the students start filing in. Carolyn, may I call you Carolyn?" She nods consent. "I want you to do most of the story telling today. Start from the very second you saw her and don't leave out any details about Rosanne, if you can. Joshua, you were here at school, when Carolyn found her, right?"

"Yes, sir, I was. I didn't meet her until she was out of the coma. Carolyn brought me to meet her in the hospital, because she wanted my approval of bringing her home to continue her rehabilitation. I was against it, at first. My grandfather is ill and needs constant care and Carolyn is single handedly running the family business, and I thought it would be too much to take on a 'project' like Rosanne."

"What changed your mind?"

"I saw her." He says, simply. Rosanne turns to look at him, tears forming again in her eyes.

"That, was it?" the Professor asks, incredulously. "No discussion, no questions?"

"No." He sighs before continuing. "I saw her, before we walked into the room, through the open door. She looking out the window on the other side of room. She had on a heavy chest brace that obviously was very painful to wear. She slowly turned and I saw her still swollen, scarred face and was ashamed at my hesitance. As we walked into the room, I looked in those big, beautiful, sad brown eyes and I was done."

"You never told me this." Rosanne says as she squeezes his hand.

He just blushes. Several students are coming into the room, now and taking their seats. They're looking at the three of them in the front, with mixed reactions. Some look as if they didn't know why they're up there. Some of them, give a nod to them, as well, as to the Professor and take their seats. After four or five minutes of them filing in, the Professor closes the classroom door and walks to the front of the room. He clears his throat multiple times to get their attention.

"Class has begun, folks. Okay, let's get started. As I mentioned in Friday's class, we are going to take some of the crime solving tools we've been talking about, to a real-world application. We have in the room with us, a real and complete mystery. If we use our minds, hearts and those tools successfully, we won't only solve the case but give a girl, her life back." He motions to the three seated in front.

"The young girl in the middle, has no knowledge of who she is. A year ago, she was found near death in the middle of deserted acreage, and her injuries were so severe that she was in a coma for months. She has amnesia and the police at the time, couldn't determine who she is or where she came from.

"A year has gone by and her case is considered cold. She has had some memory glimpses come and go and some terrifying flashbacks regarding her attack. We hope not to intensify those terrifying moments. We will start with the woman who found her and she'll give us as much of the details as she can remember from those first couple months. If we have enough time today, we will hear from Rosanne, herself. As you hear her story, write down questions that you need answered to start your investigation. We will have them come up once or twice a week to fill them in on the leads we are chasing down. Next week, I would like us, as a class, to go to the location that she was attacked and/or dumped. We may find that the attack didn't take place there. A year is a long time for clues to hang around in an outdoor setting, but we may get lucky. When Rosanne feels comfortable with us and our process, we will try take her there to see her reaction to it, if it shakes any memories for her."

A loud yelp came from Rosanne as her hands leave the comfort of the brother and sister and go up to cover her face as she shakes her head no and whimpers.

The Professor continues, "Obviously, that won't happen right away. The mind is an awesome but fragile thing. She might have amnesia from the brain injuries she sustained. Or she might have amnesia from the trauma of the event itself. Her mind could be protecting her from reliving an event too terrible to comprehend. If that's the case, forcing that 'reliving' can convince the mind to let go, and allow some if not all her memories to return. We don't know, at this point if that's even an option, since we don't know, yet, if her amnesia is injury related or not. That in of itself is part of our investigation. Let's hear first from the woman who found our subject. This is Carolyn Lewis and she owns the land that was the dump site. Excuse my bluntness, Rosanne, this is how we begin. Carolyn, if you will, please start." He goes to his desk and sits down, he pulls out a notebook and like his class has a pen in hand for notetaking.

Carolyn stands up looks around at the class and says, "Should I stand or sit? Can everyone see me if I sit?" They murmur, yes. She retakes her chair and reaches for Rosanne's hand before she continues.

"I was in my work truck with my dog, Rocco, on a Sunday afternoon. He always accompanies me when I go about my rounds on the plantation. I checked several of our operations that morning. I had been to the tomato fields, first. After the tomatoes, I went over to the cattle lands, to survey the herd. They were half way through their fattening-up period and I was just checking their progress. I was considering a new area of acreage, that hadn't been planted before, and I was going out to see if it was an area that I could salvage through my irrigation system.

"Well, anyway, I was on the outskirts of my land, riding with the windows down because it was an unseasonably hot dry September day when Rocco suddenly went crazy on me. He normally was a quiet but very alert passenger who loves to ride, sniffing the air with his head out the window. Well, he sniffed something, alright. I stopped the car as soon as I could. Before I could say, 'What is it, boy?' he was out of the car and running to something about thirty feet back. Before I could get half way to the thing he was sniffing, he ran back to me and was jumping all over me. Also, something he never does. He suddenly stopped jumping and nudged my hand a few times and took off back to the 'thing'. He started licking it then sat down, with his tail wagging looking from me to her." She nods to Rosanne.

"When I got closer, I could see it was a naked bloody badly bent body. I screamed, though there was no one for miles who could hear me. Rocco, was still wagging his tail and occasionally licking her face. She was covered in blood, so much so that I had to look away and had to . . . lose my lunch. After I stopped, I walked a little closer and saw that she was breathing, just barely, I thought. I tried to feel for a pulse and was shocked that I could feel one. She was so bent, I could tell that she'd multiple broken bones, because both her shoulders bones were sticking out, funny. I didn't want to risk additional injuries but I didn't want just to leave her alone and go get help either, but that was what I had to do. I started to go back to my truck, and out of habit, called for my dog, Rocco. He stood up and barked at me, then sat back down. He wasn't going anywhere. She was going to be safe with him guarding her.

"I went to the closest phone which was in the farm office. It was an excruciating ten-minute drive, even though I was going so fast that all I could see behind me was the plume of dust that was shooting up from wheels. I called the sheriff's police and they said that they would bring a wagon to pick her up but I knew that would make her injuries worse, so I called the private medical facility that I use for my grandfather and asked for the doctor that I knew there and explained her injuries. He agreed with me that she should only be moved by medical professionals and said that he'd come with an ambulance, immediately.

"I called my farm foreman, next, and told him briefly about the girl, then asked him to meet the sheriff and the ambulance at the front gate. I told him to escort them to the southwest corner of the property that he and I had discussed irrigating that morning. I told him bring the ambulance the minute it arrived and if the sheriff arrived first, he was to wait for the ambulance.

"I sat for a moment wondering what else I needed to do, and was at a loss. I jumped back in my truck and went back to my dog and Rosanne."

The Professor stops her right there. "Does anyone have questions for her so far?" He looks around the room. "Please continue, Carolyn."

"I got back to Rocco, and the girl. She hadn't moved even though I could tell, Rocco had been cleaning her face with his tongue. I must admit, I've a very weak stomach and even though, I thought, I had already emptied it; I had to bend over and do it again.

"Afterward, I checked for a pulse, again. How she could be alive, was beyond my understanding. I prayed out loud, thanking God for my dog's instinct and chance to help this girl, who looked beyond saving."

Rosanne suddenly hugs Carolyn, with all her might. Tears are flowing down her cheeks as well as some of the students, and the Professor. They're all feeling the raw emotion in her presence.

Carolyn struggles with her own emotions but continues, "My doctor friend, arrived first, thank God and Joseph led him to me. His assistant, Jose, waited for the sheriff. The doctor looked her over carefully, before even touching her. He said that both her shoulders and her nose were broken and possibly her neck, too. He put a neck collar pillow thing around her neck as carefully as possible. Then slowly lifted her up so that his assistants could put a back board under her. She never came to, thankfully. She'd have been in so much pain.

"The sheriff came with their wagon and were surprised if not a little put off by the fact that I had called a private ambulance. Not that I cared, I knew she was getting the best help available in the county. The sheriff wanted to talk with the doctor but he was too busy with Rosanne. Dr. Mason told them which facility he was taking her to and got in the ambulance and was gone before the sheriff could write down the name of the place. With Rosanne gone, they turned to me for answers. They asked me what time I found her, forty minutes ago. When was I here last? Two weeks, ago. Why was I here now? To determine if the land was suitable for irrigation. Then, I had to explain what that was."

The Professor, clears his throat. "For the sake of the class, would you explain it to us, please?"

"Oh, okay, um, I've an engineering degree from here and I designed a series of piping that draws water from a source, usually a fresh dug well, carries it to the rows of plants and delivers the water daily in a rotating wand type sprayer, also, of my design. It's been very successful on our farm and has allowed us to combat the drought and dust storms we've been plagued with the last few years. Does that make sense?"

A few students mumble yes, the Professor says, "Thank you,

Carolyn, that's a life altering invention of yours. Very impressive, please, continue."

She blushes, slightly. "Okay, the sheriff's deputies take a few pictures of the dirt. He says that the drought has made tire tracks impossible to see, so that would be a dead end. They did find a little bit of glass, I think. I remember them saying it could be from a head lamp. That's about all I know about the site, I think."

"Class, we need to call that sheriff's office to get copies of any evidence collected. George and Michael, that will be your assignment. Who wants to contact the doctor that first examined Rosanne?" Three hands shoot up. "Okay, Sally, Clem and Bobbie Rae, that's your first assignment. Carolyn, can you give them those phone numbers if you have them?" She nods. "Good. Is your foreman and his assistant both still employed on your farm?" She nods, again. "Excellent, is Jose, English speaking?" She nods a third time. "That helps, Sandra and Margaret, call them and see what they remember. Okay, now, Rosanne, do feel like talking to the class? We have time left. If you don't feel comfortable, Carolyn can keep going."

Rosanne is overwhelmed with emotion. Some of what Carolyn just said, she's hearing for the first time. She shakes her head no, slowly, but then stands up. "I want to thank everyone in advance, for your help. Thank you, Professor for doing this wonderful thing for me."

He interrupts, "Rosanne, this is the best use of this class, a real investigation and a mystery to solve that doesn't have an answer in the back of the book. Can you tell us about some of the things you have remembered about yourself or have discovered you can do? Joshua says that you are an awesome cook."

She sits back down and reaches for Joshua's hand, and gives it a squeeze. "Well, I seem to be a short order cook of a sort. Several times, since I've been living in the main house on the Plantation, I've had to cook for field hands, as many sixteen at a time, and I can get the main course and all the sides, ready to be served, and all at once. I'm told, not everyone could do this."

The Professor asks, "Do you remember cooking in a restaurant?"

"I don't have any memory of cooking, but I can. Weird isn't that?

"Who doesn't have an assignment?" Several hands go up. "Okay, the four of you in the back row, whose hands aren't up but don't have assignments, you are going to call diners and restaurants to see if they were missing any cooks. Start with Lawrence and work outward. Mable go north from center, Ruth go south from center, Jessie, take the east and Bobbie Jo goes west.

"What else do you have memories of?"

"She remembers picking tomatoes as a field hand." Carolyn offers.

"Excellent, Joseph-north, Anthony-south, Denise-east and Frank-west. Call all bigger farms and see if they use day laborers and if they remember someone going missing last year, last September. Rosanne anything else?" She shakes her head, no. "Carolyn, Joshua, anything else?"

Carolyn laughs, nervously "Okay, these are the things I know, she never had a phone before or indoor plumbing. She knows how to use a kitchen hand pump, though. She also doesn't think she was ever in a big city. Coming out here, she was thunderstruck by all people, cars, houses etc. She can sew, as good as she cooks and she says that she doesn't know if she can dance. And her name isn't Rosanne. I named her that while she was still in the coma. She's very easy to make laugh and is the most patient caretaker, my grandfather has ever had. We love her and want to keep her, but she needs to find out her real name and where she's from."

Joshua who has remained silent up until now, clears his throat. "The doctors told us she's about nineteen or twenty, they say that she was raped as well as beaten and run down with a car. She miscarried the baby five months after the rape. It may or may not have been the rapist's. She feels that she might have been married before the attack but has no specific memories of it. It's just a feeling. I think that her attacker is convinced he killed her, I mean, who could have survived all of that, after all. So, he's sitting pretty, thinking she's dead in an empty field, never to be found."

The Professor speaks, "That may be, or he may be sitting somewhere accused of her murder, without a body. I've seven students without assignments, according, to my notes. You guys will call all sheriff departments and ask if they've any outstanding missing persons from last year. If not, ask them if they've anyone in jail, or suspected of murder that they didn't prosecute because of a missing body. I want each team to make a report on Wednesday, our next scheduled class. You can use the phone bank in the Criminology offices. Where my offices are, for those of you who just gave me a dumb look."

He turns to the three in front. "You did great. I'll let you know, what has been reported on Wednesday. If no leads, we will keep at it until Friday's class. I'll let you know when to come back here. I'm not sure if the crime scene will be of any use, at this point but I'm not taking it off the table." He turns back to the class, "Any questions from the investigators? That's you, student of the Criminology 401, any questions for our three guests?"

One student, raises his hand. The Professor calls him Clem. Clem asks, "Do you have any memories or flashbacks of the attack or attacker?"

Rosanne starts to tremble, "I had one a week ago. I was behind the wheel of Carolyn's car. It was the first time that I had even thought I could drive. After I backed the car out of the spot, and checked my mirrors, I got a horrible feeling like I was being boarded. I was alone, behind the wheel, afraid for my life. I felt like they were coming on all sides. I had the feeling of being closed in an unescapable place. I know that I was overtaken on the road somehow."

The Professor interrupts. "That's a good clue, so we can also check with the authorities if a car was reported missing and/or damage to the head-lamp reported. Carolyn, you said that glass was found at the site, right?" She nods, again.

"Time is up for this class, I'll see you all in my office calling your assignments, and at the next class, have one person from each group give the rest of us, a report. You are all excused." They all file out, leaving the three with the Professor.

Carolyn was the first to speak, "Wow, that was impressive, Professor James. We are bound to get answers with this much man-power. Thank you." She reaches out to shake his hand and he blushes, slightly.

"No thanks needed, and call me Eddie." He shakes her offered hand and Rosanne and Joshua cannot help but smile watching Carolyn blush right back at him. Something more might come out of this than just answers for Rosanne.

TWENTY-ONE

The Third Monday in September, 1935
In EL Dorado, Kansas

The Masters family are all on the early truck to the Field. Judd cannot believe that the crop is still going. He expected the tomatoes to be picked out last week, so they're very lucky.

Matthew managed to replace the money into the valise while his parents were out visiting Mr. Harrick, the day before. He's still worried, not just that it seemed too easy and that he still could get into trouble but there was something else. He LOVED the excitement. He knew it was wrong, but he wanted to do it again, even though he didn't know what 'it' was. That's why he hung around after the service, yesterday. He was asking God to help him sort through these feelings. He didn't want to be bad. *But, wow, it was so much fun, and it pays so* well.

The Camp truck finally rolls into the field, and everyone is getting off to start their day. As they approach the paymaster's office, Matthew's heart is beating out of his chest. The workers are all lined up but no one is going in. People are mumbling and starting to get impatient, knocking on the door. After some time, Croner and Miller, the Paymaster, come out waving everyone back.

"Sorry folks, we cannot have you picking today. We've been robbed and we must get the sheriff to come out." Explains Miller.

Since the Masters are at the end of the line, Judd cannot make out what they're saying. "What's going on?" He asks his children.

Anna speaks first. "I don't know, Pa. I think he said that they were robbed." The workers get out of the line and start to encircle the building for answers.

"What does this mean for us?" Yells one fella.

"We were counting on working, today!" Says another.

The driver of the Camp truck went over to Miller and Croner and asked if he should just take everyone back to the Camp.

"I don't think so. The Sheriff might want to talk with everybody," says Miller rubbing his chin in thought.

"Why, what do we have to do with it?" Asks one elderly woman. "We don't know nuthin'." She complains.

"As far as I'm concerned, I wouldn't put it past any of you to have somethin' to do with this." Barked Croner. Then he added, "Better all just get back in the truck and sit down, Sheriff is on his way."

The driver says "But Miller, shouldn't I get the next load, so the sheriff can talk to everyone who picks here?"

"Good thinking." Miller answers. "Go get everyone. Don't say nothing to them, just get back here, quick."

Croner calls out, "Alright, everyone, come down to this side of the building and take a seat on the ground." He's waving and pointing but the workers aren't moving.

"Better put your asses over there, or else!" He starts to push people to the grassy side of the building. He grabs one young woman and pushes her so hard that she falls on her knees.

Matthew rushes forward and helps her up. He turns to Croner. "Keep your hands to yourself. We'll go, you don't must push women around. What's the matter with you?"

Croner just squints at Matthew. "What's your name, son?"

"Matthew Masters, sir. Why do you ask?" Matthew is now helping an elderly lady to sit down.

"Cuz, I want the sheriff to talk to you first. That will serve you right, buttin' in where your nose don't belong." He explains, thinking what a young punk Matthew is.

Melinda, who is already sitting, stands up and takes Matthew's hand and brings him to Judd's side. First, she gave Croner an 'if looks could kill' stare, but he doesn't even notice.

They're sitting on the ground for forty minutes before the camp truck makes its way back with the next load of workers. Henry and Mr. Harrick are both on it. The driver opens the back gate for everyone to get down but they're reluctant to do so because they can see all the workers sitting in the grass. Croner is at them in a flash.

"Come on down everyone. There's been a robbery and the Sheriff's a-comin'. We want you all to sit over where the others are. Come on, move. Think we got till Christmas to wait? Move it!" He shouts as he pushes another woman and Matthew is up in an instant ready to pounce. Melinda grabs his arm, again.

"Don't attract attention to yourself," she warns.

Henry and his father make their way to Judd's side and sit. Matthew is trying to avoid looking at Henry. Frank didn't quite hear what is happening so Anna explains what has happened so far. She adds that it's taking the sheriff a very long time to get here.

"How long will they keep us here?" "If we cannot pick, why don't they let us just go home?" "What is taking so long?" These are some of the comments and complaints that are getting louder, the longer they sit.

Finally, the Sheriffs come. Seven of them, in three vehicles. They all go into the paymaster's office and take about 45 minutes before they come out to address the workers.

"Okay, folks, here's the story. It seems that there's been a robbery and we would like get all your names, and a statement from each of you. Actually, only the workers that were here on Saturday."

"Oh thank God!" Says the elderly lady. "I wasn't here Saturday and I got to go to the outhouse and Croner wouldn't let us move. Can someone help me up?" The sheriff is the closest so he assists her.

"Sorry for the inconvenience, Ma-am, I'm sure he didn't mean to upset you." He says.

"Sure he did. That Croner likes to upset everyone. He's just a meanie!" She says as he ends up escorting her all the way to the outhouse.

When he returns, three of the sheriff's deputies are already taking down the names of everyone who worked on Saturday. Everyone's statement is pretty much the same.. We couldn't wait to get out of the fields because it was so muggy. We didn't see anything suspicious at the paymaster's office. We got our card in the morning and got our pay before noon and were took the truck home. No one had anything else to add.

When it's Henry's turn to give his information, he tries to ask them what is missing but they won't tell him anything.

When enough workers are questioned, the driver of the camp truck loads them up and takes them back to camp. Their Pa is complaining, "And here I thought we were so lucky to have the harvest last this long. Now what are we going to do? I don't know of another harvest in the area. We need to keep pickin' if we're ever gonna get the farm back. I don't know what your Ma's gonna think when we all show up, at this time of day." It's only about two p.m. When the truck starts to unload, everyone moves as in a daze. No one knows what they're going to do.

Matthew is feeling so guilty. *All these people are hurt because of something I did.* Melinda could sense his thoughts and stays next to him and squeezes his arm occasionally to give him strength. Judy is in the middle of washing clothes in the kitchen on her scrub board with a large pot of boiling hot water. She has a kerchief on her head and large rubber gloves on but looks up in shock as one by one her family comes in, each looking as if the world has ended. Matthew walks in and collapses face down on the couch.

"What's happened?" She asks, because no one has said a word. Judd goes over to her.

"Ma, it's something terrible. We might have to move on sooner than we thought. The Paymaster's office was robbed and now they can't pay us to pick, no more." Judd sits down at the kitchen table and puts his head in his hands.

Judy asks, "Well, are there still tomatoes on the vines?"

"Well yes, but they've no money to pay us." Judd answers.

"So . . . they're just going to let them rot? Won't they need the money the tomatoes bring in, now more than ever? They could just pay us when they sell them, couldn't they?"

Judd looks up at his wife. He stands up and kisses her on the mouth right in front of the children! "You are so much smarter than me, my dear. Of course, they still need to take the tomatoes to market! They still need us! Did you hear that children, they still need us, we will be alright!" He hugs Judy, then picks her up off the ground and swings her around and kisses her again. She still had dripping laundry in her hands and it makes a mess all over everything, but Judd is so relieved and happy that Judy doesn't care.

"Kids, come help me with this laundry, so we can get supper started. Since you are all home so early, we might as well eat early." She says as cheerfully as she could.

After dinner, Judd goes over to Frank's hut and discusses offering to work without pay until the tomatoes go to market. Frank and Henry both think it's risky but it's better than moving on. They go to the Camp Store to see if Mark, the young manager, can call someone in the Management Office with their offer. Mark says that he'll call Miller at home and talk with him after the store closes. He said it's 'mighty nice of you to offer them credit when they don't offer it to you.' The store has a strict cash only policy as per management.

TWENTY-TWO

The Third Thursday in September, 1935
In EL Dorado, Kansas

On Tuesday morning, the Masters family awoke, as usual, and got ready to pick. They walk to the Camp Store to load into the truck, for the first run. The driver never shows, and the store doesn't open. When the Harrick's came, they decide to drive to the field, themselves and offer to pick with delayed payment.

By this time, several other families decided that they could work that way also, and wanted to go with them. Before they could head to the field, five car loads of workers are ready to offer their services.

Henry's truck leads the way to the field. He has his father and a family of six in the back of the truck. As he pulls into the field, he sees sheriff cars parked by the paymaster's office. Henry parks the truck and goes to the door and knocks. Sheriff Lark Bailey, himself, opens the door and Henry explains that they came to pick and are willing to wait for their pay. The sheriff doesn't give Henry a chance to finish. He explains that no one from management is here because the crime scene is still being examined.

Judd is out of his truck by this time. "Can't you get a hold of someone to tell them we want to work? We need to work. The tomatoes are gonna just rot, if we don't pick-em!"

The Sheriff says that if he got someone from management that he'd get word out to the Camp. Everyone's very disappointed. Once again, Matthew feels the weight of guilt.

The Camp Store didn't open so several families are packing up to find another harvest, but the Harrick's and the Masters' tried again on Wednesday, but the tomato fields were empty. Judd is about to give up also.

The Management of the Operation is at the Camp with the Sheriffs to talk with the workers. They call everyone into the large encampment barn.

The man dressed in a fine suit starts the conversation. "My name is Grant Johnson the 3rd, and I own this Farm. I know that you all have lots of questions. It's a terrible thing that' happened but we are going to try to make this right for all of you."

"Why are you letting the tomatoes rot on the vines when we could pick them for you?" One man shouted from the crowd.

"Hang on, I plan on answering all your questions. First, let me tell you what's happened. Someone or several some ones, broke into my paymaster's office Saturday night. We had just gotten paid cash for the multiple crops that went to market last week, and we had it all in that one office, so that we could distribute it to the other fields for payment to all our day laborers. All of that money was taken."

"Do you know who did it?" Asks a young woman.

"No, there are no real clues, so far. The sheriffs suspect that it was an employee since the presence of the large amount of cash on hand was not public knowledge. Now, as far as going back to the fields ... We have no cash to pay you, right up front. I understand that several of you are willing to work and wait for your pay and that's very commendable, but . . . um, the money for the remaining harvest won't be enough to pay all your wages. I'm afraid that we will be only keeping a few of you to work."

Mr. Johnson seems ashamed at this and looks down at his impeccable shoes so that he doesn't make eye contact with the crowd. He's a sixth-generation farmer. His father, Grant Jr., doubled the size of their land and since the stock market crash, Grant the 3rd, has doubled it again. He hates making a profit on other people's tragedy, so he gives the former land owner a job somewhere in his fields. Mr. Johnson has very fair complexion with light blonde hair that's styled short in the back but left long over his hazel eyes. He is only in his early thirties and is about Anna's height but his figure reminds Anna of the 'doughboys' nickname that the Americans got in the big war.

"I had agreed to help pull the vines after the harvest, will you be keeping me?" Shouts one young man, in the middle of the crowd.

Matthew tries to see who it's. It sounds like John Walker. He hasn't seen John since 'the job' nor has he seen the Model A. Matthew just assumed both went North with the loot.

"Yes, John," Mr. Johnson answers. So, it might be John Walker, Matthew thinks as Mr. Johnson continues talking. "We are going to keep only the workers that signed up to pull the vines and till the fields after the crop is over. It's the only way that we thought that was fair. I'm sorry everyone. If you didn't sign up for that work, your time is done here. The sheriffs have a few more questions for you and Miller has all your names and is instructed to give all the other workers five dollars as a small compensation for moving on unexpectedly. I know that it's not enough but that's the best that I can do under the circumstances."

There's much mumbling and shouting from the workers.

Mr. Johnson shouts over the unruly, unhappy crowd. "If any of you can hold out, we do have two other crops coming to harvest in a few weeks. We will need to have a crew for the sunflowers and a bigger one for the pumpkins and squash fields. The harvests for each will be a quick one. Just a single picking, unlike tomatoes, that just kept giving."

One woman with kids' shouts, "How are we going to live until then, will you let us stay here and reopen the store, and give us credit to buy stuff?" She adds boldly.

"I can let you stay on here, but I cannot let you buy on credit. When the other crops are ready for harvest, you'll be paid daily like you have been for the tomatoes. I know that none of this is what you want to hear, but it's the only thing I can do to keep my operation going. Any other questions?"

One woman in the front, with a baby in her arms says, "This has been the best Camp we've stayed in and your store has very reasonable prices. And now, you are willing to give us five dollars each for having to move on, I for one, thank you for your kindness."

Some of the crowd start to quietly applaud, though they're angry at the situation. Anna and Judd stand up clapping louder and slowly more workers do the same.

The owner is noticeably moved. "If there aren't any more questions, I'll turn you over to Sheriff Lark Bailey and his deputies. Oh, umm . . . the truck will be on the regular schedule tomorrow and you'll work a whole day on Saturday to try to catch up. Miller is set up at the table, over there, to pay the outgoing workers. Please remember, there's no hurry for you to leave the Camp. Umm . . . God, Bless you all." He takes out his monogrammed handkerchief to wipe his forehead and turns away to wipe his moist hazel eyes.

Anna looks up to her Pa, "Did you sign us up for pulling vines?"

"Just Matthew and myself. I didn't add you or Melinda. It isn't work for womenfolk." Judd says disappointedly. "But least, he's givin' ya five dollars. I thought him a bad owner. I bet he didn't know how his managers treated us."

"I agree with you, he doesn't seem to be the type of guy to let Croner and the rest yell and cheat us, if he knew." She turns to Melinda, "Let's get in line for our fiver."

The sheriff and his deputies are pulling a few men at a time and leading them to a private area by the hay bales to ask more questions. They didn't approach Matthew or Henry, though.

Melinda's thinking that she might try find a job in town. Maybe waitressing at the diner? She must do something. She'll go mad if she stays home and stare at the walls of the Quonset hut. She doesn't know if Henry is signed up for pulling vines, or not. *That will make all the difference if the Harrick's move on,* she thinks.

Later that day, Henry gets with Matthew and tries to ask him questions about the robbery. Matthew just answers, "the less you know the better. I'm not talking! I didn't plan this, and I do feel very bad for everyone. I wish I could get with John Walker and ask him a few questions, myself"

After dinner, Frank and Henry are in Judy's kitchen drinking coffee with Judd, Anna and Melinda. Judd had already consulted the valise for a true count of the funds they need to live on. Henry signed up for the extra work after the crop so the Harricks are staying.

TWENTY-THREE

The Third Friday in September, 1935
In EL Dorado, Kansas

Judd and Matthew are on the camp truck with Henry, leaving Frank and the womenfolk at home. The Camp store is open and Judy sends the girls there to shop for dinner. While shopping, Melinda talks to Mark who runs the Store. "I'm glad that you didn't stay closed long. Does anyone have a clue who robbed the Paymaster's office?"

Without hesitation, Mark answers, "They're looking for someone who owns a newer Model A. It was seen on the road heading toward the tomato field, Saturday night. No one around here owns a car like that. So, that's a dead end, as far as I know."

Melinda quickly changes the subject. "Do you know of any work in town? I really need to help out the family."

Before he can answer, Anna is next to her and adds "make that 'we' need to help out the family."

Mark Collins is a tall man with laugh lines around his brown eyes. He's very good with numbers and knows all the prices by heart and barely needs to write down the sale before he knows how much is owed. Melinda knows that he's a widower in his mid to late twenties and that his young wife and their first baby died during the delivery. He's lived in EL Dorado his whole life and his wife was the older sister to John Walker's cousin Susan. He has always been real nice to the Masters family. Anna sees that he smiles sheepishly, whenever Melinda is in the store. Melinda doesn't seem to notice.

"You might go into town to the Kroger grocery, or Sally's diner. The diner needs a line cook, and the store needs a cashier. The grocery is owned by friends of mine, Joan and Petro. Tell them I sent you. The Diner is run by Ted who is my uncle. Better get there before anyone else from here beats you to it. Jobs are very scarce in these parts."

"Thank you so much, Mark, we appreciate this. We will let you know what happens." Melinda bats her eyes at him. He blushes.

The girls hurry home. Melinda says, "We need to borrow the truck to go to town." Anna looks at her like she has two heads.

"Who's going to drive it? Neither of us know how to drive."

Melinda thinks about that for a second. "Let's see if Mr. Harrick will take us. He didn't sign up for the vine pulling, so he's home."

"I don't think Da drives anymore. Henry is always at the wheel. I wish Pa had taught us to drive!" Anna says, feeling very frustrated.

"Well, there's only one way to find out, let's go to Mr. Harrick and ask. He'll do anything for you, Anna. You are the daughter he never had. After all, he picked you for Henry!" Melinda adds under her breath, "damn old coot!"

"What was that last part?" Anna asks as they're entering the hut with the groceries.

"Nothing, let's get these things put away and go get a ride to town. If Mr. Harrick cannot do it, maybe someone else can."

A few minutes later, the girls have put away the groceries and have changed clothes to look for work. They kiss their mom good-bye and head to the Harrick hut. Anna thinks that she'll try for the diner job because Melinda isn't a good cook. Melinda is good with numbers so she'd make a better cashier. If only they can get there before the jobs are filled.

Meanwhile, the men are in the fields for what seems to be the last harvest. Half of the fruit on the vines are overripe from five days of no one picking. They toss those in the aisle and put the good ones in bushels. With only a fourth of the normal workers, the job seems overwhelming. Since Anna isn't here to stay with Judd, Matthew tries to stay close. This also discourages Henry from asking him questions.

Matthew is very torn up about the loss of workers in the field. He decides that it's unproductive to feel this way. He thinks that someone else would have been behind the wheel if he wasn't. He'd no idea where they were going, what they were doing or how it would affect the whole Camp. His thoughts continue. *I'm just glad that I could replace Pa's money when I did, because Pa went straight to that valise, to see how much money they had to weather this storm. If I wasn't in on it, the family would be in dire straits!* This lightens his load, and he tries to hum while he works to clear his mind. His father smiles and joins in and several others begin to hum as well.

Croner doesn't have any womenfolk to yell at, and is made to clean up the aisles so that the men can maneuver between rows. He assigns Henry to assist. Like Croner, Henry has a horse drawn cart that he shovels in the rotten tomatoes and any dead vines that are in the aisles. The horse is very smart and Henry just needs to say, "giddy up or whoa" for the horse to move ahead of him in the row. Shoveling is a new exercise to his muscles after weeks of picking and Henry's back and shoulders are sore by noon.

Croner is very miserable having to do manual labor himself and is ready to beat any worker or horse if they don't do as told. Albert Croner inherited a small farm when he was a forty-year old newlywed, just before the first drought summer. He lost the farm and his wife that first year. He started to work for the Johnson Farm Company when Grant Johnson bought his land from the bank, a year later. He tore down the dilapidated farm house and tilled up the whole property, then planted strawberries. Croner is glad that his father isn't alive to see him shoveling rotten tomatoes and living in a boarding house.

Henry nears Matthew and Judd with his horse cart and shovel. When Matthew looks up at him, Henry says, "Guess who I saw on the other side of the ridge, earlier?" He pauses then goes on. "Your good friend, John Walker. It's been almost a week since I've seen him, how about you, Matthew?" Matthew stands to straighten his back and looks in the direction of the ridge.

"Oh, you've seen him? How far is he? I'd like to catch up with him . . . um, about his cousin." He adds so his father isn't suspicious. "Pa, my basket is full, anyway. I'll get it weighed and then have a quick talk with John. You'll be okay?" His father just nods.

"Let me know what he says, little bro." Henry says then to the horse adds "giddy up!" The horse moves forward and Henry keeps shoveling.

Matthew gets his bushel weighed and card stamped. He grabs his empty basket and heads over the ridge to meet up with John. He must be telling a funny story because those around him are listening intently and laughing.

He walks up to him and says, "John, got a sec?" Matthew has caught him off guard but he stands up right away and goes to him.

"I was going to come see you, today. I'm glad that you are still working. They're having another game night on Sunday, interested?" John smiles as if he said something funny.

"As a matter of fact, I am. I'll not bet money that I don't have, ever again, but I still want to play." He adds in a lower voice. "How are your friends Pete and Harry? I'd love to see them again, too." He gives John a little wink.

"Really, Matthew? You are a surprising young man. We did like working with you. We might have something else planned, but not right away. Things need to cool off a little, don't ya think?

"The weather is pretty hot, right now." He adds another wink.

John leans in, "Stop winking at me, kid. Folks are gonna talk."

Matthew laughs. He cannot believe that he's contemplating doing this all over again. Just think if he can earn another two hundred for the farm fund? Is it worth the risk? Hell, he enjoys the risk, and he might as well admit it to himself.

"So, Sunday? Bring Melinda if you can." He turns to head back to picking, then adds, "Leave Henry home, though. He's become a wet blanket, lately." John laughs at his own joke.

"You know I can't do that. I told you, he's my brother, John. And I definitely don't think he'll stay at home if Melinda goes."

"Oh, so you know about them now? Whatever you say, kid. Just make sure that you all have money to spend!" John squats back down to work leaving Matthew standing there confused.

TWENTY-FOUR

The Third Friday in September
Washburn University – Topeka, Kansas

Carolyn, Rosanne and Joshua thought that the first class they attended was amazing. The Students were all seniors and they later learned that this class project would be in lieu of a final. That motivated them, even more. The phones in the Criminology offices were being used non-stop at all hours. Some students took road trips to follow up leads, or to do interviews.

Carolyn and Rosanne, drive in today at the request of the Professor. He called Carolyn instead of Joshua, his original contact person, on Wednesday night, which was the first class after meeting Rosanne. The only ones with anything real to report were the students interviewing the sheriffs and the Medical staff. All the cold callers turned up nothing. They now had thirty-six more hours to make more cold calls.

Carolyn took a very long time, picking out which dress to wear. Rosanne was trying to help her, but Carolyn just told her to get her size six butt out of her room. Carolyn is nervous about her size twelve curves being appealing to the handsome Professor. She hasn't been able to think about anything except that handsome Eddie James! She was thrilled to get a call from him instead of through Joshua. *How silly is I being?*

Joshua meets them at the Campus front entrance, again. Rosanne is far less nervous for this class than she was for the first one. Carolyn on the other hand is more nervous about seeing the Professor. Joshua teased her about her crush, but Carolyn didn't pay him any attention.

Three chairs are set-up in the front of the class, again. Most of the students are already in the room, when they arrive, even though they're just as early as on Monday. The students look much more interested and friendly now that they've been working on the case. There's a feeling of excitement in the air.

Once everyone has taken their seat, the Professor gets right to it. "Welcome back, Rosanne, Carolyn and Joshua. We have several reports for you, this afternoon. I want to get right to them. George, Michael, you were assigned the Sheriff's office evidence. What did you find out?"

George stands up, "Sheriff's office was very cooperative. We saw the photos that they took and read their reports. As Miss Carolyn said, there were no tire tread marks due to the drought. The glass that was recovered was covered in long hairs, blood and even had brain matter on it. They determined that the glass was from a Ford vehicle. Due to the cloudiness of the lens, it was estimated to be a ten-year-old vehicle.

There was enough blood at the scene to convince them that it was the 'attack' site, at least for the last portion of it. They also determined that the vehicle that hit her came from the south and then turned around and went back that way. They determined that from the blood drip trail left from the vehicle."

Michael stands up very excited. "We talked with a sketch artist. He said that he'd like to do a sketch of you, as you are now; then adjust it to erase the injuries of your face and of course replace your long hair. We'd be able to send your 'before' picture to authorities all over the state."

"Excellent progress, gentlemen. Next, we have Sally, Clem and Bobbie Rae for their Medical report. Folks, come on up."

Clem starts the report, "We talked with Dr. Mason and his staff. They determined the order that the injuries took place. This might be a little hard to hear, Miss Carolyn, you might want to have the Professor's garbage can near you, if it gets bad." He jokes and everyone laughs even Carolyn. But the Professor moves the can to her anyway, which makes them laugh, again.

"Dr. Mason thinks the oldest injury was the broken nose. He could tell that it broke a second time when she was hit with the vehicle. After the first nose breaking, the rape was committed. She may have been punched a few times in between. The most injuries were caused by the vehicle. The Doctor said that she was facing the vehicle when it hit her, if you can image that. There were large amounts of broken glass in her forehead, face, and hair. She fractured her neck in two places and both shoulder bones were broken. She'd several rib fractures and one rib punctured her left lung. The most serious injury was to her brain. Her skull was cracked in several places and her brain swelled causing pressure on her already traumatized head. All the team kept saying is that they don't know how or why she survived. Any of one of those injuries would have - should have killed her."

Sally takes over, "As we were told, Rosanne was in a coma for months. They reset all her bones and even fixed her nose during the time her brain was returning to its normal size and function. They were amazed that she woke up, amazed she could walk and talk and understand language! Once awake, the psychiatrists were determining her state of mind and would have been surprised if she didn't have amnesia. They haven't been able to determine if the amnesia is from the brain injury or the mind shielding the psyche from any further trauma, reliving the experience, as you mentioned, Professor." She nods to him and he nods back to her.

Bobbie Rae is the last of them to report. "Her weeks in the hospital after she came out of the coma were pain filled. She was fitted with a double shoulder/chest brace so that those bones could stay immobilized. She weighed 99 pounds by that time and the brace that she wore weighed 45 pounds. They said that she never complained and when they would apologize for causing her pain, she'd smile and tell them 'it would be okay'. They were all amazed at her attitude and inner strength."

Bobbie Rae takes her seat next to Clem and Sally. The Professor congratulates them on their reports as well as George and Michael.

"Ruth, your team is up next."

She stands up, "Between the four of us, we've talked to almost three hundred restaurant and diners in Lawrence and a 30-mile radius out of it. None of us had a good lead. We hope, we will be increasing our radius to 100 miles by this time, next week." She goes to take her seat, but turns to Rosanne and adds, "We are very motivated to finding out if you cooked anywhere. If anyone's assignment has been completed and want to work with us in cold calling, we'd love the help. There's much ground to cover. We're sorry, Rosanne." Now she sits down.

"Joseph, it's your team's turn."

Joseph stands up. "We were calling the farms that use day laborers for tomato harvests. We've already extended our call radius to 75 miles from the Lawrence crime scene. Nothing, yet. We aren't giving up either. We will expand until we have someone who is missing you, Rosanne." He sits.

"Okay, Brad, you guys were going to call Police and Sheriff's Dept.'s looking for a Missing Girl, Missing/Damaged trucks, or suspects of murder investigations missing a girl's body. Any luck with you guys?"

Brad stands up. "No sir, not yet, but we are hopeful that if Miss Rosanne can get that sketch done, we'll mail it to all the departments we've talked to already. Knowing the vehicle was a Ford will help. We also will increase our radius. We'd like to hit 150 miles before this time next week."

"Wow, very good everyone, unfortunately, not a lead anywhere but I can tell that you are putting in the shoe leather as they say in the dime store novels. Rosanne, can you call the sketch artist at the Lawrence Sheriff Department, as soon as possible?"

Before Rosanne can speak, Carolyn answers. "I'll call them this afternoon and as soon as they can do it. I'll have her there."

Rosanne stands up and says, "Thank you all, I'm sure that this is going to lead to something. Professor, your taking this case on, means everything to me." She walks over to him and gives him a kiss on the cheek.

"Well, from what Carolyn, Joshua, and the whole Medical facility say about you Rosanne, you are someone well worth helping."

TWENTY-FIVE

The Third Friday in September, 1935 cont'd
In EL Dorado, Kansas

The girls are very lucky. Mr. Harrick is home and able to drive them. They're given interviews right away. On the ride to town, Melinda was chatting away with Mr. Harrick while Anna was trying to think of all the meals she knew how to prepare, in case they ask at the diner. Mr. Harrick parks on Central Avenue near the intersection of Main Street. Central Avenue divides the town east and west and Sally's Diner is at the end of the first block. Main Street divides the town north and south and the Kroger store is a half of a block down. Each girl had to walk in a different direction to their want-to-be jobs. Frank goes into Owl's Five and Dime to look around and kill time.

At the Kroger Grocery, Melinda meets the owners, Petro and Joan Theonopolis. The small store has a fresh meat counter as Petro's a butcher. His wife Joan bakes bread, cakes and pies, does the ordering and the books. Their grown children ran the register, but Anastacia the oldest is married, in a family way, due any day now and their son Nikko has just gone away to college. The couple thought that they could manage by themselves but found out right quick that they couldn't.

They love Melinda right away and give her a simple math test, which she passes. They need her to start, first thing in the morning. Melinda is so excited that she almost forgot to ask what the pay would be.

"Oh, dear. I didn't think about that." Says Joan as she thinks a moment, "I guess, I mean, we can pay you fifty cents an hour? I didn't pay my children, exactly so . . . I hope that's alright?"

Melinda is thrilled. It took her almost an hour to fill up a bushel basket for fifty cents, and here she wouldn't be in the hot sun getting green hands from those damn tomato plants! She assures them that that will be great and that she'll see them at eight a.m. in the morning.

When Anna arrives at Sally's Diner, she's again impressed by the clean look of the black and white décor. She asks for Sally or Ted, and says that she's looking for a job cooking, if available. It turns out that the former owner was named Sally but Ted Collins has owned it for the last ten years. Ted is expecting one of the Masters girls to come in because he got a call from Mark recommending the girls. Anna thinks that this town is too small because everyone seems to be related somehow.

Ted asks her what dishes she can cook and Anna rattles off a dozen or so. He has a good feeling about her and says so. He takes her into the kitchen to show her around. The kitchen is almost as clean as the seating area. When Anna sees the big grill surface, she's slightly intimidated. She admits to Ted that she has never cooked on something like that. He says, "Everyone has to have a first time. I think that a few hours behind it and you'll be fine. When can you start? I need some help back here, 'cuz my sister decided to run away and get married!"

"Oh, my! Well, I can start tomorrow, if you like? Sorry, about your sister. Mr. Collins, um, can you tell me how much my pay will be and how often I'll get paid?" She looks down at her feet, feeling as if she's begging. She thinks to herself, *well, that's silly* and then looks up at him.

"Well young lady, first, call me Ted. Second, I'll start you out at forty cents an hour while I teach you my recipes. If and when you can make them yourself, I'll raise you to sixty cents an hour. And third, you'll get paid every Saturday night. Sound like a deal?"

"I guess I'd better become a fast learner. Sixty cents is very good money, Mr. Collins. I mean Ted. You won't be sorry. What time did you want me to come to work tomorrow?"

"Well, I open at six a.m. but that early is too busy to teach you, come in around eight a.m." As he says this, Betty the waitress comes into the kitchen and yells to Ted.

"You have a new table, Ted, order in!" With that, she's gone.

"Get me that order slip, please Anna. It's time for me to cook. See you tomorrow morning, and wear comfortable shoes, and make sure that your hair is up and ready for our not-so lovely hair nets."

Mr. Harrick is back in his truck napping in the early afternoon heat. Melinda is the first to arrive with her good news. She rattles on about Petro and Joan who both are from Greece. She says that she'd a hard time understanding Petro but not his wife, Joan.

Anna comes to the truck a few moments later. She too is very excited about getting a job on the first try. She's nervous about the recipes but Melinda says, "You've never had a problem with cooking. You have Ma's natural talent for it. So, you might must learn a few new ones but you'll probably end up improving the menu, quite a bit."

Frank is shaking his head, no. "Ted and his sister have been cooking there for ten years. Never served a bad meal, yet, as far as I know. Henry and I've eaten there a lot. I'm sure that they'll show you what you need to know."

"Ted said that his sister has run off. He wants me, tomorrow at eight a.m."

"That's what time I start, also. Mr. Harrick, can you drive us into town, tomorrow? Maybe I can get Pa to teach us to drive so that we won't put you to any trouble."

He laughed. "What trouble? Having two beautiful ladies in my truck is bound to up my status around this town. Do you know what time you are getting off? I can have Henry pick you up if he's home from the fields. 'Course your Pa and Matthew will be home also so … well, I'm here if you need me, girls."

Anna is moved by his sweetness and would have given him a kiss on the cheek if she was next to him. As if reading her mind, Melinda is the one that gives him a peck. "Thank you, Mr. Harrick."

"Don't you ladies think it's time you called me Frank?"

Both girls shake their heads no at the same time. Then they talk at the same time "No, Mr. Harrick, we couldn't." says Melinda as Anna says, "It wouldn't be right, Mr. Harrick."

"Do you both think alike?" he laughs.

"Not usually" they both say at the same time and laugh. Then they immediately lightly punch each other in the shoulders saying together, "Jinx, double Jinx!"

"Oh my goodness, it's been a long time since we did that," says Anna quieting down. It felt good to her to be so relaxed with Mr. Harrick and Melinda. She has been feeling like something is off with her sister, but she couldn't put her finger on it. Her relationship with Mr. Harrick has always been formal, but more so now with the impending engagement with Henry. This felt more natural, like it should be.

With Melinda talking nonstop, they're back at Camp in no time. They thank Mr. Harrick profusely and they start their journey home.

Judy is very thankful that they're home. She forgot to put cream and butter on this morning's list for the Camp Store, so she needs Melinda to go there. She wants Anna to help her get dinner going. "I cannot wait until you bring home a few new recipes, I get so tired of stew, roast and fried chicken." She makes Anna bend down so that she can kiss her forehead. "And you Melinda, I'm so proud of you. Running a cash register looks difficult but I'm sure it won't be for you. You have such a good head on your shoulders." She reaches up to give Melinda a kiss on the forehead, too. "Not a day goes by that I don't think, how blessed I'm to have my beautiful daughters and my strong good looking son. I'm so grateful for my family."

"Aww Ma, don't get all gushy. We just got jobs, no big deal." Melinda says as she kisses her back. "We had to help, somehow."

"What we need to do is learn to drive so that we can get to work and back without bothering Mr. Harrick. Do you think Pa will teach us? We should get Matthew to do it. Of course, why didn't I think of that, before?" Anna words rush out as her excitement increases.

Melinda is happy to go back to the Camp Store. She wants to thank Mark for the job leads and the good references. Joan had said that he called before they arrived and spoke very highly of the sisters. He didn't know which sister would apply for which job but said both girls were very smart and ambitious. Anna said that her new boss got a call from Mark, also. How sweet he was to do that for them! When

Melinda thanked him for going out of his way to do them this favor, he said, "Shucks, I was happy to help. Your family is good folks and I didn't want to see you leave, if I could help in any way. I'm glad you are at the Kroger. You'll love working for Petro and Joan. They're very funny people who love to have a good time. My cousin Joe is married to their daughter and I was his best man. That wedding was the funniest event I've ever been to, because of them!"

***

The potatoes are washed, peeled and ready for frying. The second loaf of bread is almost done and the pork chops are washed and seasoned and ready to go into the oven so it all can be served as soon as the menfolk come in from their hard day at the field. The women are just brimming with excitement to break the news of their jobs. They invite Mr. Harrick to join them with Henry for a celebration dinner. They asked Frank not to let Henry know about the jobs so they can make an official announcement.

When Judd and Matthew got home, they look beat. Several days off isn't good for the muscles. The womenfolk fuss over them but hurry them to wash up and change for dinner. The smells that fill the hut is making Matthew salivate. He's glad that Henry is coming over because he hasn't had a chance to tell him of the next crap game.

Frank follows Henry through the front door. He winks at the girls and he goes into the kitchen. When he comes back in the room he says to Judy, "Knock, knock."

She answers, "who's there?"

"John" he's so serious as he plays this out.

"John who" Judy continues with his joke, not knowing where this is going.

He raises the ironing shaker water bottle over her head and shakes it vigorously, "John the Baptist, of course! Gotcha!" He's so pleased but Judy just smooths her wet tendrils into place and walks up to Judd.

"Judd, I think I need that big spoon again, I know you're tired but can you get that for me." She smiles up at him.

"Now Judy," He starts to say something but clearly changes his mind. His blue eyes are twinkling with humor. "Aww, why not, we need another good laugh." Everyone is shocked that he goes into the kitchen for the spoon. "Now don't take too long, dear, we are very hungry, aren't we Matthew?"

"Sure am Pa, I could eat a horse, right now."

Henry interrupts, "Don't mention horses. I feel like I still smell like one after a day of him being my partner."

Judy is still standing there with the spoon in one hand, hitting the palm of her other hand, thinking.

"Frank, I pray I must hold off your punishment for the sake of our starving children. Remember, this is a postponement not a cancellation." She warns.

As they all sit down together, Melinda offers to say grace. "Almighty Lord, we thank you for the meal before us and the company that shares this meal. We thank you for making sure that we all have good paying jobs so that we can ALL contribute to our families in a very meaningful way. It's in Jesus's name we pray. Amen."

Anna looks up. "Any questions before we pass the potatoes?" The men all speak up at once, wanting to understand Melinda's prayer. "Melinda and I went to town today. Thank you again, Mr. Harrick for the ride. I got a job as a cook at Sally's Diner and Melinda got a job at the Kroger Grocery Store as a cashier! Isn't that great news? And we will be making as much as we did in the fields! Aren't you glad Pa?" Judd looks down at his empty plate, tears threatening to break through his warm pale blue eyes.

"Girls, I never wanted you to work. It's my job to provide for my family. Being in the fields, together, seemed almost like still being on the farm, but now we are going our separate ways. All because your Pa can't keep up." His sorrow is very apparent though the tears are held at bay.

Frank speaks up. "Judd, they're grown women and very industrious. You cannot imagine that they're little girls not able to do for themselves still, are you? You should have seen their faces when they got into my truck. This makes them happy to help. It's what we as parents teach them to do. We cannot be sad when they do as they were taught. Come on, old friend, this is a happy occasion!" Frank pats Judd on the back. "Now pass those scrumptious looking potatoes!"

Henry remains quiet. He believes like Judd, that the womenfolk shouldn't be working if they've a man to provide for her. He understands their need to help, though. He feels the same way toward his father but this will change everything. He won't be able to see them in the fields for quick conversations between the rows. But whether they've jobs or not, that's already happened, he thinks. They begin to eat in earnest. Everyone is famished.

"How were the crops today?" Melinda asks the men.

"Two or three rotten tomatoes for every one tomato picked. We are pulling dead plants out, too." Answers Matthew.

"Yea, thanks for that. Then I get stuck with the horse and shovel brigade. My shoulders are killing me." Henry complains.

"Sure, but you are getting paid hourly unlike us who're still getting paid by the bushel. It's taking longer to fill the bushels with so much rot on the vines!" Matthew whips back. "So when do you start the new jobs?" Matthew changes the subject back to the girls.

"Tomorrow at eight a.m." They both answer at the same time.

They aren't next to each other to punch each other's shoulders but still say, "Jinx, double jinx." Before, they both laugh.

"I'll take them into town," Frank interjects. "But these ladies would like to learn to drive so they can use your truck while you're in the fields, Judd."

"I'll teach them!" Now it's Henry and Matthew's turn to say the same thing at the same time. They didn't add the Jinx part.

Judy comments, "Well, two trucks, two teachers, two students and all day Sunday to teach them. You can even switch up the pairing if needed. Sounds perfect." Judd looks less than thrilled. "Now Judd, don't go looking all grumpy. This is 1935. Women should know how to drive, for goodness sakes. After the girls learn, I might try my hand at it. Doesn't look too hard, after all. Matthew's been driving since he was eleven and shorter than me, so how hard could it be?"

"Well, Ma, you cannot compare yourself to me. I was practically born behind the wheel." Matthew defends himself.

"Matthew, I'm your mother and I know where you were born and it was nowhere near a steering wheel!"

Melinda interrupts, "I don't know if I've Sunday off, yet. Do you, Anna?"

Anna doesn't like the idea of working Sundays but that's a very popular time to eat out. She'd be needed that day, especially. "I don't know but it makes sense that I'll work on Sundays, at some point. I suddenly don't like this job." She starts playing with her food on her plate. "I never thought about it not being a 'weekday only' type of work. I'll ask, tomorrow."

After dinner, Matthew pulls Melinda and Henry outside and tells them of the Crap game Sunday night. "And John Walker said for me to bring you, Melinda, to the game and leave you, Henry, home. When I said that Henry wouldn't like that he said something funny. He said 'so you know about them, now?' What is he talking about?"

Henry responds, "Why are you going to the game after all the trouble it's caused you? Are you trying to live dangerously? And I wouldn't like you or Melinda going to a game without me. I was the one who liked going, first"

Matthew says, "That doesn't answer my question."

"You need to ask John, what he means." Melinda says. "Come on if we stay outside any longer, Anna will get suspicious. Why do you want to gamble again? Any way?"

"Craps is fun. The game is exciting. I'll only bring a little money to lose. I can afford to lose five dollars. That's how I look at it. I'll only play what I can afford to lose. No more, all over the place crazy bets, for me.

.

TWENTY-SIX

The Third Friday in September, cont'd
In Lawrence, Kansas

Joshua takes Rosanne and Carolyn back to his apartment in the Senior Dormitory. Carolyn didn't want to wait until she got back to the Plantation to call the Lawrence Sheriff's Department to schedule the artist sketch. Neither of the girls have been to Joshua's place and they're surprised at the neatness of the it. Carolyn kids him, "Who have you hired to keep this place this clean? They're worth every penny!"

"That would be funny if it wasn't true, I've two freshmen girls that come in together, on Mondays, Wednesdays and Fridays to clean and organize the place. They need the extra cash and I like living in a well-kept place. It's a great arrangement for all concerned. It's worth the money to have my privacy and have it looking like I like it. Don't you think?"

Rosanne is silent during this conversation. She looks all around and as he's saying that he likes to live alone, she tries to think if she ever lived alone. She tries to imagine coming home to a place where no one was waiting for her. That doesn't seem pleasant to her, at all.

Carolyn sees the telephone and goes straight to it and asks the operator for the Lawrence Sheriff's Department. When she's connected, she asks for Officer Bob, who is the artist that Michael mentioned. The Officer came on the line and Carolyn went right to it. "I'm calling about having a sketch drawn, Michael from Washburn University told us to call you . . . yes, the found person from a year ago . . . I'd like to bring Rosanne to you as soon as possible. Do you have time, this evening, or tomorrow, perhaps? We haven't left the University, yet but if we rush right down we could be there in about forty-five minutes. That works? Oh, bless you! We will see you later." She puts down the receiver. "Isn't that wonderful. He'll do it today!! Come on Rosanne, let's get going."

Joshua stops them. "I'll go to my last class of the week and then I'll head right home. If he does the whole thing today, I can bring it back up here and give it to the Professor so they can distribute it to all the authorities, that they're calling. They could even mail it to the diners and the farms, for that matter. Wait, I know! I'll have 2000 flyers made up and we'll paper the state with them!"

Rosanne is so moved by his generosity that she rushes to him, puts her arms around his neck and gives him a big kiss. "This wouldn't be happening, if it wasn't for you. Rocco saved my life, Carolyn saved my life, then the Colonel saved my life and now you are going for the gold. How many times can one person be saved?" She kisses him again.

Carolyn clears her throat. "Come on, Sister, we need to go. We will see you at home, brother Joshua."

Rosanne blushes. "That's Carolyn's way of telling me that I'm sending you mixed signals. She's right, I'm just so . . . I feel so . . . close to knowing!! This is going to work. I just know it. Good-by Joshua. See you at home, big brother." With that, the two women are out the door.

Joshua is left standing in the middle of his apartment, with the feel of Rosanne's kisses still on his lips. "Big Brother, My Ass!" He says out loud, to no one.

On the way, back to Lawrence, Carolyn warns her not to be too hopeful. "When you were found, it was in all the papers and picked up by the state news wire. There was hardly a town that wasn't notified. A picture is going to help, considerably, I admit, but now it's been a year and memories fade. I'm sure this will be a good thing, but if it does nothing, I don't want you to get all down in the mouth. Like after the miscarriage. The Doctor said you could get out of that bed, you just didn't want to. That's why I kept sending the Colonel in the room to talk with you. He was the only one that could get you up and get up you did!" Rosanne gives her a pretend pout. "Okay, lecture, over." They ride the rest of the way lost in their own thoughts.

***

Officer Bob draws her very quickly. He says that the police report stated her injuries so he'll try to imagine her without the twice broken, once fixed nose and add in back the middle-of-the-back length hair and of course won't include that big scar across the forehead either. After the first drawing of what she looked like today, he takes a little longer with the unscarred version. When he's done, and hands it to her, she sits back in the chair and stares at it. "That doesn't look like me at all!" She looks at the two sketches side by side. "The eyes are the only thing the same. Are you sure this is what I looked like before the attack?" Officer Bob just nods. "She was very, very pretty." She gets up to leave but turns to him. "Thank you for doing this. This is a long shot, but we are so desperate." She's walking out of the department, when he thinks he hears her say, "How could anyone hurt someone so pretty. He must be a real monster!"

Carolyn is waiting for her in the car outside of the Sheriff's Department. She didn't know that Rosanne was going to walk out with both sketches. Rosanne hands them to Carolyn as she gets into the Hudson and settles into the seat. Carolyn loved the 'now' sketch. "Girl, this looks just like you. What a good job!"

"Yes, but look at the 'before' sketch. I don't know that girl. I hoped that I would see myself and say 'that's me, my name is _____', but she's a stranger. She's so very beautiful, how come no one is looking for her? You were right, Carolyn, this makes me sadder than I was before. If no one loved this girl, how is there any hope for me?"

"We love you, Rosanne, you never have to leave us, you know. We are your family, now and forever. Let's go home and get the Colonel to his bed."

"Is Joshua coming home tonight or the morning?" Rosanne asks.

"I believe, he said tonight. I cannot believe his neat little apartment. Who'd have thought that he'd be a neat freak."

"Just because he likes it clean, doesn't mean those girls don't have their work cut out for them. A neat freak, won't start a mess that needs cleaning. I just hope he pays them well."

Rosanne just sits and stares at the two sketches in her lap, as Carolyn drives home. *The 'now' sketch right on the money. The 'before' sketch is amazing. I just can't believe that it's me. My poor nose had been through so much and obviously makes such a huge difference in my appearance. If my real family walked into the room, would they even recognize me?* She couldn't stop staring.

Carolyn pulls up to the front door. Rosanne looks at the Plantation main House. The Colonel had several houses built on his properties. As he acquired more land and wealth, he built house after house for his Julia. This one was the biggest and the best. It's two stories, with a formal dining room as well as a formal front parlor big enough for a dance! It has five bedrooms all with their own fireplaces, five bathrooms, a 'Dinner' type kitchen, a large laundry room, a work office, a servant's day room and a cozy sitting room. The front of the house has four huge columns that go up to the second floor. The front porch is fifteen feet wide by sixty feet long, the width of the house itself. There are several swings, chairs and tables set up for outside sitting, front and back. The Colonel's room, which is the master suite leads out onto a small balcony overlooking the front door. The house is immaculately painted white and reminds Rosanne of the beautiful houses described in the new book Gone with the Wind by Margaret Mitchell.

When they walk in they can tell that the Colonel is having a melt-down. They could hear his yelling at the attendant in the sitting room. 'I don't want to settle down. I want my Julia. Is she hiding from me? Are you hiding her from me? She'd come when I called. It's your fault."

Rosanne puts the sketches down on the front hallway table with her purse and wrap and goes straight into the sitting room to help with the Colonel. Carolyn can hear her. "Colonel, there you are, I'm so glad to see you. I was just going to make myself a little something to eat and a nice cup of hot tea. Do you want to come into the kitchen with me and keep me company? You can have a cup with me. Want one . . . Good, come with me. I think your Carolyn is hungry, also. I'll make something for all of us, okay? There you go."

Rosanne is so good with the Colonel. Carolyn thinks. *He wouldn't be the same if she left the family. None of us would be the same.*

Carolyn hangs up their coats then she goes back to the sketches, and stares at them side by side. She's carrying them into the kitchen. As she walks in, she says, "I think we will get lucky with this sketch. There must be someone, thinking you are dead and gone. Otherwise, why would they stop looking for you? I wouldn't."

She looks up and sees the silliest thing. The Colonel is on the floor laughing so hard that he's soundless and he has his little dog, Robbie, in his arms, licking him all over the face. Rosanne is sitting on the counter stool, looking down at the scene blowing on a dog whistle each time Robbie stops licking. When he hears the signal, he licks all over again.

"What is going on here?" Carolyn asks frozen in place.

"Well, the Colonel needed to make up with Robbie. I trained him to lick when he hears the dog whistle. Good dog, Good boy. Two birds with one stone, kind of a thing. Don't you agree?"

Carolyn crosses the room and goes to her, and gives her a hug. "You constantly amaze me, Rosanne. But I must tell you, one thing, I'm starving to death!!"

Rosanne smiles at the old man on the floor and says, "Ah, well, we will fix that, won't we, Colonel?"

He looks up smiling and says, "Whatever you say, Rosanne, Robbie is a good boy!" He's scratching the dog under the chin and the dog is enjoying it immensely.

TWENTY-SEVEN

The Third Saturday in September, 1935
In EL Dorado, Kansas

At five-thirty a.m., Matthew is again watching the familiar dance that happens every morning through his half-closed eyes. Though it's early and he's sore and tired to the bone, he smiles slightly at the comforting sight of his parents working in the kitchen in such perfect harmony. This is his favorite part of the day, seeing them this way. *Is anyone else as lucky as my parents to have found their other half. If anyone can be considered Soulmates, it was them. Definitely. I'll bet my life on it.*

Anna and Melinda are all raw nerves this morning for their first day at their first jobs. Anna is especially nervous of that big fry grill. She knows Ma's pots and pans; but this type of cooking will be as different as different can be. Melinda is trying to find the right outfit that looks professional for a cashier. She hopes that she can remember all the prices. Now she's wishing that she'd done more shopping with her mom growing up, so she'd be more familiar with things in a store.

Anna has her hair in a tight bun so that the hair net that Ted said she must wear will be easy to put on. Plus, it will be hot cooking in the kitchen all day.

Melinda is wearing a simple blouse and skirt set. Nothing tight or revealing. She doesn't need men to bother her on her first day. She remembers when even in her baggy work pants, Croner was trying to sample some of her wares, uninvited. *Oh, I'm so glad I don't have to put up with him anymore,* she thinks.

Mr. Harrick is waiting for them in his truck at the front parking lot at seven-thirty a.m. He takes Melinda to the Kroger Grocery first and goes in with her to ask what time she need a ride back. Joan says to come for her at five p.m. Frank will be the 'pick-up man' since none of the others will be back from the field by then.

The next stop is Sally's Diner and Frank goes in with Anna, also. Ted says that Anna's pick-up time is five p.m. also. Frank wishes her good luck with a kiss on the forehead and heads out the door. Anna turns to Ted and says, "I'm in your hands. Teach me to cook, please."

"I like your can-do attitude. Let's get to the back." He leads the way through the double doors. There are two very busy people in the kitchen. Ted introduces them as Bruce and Dana. They're a married couple that have cooked at Sally's since Sally owned it a decade ago. Ted explains that he's the breakfast short order cook and that Bruce makes the soups, roasts, meatloaves and barbeque. Dana works salads and prep. She cuts up all the vegetables that are needed in the soups and side dishes. They're both very hard at work already, and just nod to Anna as Ted continues with his explanations. He heads over to the big grill and the eight-burner stove. He says to Anna, "Here will be your station. You'll finish breakfast, work through lunch and start the dinner shift. I would like you to work Wednesday through Sunday if that's okay with you and if you can handle the job." He can see immediate disappointment on her face. "You don't think you can do it? You haven't even tried?"

"Oh, it's not that, I'm sure that I can do it. It's just that Sunday has always been a family day. Even when my father had his own farm, he never worked on Sundays, except to feed the animals. I know that's a very busy day for eating out but I would like to have that day off. Maybe I can work one week Tuesday through Saturday then the next week work Wednesday through Sunday? I know it's bold of me to ask before I've even started but . . . um, it's very important to me. I'd be even willing to work six days and only have Sunday's off if that would help." She's very flushed from asserting herself.

"I'll take that last offer. Monday through Saturday – nine a.m. to six p.m. But let's see if you make it through today first." Ted is smiling as he turns to the grill. "I like to call her Big Bertha. She's hot, large and in charge. I've been married to her or grills just like her my whole life. Most of the breakfast is done on her as well as the burgers and meats for the other meals. Let me show you how to make ..." He pulls the order slip from the counter. "Two orders of eggs up with hash brown potatoes, bacon and toast." He shows her how to grease the grill before putting down any of the food. The bacon gets a weight put on it while frying so that it stays straight. The hash browns are the next to go on the grill. They sizzle loudly. He takes two eggs and breaks them into a small pan and puts it on one of the burners. He repeats that for the next set. A second later he's turning the bacon and shifting the potatoes around then back to the eggs, where he swirls them in the pan. Then he's off to the toaster to put down four slices. Back to the bacon and the hash browns. Anna is getting tired watching him but confident that she could mimic his moves and with time, his speed. The morning just flies by as she's shown step by step each item as it comes in on the order slip.

The lunch service is fast paced also. She's working the grill by now and is flipping burgers and making grilled cheese sandwiches and loving this.

Meanwhile, Melinda is having a difficult time understanding Petro as he yells from the meat counter. He's telling her the cuts of meat that he has wrapped and given to the customer. When they're done shopping, and come to her to be checked out, Melinda must ask them what meat is in the wax paper package. Joan sees this and goes to

Melinda and asks if she can hear okay or if she cannot remember. Melinda feels ashamed but admits that she cannot understand Petro with his thick Greek accent. Joan sympathizes with Melinda. "Many of our customers say the same thing."

"What if he writes on the butcher paper what the meat is and the cost that I'm supposed to ring up, instead of yelling across the store? I'm sure that your children didn't have a problem with the system but . . ." Melinda is nervous that she'll hurt their feelings with this suggestion but continues, "I think it would be more professional this way, don't you Joan?"

Joan thinks for just a second. "We could use more professional." She heads toward the meat counter speaking loudly in Greek as she went.

Petro is leaning over his counter, nodding his head as she was explaining Melinda's idea. "More professional? Good! We need that! Good idea, Melinda, good idea. But can you read Greek?"

Melinda is dumbstruck for a second, she hadn't thought that he didn't know how to write in English. She was about to say something when Joan and Petro both bust out laughing. Joan says, "Petro is never serious about anything. He can read and write in English, Greek, Spanish and Portuguese. But don't believe anything he says, in any language. Learn from my mistake. In Greece, one day he said we were going on a boat ride and I ended up here, in America!"

Again, Melinda is at a loss for words. Now it's Petro's turn to say, "Don't believe her either. She's a bigger liar than I am and that's no lie!" *It's going to be real fun working with these two crazies. Mark was right.* When no one needs to checked out, Melinda is supposed to price merchandise and stock shelves. Joan shows her how and then disappears into the bakery part of the store. Not only does she sell what she bakes to store customers but she also supplies Sally's diner with baked goods as well. Joan has been at the store since four a.m. and Petro made the diner delivery just before six a.m., well before Melinda got to work.

Before either girl knows it, it's the end of their first work day. They each feel very satisfied with their new jobs and when they meet up in Frank's truck. They don't stop talking for a minute their whole ride home.

Frank cannot believe that two people can talk so much and so fast. They're both going a mile a minute. He manages to get a word in, "Do either of you work tomorrow?"

"No, thank God! -- Jinx, double Jinx!" then comes the shoulder punching between these two very different giggling girls.

Once back at home, the girls kiss their mom hello, then continue their constant chatter, while setting the table. Judy has the meal made and once the men are home, they sit down to supper. Judy is so proud of her girls having jobs but Judd is still having problems with it. She talked to him about it last night, prior to going to sleep and Judy thought she convinced him that this is a good thing for them. But Judd is being very quiet and barely looks up from his plate as they talk about their first day.

After supper, Henry comes over to find out how things went. He's amazed at the difference in Anna in just a single day. She's just glowing with satisfaction as she describes making Big Bertha do as she commands. It's as if she has gained all the self-confidence she was lacking. He also wants to know if Anna will go to Service with him tomorrow, and then maybe have a driving lesson afterward. She rushes to his side and kisses him on the lips! This is their first kiss on the lips, and she does it in front of Melinda and the whole family. She immediately blushes bright, bright red and looks ashamedly at her parents. Melinda, of course, seems to be the only one to mind. Henry doesn't seem to notice Melinda is even there. He asks Anna, "Are you very tired? Do you want to go for ice cream in town?" She turns to her parents and asks, "It's not too late, is it?" They both shake their heads no, so Anna and Henry leave, just like that.

Matthew looks over to Melinda and says, "Want to go for a walk, sis? I'd like to ask your opinion about something." Melinda was still staring at the closed door. "What did you say, Matthew?" She says without taking her eyes away.

"I said, want to go for a walk with me? I'd like to ask your advice." He leads her by the elbow to the door then turns to his parents who were sitting on his couch. "We are just going to get a little night air. We won't be long."

Once outside, Matthew turns on Melinda. "When John said, 'so you know about them' he meant Henry and you have something going on, don't you? You cannot lie to me, Melinda, I can see how you look at him. Especially when he looks at Anna, like he did just now. Come on, 'fess up!"

Melinda is ashamed of herself, mad at Henry and jealous of Anna right now. *How could I have been so stupid as to let Henry keep leading me astray? Or did I lead him?* Matthew was waiting patiently as he could tell Melinda was working through her feelings. She finally said, "I cannot take it anymore, Matthew. I do want Henry. He and I've been meeting secretly for weeks. He keeps saying that he's obligated to try to make things work with Anna for his father's sake but the look that he had for Anna, tonight. That was not obligation on his face. He's falling for her, after all! What am I going to do?"

"If Mr. Harrick was looking for a wife for Henry, why can't it be you? Why Anna? Anna and Henry aren't a good match, Melinda. Melinda, look at me." She's looking down but raised her head to face him. "You have nothing to be ashamed of. Anna is wrong for him. Henry should have said that from the beginning."

"Matthew, I'm ashamed. I want Henry, but I don't want to get married. That's why Anna is the one. She's the marrying kind, not me. I want more out of life than a husband and kids. I want to travel and see things. I want to live, not settle down, but that doesn't lessen what I feel for Henry. He makes me feel alive, when he touches me." She looks down as she says this. "I don't want him to be with Anna. I'm ashamed for feeling this way, with my sister's fiancé, yet." She cannot believe that she's telling her fifteen-year-old brother all her deep dark secrets. *What will he think of me? How will he handle this kind of knowledge?*

"Melinda, you say that you don't want to settle down, but that Henry's touch makes you feel alive, isn't that living? Look at Ma and Pa. I watch them every morning. They're made for each other. They live for each other. I can see that's possible between you and Henry. He wants the same things you want. He doesn't seem to want to get married any more than you do." He shakes his head. "I don't know how he feels about Anna right now, but it can't be as powerful as what he feels for you."

"So what should I do, Matthew? I don't want to do this anymore. I'm torn up with all the lies I've told, especially to Anna. She deserves better from me and from Henry."

"I said sort of the same thing to Henry, just the other day. Anna isn't like us. We like the excitement, and the risk taking. She doesn't like it or need it. She's too good for us, I think were my words."

"Matthew, you're an amazing young man. I'm very proud to be your sister; you know that don't you? I'd do anything for you. But what am I to do about our Anna and Henry situation? If I tell Anna that I've been seeing him, she'll be so crushed and mad at the both of us. If I just break it off with Henry, I'll still see him and want him. I don't see a win in this game."

"Well, with your new job, you won't see him as much and you should try to date someone else. I'm sure you get offers all the time. I know that you're not sweet on John Walker but I'm sure that someone else is out there for you. Isn't Mark at the Camp Store a little sweet on you? As you say, you aren't interested in marriage so play the field."

"I never thought about Mark, that way. He's a very nice guy. He's 'sweet' on me? Oh, I don't know. I'll take it one day at a time, I guess. By the way . . ." She says changing the subject. "You ARE going to teach me to drive tomorrow, aren't you? I can't let Anna learn first. What fun will that be?" Melinda's spirits rise.

"Sometimes I think you came out of the womb in competition with Anna. Why are you like that?" Matthew see Melinda pout. "Of course, I'll teach you. Stop pouting and smile. Tomorrow night is the next game and I'll have you driving me there."

Henry and Anna are having a wonderful time. She's still talking about her work and learning to drive. He thinks she's spectacular when she's excited. *What if I can excite her in other ways?* They're on their way back from the Soda Shoppe, where they each had two new flavors New York Cherry and Mint Chocolate Chip in a bowl, not a cone. Anna is leaning on his arm as he drives. She puts her head on his shoulder and sighs loud enough for Henry to hear it over the truck engine.

"What was that sigh for, Anna? Are you tired?" He asks.

"No, Happy. That was my Happy sigh. This was a surprising, wonderful evening. Thank you, Henry."

"The pleasure is all mine, Anna. I love seeing you like this. Seeing you happy. You deserve to be happy."

"How about you Henry, are you happy?" She murmurs into his neck. "What makes you happy?"

"Being with you and your family. I could be happy with you, Anna, I believe I can." He realizes that this is the truth. He can be happy with Anna at his side. She'd give him all the support and comfort that he could want. And she was as sweet as a new day. For the first time, he thought that his father made the right choice, when he chose Anna.

He's gone quiet, so Anna nuzzles herself deeper into him. She's having strange new feelings stir up inside her. *These must be the feelings her Ma told me to keep in check until marriage. For once, I don't want to listen to Ma.* She wants to see how this feels. When they pull into the Camp lot and Henry shuts off the truck he turns to her and lifts her chin and leans in to give her first sweet long kiss. He can feel her kissing him back. He puts one arm around her back but keeps the other on her face. She's thinner than Melinda but has hidden curves. She tastes of Mint Chip and her hair smells like French fries from the diner. He takes it all in and it's wonderful. She breaks away for a moment and looks in his smoldering eyes. "I'm trying to be a good girl, Henry but . . . " She doesn't finish her sentence because her lips are on his with a passion that's surprising them both. He moves his hand to her breast and she lets a surprised breath out. "Oh Henry, we shouldn't."

Henry doesn't want to stop, but he breaks away. Anna would regret it, if he takes liberties too quickly. She seems willing but he doesn't want to push things too fast for her. "Then we won't, Anna. But if you keep kissing me like that, I won't be able to help myself. You seem to have become a woman today. So, confident, so sure of yourself and it's as sexy as hell! Just one more kiss, and I'll walk you to your door." She leans in and kisses him lightly at first then her own passion takes control again and she presses against him. She doesn't know if she can control this urge for more.

"Henry, I don't know what I'm doing." She says, breathlessly.

"But you're doing it so well." He laughs. "Just a little more."

"That's the trouble, I want more, too. I thought a good girl doesn't have those feelings." Anna says just barely above a whisper.

"No, a good girl ignores them. Please, don't ignore them. I just want to keep kissing you." Henry means this. He just wants to keep kissing her. *After all the passionate nights with Melinda, why am I so content with so little from Anna?*

"Yes, keep kissing me, please." She begs softly. She can feel the urge to lean into him and she can feel herself moisten as his tongue hesitantly probes her mouth. She thinks to herself, *why does it affect me down below.* She nervously lets out a small laugh.

Henry pulls back. "Is my tongue amusing you, my dear?"

"No, it's that …" she hesitates and decides that she can't explain it to him, it's too personal and silly. "it's nothing, I've to say that we should get going. My parents will be waiting up for me. I know when they ask me if I had a good time, I'm going to blush from the thought of how your kisses make me feel."

"And how is that?" His voice is at its sexiest when it's just above a whisper.

"Like I want more than just kisses." *There, I admitted it.*

He smiled and took her face into his hands, once more. "I think this is just the beginning for us, Anna. We've crossed whatever barrier was between us. Doesn't it feel that way to you?" With her face, still in his hands, she nods. He bends down and chastely kisses her forehead. "I think we will leave it at that, then." He lets go and turns to open his door and get out.

Anna starts to object but knew that it's the perfect time to say good-night, before anything happens that they might regret. He opens her door and puts his arm out for her to lean on as she gets out. She looks in his eyes again. *I can live in those eyes*, she thinks. When she's standing next to him looking in his eyes, he leans down and slowly softly kisses her. She puts her arms around his neck and leans into him. "Oh, this is too good." She says out loud.

"I agree, sweetheart. I cannot wait to see you tomorrow. I hope I can be good and not touch you during Service, at least."

"Oh, Henry, you'd better not! I'd be so embarrassed!" She blushes again. "In front of God and everybody, really?"

"How could it be a sin, to want to love you, Anna?" Henry asks.

"I think wanting to love me is different than wanting to make love to me." She says matter-of-factly.

"Well, I want both, Anna." He says with a smile and a look that sends quivers to her insides.

How can he do that to me with just a look? She thinks. They're now at her hut. She leans in and kisses him on the cheek and opens the door and goes in before he can do anything else to her insides.

Ma is darning socks and Pa is playing checkers with Matthew. Melinda must be in the bedroom. They all look up as she enters. She's smiling. She twirls around the room until she gets to her bedroom door. "This has been a magical day, and night. I'm so happy but tired, good night everyone." She goes into the bedroom before anyone can say goodnight back to her.

Melinda is on her bed thumbing through a magazine. Anna sits down at the mirror and starts to undo her hair. She's still smiling. Melinda puts down her magazine and simply asks, "Happy?"

"Oh my darling, sister, I couldn't be happier. I cannot stop smiling. I swear that I'll smile in my sleep, tonight. I think Henry and I are going to be a good couple. I think we've finally hit it off."

"How did that happen?"

"Well, I kissed him, I mean, really kissed him, on the mouth. Then, I couldn't stop, I didn't want to stop." She pauses.

"Did you stop?"

"Well, Henry did actually. He said that we will take this slowly. I don't know why I was so hesitant about him. He always was the one, wasn't he? I don't know, but it feels so good! I want to sing, cry out and dance! I think I'm in love, Melinda, I think I am!"

Melinda deadpans, "That must have been some ice cream!" but Anna is too lost in her own thoughts to hear her.

Melinda went out after Anna was asleep to the camp truck but Henry was a no-show. She went there to end the relationship. He needs to concentrate on Anna, now, because Anna's in love with him. When she snuck back into the room, Anna was smiling in her sleep, just as she predicted. *He'd better be good to her!* Melinda thinks.

TWENTY-EIGHT

The Third Saturday in September
In Lawrence, Kansas

Once again, Carolyn wakes at her usual time, and is told that Joshua is home and asleep in his old room. He came home, after midnight, far past Carolyn's bedtime. She hesitates going into his room, this time. She didn't think that he has had a chance to see Rosanne's sketches, yet. *If he loves her as she's now, what would he have done if he'd met the 'before' Rosanne?* She'd have a worse time, trying to get rid of him as her suiter. But then again, her excuses of being broken and damaged, wouldn't be in the way of her happiness, either.

She smells Rosanne's coffee and she heads downstairs, still in her nightgown and robe. She can hear Rosanne talking in the kitchen and assumes it's Joshua. She enters the room saying, "Joshua, you're up early." but to her embarrassment, she's looking in the face of the Professor, instead. He's sitting at the counter across from Rosanne, sipping his coffee.

Rosanne sees the embarrassment on her face and tries covers for her with, "Carolyn, don't worry, the Professor didn't drink all the coffee, I made enough for you and Joshua and the Colonel, too, if he'd like some."

"Oh, thank goodness, you know how I get without my coffee. Good Morning, Professor, I didn't know you were making a house visit. I would have, um, I don't know, dressed?"

"My apologies, Carolyn, Joshua told me last night that Rosanne was getting the sketches done, and we both got too excited to wait to see them. I came up with him last night and slept in the guest room. I didn't realize that he didn't warn you of my presence or ask your permission, for that matter."

"He doesn't must ask permission. This is his home and he's welcome to have anyone come stay that he wants. Notice is appreciated, but no permission is needed." She goes around the counter to get her coffee from Rosanne, who was pouring it hot from the pot on the stove. "Thank you, and good morning, Rosanne."

"Have you seen the sketches, Professor?" Carolyn asks.

"I'm sorry, I thought you were going to call me, Eddie? No, not yet. Rosanne wants Joshua to see them, first."

"I bet she does. What is up your sleeve, sister?"

"Well, I don't know, this college investigation is Joshua's doing. I just want him to see what I looked like before anyone else. Professor, you don't mind, do you?"

"No, I'm just happy to be helping." He smiles at Carolyn not Rosanne when he says this.

"What does Mrs. James think about you spending the night away from home for a Found Person sketch?" Carolyn baits him.

"I don't know, I didn't call my mother before I made the decision to come here. I'm not married, Carolyn. The right girl has thus far been elusive." He blushes but doesn't look at her.

Carolyn blushes past red and tried to cover up her embarrassment by sipping her hot coffee and just ended up choking on it, instead. She puts the coffee cup down. "I think I'll go and get dressed and wake our brother. If you can stay the day, I can take you to the place, where I found our Rosanne." She blushes again and doesn't wait for a reply but leaves the kitchen quickly.

Rosanne says, "What do you like for breakfast, Professor? I can make just about anything you'd like."

"So I've heard. You can call me Eddie, too, you know. I'll wait until the others come down to eat, thank you, anyway."

Just then, the bell starts to ring from upstairs. Rosanne smiles, "Looks like you are going to breakfast with the whole family, this morning. Excuse me, while I go get the Colonel dressed and ready to come downstairs."

"Of course, Rosanne, I'll just help myself to another cup of coffee."

It's about thirty minutes before Rosanne is back in the kitchen with the Colonel on her arm. The Colonel is very lucid this morning, thank goodness. It's much easier and more pleasant if the Colonel is having a good day. Carolyn and Joshua are both already in the kitchen talking with Eddie. Carolyn's wearing a very feminine dress that accentuates her curves. She's voluptuous, and it shows. She even put on a little rouge and lipstick. *Oh, she, really, likes this professor!* Rosanne thinks.

Rosanne introduces the Colonel. Then says, "What does everyone want for breakfast? Eggs, bacon, hash browns, toast, oatmeal, grits, French toast, waffles, sausage, ham? Come on, folks, I don't have all day."

The Colonel speaks first, "I want my eggs scrambled with bologna, please, with hot tea."

Joshua says, "I'll just take coffee and toast, please."

The Professor says, "Eggs fried and some Oatmeal, if it's not too much trouble."

Carolyn is last to decide. "Well, that leaves me. Um, Sausage, eggs scrambled and toast. Do you need help?" Carolyn offers but is dressed too nice to get near a stove."

"I've got this, Carolyn, stay with your guest. Here is your coffee, Joshua."

In less than twenty minutes, they're all eating including Rosanne. Carolyn is on Colonel duty to make sure he doesn't give half of his food to Robbie. As everyone, pushes their dishes away, Carolyn, impatiently says, "Rosanne, please show Joshua, the sketches."

Rosanne gets up and walks to the cereal cupboard and pulls out the sketches. She's smiling as she hands the 'now' sketch to Joshua. "Wow, Rosanne, he captured you so well. This is good, you are so beautiful." She smiles at him.

"You haven't seen anything, yet. Look at what I looked like before the disfigurement. I don't understand, who could have wanted to kill 'her'?" She points to the sketch as she hands the 'before' one to Joshua.

"No way, the only thing the same is your eyes. This girl is a knock-out but she doesn't have your spark. The guy should have added your spark. This girl is very pretty but she looks empty. Well, if this is what the Artist thinks is the 'before' look, I'll go down to the print shop in town, this morning and have two thousand printed up and we will start mailing them around the state. What do you think, Professor?"

"Two thousand should be a good start. We have all the authorities, and we can see if local newspapers can run a smaller picture with a press release giving my college number for leads. I'll get the class on this Monday."

"Yes, but missing the spark that makes her Rosanne." Joshua repeats as he stares at the 'before' sketch.

Rosanne walks behind him to look over his shoulder and hugs him from behind. "Dear brother, you are seeing me with your heart and not your eyes. I was stunning, I wonder if I knew?"

"Probably not because you don't believe me when I tell you that you are beautiful, now." Joshua says. "And I'm not saying that as your brother."

The Professor interrupts. "Ah, I see what's going on here. You call each other brother and sister but there's more to it, isn't there?" He asks.

"Yes!", Joshua says. "No!", Rosanne says. They both say it at the same time. The Professor looks over to Carolyn for clarification.

"It's complicated. Joshua says he's in love with her and she says she loves him as a brother. She says that she isn't free to fall in love with someone until she knows if she was married or involved with someone else."

Rosanne adds, "When I miscarried, my fear was that this wasn't my first child. What if I have a baby, missing her Mommy? I asked the doctor and he said that it appeared to be my first pregnancy. Thank God. How can I get involved with anybody with all these questions left to be answered?"

The Professor says, "We are doing all we can to help. These seniors have until May to work on your mystery. If it's not solved by then, I promise you, I'll request a summer course, that will pick up where they left off, and if that doesn't work, there's next fall's class.

Joshua interrupts, "Professor, we must get to the printer early. He isn't open past two p.m. on Saturday."

"I was hoping to go with Carolyn to see where Rosanne was found. I'd like to see that irrigation thing she designed, also. I think that's a fascinating invention."

Carolyn blushes, "It's nothing, but I'd love to show you."

"Oh, oh, of course, Professor, I can run to town, myself. You have a good time." He turns to the girl behind him. "Rosanne, can we go for a drive later?"

"Um, I don't know."

She isn't making this easy, he thinks. "Okay, later tonight, why don't the four of us go to town, have dinner and see a movie."

"Like a double-date?" She asks.

"Sure, you can call it that." Joshua answers.

"No, Joshua, I don't think so. I'm taking my stand, brother, no dating."

"Well, you can't blame a guy for trying, though." Joshua laughs.

TWENTY-NINE

The Fourth Sunday in September, 1935
In EL Dorado, Kansas

Anna slept like a rock, and is up at first light. She feels light as a feather. This is the feeling that the songs are written about. She cannot believe this is finally happening. *She has struggled with her feelings about Henry but not anymore. I cannot wait to see him. I cannot wait to learn to drive. Oh, the feeling of freedom, never having to wait for someone to take you somewhere.* Anna is so happy to be pulling her own weight for a change. She's going to make an extra dime an hour plus work an extra eight-hour shift. *I'll be finally making more than my little sister, the 'small but mighty' one.*

Melinda said last night that Matthew was going to teach her today. She hopes one of them will learn enough to drive to work on Monday. They're working shifts with an hour difference. Melinda will start at eight but Anna will start at nine so she'll have an hour to kill in the morning, then Melinda will have an hour to kill in the evening.

Henry gets to the Masters' hut a half hour early and catches Anna still not ready. She was trying to pick out the cutest outfit to wear. She even considered borrowing something from Melinda but their sizes were too different for it to work. Besides, Melinda had more curves than she'll ever have. *Oh, why would Henry come so early?* Anna questions as she puts on her 4th dress.

Matthew is keeping Henry company in the front yard. "I'm looking forward to tonight's game. I'll be bringing Melinda with me. If I can teach her to drive successfully today, she'll be driving tonight. About Melinda . . . she wants a private word with you and I suggest you take her seriously." As he says this, Melinda comes out and walks to him with her head down.

Matthew turns to give them a moment of privacy but Melinda puts her hand on his arm and says, "Stay Matthew, you know what I'm going to say to him, anyway." She turns to Henry, looks up briefly at him then looks back down. She's afraid of looking in his eyes. She says, "Henry, it's been fun, but <u>we</u> are over. I want you to make my sister happy. I'll no longer be in the way."

"What are you talking about? Over . . . what's over?" He tries to look innocent to Matthew. "Is she pulling my leg, Matthew?"

Matthew pulls himself to his full height. "No, Henry, she's saying that the late-night meetings in the camp truck are a thing of the past and that she loves her sister and wants YOU to not hurt her. It's simple, brother. Anna is your only mission, here. She's going to come out at any time, so we need to wrap this up. I just have one question, is this going to be a problem?"

"Matthew, you misjudge me here. I've tried to do right by Anna and Melinda. I . . . I . . . ." He's at a lost to say more.

"I'm not judging you Henry. You and Melinda had a good time. She wants to stop, so I want you to stop. No hard feelings. If Anna doesn't get hurt, no harm, no foul."

Melinda has just been standing there, ashamed. *Why is my little brother standing up for me? Why can't I do it myself? Why can't I look at Henry? Why do I want to cry?* "I've to go get ready for service, I'll see you both later." She keeps her head down and heads into the hut.

They watch her go in, Henry is shaking his head. "What just happened here?"

"Melinda loves Anna more. She doesn't want to stand in her way for happiness. This wasn't an easy thing for her to do, Henry. I hope you'll respect her decision."

"Matthew, I never meant to hurt either of your sisters. As you have said yourself, Melinda and I are more alike. We were attracted to each other before our fathers got involved. I hope I don't lose her friendship or yours, over this." He holds out his hand hoping, praying, Matthew will shake it. "Still friends?" He says, waiting.

"No Henry." He takes his hand. "Still Brothers." Matthew shakes his hand then pulls him in for a hug. Henry hugs him back and suddenly feels choked up. This young man is so smart, so sure of himself, so mature. He'd have hated losing this relationship.

Anna comes out just as they let go of each other. She's so excited to see Henry that she doesn't notice the awkwardness between them. "Oh, there you are Henry, sorry to keep you waiting." She turns to Matthew. "Young man, you're not going to service in those old pants, are you?"

"No sis, I'll go change, I just didn't want Henry to be lonely out here. Pretty dress." Without another look to Henry, he goes into the hut to change.

"Matthew is amazing. I've said that he's fifteen going on forty. He's an old soul, in a young man's body."

"Do you think so? I don't think I've ever thought of him that way."

"Maybe I notice because I've not seen him for a while. Speaking of not seeing someone in a while, get over here." He reaches for her and pulls her to him. "I've missed you, that's why I'm early." He lowers his voice to a silky whisper, "I couldn't wait to see you again." He leans down to kiss her but hesitates. "Can I kiss you?" He asks. She silently nods. He whispers in her ear. "Don't just nod, say it, give me permission."

She's blushing already. "You may kiss me, Henry." He still hesitates so she adds. "Please kiss me, Henry." She starts to look down in embarrassment.

He softly tilts her face upward. "Say it again, and say it like you mean it, or I swear I'll not do it."

She's feeling weak in the knees and isn't ready to be so bold. She straightens her shoulders and says with quiet authority, "Henry kiss me, kiss me now." He leans in so that his lips are lightly on hers, forcing her to go the rest of the way. She leans into his embrace. *The sound of his voice, the softness of his lips, those wonderful smoky gray eyes, he's the total wonderful package. How have I not seen him this way until now?*

He finally pulls away. He didn't want to, but they had to get going to Service. "You are getting very bold, my girl." She blushes again. "I'm not saying that I disapprove, mind you. I definitely approve, but we need to walk to Service, unless you want to play hooky and get straight to the driving lesson." He raises an eyebrow.

"Henry, you are the devil, trying to get my very soul!" She elbows him, as they start to walk toward the barn.

"I'm trying to do no such thing. I do want to hold your hand, though." He holds out his hand and she readily takes it. "I cannot believe that I can feel this way." His heads shakes.

"What way?" She's holding the hand that's holding hers.

"Like a kid back in school, afraid to give a girl a Valentine."

She smiles. "I remember you as that kid in school. I got a Valentine from you, I believe. It wasn't signed but I always thought it was from you." She stops walking. "It was you, wasn't it?"

Now Henry blushes. "Of course, it was from me. I would have beat up any guy who tried to give you a Valentine. You were always mine." He thinks about it. *It's always been Anna. Why have I fought it?*

"Then why has it taken us this long to get here?" She smiles. "I don't think I was helping. You seemed so different that I couldn't see you in this new person."

"And I wouldn't look at you. I was trying to prove that I had outgrown you. Do you forgive me?"

"Nothing to forgive. Wait, stop. Come here." He does so immediately. She takes his face in her hands and gives him a lingering kiss. "You are forgiven, don't ever do it again, okay"

"Yes Ma-am." She's so playful. So, sweet. So, beautiful. He's so lucky to have run into her family here and finally wised up to see her for what she has always been – his Anna.

THIRTY

The Fourth Sunday in September, 1935 cont'd
In EL Dorado, Kansas

After Service, Henry and Anna head to the parking lot to start the driving lesson. Henry says that he'll show her how to start the car and drive a little then let her take over and drive them to town to have lunch at Sally's.

"That will be so nice. I can introduce you to everyone." She beams.

"I pretty much know everyone there. Da and I've eaten there many times."

"They know you as Henry but they don't know you as my boyfriend. Let me show you off to my new co-workers."

"Boyfriend, huh? Is that how you're going to introduce me? Just your boyfriend?" He was looking at her as he says that.

"Henry, keep your eyes on the road. What a bad example you are setting for me." She chides him.

"You haven't answered my question." *Why am I getting nervous? I never wanted to get married, never wanted to be tied down. Why is it so important now that she declare herself to me?*

"I'll introduce you as my boyfriend Henry." She adds, "Now let me have a chance at the wheel." He pulls over and turns off the engine. They change places and she starts the engine on the first try. She has a little trouble getting it in gear but pulls out onto the road without hesitation. "This isn't so hard!" She exclaims.

"Big Fat Liar! Anna Rose Masters, you've driven before, haven't you? No one pulls out like that the first time driving."

"Henry, I swear, this is my first time. I've started an engine or two, but I've never been behind the wheel on a road in my life." She smiles at him.

"Have you driven in a pasture, maybe or in a cornfield?" He elbows her lightly. "Come on, 'fess up. Where have you driven?"

"Okay, one time, I was the only one with my Pa and he was fixing a fence. He threw his back out and I had to get him in the truck and drive him back to the house. But we never went on a road the whole time and that was before you left. Don't you remember that my Pa was down for a week and your Da had to come to help him out?"

"Anna, that had to be four years ago! I'm very impressed with how you are doing. You're a natural. Now pull over on the side, just up ahead." She does as he says. "Now shut off the engine." Again, she follows his instructions. "Now tell me why you are going to introduce me only as your boyfriend."

"I thought this was part of the driving lesson! Oh, you are being so silly Henry." She starts the engine again. He reaches over and shuts it down and removes the key.

"I'm not playing, Anna. I want to know what is going on here." He looks mad and it's scaring her a little. "I'll not give you back the keys until you give me an answer."

She sighs. "Henry, that night your father said we were engaged, my Ma said that I don't have to be engaged until you ask me proper. We have only just reconnected. Give it some time. Court me for a little while. Then the proper thing will be for you to ask me to marry you. I'm not going anywhere. You are my boyfriend, are you not?" She leans over to him and kisses him.

Well, she sure told me. She has her head on her shoulders and isn't willing to be easily manipulated, just like Matthew. "I'm your boyfriend and I'm very happy to court you. You deserve to be courted. You deserve more than I can give you, actually." He hangs his head. Now it's her turn to lift his face up so she can kiss him.

"Start . . . by giving me more . . . of yourself. Can I drive now? I really like to drive!" He hands her back the keys. She's smiling that smile that fills his heart with gladness.

That's the difference, he thinks. When Melinda gave him those looks, he felt them deep but it wasn't to his heart that it went. That's why this is real. Not that she can't give him those other feelings, they'll come, he's sure of it. But right now, his heart is content just to FEEL that smile. He smiles at the realization.

She's driving but steals a peek at him just in time to see a slow smile spread on his face. "A penny for your thoughts."

"In time, Anna, in due time." He changes the subject. "I'm starving. Are you going the speed limit? Can't you go faster?"

"Henry, I'll not get a ticket before I'm licensed."

When they get to the diner, she pulls into a spot directly in front of the window. Henry says to her, "You are lucky that they've diagonal parking in town and not parallel. That could take days for me to teach you."

Before he can reach for the door, she puts her hand on his arm. "Henry, what I said, I didn't hurt your feelings, did I?"

"The only way you could have hurt my feelings is to say that I'm NOT your boyfriend. Anna, is it too soon to say, um . . . I think I love you."

He looks in her eyes to gage her emotions. Her soft browns were moistening as she replies just barely above a whisper. "I love you, too, Henry." Then she lowers her head.

"This is wonderful. Look at me Anna." She raises her head just as one tear escapes her right eye. "Why are you crying? Is something wrong?"

She nervously laughs. "My silly man, don't you know women cry when they're happy? These are happy tears. They are 'he finally said he loves me' tears. Now do me a favor, kiss my tears away or hand me a handkerchief." She laughs again.

He decides that he wants to kiss her tears away. He wants to kiss her fears away. He just wants to kiss her and he does. He showers her whole face with kisses until they're both laughing.

They finally go into the diner, both smiling from ear to ear. Allison and Betsy are waitressing and Henry knows them both but Anna doesn't so Henry introduces her as his girlfriend and their new cook. They both had heard that Ted finally hired someone, but they didn't think it would be someone so young and pretty and they both say so.

Both Henry and Anna order the meatloaf. Henry raved about it so much, and she now she knows Bruce is the meatloaf king. Allison takes the order slip to the kitchen and moments later Ted is out front grabbing Anna and pulls her to the kitchen. She objects and introduces Henry and Ted says "So bring your boyfriend back to the kitchen. I want you to see your meal being plated."

They both watch the chaos/poetry that takes place behind the scenes and Henry is amazed. Anna just smiles and turns to him. "Exciting, isn't it? I had so much fun back here that I can't wait to come back tomorrow."

When their food is ready, they take it to the table themselves to eat it. Bruce's meatloaf is very different from her Ma's but very, very good, too! Anna says between bites. "Did you see Big Bertha? She's all mine. The sizzle sound that the food makes on it's delicious. I'm so glad that you brought me here today."

"Anna, the size of that grill and the heat from that eight-burner stove, aren't you intimidated by it at all?" Henry couldn't believe it.

"I was at first, but as soon as I saw Ted start the cooking, I knew I could do it. It's a little hotter than the fields, but it's so much more satisfying than filling bushel baskets. I've a lot to learn but Ted seemed to be impressed by what I could do already. I'm sure that I'll be making the full sixty cents an hour in no time."

"I'm sure you'll be. Good for you, sweetheart. You know, getting this job has made you bloom. I think that's why I was hesitant about you. I didn't think that you had blossomed yet. You seemed stuck as the girl I knew instead of the woman you are right in front of me. I love the woman you are, right now." He leans over and kisses her on the forehead.

"Henry, we are in public." She blushes. "Behave yourself."

"Believe me, Anna, I'm behaving myself." He reaches for his water, when he feels her hand on his thigh. He looks down and smiles as he looks up at her. "Did you lose something?"

"No, more like I found someone." She slightly blushes but keeps eye contact and smiles.

"Anna Rose Masters, you are surprising me more by the minute. Are you done eating? I would like to get you back into that truck." He says with a wink.

She slowly removes her hand from his thigh. She reaches for her napkin and dabs her mouth as she says, "Yes, let's get out of here."

After they all say good-bye to them, Henry goes to pay the check and Allison says, "Ted won't take your money tonight, Hon, you know, he likes you kid." She nods to Anna. "He doesn't give away free dinners to anyone!" She laughs and adds. "He's the original cheapskate!" Then she calls to Betsy. "Am I right, Betsy?"

"You're right, he's the head of cheapskates!" She yells from the back of the room.

When they get back to the truck, Anna gets into the driver's seat. She goes to start the car but turns to Henry instead. "You never showed me reverse. Why don't we change places and you can show me how to back up this thing? In fact, why don't you just drive, take me someplace where we can be alone." She puts her hand on his thigh again.

"Anna, darling, I don't know if you know this, but your hand, there, is a little um . . . distracting."

"Oh, I'm sorry. Is it bothering you?" She asks but doesn't move it.

"It's giving me ideas, that you might not be ready for . . . why don't I drive and you keep your hands to yourself." They change places. Henry starts the car, shows her how to put it in reverse and shows her how to look out all her mirrors. Then he suggests that when she turns to look out behind her that she place her right arm behind the passenger seat as the proper form for backing out. She laughs and asks why. He says, "It gives you more stability to handle the steering wheel as the truck goes in reverse."

He drives along toward the Camp and finds a nice area on the side of the road with lots of trees. There's no grass or even a road but he pulls in under the trees for shade from the afternoon sun and shuts off the engine. "How's this place for being alone?" She smiles. He feels that feeling again, it's like his heart is singing.

She slides closer to him and puts her head on his shoulders. "This is a perfect spot." She murmurs into his neck. She suddenly notices that he has toilet water on. She has never noticed that before. "Henry, is that a new scent?" She asks.

"My Da bought it for me at Owl's Five and Dime, when he took you for your interviews. He thought you'd like it on me," he said. "Was he, right?" She leaned in and took a larger sniff.

"Tell Da, he did good. I do like it. I was just surprised. I don't think my father has ever had on toilet water."

"Is it manly? When I was putting it on, I felt like Claudette Colbert dabbing perfume behind my ears like in "It Happened One Night." My

Da has never used the stuff, either. He says the girl at the store told him it's the newest thing for all men to smell their best."

"It smells very manly. I like it very much. Come here, let me smell it again." As he leaned in to give her access to his neck, she turned his head and kissed him instead. She kissed him long and slow. His tongue sought entry inside her mouth and she let him in. She didn't taste the same as last night. This taste was all Anna. He has known that she'd taste like this, his whole life. *Why didn't I remember that?*

Anna feels herself melt in his arms. His tongue is once again, doing crazy things to her. She feels brave enough to pulls him on top of her. She could now feel his 'down below'. She suddenly had an image of her Ma telling her about teasing a man. Ma had said that when a man's part was going north, it was time for her to go home. It's funny, she never knew what she meant by that. She can feel his part is, north. Definitely! Anna didn't know what to do. Her body wanted to arch toward his. She wanted to feel his hands on her breasts. She wanted to do all the things her Ma warned her against.

Henry is being as good as he could take. He's keeping his hands on her face and neck. He was mildly surprised when she pulled him down over her. He knew she'd feel his hardness. He could feel her surprise but acceptance of its presence. This was going further than he intended. He pulls away. "Anna, we shouldn't. I love you and I don't want to use you this way." She sits up and looks ashamed. He didn't mean to make her feel that way. "Look, we are just starting to get to know each other."

"But Henry, I want to show you that I love you." She looks down as soon as she says it. He lifts her chin so he can look in her eyes. "There's no hurry, my love. I don't want to hurt you; I don't want to do anything that you can't look in my eyes about. I don't want you to look at your Ma and lie about being a good girl. I know how important that's to you."

She looks in his eyes. "Henry, can I ask you something?"

"Anything."

"I want you to be honest. If you can't be honest, just tell me you don't want to answer, okay?" She was turning red and now looking down.

"Anna, what is it?"

"Have you been with a woman before? We've been separated a long time. It's not like you knew to wait for me, but I do want to know. Have you made love?" Now she was bright red.

"Yes, Anna, I'm sorry, I have." He was sorry. He'd waited until he couldn't resist the temptation. He wished it had never happened. Especially since it happened with her sister. It's his turn to look away. *Why hadn't I waited? I knew my father's intentions. I could have tried harder.*

"Henry, look at me." He turns back but cannot look her in the eyes. *How can I hurt her like this?* "No Henry, look at me." He slowly looks in her loving eyes. He wants to be swallowed up by them. "Henry, did you like it? Was it like you expected?"

"Anna, what kind of questions are those?" He thought she was going to be mad or disappointed.

She straightens herself up. "I want to know. I love you and I need to know if . . . I don't know . . . if you liked it but then don't like it with me, what will I do? Or if you didn't like it and that's why you don't want to do it with me, how can I fix that? I've never been with a man, well, you knew that but how will I know if I'm any good to keep you interested. Ma says that good food and good sex are the things that make a marriage successful. But she says that I'm to be a good girl until marriage. So, one of us should bring some experience to the marriage bed, don't you think?" Now, she's talking out of nervousness.

"Oh, Anna, such thoughts. I'll admit that sex was very nice. I liked it plenty. Don't worry if you'll be good at it. When we do it, it won't be sex. We will make love. Making love won't disappoint. I never thought I'd have a conversation like this in my life. Can we go back to kissing, now or do you have any other embarrassing questions?"

"Have you been in love with anyone before me? Since me? While we were separated?"

"I've never said I love you to anyone else. I've never been close. Have you?" She shook her head no.

"Anna, can I tell you something about you?"

"Please do." She blushes but smiles and keeps eye contact.

"Do you remember when you said 'a penny for your thoughts.' A while back?" She nods yes.

"Well, you had looked in my eyes and smiled. I felt that smile in my heart. That's why I know I love you. No one has made my heart feel that way. It wants to burst with joy. Only you have done that. Yes, I've quivered in my loins, but I've never had joy in my heart from a simple smile. So, calm your fears about making love, you have made love to me with your smile."

"Oh Henry! I never knew a man could feel like that. Let alone put it into such words. I do love you. I'm so happy." She says, then sighs.

"I know that sigh, that's your happy sigh." He leans to her to kiss her.

She looks up at him and smiles. "See, I'm making love to you with my smile." Then she sweetly kisses him. "But I would love to make love to you with more." She blushes for the hundredth time.

"In time, my love. Should we be heading home, do you think? I think your Ma would see you safe and sound and in her presence. I think my Da was going to visit them. We could show him your smile? Or I could take you to a Crap game, tonight? Or I could make love to you, right here right now, since it was your suggestion? Pick one, darling for they're all good to me."

"I don't want to share you just yet. I want to . . . um . . . please, let's stay here and see what happens."

"It's not like I didn't warn you or give you a few options." He kisses her and lowers her to the seat. He's just happy to have her to himself. He runs his fingers through her hair and traces the outline of her heart shaped face as he looks in her eyes. He smiles as he kisses her eyelids. "Such beautiful eyes." He says. He kisses the tip of her nose. "Such a beautiful nose." He says. He traces her lips with the tip of his finger. "Such a Lovely smile." His mouth is suddenly on hers with a passion that she hasn't felt before. She returns it with equal hunger. Once again, his tongue searches hers. She arches under him and pushes her tongue inside his mouth and he sucks it slightly before they both come up for air. He lifts off her enough to look in her eyes. She smiles again. "Now cut that out, I'm trying to hold myself back, here. Stop smiling at me."

"But Henry, you don't seem to know it but you were smiling first. And I do feel it in my heart, just like you do. I think we are doomed to be hopelessly in love."

He knows that he cannot take anymore of being with her and not having her. "Anna, we need to leave here before something happens."

"So what time is this Crap game?" *She must be joking*, he thinks. He looks to see if she's smiling. She isn't.

"Why do you want to know? I thought that was the last place you'd ever want to be?" He can't believe his ears.

"It is but if it's something you like . . . can you tell me why you like it? Is it just craps or are there other games being played?

He'd to think fast, why did he mention the damn game? Melinda and Matthew will be there, so it's the last place Anna should be. "Well, there's a bar, of course. Nothing makes you gamble and lose better than booze. They've a few poker tables, a blackjack table and a roulette wheel. I go for the game of Craps, though."

"Where is this game? Is it always at the same place?"

"No, actually, since booze and gambling are both illegal in Kansas, they move it around and play random nights."

"How do you know when and where, then?"

"Word of mouth, John Walker has a hand in it, I think. He's always the one who tells me when, where and what the code word to get in is. No code word, no admittance."

"Does Melinda know that John Walker is in on this?"

Now he's in deep water, but he might as well answer. "Yes, he's brought her to a game or two." Well, that's the truth.

It takes her just a second or two to put it together. He can see it in her eyes. She's working it out.

"Wait, Matthew has been with Melinda each time, she went out with John. Have you seen my baby brother there?"

He hangs his head. His bliss is about to blow up. "Yes." He says simply.

"Well, I'm glad it wasn't you, at least." She shakes her head side to side. "Do they drink there, Matthew and Melinda?"

"Melinda has had a few drinks, but I've never seen her drunk. But not Matthew. Anna, please don't be mad. I'm responsible for introducing them to this, before you said you didn't like it. This is one of the things that's been between us. You said that you didn't like crap games and that you didn't want me to talk to Matthew about it. Matthew did get the idea from me but once he'd hold of the notion, there was no talking him out of it. Not that I tried too hard, to be honest. This is their secret and I shouldn't have shared. I just don't want anything to get between us. I love Matthew and I've tried to be a brother to him but I love you more and I swear I'll never go to another game if that's what will make you happy. Just don't hate me for something that happened before I knew your feelings."

She's silent for a minute. This is a lot to take in. She looks up at him. "Henry, take me home." She adds, "I'm not mad but this is too much to think about sitting in your truck."

"How about an ice cream before I take you home?" He nervously looks in her eyes.

Anna looks back. His smoldering eyes are pleading. He gives her a nervous smile. "That smile, Henry, doesn't make my heart sing." She gives him a true smile that he can return honestly.

"That's my girl, can you forgive me?"

"I'm trying. I've more questions but as you say, these aren't your secrets to tell. I'll take that ice cream, though."

"Can I've a little kiss, first?" He starts to lean in but stops because he sees that she doesn't lean in with him. He shakes his head, "No?".

"I didn't say no, Henry. You can have a kiss first, second and third." She leans in to meet his lips. "I have to forgive you for something that happened before you knew of my feelings, don't I?"

Henry starts the engine, then turns to her and asks, "Did you want to drive? You need a little more practice before you take your dad's truck, tomorrow."

"I know that I should but my mind isn't on it, but thank you for asking." She says with a wrinkled brow from concentration on her face.

"A penny for your thoughts, or do I not want to know?" He asks hesitantly.

"I'm just wondering what I should do, talk to them at home or at the Crap game? It doesn't bother me that Melinda is there; she'll be eighteen soon but Matthew is too young. He's too impressionable. He has always liked taking chances and I'm afraid he'll like gambling too much. What do you think that I should do? I almost feel like going straight to Pa."

Henry has turned the truck around and is heading back to town. He cannot believe he opened this can of worms. "Anna, I don't think going to your parents is a good thing. Of all those options, I would say going to the crap game is the least of all these evils. Or you could sleep on it and discuss it with Melinda on the way to work, if it's just the two of you. She most likely has had more time to drive in her lessons, since she hasn't stopped to neck a few times." He smiles at Anna. She doesn't notice.

"But it's Matthew that I really want to talk to. I don't know what to say to him, though."

"Look, Matthew has this in check, he has a good head on his shoulders. He's very quick and I don't think he's impressionable. He's responsible. There are things that I know, that I can't tell you but they've proved to me that we don't need to worry about Matthew."

"What things? I appreciate that you are keeping their secrets like a good big brother, but I'm so worried."

"I was very worried about him at first but he's handling himself better than I would. And I mean now that I'm older. I would have been a complete mess at Matthew's age. You remember me back then? No way was I as smart or observant or mature as your brother. You can relax a bit about him, Anna. I swear he's fine."

They were almost back to town. Henry wished that she'd drop this whole thing. This can still blow up completely if she knows about Matthew's other activities.

"Henry, I feel that I don't know my siblings, anymore. They've been keeping so much from me."

"They don't like it any more than you do. They've both said so, several times. They love you so much, Anna, but they think that you are so different from us that you'd just wouldn't understand."

"Us? You think you are more like them than I am?"

"Hasn't that been part of the problem between us? I want more out of life than roaming the harvests. I've liked walking on the wild side as a distraction to this bleakness that's become my life. Anna?"

"Yes?"

"The bleakness of my life has gone away, since we've met up with your family, by the way. Having them all back in my life has erased all that gray away. Then discovering my feelings for you, I cannot tell you how different I feel about everything. It's like I was walking under a low-lying cloud but now the clouds are all gone. I'm not explaining it to you, correctly. But what I'm saying is that, I have my family back and I don't need to look for the next kick of excitement. Oh! That isn't it either."

"Henry, I think I understand what you are saying. We have been working so hard with no light at the end of the tunnel, also. I think that if

Pa hadn't met up with your Da, well, he was in a very discouraged place. Being with your father has been very good for him."

They were in front of the Central Avenue Soda Shoppe, now. Henry turns to Anna, "Do you know what flavor you want?"

"That Mint chip was so good! I'd like that again, please." Henry gets out and goes around to her door, to open it for her. He holds out his arm to assist her. Once out of the truck, she says, "You get your second kiss, now . . . or is it the third?"

"Don't know, but say no more." He takes her face in both his hands and looks in her eyes. *Those beautiful brown eyes!* "Anna, I cannot get over that I . . . can love you so much. I feel like I'm falling endlessly. It must be that I fought it so hard." He kisses her tenderly. She returns the kiss, and puts her arms around his neck.

"I love how we are a perfect fit." She says as he begins to pull away. She doesn't move her arms. "Whether we are standing here or I'm on your shoulder in the car, we just fit together." They walk into the Soda Shoppe, hand in hand.

THIRTY-ONE

The Fourth Sunday in September
In Lawrence, Kansas

Joshua and the Professor stayed the night. Yesterday, Carolyn had a great time with him, explaining her inventions, showing him different aspects of the Farm business and then taking him out to the site where Rosanne was found.

He walked around looking at the dirt. Carolyn was back in the car. She'd gotten out and showed him the exact spot where Rosanne was laying. They could still see the bloody ground. The lack of winter snowfall as well as the drought of the spring and summer meant that the blood was not washed away.

The car was facing Eddie, so Carolyn was watching him as he walked around and occasionally bent down to kick the dirt or pick something up. *What a handsome man*, she thought. He'd a very thin moustache and a full head of jet black hair that he combed straight back. He wasn't as tall as Joshua. Carolyn is guessing about 5'9". A good height difference since she's 5'5". He has a medium build. He does look like he keeps very fit.

He's looking around intently for about twenty minutes. Carolyn didn't mind, she loved looking at him. On the way, out there, he told her that he grew up on the northern-most section of the city of Topeka. He'd worked in Chicago for two years for the Retail Credit Company of Atlanta. He was friendly with Eliot Ness, another employee, who at that time had an economic degree. He claimed he'd influenced Ness to go back to school to earn his master's degree in criminology like he had.

"You're telling me that you knew the Eliot Ness, who started the *Untouchable* Squad in Chicago? Why weren't you working with him, as a Prohibition Agent?

"Because I wanted to teach. My enthusiasm for the field was contagious enough to encourage Ness to do it. I was a molder of young minds even back then." He laughed at his own joke.

They had dinner at the Plantation. It was so nice to have a full house again. It was good for the Colonel. He attached himself to Joshua, and was on his best behavior. After dinner, they all sat in the sitting room and talked for hours.

This morning, they went to early Service, the four of them. The Colonel didn't want to rise that early, so they left the attendant, Andrew, in charge of him.

Carolyn felt a little strange inviting Eddie to attend, not knowing how to broach the subject. Joshua had asked him the night before when they were talking about what time to leave and, so, which Service to go to, before heading back to Topeka.

After Service, Rosanne makes a huge lunch of homemade Tomato soup, a salad and sliced turkey sandwiches. Joshua jokes, "If I ate this way, daily, I'd lose my girlish figure." Carolyn takes offense and hits him.

Joshua insists on helping Rosanne with the clean-up as he did the night before. This gives Carolyn a little more time with the Professor.

"They're hitting it off quite well, don't you think? He asks Rosanne.

"Extremely well. You must bring him down again. Very soon."

"It can't be next weekend, that's the College dance. You know that I'm on the organization committee for it? Any chance that you've changed your mind? It would be a great excuse to bring Carolyn so that she can dance with the Professor."

"I think that since you have less than a week to ask someone else, you'd better get on that. Let the Professor, get his own dates." Rosanne is washing the dishes and she splashes Joshua with the soapy water. "Seriously, brother, Get A Date for the Dance!!! I'm not kidding. I'll not change my mind!"

"Rosanne, there's no one else that I want to go with, and you can't make me!" He sticks his tongue out at her like the twelve-year-old he used to be.

"You stuck your tongue out at me, I'm going to tell the Colonel!"

"See, my love, you got me. That's all I'm saying. You get me, you got me, you're stuck with me. Get used to it." He takes his dishtowel that he was drying with and whacks her on the bottom.

Robbie sees that from his bed which is under the sink, and starts barking at Joshua.

"Apparently, Robbie disagrees with you. Come on, Boy, good boy!"

"You even have him seduced by your charms." Joshua uses this as Robbie's excuse.

Meanwhile, Carolyn and Eddie are in the parlor discussing seeing each other again, also. "Of course, I'll see you for the next class report and I'd like to take you to dinner afterward, except you'll have Rosanne with you.

"That's a bummer, we could all go out together? A Foursome." Carolyn suggests. "Rosanne wouldn't like that, it's too much like a double date."

"I'd like you all to myself though. I'm an only child and I'm not big on sharing. Next Saturday is the College dance. Would you be my date for that?"

"Yes sir, I think I would."

"Carolyn, I do think you are amazing. You are extremely smart. You run a very large company. You take care of your grandfather and

Rosanne, you're an inventor and you have the prettiest hazel eyes! I've a crush on you, as my kids in my class say."

"Do you want to know what I've been thinking?"

"Absolutely."

She motions to him to come closer. "It's a secret, come here." He moves in. She whispers, "I've been wondering what that moustache will feel like if you kiss me."

"Well, wonder no more." She looks up at him, still shocked at her own boldness. He looks around to make sure they're alone. Then he leans in and kisses her. The moustache's thin enough that she still can feel his full lips take hers but it leaves a little tickle that she thinks she likes.

He pulls away and looks in her hazel eyes and asks, "Well, what does it feel like?"

"It tickles my top lip. And I think, I liked it."

"Good, since I'm not sharing you, I'll tickle you some more." He leans in and kisses her again. This time, he takes her fully into his arms.

Before two o'clock, Joshua, Eddie and two thousand sketches of the 'before' Rosanne are on the way back to the University. Carolyn and Rosanne wave them good-bye from the front step and then go back into the house.

"Well, you like him, don't you? Rosanne chides.

"Oh, Rosanne, I've never felt like this about anyone!" Carolyn says with all seriousness.

"I did once. I can almost see those eyes looking down at me with so much love that I thought my heart would burst." Rosanne looks down at her hands, as a single tear falls from each eye.

THIRTY-TWO

The Fourth Sunday in September, 1935 cont'd
In EL Dorado, Kansas

Henry thought he'd convinced Anna into waiting until tomorrow to talk with her brother. He seemed to calm her fears down, somewhat. He finished his ice cream before she has. He leans over her dish and says, "Look out the window." She does as she's told, and he steals a spoonful from her bowl, of course he gets caught.

"Henry, where are your manners? I know you were not raised like that." She kids. She takes the last spoonful and goes to feed it to him but quickly puts the spoon into her own mouth.

"Anna, you have a mischievous side. I think I like it." He leans in for a mint kiss. She looks around to see if anyone is watching before she gladly gives him some minty pleasure.

"Delicious, I want more." He gives her a wink.

"Ice cream?"

"No, you."

She blushes. "Henry, what am I to do with you?"

"Whatever you want. I'm yours."

"I want to go to the Crap game and see Matthew. I know you said not to worry but until I see him, I will be. Will you take me?"

"Okay, okay, on a few conditions, though. Let me introduce you to everyone as my girl and when you see your siblings, just smile and ask them how their night is going. Don't embarrass them in front of the people at the game. They're a very different crowd."

"I can live with those conditions. I'll try to be good."

"Anna, you're good without trying."

Before getting back into the truck, again, Henry asks if she'd like to drive but she declines. "I'm too nervous about going to the crap game." And she remains silent for the rest of the way.

It takes a few minutes to get there. The game is in an old house on the outskirts of town, opposite of the Camp. When they do find it, it's dark out but the house is surrounded with cars and trucks.

Anna asks, "Are all these people here to gamble?

"This is the usual amount for a Sunday night."

He parks and opens the door for her. He can tell she has lost her self-confidence. She isn't standing as tall and is looking around sheepishly. "Anna, we don't need to go in, if you don't want to."

"I do feel a little intimidated."

"If you can tame Big Bertha and that eight-burner stove, this will be nothing. Chin up, go forward, and smile. I'll explain the game to you, if you want. It's not too hard. Matthew picked it up in one afternoon in the field."

"I couldn't pay attention, Henry, I just want to find Matthew and Melinda."

"Fair enough." They enter the house arm in arm. Henry gives the code word to the man at the door and he lets them into the basement where everything is set up.

Anna is shocked at how many women are there. She expected her sister but a good third of the crowd are very well dressed women. They're all wearing jewelry and holding drinks. Wow. She cannot stop staring.

"Anna, I see John Walker, let's go say hello." They head his way. Anna is smiling, though it feels forced. "Hey John, thanks for the invitation. Look who I brought, my girlfriend Anna." Henry holds out his hand for John to shake it but John just looks at Anna, confused.

"What's she doing here? I thought she didn't like Crap games?

"Don't talk about me as if I'm not here, John." She corrects him, still smiling. "If my Henry likes coming here then I need to see what the attraction is. Have you seen my sister and brother?"

"Yup, they're around here, somewhere." Still staring at Anna, he says, "Can I buy you a drink?"

Henry jumps in, "No one is buying my girl something to drink besides me."

"Your girl, huh? Okay, Henry, I'll go along. How about I buy you both a drink? I've won a few hands at poker tonight, so I'm feeling generous." He walks them to the bar, and puts a few dollars on the counter and says, "Bartender, their drinks are on me, keep the change." He steps aside and waits for them to order.

Henry leans in to Anna "What do you want to drink?"

"I don't know, Henry, I've never had a drink before."

"I'll order you a screwdriver, then. You like orange juice, don't you?" She nods. He orders two of them and hands her one. Before he can say, here's mud in your eye, Anna tastes it, likes it and drinks the whole glass at once.

"That screwdriver was delicious." Both Henry and John watch her, they know that the booze was going to hit her at any moment. Suddenly, she reaches out for Henry's lapel, Henry puts an arm around her waist to steady her. "Wow, that's a kick, what was in that?"

"A shot of vodka, of course." John says in a demeaning way. He reaches back into his pocket and orders three more screwdriver drinks, one was for him.

"Anna, just sip this one, okay? I don't want to carry you home. This drink tends to get you very drunk very quickly."

The three of them, with drinks in hand, walk toward the craps table where her brother was playing. Matthew was concentrating on the board and didn't notice them watching him.

John offers, "Matthew is on another winning streak." Matthew hears his name and looks up. Anna is taking another large gulp of her drink then makes eye contact. She smiles slowly. Matthew is standing with his mouth open shocked to see his sister in a gambling house drinking booze.

He looks at Henry, "What's going on here, brother? Hi, sis, what are you doing here?"

She finishes off her second drink before answering. "Just came to see if you are all right. I was worried about you, Whoa!" She grabs Henry's lapel, again. "Did the room just start to spin?" She slurs.

John is behind Henry and he starts laughing outloud. "She can't handle her booze like Melinda can. Want another, Anna?"

Henry glares at John, "I don't think she needs another one right now." Then turns to Matthew, "You're on a winning streak? Great, let's call it a night, then? Where's your other sister?"

"I don't know, but I don't want to quit now, I'm hot."

"Matthew, I've spent the better part of the evening with this sister," he points to Anna, "trying to convince her that you have a handle on this. Don't make a liar out of me, here."

Anna suddenly sees Melinda. She's leaning over a poker player and seems to be advising the card holder on what to play. As he wins the pot, he gives Melinda some cash that she puts in her bra. Without taking a step to get any closer, Anna shouts "Melinda, what are you doing there?" Melinda looks up, mortified. She sees Anna, John, Matthew and Henry all staring at her.

Henry is over to her in a few strides. "I've come with Anna to take Matthew home. I think you should come home, also."

"You brought Anna, here? Have you lost your mind?"

"Pretty much. She was worried about Matthew, but by what I just saw, I'm worried about you."

"Henry, you mind your business, and I'll mind mine."

Anna has followed Henry. "Melinda, you took money from that man? Why?"

"Because he gave it to me, I helped him win."

"Well, Matthew won't leave because he's on a 'hot' streak. Will you help us get him home?" Henry says as he puts his arm around Anna's waist because she was swaying slightly.

"Is she drunk?" Melinda asks Henry.

"Why is everyone talking about me as if I can't hear them. I hate that! I'm not drunk. I've only had two drinks." She straightens up and squares her shoulders, in defense.

"The problem, Anna darling, is that you drank them both in the less than ten minutes we've been here. The alcohol becomes a race car heading toward a brick wall when you drink them that way." Henry explains. He's getting overwhelmed with whom to help first. Anna is tipsy, though she won't admit it. Matthew is still at the table gambling and Melinda, well, is being Melinda, doing what she damn well feels like doing.

"Melinda, please help with Anna and I'll go talk to Matthew, again." Melinda comes to Anna's side and puts her arm around her sister's tiny waist. Henry is back to Matthew. Just as he walks up, Matthew is called to be shooter. *Damn, I'll won't get him to leave until his roll is over,* Henry thinks.

Melinda walks Anna over to watch. Anna uses the sides of the table to keep her from wobbling. The caller of the game, says to Anna, "Are you betting, young lady? If not, I've to ask you to step back for the players to bet."

Henry comes forward to take her place and puts money down on the pass line. Matthew holds his dice out for his sisters to blow on them for good luck. No one told Anna about this so just Melinda blows. He throws the dice and Matthew shoots a seven. He and Henry win with this roll. Henry bets the Come line. The next roll is a six. Bets are placed all over the table before the caller gives Matthew the dice again. He holds his dice out for another good luck blow and Anna participates this time. He sends them hard across the table. He shoots a three and wins another round. Henry smiles at him. His next roll is a five and he makes more money.

Matthew looks at Henry and says, "it's time." He and Henry both put a new bet on the Don't Come line and sure enough, Matthew throws a seven!! He has doubled his money as the shooter!

Both Matthew and Henry turn to Anna and Henry speaks first, "See Anna, how exciting it's?"

She shakes her head no, "I didn't understand any of it." Matthew and Henry just throw their hands up in the air. "Well, I can see that you made money, Matthew, but I don't understand why, yet. Is hot in here, or is it me?"

Henry says to all of them, "Okay, time for all of us to head home. Who is driving what truck? Never mind, Anna, you are in no condition to be behind the wheel." He leads them all to the door. "Melinda, did you have driving lessons, today? Anna was doing very well. She's a natural like her brother, I think." He gives her a squeeze as they're walking out.

Anna beams, "I really didn't drive as much as I think I should have but it was very fun. Did you like driving, Melinda?" She slurs out the sentence.

Melinda scowls, "I think I need a new teacher, Matthew made it very confusing." She winks at Henry, "Want to take me for a spin?" She gives him a look that used to make him crazy. He ignores it and turns to Anna, "Do you mind if Melinda, comes with us next time?"

Melinda just storms off to their father's truck without saying another word. Henry and Matthew both know that she doesn't mean to be the third wheel but to have Henry to herself. Matthew says, "I don't know why she said that, she drove pretty good. Driving can be confusing with all the things that you must think about at once, but she did good, for her first time."

Matthew's walking backwards talking to Anna and Henry but suddenly stops and says, "Wait for me, I'll be just a minute." He heads off back toward the building. Henry turns to see where he was going and he saw John with two other fellas talking next to John's car. After just a few words, Matthew comes back to them.

"Who were those guys with John? I didn't recognize them." Henry asks. Something didn't seem right to him.

"Friends of John's. I was a . . . asking about the next game night. They said they didn't know of one, yet."

THIRTY-THREE

The Fourth Sunday in September, 1935, cont'd
In EL Dorado, Kansas

The two trucks follow each other back to Camp. They all walk to the hut together. Melinda still seems mad about something. Anna is feeling much less tipsy after the drive with the windows down. She feels that she can talk to Matthew now and make some sense. She was very impressed with how Matthew handled himself tonight. He seemed to know exactly when to bet against himself. Melinda is the first to enter the hut. She doesn't say to good-night to any of them. either. Matthew's manners make up for Melinda's rudeness.

"Henry, I know I was upset when I first saw you at the game, but I want to thank you. I hated lying to my sister so much."

"I can't believe you all had so little confidence in me." Anna acts severely wounded by putting her hands over her heart and pretends to swoon.

"We were wrong about you, sis. I apologize, for my part." He goes to her and gives her a kiss on the cheek. He turns to Henry and puts his hand out for a shake. When Henry takes his hand, they pull each other in and hug. This seems to be a practiced thing between them, Anna notices. Matthew says good-night and walks into the hut and closes the door, to give them a little privacy.

"Are you feeling better, now, Anna?" Henry has his hand in hers. He bends down and gives it a kiss. "You were so damn cute tipsy. For a moment, there, I really had my hands full." He laughs at the memory of her swaying back and forth.

"I cannot believe those drinks, I never tasted the alcohol in them. What kind was in there?"

"Vodka, it's basically a hell of a kick with no taste. It's made for blending with juices and other alcohols. You would have been fine if each drink was sipped for a half an hour or so." He lets out a small laugh. "Even after you were warned on the first one, you downed the second one. That's so unlike you."

"It brought Melinda to my side and away from that poker table, didn't it?" She smiles slowly.

"Anna, you, sly dog, you did that on purpose?"

"I knew she wouldn't leave because we said so. Melinda will fight you on everything that's your idea. But if it's her idea . . . She'd never let me fall down, not in a million years."

"So you weren't drunk, my scheming beauty?"

"I didn't say that. The room was moving on me so I intensified the sway affect, that's all. I didn't want either one of them to be upset with me for making them leave so after I accidentally drank the first one too fast, I thought of doing the second as a way out."

"Brave, yet timid, shy and . . . a genius. You amaze me. Anna. How did I not see this in you at first? We were all wrong about you, and my father was so right." He pulls her to him, and traces her face with the back of his hand. "I'll give it one more week, I think. That should be about enough."

"What are you talking about? A week for what?"

"That's how long I think I can hold out before marrying you. I want to take you so bad right now, but I promised myself that I wouldn't. A good girl is going to walk down that aisle dressed in white. It may kill me to do it, but that's what you deserve." He leans in and gives her a sweet kiss. She returns it and starts to hunger for more and he can feel it, too. He pulls completely away. "Oh, keep kissing me like that and I might wake up the preacher tonight."

"Henry, I can't get married tonight, I have to work tomorrow." She says with a straight face. She gives him a peck on the cheek and turns to go into the hut.

"Anna sweetheart? A driving lesson tomorrow? Can I pick you up after dinner? I can teach both you and Melinda if you like. This way both my lips and my hands will stop trying to ravage you."

"I would love another lesson. I'll let you know about Melinda. If she's this moody, tomorrow, I don't want her ruining our date, I mean lesson." She walks to the door and has her hand on the knob but stops and calls, "Henry?" When he turns back to her, she runs to him. "I don't want to say good-night. I want to be ravaged, instead." She clings to him, with her head on his shoulder. "Have I told you that I love you, this evening?" She lifts her head and his mouth is on hers, instantly. Her arms are around his neck and she's arching herself against him.

Henry is really . . . trying NOT to ⠇. . . but she tastes so good and she's pressing up against him with her whole body. Her hair smells like fresh air, and now her tongue is teasing his lips, seeking entry into his mouth. He thought of taking her to the camp truck but that idea sickened him. He could never have Anna that way, especially there! This was enough to break the spell of her intoxicating kisses. "Stop, please stop!" He pleads. He forces her to arm's length. "We mustn't, we can't, seriously Anna. I will not!" Then smiles up at her, "Good girls don't do that to the men they love. Ask your Ma, if you don't believe me." He smiles at her, knowing that this is the way to get her.

"Henry, there are somethings that I cannot talk about to my Ma," she nods to below his waist, "that's one of them!"

"That may be but," he takes her by the hand and leads her back to the front door. "you are going in now." He opens the door and gently pushes her inside. "Good night my love." He whispers before he slowly closes the door.

Matthew is sitting at the kitchen table with a glass of water in his hand. Perfect, she thinks. I can use a cup myself. As she approaches, Matthew says, "This is for you. They say that drinking dehydrates you." He hands her the cup. She sits across from him.

"Where did you hear that? And when did you get so smart?"

"Anna, I'm anything but . . . I checked on Melinda, she seems to be asleep and there's something I want to tell you. I'm tired of secrets and I hope that you won't think less of me when you hear what I've done." He tells her of his farm fund loss and he gives her just the bare facts about how he replaced the money. He did add that Henry offered to take his place but still put all the money back.

She sits back with her water in hand, quietly listening. She cannot believe that all this has been going on behind her back. She takes a few sips of the water between his words. When he has caught her up, he hangs his head, holding his breath, waiting for her condemnation.

"Oh, Matthew." She says at last. "What you have been through! Henry did say that he knew things about you that made him think you can handle yourself in sticky situations. I would have never guessed, though." She shakes her head as if to clear it, and takes another sip of the water. "You are a surprising young man. Now after all that, why did you want to go back there tonight?"

"I want to prove to myself that I can do this. I decided that I'll only spend a few dollars, that I've on hand each night that I play. If I win big, I'll sneak it into the valise. Tonight, I started with five dollars and walked away with fifty. I'll keep out the five for the next game and put the forty-five into the farm fund. If I lose the five one night, well that's the cost of an evening, pity. You must admit it that I've skills at the game."

"What I saw was luck, Matthew. Just luck. I know that I don't know the rules but there's no skill to rolling dice, just luck. Pa wouldn't like you adding to his fund this way, and you know that, otherwise you would give him the money outright." She finishes the water with a few gulps and hands him the glass. She stands up and stretches. "I've to get some shut eye. I've Big Bertha to conquer in the morning." She ruffs up his hair and tilts his head up to look him in the eye. "I'll try not to worry, but I think I'm going to be looking after you, with Henry by my side."

"You two, have really reconnected, haven't you? I'm very glad for you. I couldn't love Henry more if he was my brother by blood." He stands and Anna suddenly thinks he has grown three inches since she has found out all that he's done. "I couldn't have picked a better guy for you, Anna." He gives her a kiss good-night on the cheek.

As she starts to walk to her bedroom, she starts to hum the song 'Day and Night' from the Fred Astaire movie she saw a few months before. With her eyes partially closed from sleepiness, she dances in small circles with an invisible partner all the way to her room. She quietly walks into the room and sits down at the mirror to brush out her hair. She sneaks peaks at her sister to see if she's awake. She feels that she needs to discuss her behavior and now.

"Melinda, darling, are you sleeping?" She whispers loudly.

"Anna, darling, are you still drunk?" Melinda returns.

"I don't think so, but thanks for your help, tonight. I thought those drinks were just orange juice and I was so nervous about going to a gambling place and nervous about what you'd say to me when you saw me there. I was just real thirsty. Can we talk?" She turns and looks at her sister.

"Depends on what do you want to talk about?"

"Things. It seems that I've a lot of catching up to do. I know that John Walker has been taking you and Matthew to the games. Matthew just told me about what he did to replace the money he gambled. I feel like everyone has been leading secret lives behind my back and I want it to stop. Whether I agree or disagree with what you are doing, I beg you to just not lie to me anymore. Like I said to Henry, I may not get the whole story about what has happened to him before we reconnected but, instead of lying about it, I would appreciate him just saying, 'I'm not comfortable telling you about that.'" She changes the subject. "He's told me he has been with another woman, and from what I can tell, it was recently. He said that he should have listened to his father instead of his hormones, so I think it's happened since his Da wanted us to be engaged."

Melinda is sitting up now, with her arms around her drawn up knees, listening intently. "What did he say about her?"

"He wasn't comfortable telling me about her. He just said that when he looked in her eyes, it was if she was controlling his man parts. He added that when he looks in my eyes, I control his heart. I make his heart burst with joy, he said several times. Melinda, I want to . . . can I be honest?" Melinda shakes her head yes. "I want to . . . oh, I cannot say it out loud. I want to be bad. Let me call it that. When he kisses me, when he talks to me with his voice just above a whisper, it talks to my lady parts. And his smiles make my heart sing."

"He does have a great voice. I'll grant you that. Do you think that you'll do . . . IT . . . with him?" Melinda cannot stop thinking about Henry's voice, his touch, and what she's done with him. Now, she must let him go. She has told him so but her mind refuses to go along with the plan.

"Well, he said, 'if we don't get married soon, I won't be a good girl when I'm dressed in white.' I suddenly think that isn't as important as I thought it was. What I want is to . . . know what it's like to love a man – all the way. Do you know what I mean?"

"Sure do." Melinda is looking down. She has had a good time with

Henry, but not the way Anna is describing it. *I don't love Henry, I just like what we did together. I must find someone else so I stop thinking about the soon-to-be-engaged-to-my-sister-Henry.* "I think we need to get some sleep. Tomorrow is a work day." She lays back down on her back, staring at the ceiling. "Anna, will you go to more games?"

"I'll go if Henry does, I want to be by his side, no matter what. I'm so in love with him. I love the friend that he was growing up and love the man that he has become. I felt we were so different, before. Now I barely see those differences."

"That's because YOU'VE changed, Anna. Overnight, you've become this Big Bertha dominator, gambling house attender, a bad girl want-to-be and I might add . . . a drinker. Your head must be spinning from all these changes, and not the booze." Melinda laughs.

"I guess you are right. I've had a lot going on the last few days. Can we talk about you, now? And answer me truthfully or not at all. Where do I start? Do you gamble?"

"No, I don't understand the crap game at all but I understand poker. I haven't played but I like to help other players. What else?"

"If you don't play, what do you do there?"

"Talk to guys. They're all risk takers and I like that in men."

"You are a risk taker, just like Matthew."

"Please, he's smarter than all of us, including Henry, I think. Nothing gets past him, anywhere. He's a bit like Sherlock Holmes with his observations. I think that's why he's a good gambler. I just thought of something. He should switch to poker. It's a game with guessing what the other players have and bluffing when necessary. Matthew would clean up in that game. Remind me to tell him that tomorrow. What else do you want to know, Anna, I'm getting sleepy here?"

"Why did you take money from that guy? And don't say because he gave it to you. You were expecting it. I saw it on your face."

"So you weren't as drunk as you pretended to be? Okay, I've my own fund started. I'm saving up to get out of EL Dorado and move on to more exciting place. I'll be eighteen in a few months. By then, I should have a few dollars set aside to get to wherever I'm going." As she says this out loud, she realizes that she has been planning this subconsciously all along.

"You want to leave us? We'd never see you again? I don't think I could live without you, Melinda. You've been next to me my whole life, and I love you."

"I'd be in touch. I wouldn't go far, at first. Maybe just to Wichita. I'll get a job and see what the city can offer in terms of excitement and adventure." We won't be staying here after the next two harvests anyway, so that will make it easier to move on.

"I'm shocked. Won't you be afraid to be on your own? No one waiting for you to get home safe and sound?"

"Anna, after lying to you these last few weeks, I'm looking forward to not must lie or sneak or explain myself to anyone. That's the freedom I want; to do what feels good without going through all that."

"Sounds a little Brazen of you, if you don't mind my saying so."

Melinda sits up again. "Anna, truth be told, I'm a bad girl and I like it. I'm sorry if you are shocked but I've never wanted to walk down the aisle in any kind of a dress. I'll just say it as plain as day. I've had sex, I liked sex and I want to do it with someone else to see what else there's to do. I'm about as brazen as they come, sis."

"Oh, Melinda." Is all Anna can think to say. She cannot believe her ears. She doesn't know her sister or her brother at all it seems.

Anna gets up from the mirror and undresses while Melinda lays her head back down. Once her nightgown is on, she grabs her toothbrush and heads out to the water pump in the kitchen to brush her teeth and rinse out her mouth. She drinks another glass of water, before heading back to her room. She shuts off the light and climbs in bed.

"Anna, are you mad at me? I didn't mean blurt that out that way. I just was being honest, like you asked."

"I'm not mad, shocked a little but not mad.

"Please Anna, let's get some sleep."

"Good night, dear sister. It's nice to finally get to know you."

THIRTY-FOUR

The Fourth Monday in September, 1935
In Eldorado, Kansas

At five-thirty a.m. Anna is the first of the Masters to wake. Those two glasses of water she had before bed are screaming to be released. She bumps into her Ma on her way out of the hut to use the outhouse. When she came back in, her Pa was up, also. Anna is humming the Cole Porter song sung by Fred Astaire, again. Her Pa joins her and then Matthew starts singing the words from his couch without getting up:

"Like the beat beat beat of the tom-tom
When the jungle shadows fall
Like the tick tick tock of the stately clock
As it stands against the wall
Like the drip drip drip of the raindrops
When the summer shower is through
So, a voice within me keeps repeating you, you, you"

Judy Masters is smiling at her happy family. "Where is Melinda? She's missing this." Suddenly a low female voice adds to the singing:

"Night and day, you are the one
Only you beneath the moon and under the sun"

Melinda comes out of the bedrooms, she moves gracefully about the front room and continues singing with Matthew while Anna and Judd do the humming

"Whether near to me, or far
It's no matter darling where you are
I think of you, night and day.
Day and night, why is it so
That this longing for you follows wherever I go
In the roaring traffic's boom
In the silence of my lonely room
I think of you, night and day.
Night and day,
Under the hide of me
There's an oh such a hungry yearning burning
Inside of me

And its torment won't be through
'til you let me spend my life, Making love to you
Day and Night, Night and Day!"

As they finish the last stanza, Melinda joins Matthew on the couch and they're holding hands like star crossed lovers.

Judy is the first to speak, "Where did all this talent come from? Not from my side of the family to be sure." She goes to each of the singers and kisses them on their foreheads. "What a beautiful way to start the morning! I'd say good moods, all the way around!" The singers smile and get up to start their morning routine. Soon breakfast is on the table and they were all eating, with gusto.

Judy asks the siblings. "How did the driving lessons go, anyone comfortable to take the truck to work today?" She looks from Melinda to Anna.

Matthew is the first to speak. "I think they need another lesson or two, before we release them to reign havoc down on the unsuspecting world." Melinda lightly punches him in the shoulder.

"Not nice, little bro. He has a point, though, I don't feel ready, yet."

"Same for me, Henry's coming over after dinner to give me another lesson. He did say that you can join us, if you want." She says to Melinda.

"I don't know," she turns back to her brother. "Matthew, I'm sorry for harassing you last night about your teaching abilities. You are a great teacher. Will you still take me out?"

"Sure Melinda, we can work on our singing career, while we are at it." The whole family laughs. Why did it feel to Judd that they as a family haven't laughed together in a long time?

Soon, they were all ready for their jobs. Henry and Frank Harrick were at the hut a little before seven a.m. Frank is there to drive the girls and Henry is there to say good morning to Anna. There isn't much time before that first Camp truck will load.

Henry pulls Anna outside and says, "Da and I had a long talk about you last night. He's so happy. I hated to tell him that he was right all along but I had to do it. I asked him how he knew and he said that when we left Hope, I was very hard to handle. He knew it wasn't leaving the farm or having no mother, it was leaving my best friend – you. He said that I called your name in my sleep for at least a year. I deny all of it, of course. Come here and let me taste you in the morning." He pulls her to him and she kisses him with all the passion pent up inside of her. Henry hears the door to the hut open and he reluctantly pulls away from her ardent embrace.

They're both out of breath, when Judd and Matthew come out. Judd says, "Come on, Henry, we don't want to be late." He doesn't look at them but Matthew does. He smiles at them and gives them a thumbs-up sign.

Anna laughs at not just getting caught kissing but being rated at it. She grabs Henry's face for one more quick kiss before he runs to catch the truck.

Mr. Harrick is in the hut, having a cup of coffee with Judy. When Anna comes in, he says, "I'm ready, when you girls are. No hurry, I'm not going to be late for anything." He laughs at his own joke. "Are you ladies going to be driving soon?"

"I think one more lesson should do it." Anna says confidently.

"Good answer, want to drive now?" He winks at her.

"Oh, yes please." He tosses the keys across the room, just in time for Melinda to come out of the bedroom and see her catch them. "I'm driving to work, you can drive home, sister. Let's go, I'm so excited."

Being familiar with the Harrick's truck, she's able to start it and put it in reverse with ease. When she puts the gear in drive, she turns to her sister and Mr. Harrick and says, "Hang on to your seats, it's going to be a wild ride!" and she laughs at the irony.

She pulls out of the Camp lot, slowly and increases her speed steadily. Melinda and Frank look at each other and both raise an eyebrow in a question. She's driving very carefully and very well. Mr. Harrick laughs out loud. "Henry was right, you are a natural. I don't think you needed me here at all."

"No, Mr. Harrick, I need you for when I take the wheel." Melinda says. "Obviously, Anna has been driving for years."

"You know that I haven't! I just had a great teacher."

"Please, you have Matthew's – behind the wheel – genes. That's all. That boy could drive anything with wheels."

"Is there anything Matthew can't do?" Anna still can hardly believe all that he has been through in the last few weeks.

They're quiet for just a moment, when Mr. Harrick says, "He can't give birth to a baby." Both girls laugh, hysterically. Each time they try to stop, one of them starts laughing again. It comes to the point that Anna can't see through the tears in her eyes from laughing so hard.

She drives to the Kroger store and lets Melinda out. "Have a great day!" They say to each other at once.

Anna backs out carefully, with her arm behind the passenger's seat just like Henry taught her. She looks at Frank Harrick. *How did she not see that Henry looks just like his father? Same Roman nose, same hairline, same jaw and those eyes!* Frank notices her staring. "Did I forget to shave this morning, or do I've hair coming out of my ears again?"

"No, sir, I was just noticing how much Henry looks like you."

"I know, poor kid. So, in twenty years, this is what you'll be married to. Can you live with that?"

"You betcha." He reaches over and takes her hand and gives it a modest kiss on the back of it. She blushes immediately.

"And you my lovely Anna, are your mother's daughter, through and through. Did you know that I almost had a shot with her? She and your Pa were fighting. They broke up for a about a week, back in high school. As soon as I heard, I asked her out on a date. We went to out to dinner but your father found us and punched me right in the nose the next day. Your mom saw, and wanted him to apologize to me. He said he would but only if she'd take him back. Just think, she has been paying for that apology for over twenty years. Poor lady, I owe her so much." He smiled but grew quiet.

"Mr. Harrick, they might not have gotten back together if it wasn't for that punch. I think I owe yo my life, literally."

"Glad to have been of service." He's smiling again. "Seriously, I had it bad for your mom. But Judd was my best friend, and all punches aside, the best man won. I never had a chance, really. About two years later I met Henry's mom, she was out of my league, but she married me, anyway. Unfortunately, she figured out that she could have done better and off she went. I feel guilty that Henry was the one to suffer, for my mistake."

Anna is in a spot close to Sally's Diner. She still has forty minutes until she needs to be in front of Big Bertha. She decides to ask a few more questions. "Mr. Harrick, how did you know that I was the one for Henry? Was it because of your feelings for my Ma?"

"What a thing to say!" but he thinks for a second. "No, Anna, I just knew how much you meant to Henry, growing up. How you helped him when his Ma run off. And maybe because you are your mother's daughter. She's a great wife and a great mother and Henry deserves to have both, since I failed in that department for him." Frank hangs his head, feeling guilty all over again.

"Frank, look at me." Anna has never called him Frank. He looks up in surprise. "You are the best father out there. You have raised one amazing man. You know that I'm completely in love with him, don't you and I've you to thank for it."

"Well, I um . . . your welcome?" He laughs at being speechless for once. "I'm sorry that you are such a good driver. I loved having both of you in my truck. You are a breath of fresh air for an old, sick man. I still have tonight, though. Can I buy you a cup of coffee? I hear that they've a great new cook at the diner."

"I'd be honored, Mr. Harrick." They both go into the restaurant and Betty is the one waitressing today.

"Frank, it's been ages!" She says and rushes to the front to give him a hug. "Where you been keeping yourself?" She leads them to a table and leaves them with menus and goes to grab a fresh hot pot of coffee. "What'll you have?"

"Just coffee," they both say at once. Anna is looking over the menu. She suddenly gets a little nervous about making all these different dishes.

Frank can see the look of panic on her face. He gently takes the menu out of her hands. "Just concentrate on what each order slip says. Take it one dish at a time. You'll be fine."

"Just like Henry, you always know the right thing to say."

Betty overhears Henry's name and says from two tables away, "Where is that good-looking boy of yours, this morning, Frank? I've never seen you without him."

"He's working at the Johnson Farm finishing off the tomatoes. Have you met his girl Anna, your new cook?" Frank beams.

"I know Anna. We are happy to have her aboard but I didn't know she was Henry's girl. I was always under the impression Henry wasn't the one to get serious about anyone. Pardon me for asking, but when did this happen?"

Anna answers, "Friday" and Frank answers, "Grade school". They both laugh then switch answers, then laugh some more.

Soon it's time for Frank to leave and Anna to get control of Big Bertha. She squares her shoulders as if about to do battle and enters the kitchen.

Melinda spends the morning learning the stock room and how to face products for display. *Not exactly mind blowing difficult,* she thinks. Mondays and Tuesdays are the bulk shipment days of the week, but each day something comes from somewhere. Just because she's stocking shelves doesn't mean that she's not running the register. There's small bell on the counter for customers to ring when they're ready to be rung up. It seems to Melinda that every time she gets in a rhythm of stocking, she's summoned by that damn bell. By the third ring, she feels like the dogs in Pavlov's experiments.

Joan has a small name tag for Melinda and made a little ceremony of putting it on her. She has several cakes/breads needing to come out of the oven, so she's off to the kitchen a second later. Petro starts to call out the meats again and after Joan comes out of the kitchen she reminds him to write it down on the meat wrapper and 'don't be such a loud stubborn Greek all your life.' Melinda loves these two people already. Never would her Ma talk to her Pa that way. Petro never even blinked at the insult. Such passionate people, they were.

Joan's very pregnant daughter comes for some groceries and the couple can't get to her fast enough. Anastasia, Stacy for short, is due in a week and looks like she swallowed the biggest watermelon in the patch. Melinda wonders how she can even move shaped like that and with all that weight in front of her. Stacy is about twenty-eight and has been married for four years. This is their first child, and the first grandchild for Joan and Petro.

Petro says to Stacy, "How you get here? Walking no good for you and the baby. No good husband you have, let you walk here. My poor Stacia, I drive you home. Go in my office and take those swollen feet off floor. Now Stacia, now!"

Joan is just as worried. "You really shouldn't be here in such a state, Stacy. You could go into labor from all that walking. Where is Joe? I should ring him and tell him to come get you."

Stacy answers, "I'm fine and Joe is working. He left at seven a.m. to go to Wichita to bring Grant Johnson's tomatoes to market. He won't be home until late tonight. I was bored at home. I can't do anything because I'm as big as a house."

As she says this, Petro has brought a wooden chair from his back room for her to sit on, right in the middle of the store. She reluctantly sits down. Joan sees her swollen ankles for the first time. Oh, Stacy, have you been eating salty pickles again? Your ankles are the size of my calves.

"I can't help it Mama, I crave them so." Stacy admits

Just then the bell rings and both Melinda and Stacy start to go to the register. Stacy laughs, "Old habits die hard, I guess."

When Melinda goes to the register, it's John Walker. "Why aren't you in the fields today, John?" She starts to ring up his few items. He's staring at her as if he doesn't know her. "John, why aren't you answering me?"

"I was just wondering if I can trust you to deliver a message."

"Message to who? Your total is ninety cents, please." He hands her a dollar.

"Keep the change. Can you tell Matthew that if he's still interested, we might have something else lined up for next week? Tell him to come see me at the next Game night. That might be Thursday night, as far as I know."

"Why would he be interested? He replaced his losses."

"How the hell do I know? He's your kid brother. He told me he wanted in on the next job, all's I know. Just give him the message, huh?" He takes his small bag and turns to leave. He suddenly turns back. "Melinda, since Henry has picked Anna over you. Do you want to go out with me, sometime?"

"Gee, I don't know John, you're such a smooth talker, I might get swept off my feet." She runs a handkerchief over the back of her neck. The day is getting warm and the sun is shining through the window right on Melinda. "How 'bout we talk on Thursday night about it." He finds this an acceptable offer and turns to leave; but again, turns to look at Melinda. "I don't like your sister coming to the games. I don't trust her. She looks like the type that will call the cops. Tell Henry to leave her home, in the future."

"Now that message, you'll must deliver yourself and take your chances. Neither Henry or Matthew will let you talk about Anna that way. And damn it John, neither will I. I don't care what you like, Anna is free to come and go as she pleases."

"That's what you think! Don't you know that I've a hand in running those games and if I say Anna ain't allowed. Then she won't get in!"

Melinda softens her approach. "Listen John, you've misjudged her. We all did. She's learned about Matthew replacing the money and she has accepted it. Don't be so rash, about banning her. She hasn't done a thing to deserve that."

"Say you'll be my date on Thursday and she can come."

"So you want to black mail me to date you?"

John just nods as if he didn't hear her. "See you Thursday," he says and leaves.

THIRTY-FIVE

The Fourth Monday in September, 1935 cont'd
In EL Dorado, Kansas

Henry comes over after dinner, as expected, for Anna's final driving lesson. His father comes with him. Frank thinks that the girls drive well enough to go solo tomorrow even though he loved accompanying them. Anna and Henry leave for their lesson.

Melinda and Matthew do the same. Melinda tells Matthew about John Walker's visit to the store and all he said about the next job and his opinion of Anna. "Matthew, you aren't going to get involved with him again, are you?" She says as she drives her Pa's truck out of the Camp. She looks to him with concern.

"I was hoping to do one or two more jobs, to help with the fund. I don't trust John Walker as far as I can throw him. You remember how he treated Anna, last night? He was more than rude and for no reason. What's she ever done to him?"

"I don't get it, either. He was jealous of Henry when I was going for him, but now that Henry has picked Anna, you think he'd just be glad I'm free to date him. Of course, I'm not going to do that again. I think you should distance yourself from him, also."

"Well, I'm definitely not going to date him, be assured of that." Matthew quips. Melinda tries to mock punch him but cannot reach him.

"Gosh, I hate being short."

"I find it advantageous." Matthew laughs.

Anna is behind the wheel, also. Henry says, "How was Bertha today? Did you tame her to your will?" He watches as Melinda and Matthew pull out of the camp.

"Don't go anywhere just yet. I've something for you." He pulls out a small velvet bag. He takes out a little necklace with a Cameo attached. "Will you accept this small token of my affection? It was my Father's mother's. It was one of the few things my mother didn't grab before she left."

"Oh, Henry, she's beautiful. Is the Cameo wearing a diamond necklace? I've never seen anything like this." She turns it over and sees that it can be worn as a pin, also. The cameo is on a heart shaped background with a tri-gold overlay rim and her diamond necklace is heart shaped, too. "Can you help me put it on?" She hands it back to him. She turns away from him and holds her hair up.

"Darling, with that beautiful neck, give me a minute." She's about to ask him why, when suddenly his cool lips are on her warm flesh. He gives her small kisses at first, at the base of her spinal column. Each kiss lasting longer than the last. He's moving up to behind her ear. "You didn't have anywhere to be, did you? I could do this all night."

"Henry, you are driving me crazy. I thought we are supposed to keep it cool? If you want me to turn around and have my way with you, just keep it up. I think you should put my necklace on my neck now."

He sighs. "If you say so, dear." He puts the necklace on her. She turns around and before he can move away, her lips are on his. She's so happy. She loves him so completely and her body is moving to him to prove it. She told him to put on her necklace so she didn't wait to kiss him. He isn't surprised by the passion in her kisses anymore; he welcomes it.

As they start to reach and touch each other in a rhythmic way, they both realize that this is, again, going too far. They break away at the same time. Henry says, "As much as I love being alone with you, I think we need a chaperone or we aren't going to last until our marriage bed."

"Couldn't agree with you more. I don't think we can be alone, but who can we get to be our third wheel? Matthew? I don't think Melinda, she's still a little off, about us. But Who?"

"Your parents or my Da. They're the natural choice. I know Matthew wouldn't mind, but not always. Melinda, as you say, isn't a good choice. I would love to take your parents out to dinner with us, though. When was the last time your mom was served food, that she ordered? It would be wonderful to watch her see the menu that you are mastering."

"I would love that Henry. Can you afford the four of us? I can chip in after my first paycheck. I can't wait to tell Ma that you want to take her out to dinner. She will be so touched by that. Okay, now where to?"

"Well, head to the Soda Shoppe. Maybe that will cool us off." He smiles. He remembers one of their first passionate kisses were Mint Chip flavored.

"I'll go there but I don't have high hopes for anything cooling us off." She backs up the truck perfectly, and drives out of the Camp with perfect ease. She's smiling ear-to-ear. Henry slides over to her and puts his head on her shoulder as she has done to him, many times. Anna maneuvers to kiss his forehead.

"Melinda says that Thursday is another game night. Are we going?" Henry's head shoots up and looks at her. She continues, "What? I want to keep an eye on my baby brother. Will you teach me how to play craps? I want to follow the betting, at least."

"If that's what you want." He smiles and kisses her cheek before he puts his head back down.

Anna continues, "Melinda had the idea that Matthew's talents would be better used to play poker. Matthew is very observant and we both know that he can bluff, well, lie. She wants him to stop the crap games, also, because it's too luck based. Do you know how to play poker, also?"

Is this Anna, talking? Henry thinks. Matthew told him, today in the field, that he told Anna about the 'job' last night and that she didn't judge him. Now she's condoning his gambling. *How does someone change so much, so quickly?* "I do know how to play poker. Melinda is right. Matthew would be able to see the cards, and the opponent's reactions and he'd be able to tell who was bluffing and who wasn't. Poker is more about that, than the luck of the cards."

"Wow, I wouldn't be good at that at all. I'll stick to cooking. How did it go in the fields today? Were you on horse cart duty again?"

"Yes, one day more of picking, I think, then just pulling and tilling. That will go very fast, unfortunately. Then we will be all on a break until the next harvest. Your father is worried about the funds, I'm afraid. He has said that he doesn't want to take your pay or Melinda's. Matthew told him how silly that is, since he did when you were in the fields. Matthew told me that he could just sneak the money into the fund for you and Melinda. That way your Pa won't feel like he's taking charity."

"Matthew has it all figured out, doesn't he? How did I not see him grow up? He was right in front of me the whole time and I didn't see it. I'm so proud of how he handles himself. I hope he doesn't make any other bad choices but he handled himself through those, too"

"Yeah, he did. I've never been so impressed by someone. He's something."

Anna starts to laugh. Henry raises his head and looks at her. "What's the joke?"

"In your Da's truck, Melinda and I said that there was nothing that Matthew couldn't do and your father said with a straight face, 'he can't give birth.' We laughed for miles!

Henry laughs too. "My Da is a sharp one, isn't he?"

"I love his sense of humor. That time that he lifted Ma off the ground and pretended not to see her, that was so funny!"

"My Mom, seemed to hate his humor. She always said that he couldn't be serious about a heart attack. Then after she leaves, he has one. Proved her wrong." Henry shrugs his shoulders. Anna has pulled into a spot in front of the Central Avenue Soda Shoppe and Parlor. "Let's go in, I don't like talking about Mom." He gets out and waits for Anna. He links his arm with hers and they enter the Soda Shoppe.

To their surprise, Matthew, Melinda, John Walker and a cute girl that resembles John are seated together in the corner booth. Henry orders for the two of them. Anna goes straight to her siblings. "I didn't know you'd be here. Hello John." She says with forced politeness.

Matthew says, "Anna, have you met John's cousin, Susan?"

Anna thinks, so, this is Susan, oh wait, the 'love' affair was just a story Matthew told to get out of the house. The confusion was apparent on her face. John says, "Aren't you going to say hello?"

"Of course, John, I didn't mean to be rude. Hello, Susan, very nice to meet you. I was just struck at how pretty you are, yet still look like John. You are very pretty, indeed."

Henry comes over with their two bowls of Mint chip and they move seats around so everyone can sit together.

Susan says, "Matthew was just telling us that you are the new cook at Sally's. That must be hard work."

"It is, but very satisfying. I'm still learning all the dishes on the menu, so I'm still an apprentice. Do you work or attend school?

"I work at the library. Very quiet job. No stress and I get to read all I want. It doesn't pay much, but I was at the library so much that they thought they should give me a job to make it official."

Matthew smiles. "I haven't had a library card in years. I need to pay you a visit, soon. I love to read."

Anna and Melinda look over at Matthew. He was never a great reader. He and Melinda could never sit still long enough to like to read. Matthew must want to impress Susan, they each thought.

Henry devours his ice cream and is now trying to get Anna's. She lets him have the last spoon, and she kisses his cheek while the spoon is still in his mouth. She whispers, "Only because I love you." into his ear. He smiles and kisses her cheek as payment.

"How cute, you two are." John says, but it doesn't sound as if he means it.

His cousin elbows him. "Why do you say it like that John? They are cute. You can tell they're in love, can't you?" She looks around the table to see if anyone else sees it also. Matthew and Melinda are both nodding but Matthew is the only one smiling.

Susan sees the cameo, that Anna is wearing. "That's so unusual. I've never seen anything like it. Can I see it closer?"

As both Susan and Anna get up, Melinda stands also and asks, "Where did you get that? It looks old."

"It was Henry's grandmothers. He just gave it to me. Isn't it gorgeous? I just love it." Anna beams

Susan exclaims, "It's lovely. I'm so jealous! Henry, do you have any brothers?"

"Just the one, you know Matthew, don't you?" Matthew nods hello, then everyone but Susan laughs. They all know how Henry and Matthew call each other brother, all the time.

John changes the subject. "I think Thursday is the next game night. Melinda says that she's my date. Anyone else going?" Everyone nods yes. "Great, the more the merrier." Again, he says it as if he doesn't mean a word of it.

Susan elbows him again. Melinda says, "Susan, are you coming too? You seem to be a John tamer and we need one."

John scowls at her. "Not funny, I don't like being elbowed."

"Then behave." Melinda and Susan say at the same time.

Everyone, including John laughs.

When everyone gets up to leave, Matthew pulls John to the side. "Melinda gave me your two messages. I'm saying yes to the first and you'd better watch yourself with the second." Matthew is smiling as he says this. John looks more than confused. Matthew explains. "I'm saying that I'm in for another job." Matthew looks around before continuing. "You'd better be nice to Anna, John. I don't think you want to see me or Henry mad."

"Take it easy kid, I was joking with Melinda."

"Will I see you in the fields tomorrow? Can you tell me anything then about the new job?"

"I'll be around but I don't know if I'll have any details until Thursday night. Don't be in a hurry, Matthew. You'll know when the time is right. See you around."

John grabs Susan, who is in mid-sentence, and pulls her out of the shop. Henry looks at Matthew. "What's got into him?"

"I don't know. I can't figure him out. He wanted to drive Melinda home but I don't think that's it. I don't think he has a firm grasp of reality. He doesn't like Anna for some reason. You better keep an eye on her where he's concerned."

"You aren't thinking of working with him again, are you?"

"Yeah, well, waiting for the next harvest to make money is bull. My Pa is beside himself with worry. I'll do whatever I can to help him out. But don't say anything to the girls."

"I'm done with secrets, Matthew. You need to be also."

"Look, let's take the girls home, and we can talk in the fields tomorrow." They walk out to the trucks.

Anna is back behind the wheel, waiting for Henry. "What took you so long?" He didn't think he took a long time. She smiles at him. "I missed you. Get over here."

He's in the truck and to her in seconds. "Yes, my love?" He doesn't wait for an answer. His lips are on her willing mouth.

Suddenly, someone from the truck a few spaces down, starts beeping the horn. It's Matthew, he's giving his thumbs up sign again. Melinda is behind the wheel and she backs out of the spot, and pulls away in the wrong direction. In a moment, they're turned around and beeping, again, as they pass.

Henry kisses Anna again and returns to his side of the truck. "I think we need to get you back home also. You need your rest. We don't want Bertha to overpower you, from your lack of sleep."

"Henry, always looking out for me?" She starts the truck engine, and carefully backs the truck so it faces the correct direction. She puts it into drive and they slowly proceed home.

"Looking at you or looking out for you, either way. I'm at your service." He winks at her. "Look out for that car with no lights. He's coming our way."

"I see him. Why would he be driving with no headlights on?"

"I don't know" Henry says aloud. He recognizes John's car. *What is he up to?*

Anna drives so well, even in the dark, that Henry cannot believe that she has only driven once before the lessons started. Now she'll not need his father to take her and Melinda to work. Frank is very sad about that. He loved being helpful.

Back in the camp parking lot, after Anna shuts off the engine, she turns to Henry, "I had a wonderful evening. Thank you for the cameo necklace. I cannot wait to tell Ma of our double date. She yawns. "I think we've had too many late nights."

Henry is yawning back. "I agree." He was walking her back to her hut. They've hardly kissed today. He hopes that he can catch up in the future. They're at Anna's door. She sees her bedroom light on. Melinda is still up. Anna yawns again.

"Henry, will I see you in the morning? I like starting my day, with your kisses. Well, I like ending the day the same way." She reaches up and kisses him before he could answer or yawn, again.

"Anna, I look forward to ending my day with you in my arms and waking up with you still in them." He smiles at her.

"Watch it Henry, I could take that as a marriage proposal."

"Take it in what sense thou wilt."

"Isn't that a line from Romeo and Juliet? Did you know that was my favorite play of Shakespeare's?"

"Of course, I remember. Now go to sleep so Queen Mab can be with you!" He gives her a good-night kiss.

She puts her arms around his neck, and says, "Oh, I love you so, my Romeo." She kisses him sweetly, and then with more passion. His tongue is entering her mouth and she's playing with it. *Oh, she tastes so good and feels so good. How am I not going to take her, one of these nights?* he wonders. *God give me strength.* He breaks loose of her and puts his hand on the door knob.

"It seems that we are always ending our evenings with me pushing you into your home. Now go to sleep. And dream of me." He adds. He has the door open, he gives her a little push and closes it behind her.

Anna shrugs as she tip-toes to her bedroom so as not to wake Matthew. She opens the room door to see Melinda snuggled in the bed with the light on.

"Are you sleeping, sister?"

"No, but very sleepy. Did you have a nice night?"

"Always with Henry," Anna says again with a sleepy sigh. "Always."

THIRTY-SIX

The Fourth Tuesday in September,1935
In EL Dorado, Kansas

Anna and Melinda go to work by themselves for the first time. Anna drives to work and it's decided that Melinda will drive home. They chatted the whole way there, like long lost friends. Anna parks in front of the store and goes in with Melinda. She'd been in there last night but was not able to look around at the selection of foods and other products. Anna feels that she should get something for Henry as a thank you for the cameo.

Joan is thrilled to see Melinda. "My girl, I couldn't wait for you to come in store. My Stacy had babies last night, twin girls! She'd a bad time and they had to cut them out. They started to close her when they saw the second baby hiding in her womb."

Anna introduces herself and says, "Tell us about the girls."

"Stacy is doing fine. The doctor wants her to stay in his clinic until she can walk around, easily. He had to cut the babies out." She repeats. "One baby's half the size of the first. She might not make it, unless she can take milk from Stacy." Joan struggles not to cry. "She's so tiny!"

Melinda puts her hand on her shoulder. "Do they have names, yet?"

"Good strong names, Diana is from the Greek Goddess. She's the firstborn. Athena is the little one, also a Greek Goddess."

"I'm sure they're both beautiful. I can't wait to see them." Melinda says. Just then, the counter bell rings. "But first, my bell has been wrung." She goes to the register.

Anna is left with Joan. "I understand that all the breads, cakes and pies at Sally's come from your bakery. That's quite an order to fill, plus run the grocery. How do you do it all?"

"I had both my children working, since they were young. I started baking for Sally's when Ted took over. He didn't want to hire a baker so . . . It all grew slowly but when our Stacy got with child and my son went to college in August, it finally got to be too much. Your sister is such a great help. I cannot believe I waited so long to look for help."

"If you looked any sooner, you wouldn't have Melinda. We just asked Mark about work last Thursday."

"Well, then the timing was perfect!" She hears Petro behind the meat counter, yelling out the meat, again. "Damn, Greek fool, cannot remember from one day to the next." She turns to go to correct him, shouting in Greek, as she went.

Anna looks at the time, she's going to be late for the work. She waves good-by to Melinda then gets in Pa's truck and drives to the diner. She runs in and goes straight to the kitchen. Ted is waiting for her. It's exactly nine a.m.

The day flies by for both girls. The boys, on the other hand are having a tough day in the field. It's another hot one and its mostly vine pulling, which is very physical work. They each have a bucket for throwing in the rare good tomato. Matthew and Henry see that Judd is having a hard time with the labor, and try to tell him to sit it out.

Croner comes past and tells them all to get moving. "You aren't getting paid to stand around and talk."

Matthew stands to his full height and says, "And you're not getting paid to treat people like dirt. You lost your farm, just like us, so why do you think you're better than us?"

"Because I'm the foreman here and you ain't. Would you like to be done for the day?"

Matthew looks at his father's exhausted worried face. Matthew knows that they only have two more days left. His father is shaking his head no, but Matthew looks at Croner and says, "Yes, my father and I would like to be done for the day. We've had enough of your shit!" He drops the tomato he's holding and puts his arm under his father and helps him to the paymaster's office to sign out for the day. "Pa, you just looked too bad for me to let you work for that asshole one more minute." Matthew explained.

Judd looks up at him, "Who is this man child in front of me, taking care of his broken down ole Pa?" He hangs his head.

"Pa, we will be fine, you'll see. You just need a few days of honest rest. I'll come back tomorrow and work, promise." Matthew takes him into the office to turn in their pay card. There's no camp truck to take them home until four, so Matthew takes his father to the shady area next to the office and they sit on the ground.

Matthew sees Henry, coming toward him. He tells his Pa that he and Henry are going for a smoke. His Pa just stares at him. "Pa, I'm kidding, I don't want to stunt my growth like Henry did." He and Henry go for a walk, and wait until they're out of earshot from everybody before speaking a word. They haven't had a chance to talk about John Walker today. Matthew asks, "Have you seen John anywhere?"

"I don't think he has showed up today. He comes and goes as he pleases, if you noticed.

"I know, but now it's even more important that I make extra money. My Pa looks like he's going to have a heart attack from all this stress."

"Did you ever consider what it would do to him if he found out where the money comes from? You are playing with matches here, Matthew, and you're standing on very dry kindling."

"That's why I want to talk with John. I want more details than I had last time, before I decide to participate. And a bigger cut! They made a huge haul, probably thousands, and I just got paid two hundred dollars. But I'm not desperate, like I was. I'll pick a safe job that doesn't hurt other people like this one did." He changes the subject. "Henry, can you show me how to play poker? Melinda is convinced that I'm made for poker. Do you think Anna will mind?"

"She has said that you should play that also. Shocked me that she's even considering it. Look, I'd better get back to work, I'll try to be on the four o'clock truck with you, to help with your father. If I can't, I'll see you tonight after supper." Henry says as he walks back to the horse cart.

An hour later, the three men are on the truck heading back to camp. They decide that Matthew will go to Henry's to learn poker before the girls get home. They talk about it a little but they don't want to say too much near Judd.

The two girls are home by six-thirty. Judy has supper ready and Matthew comes in from visiting Henry. They're filled in on Matthew telling off Croner and leaving. Judd says, "We must go back tomorrow. It might be the last day for that field."

Matthew says, "I told you that I would Pa, but you don't need to go. You don't need to work one more day. You are exhausted."

Judy adds, "I agree with Matthew, you are working too hard and worrying even harder. We have money to live on. The girls are working full time and the next harvest won't be but a week or so away, and we can stay right here."

Melinda says, "Did I tell you that I get a twenty percent discount at the grocery? Kroger's prices are cheaper than at the Camp store. You can give me a list of what to buy every night, Ma, and it will save us money."

"See Judd, we are living on easy street! Our beautiful children are providing for us in our old age!" She strains her voice to sound like she's on her eighties instead of forties. He laughs at her imitation and takes her hand and kisses the palm. Anna is touched by the intimate gesture.

After dinner, Henry comes calling. Matthew suggests that they all stay in and practice playing poker. Melinda knows how but Anna doesn't. Henry lets Matthew teach her as a way of reinforcing what he has learned this afternoon. Henry has brought with him cards and poker chips and they set up around the kitchen table.

Matthew rearranges the cards to show Anna the types of winning hands from the Royal Flush, the strongest hand to a lowly pair, being the weakest hand. She seems to understand Straights and Flushes, Full House etc.

Anna isn't grasping the concept of bluffing. She's just terrible at lying and cannot do it. Matthew tries to explain that by watching the up cards come out and seeing your own hand and the faces and actions of the other players, you can tell if they've a better hand than you. If you think they're lying, you can call them. He also explains that betting goes around the table to each person. They can raise, hold or fold.

They try to play a hand or two but Anna just doesn't get it. Judd come in from the living room and watches them for a moment. He's standing behind Anna and sees her hand. Matthew is holding his breath waiting for his father to object to the game when Judd bends over Anna and tells her to ask for two cards and he points to the cards she needs to trade. Matthew, Melinda and Henry are speechless. Judd says, "I wasn't always just a farmer, you know. Frank and I had regular poker nights when we were newlyweds."

Judy comes in the kitchen and adds, "No one could beat your Pa. He was the best poker player in Hope. He stopped playing because I didn't approve of gambling. I had no reason to be upset, he always brought home money but it didn't seem right once you babies started coming." She goes to get herself a glass of water, then returns to the living room.

Melinda is the first one to regain her speech. "Well, blow me down with a feather! Pa, can you sit in where Anna is? We are trying to teach Matthew for a game on Thursday night."

THIRTY-SEVEN

The Fourth Thursday in September
In Lawrence, Kansas

Rosanne is looking at herself in the mirror in the indoor upstairs bathroom. She has the original 'before' sketch taped on the mirror so that she can look from the sketch to her reflection. She squints at the girl in the mirror. No matter how she looks at herself, she cannot imagine looking like the sketch. She can't remember her face, at all. She still thinks that the artist might have made her prettier than she was. She looks at her hair in the 'before'. She tries to imagine fixing her hair that long. She closes her eyes and pretends to put the long locks in a bun. The movements feel natural. Of course, it could be because Carolyn, the doctors and the sheriff's statements all say her hair was long.

After her coma, they kept her from mirrors so she knew that she'd to look awful. She'd run her hand over her scalp and feel all the scabs, scars and all the short hairs that they would cut again and again to keep the wounds clear and clean. Each time they shaved her head, she'd go back to her room and cry herself to sleep. She cried so much during those months. She turned crying into an art form. She never wanted the Facility staff to know, so she forced herself to cry soundlessly. They knew though, because they would find her bed and pillow tear soaked every morning.

The Colonel's bell is ringing, suddenly. She leaves her reflection and her sad memories in the bathroom as she goes to work.

The Colonel, is still in his bed. He's crying, something he rarely did. She goes to his side. "What is Colonel, did you have an accident? Are you in pain? Tell me so that I can help you Colonel."

"My back, pain in my back. I've got to pee, and I can't. I hurt so bad."

She goes to him and checks for a fever and he's burning up. "Oh my, Colonel, when did the pain start? How long has it been since you've made water?" As she's asking this, she knows that any answers he gives would be unreliable. Time and place are the first things that become demented on the Colonel. They get even more elusive with pain, stress or illness. The Colonel is experiencing all three. "Sir, I'll go call Dr. Mason. He'll come with his ambulance for you. He'll make you all better."

She rushes to the upstairs phone in the hallway, and she calls the Farm office. Carolyn picks up on the first ring. "Carolyn, the Colonel has another kidney stone. This one seems worse than the last one. Please call Dr. Mason for the ambulance, I'll be in with the Colonel. See you shortly."

She goes into his bedroom. He's still writhing on the bed. She goes to his bathroom to run cold water on a cloth. She's back at his bedside in an instant and wipes his face and forehead. He holds still as she does this but his eyes are wide with terror. "You'll be okay, Colonel . . ."

Suddenly, both his hands grab her two wrists, tight. "Leave me alone, soldier, get back in the ranks. I won't have this kind of behavior on my watch!" With all his strength, he pushes her away. She isn't expecting this and cannot brace herself in time. She falls back hitting the nightstand before landing on the ground. The ceramic lamp on the night stand falls over and shatters in pieces. Rosanne's neck, back and shoulders are throbbing. The Colonel is yelling at her to get out and go back to the fort.

"Colonel, I'm Rosanne. You are on the Plantation, not in the Cavalry anymore. You are home and sick. Please calm down." She struggles to get up. "Colonel, help is on its way, I promise."

He's in so pain, he cries silently with his mouth open. This isn't going to be good. His dementia cranks up with illness and pain. He'll fight the orderlies that come to get him. She doesn't know what to do. She hopes that Carolyn gets here, before the ambulance arrives. If the doctor comes and brings a sedative, maybe she can distract the Colonel so the doctor injects him.

She hears Carolyn come in downstairs. Rocco is coming up with her. Rosanne looks at the Colonel, "Your granddaughter is here, Colonel, now stay calm, she gets so nervous when you aren't calm. Okay? You've got to behave. The orderlies will be here soon and they'll help you.

Carolyn rushes into the room. "Grandfather, are you okay?"

He looks to her. "My girl, I hurt. Tell the Sargent that I can't go on duty. I cannot go on that damn horse. He threw me and now I'm in so much pain."

"I know, Colonel, we are getting someone to help you. Just lay still and let Rosanne help you."

"She's the enemy! She tried to drown me with that cloth. I pushed her away. I won't put up with that behavior, I tell you."

Carolyn looks at Rosanne, "He pushed you? Are you alright? Did he hurt you?" Carolyn now notices the broken objects from the nightstand and is concerned.

"The lamp got the worst of it." Rosanne says as she tries to bend down and to pick up the pieces. "I'm worried. He's never been this bad. He was fine at bedtime. The attendant didn't mention any problems during his shift. Kidney stones don't just appear suddenly. Do they?"

"Why is she still here? I just told you that she tried to drown me!!"

Rosanne sighs. "I'll go downstairs and wait for the ambulance. I'll call Joshua, and let him know that the Colonel is going into the hospital." She struggles to go down the stairs as the pain from the fall increases.

Dr. Mason soon arrives with the ambulance. Rosanne tells him about the delusions. He says, "That tends to indicate how hard the body is fighting."

"I'm just worried that you might must sedate him to get him into the ambulance. He pushed me down when I tried to put a cold towel on his brow."

The Doctor stops in his tracks. "Are you hurt, Rosanne? You should come into the clinic with him and let us look you over."

"I'm fine, Doctor." She lies. "Please concentrate on the Colonel."

"There's nothing that says that I can't do both." He smiles and rushes up the stairs to the Colonel's room.

Rosanne hasn't had a chance to call Joshua, yet. She goes into the dining room and dials his number. She tells him quickly what is happening, and he says that he'll come to the clinic after his last class.

As she places the heavy receiver back on the cradle, a painful spasm runs from the back of her neck down her spinal column. It feels as though her neck is being separated from her body. Her hand is still on the telephone. She can't move. *It hurts so bad. This has never happened before.*

She can hear the orderlies come in with the stretcher and go up the stairs. She must call out but they're gone before she can gather up the courage to call attention to the fact she needs medical attention, again.

Just then, Carolyn comes down the stairs and comes into the dining room. Rosanne is standing still frozen in place. Silent tears streaming down her face. Carolyn goes to her, "Rosanne, what is it?"

"My neck, it hurts so bad, I cannot move."

"I'll go get Dr. Mason. Don't try to move, anymore." She runs up the stairs. Rosanne thinks, *I didn't want this. The doctor has his hands full with the Colonel.*

The doctor takes one look at Rosanne and calls to an orderly, "Glenn, go get a cervical collar for Rosanne." He turns to Carolyn. "We will get her in your car. Follow us so we can x-ray her neck. I think when she was pushed, she may have re-fractured or sprained something." Glenn is back and the collar is put on her neck. The Doctor takes her hand off the receiver and lowers it, slowly, to her side. "Take small steps now, Rosanne. We will get you some help, I promise."

"I can't go back into that brace, doc. Anything but that brace." Her tears fall onto his hands which were wrapped around hers as he was leading her slowly out.

"I can't make that promise, Rosanne. We will see what the x-ray says. You might be spending the night with us tonight, as will the

Colonel.

Carolyn's Hudson is still at the back of the house. She pulls it to the front, so that she'll be behind the ambulance. Her head is spinning.

They had warned her. *The next set of kidney stones in the Colonel, could be fatal.* There's little they can do for them to break them down, or go in to get them out of the way so that the Colonel can urinate. There isn't enough known about the kidneys. The added stress of Rosanne's neck is almost too much to take. She prays that the Colonel didn't do lasting harm to her. It's not like she isn't accustomed to pain, but she was on the home stretch of being free of all that.

Dr. Mason is placing Rosanne in the front seat. Rosanne doesn't complain, she never does, but Carolyn can see that she's in a lot of pain. The doctor says, "The ambulance is going to go fast with lights and sirens, Carolyn, but I want you to take your time. Drive like you have a raw egg hanging from a string in the car. Any bumps, or turns taken too fast will slam the egg against something and break it. Rosanne's neck is that egg."

"Doc, do you think she should wait for another ambulance? I don't want to cause her anymore pain." Before he can answer, Rosanne put her hand on Carolyn's arm.

"It will be okay, Carolyn. Don't worry."

We've heard her say that before, thought Carolyn. 'It will be okay' was her answer for anyone who caused her pain. *Where does she get that inner strength?* Carolyn wonders. She's now on the road, driving at a snail's pace, trying not to break that precious egg.

Carolyn gets to the clinic, where they're met out front with a wheelchair for Rosanne. They have the Colonel already sedated and feeling pain-free. Dr. Mason wants to try and force the stones by flushing him with fluids. He says that it's a tricky procedure because if he cannot release the urine, he can be poisoned by it. Carolyn needs to give permission for the procedure. *Permission to poison her grandfather?*

"Dr. Mason, I trust you completely but are <u>you</u> sure about this? What can be done to release the urine if he's blocked. Is there anything?"

"We plan on doing a procedure where we insert a small penial tube and we hope to push the stone or stones out of the way to release his waters."

"Please do everything you can for him. Where did they take Rosanne?"

"She's being x-rayed. I'll have someone come get you when you can be with her. She might just have a sprain or strain, Carolyn, so try not to worry about her."

"Easier said than done. I've been worrying over her for a year now."

"Has it been that long?"

"Yes, this Tuesday will be a year, what a long year for her, too!"

The doctor takes his leave and goes in by the Colonel, leaving Carolyn, alone to wait for Rosanne. She is praying that both people she loves so much can be relieved of all the pain that they're going through. Please God!

Time ticks by. Rosanne is put into a small room and Carolyn sits with her. Rosanne still has on the collar and is in a traction bed so she doesn't move until the x-rays can be read. She feels less pain now in her third hour but it still hurts and she's very afraid to move.

Joshua finds Carolyn in Rosanne's room. He has the Professor with him. Carolyn rushes to Eddy's arms for comfort as Joshua rushes to Rosanne's side.

"How did this happen, you were fine on the phone, weren't you?"

"I thought I was. You know how I hate that heavy receiver."

Carolyn cuts in. "It's the Colonels fault. She was putting a cool rag on his forehead, and in his delusion, he grabbed her and pushed her off him. She fell over the nightstand and landed on the floor."

"He didn't know what he was doing. How could he? Have you gotten an update on his condition? I'm so worried." Rosanne tries to sit up, just a little so that she can see their faces better. The spasm in her neck revives and takes her breath away. Immediately, tears spring to her eyes.

Joshua leans over her. "Darling, you can't move, that's why they have you like this. The Colonel is still asleep and they've a tube in him to empty his bladder but it isn't working, yet. They're still talking about a more aggressive procedure but are waiting until the very last minute before they do it. His dementia will play a factor in his recovery, either way. He's in good hands, Rosanne. You need not worry about him right now."

The Professor has his arms around Carolyn. "Is there anything I can do for you?"

"Tell us about the classes. We need some good news. What did they think about the sketch?" Carolyn asks. Anything to stop thinking about the Colonel.

"The students have been working overtime. They've just about mailed out all the flyers. They're still making lots of calls, too. I do have very good news. I was talking to a colleague at Butler Community College, down in EL Dorado, about an hour and a half southwest of here. He heard that I'm doing a live cold case investigation. He'd like to join us in the search. I didn't get the chance to tell him any of the details. I plan to present the material to him tomorrow. If he's interested, he has two classes that are going to help with the calls and the leads.

I was hoping to bring you, Carolyn and Rosanne but that was before I found out about . . . this situation. I couldn't reach anyone at the house so I called Joshua and his cleaning girl told me that he was coming straight here from his last class. So, I went to his last class and waited for him and we rode down together."

The Doctor came into the room, with a very grave face. Carolyn saw him first and rushed to him. "Is it the Colonel?"

"He's holding his own. We are starting to see a urine discharge. It's very cloudy but where there's a little, we expect it to be more. No, it's Rosanne's neck. Is it any better?"

"It was but I moved and now my head hurts in the back. I'm a little dizzy. How can that be if I'm lying down?"

"That's because you have a serious neck sprain. The Colonel must have jerked you hard, it's like a whiplash. My concern is that like your original neck injuries, your spinal column might also be compromised. Neck sprain symptoms develop over the first day or two so I'm going to keep you here until Saturday. You must stay in traction, like you are, to avoid additional injuries."

"Aww, do I've to? I wanted to go dancing Saturday night?" Rosanne looks at Joshua and watches his jaw drop. "Just kidding. But do I've to stay like this until then?"

"I'm afraid so, my dear. I'm ruling on the side of precaution, knowing all that you've been through."

"You'd think that with all that I've been through, you'd go easy on me."

"Rosanne, is that your first complaint in the year that I've known you?"

THIRTY-EIGHT

The Fourth Thursday in September, 1935
In EL Dorado, Kansas

The day for the big game has arrived. Matthew didn't go to work yesterday or today. He and his father and Frank played poker. Yesterday, after dinner, Melinda and Henry also, joined in the game. Matthew gave all of them a run for their money, well, chips. Henry thought he was ready. He got the location of the game from one of the other regulars that also works in the fields.

Judd is very proud that his son picked up the game so fast. He gave Matthew a twenty-dollar bill to bet. Melinda looks at her father and asks, "What happened to my father who was afraid to spend money?"

"He's proud of the chip off the old block and I expect him to return my twenty and keep the rest." Judd smiles at his only son.

Anna and Melinda had rushed home to get ready for their evening out. Anna was very impressed with the women at the game and tries to dress up as best she can. She's wearing a beige frock with a ruffled low neckline and she's wearing Henry's cameo.

Melinda isn't happy being John's date. She liked him as someone to make Henry jealous but he's too full of himself and too erratic. She's happy that Susan will be there. She likes Susan. She has a very good sense of humor. Melinda never had any female friends other than Anna. She thinks Susan can be the exception. Melinda is dressed very plainly on purpose. She doesn't want to lead John on, but her curves show through everything, even those damn field workpants.

Earlier in the afternoon, Matthew went to town to get his long overdue shave and haircut at Wm. Mooney's Barber Shop. Then Matthew borrows a shirt and jacket from Henry. He looks so grown-up. Henry is at the Hut before eight o'clock to pick up Anna. Melinda isn't sure if John plans on picking her up. He never said and no one has seen him, since they left the Soda Shoppe.

Matthew thinks that they should drive separately. He takes Melinda with him. He's more nervous than his first crap game. He still cannot believe that his father worked with him and gave him such an enormous amount of money to spend. "Melinda, do you think that I'll be able to win?" He asks when they were in the truck driving to the new location.

"Matthew, I think you can do anything you set your mind to do." She laughs and adds, "except give birth!" Matthew looks at her oddly. She explains that's what Frank Harrick quipped, one day when he drove them to work.

Anna and Henry are at the Craps table, when they arrive. Henry is shooter and Anna is blowing on his dice. Matthew joins the betting and places money on the 'Don't Come' line. Henry looks up at him. "Brother, you wound me. Don't think I can win?"

"Not on this roll, you can't." Matthew winks at Anna. She's just glowing with excitement of watching her men play.

Henry throws the dice hard and they come up as seven. Lots of people at the table lost money except Matthew. Henry comes around to the other side of the table and roughly grabs Matthew around the neck. "You brought me bad luck, brother, I outa . . ." He bends Matthew down to ruff up his hair! "Don't ever bet against me, we are a team, remember!" To all those around the table, and to Anna, they look like they're going at it. Both of her men come up smiling and pat each other on the back.

Anna laughingly says, "Where is Melinda? She's missing the fun!" She looks around.

"She went to talk with the guy that runs the poker game to see if she can get me a seat." He tries to put his hair back together. "Gee, Henry, I paid good money to get my hair just perfect. Anna, does it look okay?" He turns side to side so she can appraise it.

Anna walks over to him to run her fingers through it to straighten up where it was sticking out. "There you go, all better. Oh, here comes Susan and John." Susan comes right to them.

"Hello, Susan, I'm glad to see you. I was hoping that you didn't change your mind." Matthew says then adds, "You look very pretty, tonight."

She's standing next to Matthew but needs to look up at him. She's only about five foot three, and only when she's wearing high heels. Her blonde hair is very curly but she has it waved and bobbed just like all the movie stars are wearing it. "Why thank you Matthew, that's awfully nice of you to say."

John is smiling at Anna. "I see you've graced us with the pleasure of your company again, Anna. Can I buy you a screwdriver?"

Henry answers for her, "Why don't you start buying one for your date first. Melinda is looking for you."

John looks around but doesn't leave them. "Oh, Melinda came after all? Did you bring them both Henry? Or are you strictly Anna's man now?"

Now, it's time for Matthew to answer before Henry does. "I brought my sister, Melinda, she waited for you but you didn't show. Susan, didn't he say at the Soda Shoppe that he was to be Melinda's date?"

"John says a lot of things. We only believe half of what comes out of his mouth." Susan elbows John in the ribs.

Matthew says, "Susan, I really like you. Will you stay by my side and bring me luck?"

"Matthew, I would be honored." She blushes, slightly. "Are you playing craps, tonight?"

"For now, but later I'd like to try my hand at Poker." He nods to the other end of the room where the poker tables are.

Matthew offers Susan his arm and he takes her just a few feet away to the Craps table. "Do you know how to play?" She shakes her head, no. "Well, the most important thing for you to remember is that when the shooter asks you to blow on his dice for luck, you do so immediately." She laughs at this and squeezes his arm.

Anna and Henry are behind Matthew. Anna says into Henry's ear, "Can you believe my little brother is a Lady's Man?"

"Anna, at this point, I almost believe that Matthew CAN give birth." They both laugh. "How about that screwdriver, now? Promise me that it will last for a half an hour, at least."

"I'll try, Henry, but must I promise?" She looks at him with the devil in her eyes.

Henry leans in and kisses her cheek, then says into her ear, "Whatever mischief you have planned, just know that I'm in."

She smiles. He goes to kiss her cheek again but she turns to meet his lips. He pulls back and looks at her. She's still smiling. This Anna isn't looking around to see who saw. This Anna isn't even blushing.

"Maybe you don't need the alcohol. You are pretty bold, without it." He smiles back at her. "I like it."

"But Henry, I'm thirsty. Let me have just one drink?"

"Anna, how can I ever say, no, to you." He goes off to get the drinks. She gets closer to Matthew and watches him with Susan.

Suddenly, John taps her on the shoulder. "I brought you your drink." It's a screwdriver. She looks toward the bar to see if it's the one Henry is buying for her. "Here take it. You were so cute when you were tipsy last Sunday."

"John, Henry is getting my drink, but thank you for thinking of me. Maybe your cousin, Susan, will want it?" Susan hears her name and turns around to see who said it.

John is upset. "What, are you too good, for me to buy you a drink? Take it, there are no strings attached to it." He tries to force it into her hand. Some of its spilling in the attempt.

Susan tries to reason with him. "John, it's not polite to buy someone else's date a drink. I love screwdrivers, I'll take it." She removes it from his hand.

Matthew turns around, "Anna, is there a problem?"

"Oh, no, just a misunderstanding, I think. Oh, here's Henry with my drink." She takes it from him and forgets about the alcohol and starts to drink the awkwardness away.

"Anna, you promised that you'd nurse it." Henry says worried.

"Actually, I didn't promise. I just forgot."

Melinda has come back to the craps table. "I talked with Roger and he said that Matthew can get into a game around ten o'clock. Hey John, nice of you to pick me up for our date." She says with all the sarcasm she can muster. "I see everyone here is drinking except me. John, what do I've to do to get a drink?"

"Go to the bar and order one, I assume." He's not looking at her. He's still staring at Anna.

Susan elbows him. "Is this how you treat dates? Don't pick them up, make them get their own drinks? You'll be single till your dead. That isn't how to treat a Lady."

"If I look real hard around this room, I might find just one lady, the rest are just dames." He sneers.

"John, does that include your favorite cousin? Where did you get this terrible attitude? Who stomped on your heart and flung it into the trash? Lighten up John, we are all here for a good time. Try having one, will you? I swear I'll elbow you so hard that your spine will say ouch. Do you hear me?"

"Yes, I hear you. Whatever you say. Matthew, do you have a minute, I want to talk to you regarding . . . um . . . future endeavors." Matthew excuses himself from Susan and walks toward the bar with John."

Susan looks to Melinda and Anna. "I don't know why he's like this. He's so paranoid and uneven. My Aunt Molly, God rest her soul, tried to get him in a sanitarium but she wasn't able to because he'd always 'recover' enough to seem normal."

They all look at her with their mouths open. "Just kidding, I don't know what's come over him."

Melinda adds, "He wasn't like this with me at first. He was impatient but not mean or sarcastic. Has anything happened that you know of?"

Susan thinks about this for a second. "He was just like this after he was fired from the oil fields for taking care of his mom when she was dying of dust influenza. He kept saying that he'll make them pay. He was acting very funny when the tomato fields closed for a few days. John's other cousin, Miller, was almost fired for the theft, you know. John has been different since then. He keeps saying he has won at cards, and he has been throwing money around like it's dry dirt, and we all know how hard dirt can fly"

Anna is listening very carefully but something sticks out to her. "John's 'other' cousin is the paymaster? Mr. Miller?"

"Oh! He gets that all the time. His name is Miller Johnson. He's barely related, a third or fourth-cousin, I think, to the owner of the Farms, Grant Johnson. I think it's that relationship that saved his job, from what I hear."

"This town is so small, almost everyone is related." Observed Melinda.

"Take Mark at the camp store, he's your late sister's husband and Ted Collins' nephew." Anna adds.

"He is, and is, also, cousin to Joe Bartlett, whose wife Stacy is Joan and Petro's daughter at the Kroger Store. His mom is Grant Johnson's cousin, too." Susan adds. "Mark was a wonderful husband. He went to pieces after my sister died." She pauses a moment as tears well-up in her eyes.

Melinda goes to her side, and changes the subject. "Did you hear that Joe and Stacy just had twin baby girls? They're still at Doc Johnson's clinic." She pauses for a second. "Is the Doctor related to the farm owner also?"

"Yes, um . . . He's Grant's father's first cousin." Susan is recovered enough to answer. Matthew comes back with John.

John looks at Susan. "Have you been talking about me?"

She responds, "Only if your name is Mark or Grant or Joe or Stacy. Geez, John, not everything is about you." She goes to elbow him but he moves away. She catches his move and turns her arm in time to lightly punch him, instead.

For the first time of the night, a genuine smile reaches John's lip. "If you don't stop trying to hurt me, I'm telling your mother."

"Like she wouldn't give me an 'Atta girl'! Come on, John, go buy your date a drink, and stop acting weird."

"Fine, come with me, Melinda. Tell me what you'd like to drink." They head to the bar.

Henry pulls Matthew over, a little, and whispers, "Does he have another job lined up for you."

"Apparently, but as usual, he's very sketchy on the details. No date, time or place or what I'll be doing. I told him that I'm out if I'm not told everything."

"How'd he take that?" Henry whispers

"He laughed, and said he likes working with me so he'll tell me when he knows something."

Susan walks up to them. "Matthew, did you still need me to bring you luck?"

"Absolutely, let's get back at the Craps table. Coming Henry?"

"Yup, we are a team, bro." Henry puts his arm around Anna's waist and Matthew does the same with Susan, and they all go to a Craps table.

John and Melinda come to the table, drinks in hand. Matthew, Henry and John place bets on the Come line for the shooter. On the next roll, Matthew signals to Henry to bet on the Don't Come line. Sure, as a rainbow follows rain, the shooter rolls a seven. John lost all the money he had on board but Henry and Matthew didn't.

They pick Matthew as the shooter. He palms the dice and opens his hand to Susan to blow on them. She cups his hand in hers and blows very seductively. Matthew smiles and throws the dice to the other side without breaking her eye contact. His dice come up eleven! He doesn't turn to look at them until the other gamblers yell at his luck. John bets a Don't pass bet on Matthew. Matthew lets Susan blow on them again. And again, he throws them without watching. The caller says his number is six. Matthew places bets on four and nine. The caller gives him the dice. Susan blows and off they go. It falls on nine and Matthew gets paid. He leaves his original bet on four and nine and his next roll is four.

Henry raises his eyebrow to Matthew as a signal that maybe he should slow down. Matthew just smiles. Now he bets the Don't Pass line and Henry joins him. Susan sweetly blows on the dice and Matthew leans in to her and says, "Thank you for bringing me so much luck." And he kisses her cheek and throws the dice at the same time. He gets a seven and is done shooting but he makes money on every roll of the dice.

Time is flying and it's almost ten o'clock. Matthew makes his way down to the Poker tables, with Susan on his arm. Melinda wants to join them but John tells for her to stay put.

Anna needs use the powder room and asks Henry to get her another drink, please. She looks to Melinda, then says to John, "Do you mind if she joins me? I won't keep her but a second, I promise." She smiles her sweet smile at him.

John seems taken back by that and says, "Sure Anna, just bring her back soon. I don't want my lucky charm to leave me." He smiles his second smile of the night at her.

With Anna and Melinda gone, Henry comes back with their drinks and approaches John. "So John, what do you have for Matthew? Just like last time, you'd better keep him safe or you'll have me to deal with. "

"Do you think that I'm afraid of you Henry? You think you are hot shit, switching back and forth between Anna and Melinda. What does Anna have that Melinda doesn't?"

"Anna has my heart, John. Melinda and I are good friends and nothing else, so quit hinting otherwise."

"Anna has your heart, ain't that cute? What did Melinda have, your cock? I need another drink." He's looking down at his nearly empty glass when Henry's right hook lands right up his nose.

John falls flat, not knowing what hit him. Lots of people stop everything to look around at the sound of John hitting the floor.

Anna and Melinda are back from the bathroom, just in time to see him land. They look from John on the ground to the standing Henry. Henry is shaking his right hand from the pain of breaking John's nose. Melinda says, "What did he say or do, this time?"

"You don't want to know, but believe me, he deserved it."

The caller from the nearby Crap Table starts to yell to the doorman, to get John out of there. Bouncers come from nowhere and they get John to his feet. He's awake, but doesn't know what's happening. Why does he have to leave when he was sucker punched? No one is listening to him. He suddenly yells, "I'll make you pay for this Henry. Just you wait!"

"Henry, he's off his rocker, but I don't think you should have hit him." Anna says without sympathy. "He hurt your hand and now poor Matthew will need to take Susan home." She giggles.

"Here is your drink, by the way, Anna. This is serious, he's not stable in the slightest. I think we all need be careful from now on, as long, as John is free to roam."

Melinda looks over toward the Poker tables, "I wonder how Matthew is doing? We need to go over there and watch."

Anna smiles and chides her little sister. "No sympathy for your date's broken nose, then?"

"Oh, I've sympathy, plenty. Henry hurt is hand and I feel terrible about it." Henry smiles.

She looks up at him. "Whose honor were you defending just now? Yours, mine, Melinda's or Matthew's?"

"I guess when it comes down to it, mine. Let's get to Matthew. I don't want to miss a thing."

THIRTY-NINE

The Fourth Friday in September, 1935
In EL Dorado, Kansas

It's so hard for the girls to get up for work this morning. They didn't get home until almost two in the morning. They had such an exciting night.

Matthew did well, last night. Some of it was from the craps table but most of it was from poker. Susan was by his side, well, sitting right behind him. Each time he received a down card, he didn't look at it until she blew on it. This was starting to make the other players very impatient but Matthew was using that to his advantage. Melinda, Henry and Anna were sitting well behind Matthew and couldn't see the table action but they knew when Matthew won each hand. He didn't win every hand but when he did, he'd upped the ante so much that each pot was rich. Henry was sitting between both Melinda and Anna and would lean into each and exclaim his amazement of this fifteen-year-old.

At the end of the night, after Matthew stood up, stretched and thanked all the players at the table, he turned to Susan and said, "Can I take you home?" Then he blushed at his own boldness.

"You might have to. I haven't seen John since you started playing Poker. Has anyone seen him?" She asks the three behind her.

Henry admits, "He was removed from the place for um . . . loitering." Susan cocked her head and raised an eyebrow in confusion. "Okay, he went a little too far with his comments and I clocked him. The bouncers assumed he was drunk, I think. They roughly tossed him out. I was going to stop them, but he was still threatening me."

Susan starts to laugh. "I wish I could have seen it. Did he see it coming?" Henry shakes his head no. "I hate to tell you this but my cousin doesn't forget or forgive easily, so you'd better watch your back." She looks to Matthew. "Sir, I would be in your debt if you would escort me home."

"Nothing would make me happier." He held out his arm for her and they all headed to the parking lot. To give Matthew a little privacy, Melinda goes home with Anna and Henry. They were happy for Matthew, that he won and found a girl.

"Susan better be careful," Henry warned as he drove to the Camp. "If she gets with Matthew, he might be the one giving birth." The girls laugh as this private joke keeps going.

When they walked to the hut, Melinda turned to Henry, "Did I thank you for getting rid of my unwanted date? It was awfully nice of you. Anna, can I give him a kiss on the cheek as a thank you?"

Anna smiled, "Just a quick peck, I want him all to myself for a few minutes."

"I don't blame you, at all, Anna." Melinda tippy toed a kiss on his cheek.

Melinda quickly bid them goodnight and went in the hut.

Anna turned to Henry and put her arms around his neck and says, "How do I love thee, let me count the ways . . ."

Henry continues the sonnet, "I love thee to the depth and breadth and height my soul can reach." Anna couldn't let him go any further, her mouth was on his. She couldn't control herself any longer.

"Anna, you must stop. We will have our time, I promise."

"Henry, I don't think I'll be able to wait. Don't you want me"

Henry just laughed. "Anna, if you knew how hard it's to not to make love to you, each and every time you smile. I'm doomed, my love."

Anna smiled at this thought. "Why are we waiting? I'm so in love with you, I know that we will together forever, but I want forever to start NOW!" She looked in his smoky eyes. "Henry Francis Harrick, I want you to make love to me. I don't want to wait any longer." She's keeping eye contact, but blushing just a bit.

"You are serious, aren't you? But what about being a good girl? I don't want you to do anything you'll regret."

"Henry, we will be married someday, right? I mean, that week you were talking about is almost over, isn't it?"

"I think you are right. It's time . . . time for you to go to bed!" He turns the knob of the door and for the third night this week, he pushes her inside. "I love you, see you tonight." He whispers.

Anna wanted to wait up for Matthew to see how his drive with Susan went but she couldn't do it.

Now, it's morning and her Ma comes in with cups of coffee in both hands. "Girls, you are going to be late for work if you don't get started. Did you see what Matthew did with is winnings, last night?" This gets both girls up.

"We went to bed before he got home. What did he do?" Asks Melinda as she sips her coffee sitting in bed.

"Well, you must come look. I can't wait for your Pa to see it. Matthew is still sleeping. I didn't want to wake him, since he isn't going to the fields today."

Both girls follow their Ma, out of the bedroom. On the kitchen table, Matthew placed one bill at a time, in rectangles from the outer rim of the table inward. There are seven rectangles on the table, in all. It must have taken him a while to do this, but it's an impressive display. Their Pa is coming out of the bedroom.

"Good morning, Judd dear, come look at this." Judy whispers while beaming. "Our boy did good last night from what I can see."

"Oh, boy, he sure did!" Judd is smoothing down his bed messed hair. "That boy has true talent! How much do you think it's?"

Matthew says from the couch, without getting up. "One hundred and twenty-six dollars. Leave me the twenty-six for the next game night and you put the rest in the valise, Pa. We'll have that Farm back, before you know it."

"Pa, Melinda is getting paid today and I get paid tomorrow, we'll be able to give you most of that, too." Offers Anna.

"I'm so grateful, my sweethearts, but I cannot take your wages." Judd shakes his head no as he says this."

"Well, that makes no sense at all, Pa. We gave you the harvest money, you are still taking Matthew's harvest money and now his winnings but you won't take from us?" Melinda makes a strong argument. "Explain that logic to me, Pa."

"Can I go with, because I said so?" They all laugh. The girls both kiss him on the cheek and head back to the bedroom to dress for work. Judy and Judd do their morning routine and Matthew watches from the couch, again, praying that life can stay as good as it's, right now.

At seven-thirty, the girls are in Pa's truck and headed downtown. Melinda is driving. "We didn't get to hear Matthew's story of what happened with Susan, last night. He was so smooth with her, wasn't he? It was like watching Errol Flynn, Tyrone Powers or Cary Grant."

"I really like Susan. She's very funny. I think she fits right in with us, don't you? Now if we can only find someone for you, Melinda, we will be all set." Anna was about to suggest Mark, Susan's brother-in-law but before she can, Melinda interrupts her thoughts.

"Whoa, wait a minute, Sister, I told you that I've no desire to settle down! I don't plan on hanging on here for very much longer. I've told you that. Don't you believe me?"

"I don't want you to leave. I want you to be around to watch me get married and babysit your nieces and nephew."

"Well, you'd better do all of that quick, because I'm not sticking around." Melinda says as she pulls in front of Kroger Grocery. "Oh, I'm so tired, today. I hope I can stay awake. Have a great day, Sis. See you at six." With that she's out of the driver's seat and into the store.

Anna slides over to drive when she sees that Melinda took the keys with her. Anna gets out of the truck and goes into the store. She calls out. "Melinda, you took the keys for the truck." Melinda comes out of the stock room and looks surprised to see Anna. "Did you hear me? You took the keys. I can't drive to work."

"Why are your legs broken? It's only two blocks away. If the truck stays here, I can drive it to pick you up after my long day."

"Well, I like that idea. Okay, keep the truck, it's a beautiful morning and I'll be cooped up in the hot kitchen all day. I can get my fresh air now. We should have talked about it first, though." She sees Joan coming out of the bakery. "Good morning, Joan. How are Stacy and the twins?"

"They're improving by the hour. Praise God. Athena is still so tiny. She can hardly suckle at the breast but Diana does beautifully. My poor Stacy ends up lopsided with one breast drained and the other not. It looks funny, too."

"I'm glad that Athena is hanging in there. I'm off to cook, have a great day. See you tonight, Melinda."

On her way to the diner, she stops at Haberlein's, known as 'The Corner Clothier" to see if she can get Henry something. She walks around for a while before a girl approaches her and asks if she can help her find something. "I'd like to get my boyfriend a little something. I think he'd look dashing in a new hat." The girl shows her several items before she picks out a black Fedora made by Stetson with a red silk band. It costs Anna six dollars but she's confident that he'll love it.

Anna's day in the kitchen is the hardest yet. She knows it's from the lack of sleep. She's having trouble keeping up with Ted's instructions. He asks her, repeatedly, if she's okay. She explains that she didn't get a good night rest, and that's all.

When they're, finally, on their way home, Anna says, "Did I mention to you that Henry and I are taking Ma and Pa out to eat at the Diner on Sunday? It was all Henry's idea. I cannot wait until she sees the menu that I'm trying to learn."

"How nice, Ma hasn't had a meal out in a very long time. She deserves it. We should all go. I can afford to pay for my own meal and so can Matthew."

"In that case, we should ask Frank, also. I get paid tomorrow, so we should be able to swing it if we all pool our funds. I just don't want Ma & Pa to pay. I want to do it, and cook their meals for them. I cannot wait!"

"That sounds so nice, Anna, I look forward to it. Matthew has enough money, that he can invite Susan. Ma would love her! Or do you think that's too many people? You don't need to cook the meals for everyone, just Ma's."

"That sounds like heaven, Melinda, almost like a party." Anna is pulling into the Camp lot. "I'm looking forward to it. Boy, I'm tired. Henry is coming over tonight and I bought him a fedora hat. I can't wait to give it to him. But I almost wish I could just go to bed, I'm just so beat."

"Splash lots of cold water on your face. You'll catch your second wind as soon as you hear his silky voice."

"He does have the sexiest sound, doesn't he? When he left Hope, his voice was going through the change, remember? He sounded like a frog sometimes. My poor Henry. He was going through hell. His mom was gone, his dad was sick, the farm was failing and his voice was going through puberty all at the same time. No wonder he wanted to leave Hope and never return. Wow, that's why he doesn't want to go back. All it was, was bad memories for him. I finally understand my poor Henry."

"Well, I didn't have any of those problems and I don't want to go back, either. Henry and I are similar that way. Forward is our only direction."

They walk into the hut. Anna puts down her things and goes straight to the pump to splash water on her face. To her surprise, Henry, Frank, Matthew and her parents are all in the tiny kitchen.

"Oh, Henry, I didn't think you'd be here this early. I wanted to change out of these work clothes and freshen up a bit." She looks from face to face. They all are looking at her.

Judy is the first to speak, "Come on, everyone, let Anna freshen up in private and we'll just be in the living room." They move as told.

Melinda comes in the room now. "What's going on?"

Matthew speaks up. "Henry and I were just telling Frank, Ma and Pa about the poker game, last night."

Melinda says, "Did you tell them that you have a girlfriend?" She smiles, as he blushes.

"Susan isn't my girlfriend, quite yet. I did ask her for a date tonight, though. She said yes."

"Of course." Melinda mocks him. "You are a Lady's man, Matthew, a regular Lady's man."

After Anna washes up, she goes and changes into a pretty blouse and skirt. She took her hair out of the tight bun but still has it gathered high on top of the head with a beautiful ribbon and a bow. When she comes out of the bedroom, Henry walks over to her and gives her a kiss on the cheek. "Do you feel fresh, now?"

"Yes, thank you. So, what's going on, are you and your father staying for dinner?" She sits down on the couch. Melinda, is changed and finally out of the bedroom, also.

Henry says. "Anna, I was wondering. What are you doing, say, the Sunday after next?"

"Nothing that I know about. What do you have in mind?" He comes and sits down, next to her, and takes her hands in his.

"Well, we were talking about timing, last night, do you remember?" She isn't sure what he means so she shakes her head no. "Silly girl, I said that I'd only be able to last about another week of just being your boyfriend and you told me that my week was up, do you remember that?"

"Yes, but what does . . ." She looks around the room, everyone is paying attention to every word. She feels herself blush. "I don't understand . . . Henry, that was a private conversation."

"Anna Rose Masters, will you marry me on the Sunday after next?

We can ask the preacher if he's available and then, you'll be all mine."

Anna just looks around the room. "Did he just ask me to marry him?"

Matthew speaks up, "Yes he did, but you haven't answered him. What, don't you like that day, I'm sure Henry will marry you any day you pick."

"I'll marry you this Sunday if you want, then we can all go to the diner for the dinner to celebrate. Anna, what will it be? Will you have me, and love me, until death us do part?"

"Oh, yes, Henry, yes, I'll marry you – this Sunday or next, as soon as that Preacher can say his words, I want to be all yours, forever."

Henry hasn't let go of her hands. He looks down at them. "I don't have an engagement ring for you yet, but I'll make it up to you. I saw an ad in the *EL Dorado Times* for the Kimball Diamond Company on Central, we can look there to see if you like anything. There's also Kirkpatrick's on Main St."

"Henry, I don't want jewelry, I want you to kiss me, right here, right now." She stands up, as does Henry.

He takes her face in his hands and says, "Your wish is my command. You've made me so happy." Then he kisses her, very sweetly, but she puts her arms around his neck and kisses him back with all her heart.

After a moment or two, they hear an "Excuse me. Do we get to kiss the bride-to-be?" It was Frank, standing behind Henry, with tears in his eyes. "You've made an old man, so very happy." He kisses her cheek. Then it's a free for all, everyone is up and kissing Anna and shaking Henry's hand. Matthew, of course, hugs Henry.

"Now, I can call you my brother, and mean it." Matthew says.

"Why, didn't you mean it before?" Henry ruffs up his hair.

"Not as much as I do now. Listen, I'm late for my date with Susan. I've got to run." He says as he runs his fingers through his hair to put it back together.

"Take the truck, it will be faster!" Henry calls after him.

Judy is back in the kitchen at the stove. She didn't kiss Anna like everyone else did. Anna goes to her, "Ma, do you need help with dinner?" Judy turns around, tears streaming down her cheeks. When Anna sees them, she hugs her, tightly. "Mama, don't cry. I'm sorry, do you want us to wait?" Judy cannot talk. She just shakes her head no. "Well, what is it Ma? Tell me," she lowers her voice, "Don't you like Henry?" Judy's tears turn to laughter.

"Henry has been like a son to us, his whole life. I knew he was the one for you, but you had to see it for yourself. I'm so happy for you, Anna. I prayed every night for this. Now, you're going to leave us and start your own family. I won't be bringing you coffee in bed in the morning or brushing out your hair at night. Nothing will be the same.

I'm so happy for you and so sad for me. I'm just an old fool who loves her daughter so very much." She cries in Anna's arms. Anna is crying, too.

Judd walks into the kitchen and sees his lovely wife and her look-a-like daughter crying in each other's arms. "There's only so much a good man can take." He says to them. "I've had to wait thirty minutes too long for my supper, and now you two are standing there, watering it down?" That's all it takes for them to stop crying. Judd has spoken. He walks over to them and embraces them both. He whispers, "My heart breaks when I see those I love in tears." Then he adds loudly. "Let's get dinner on the table!!"

Henry walks into the kitchen, "How can I help?" Anna wipes her eyes and hands him a stack of plates. "What do I do with these?" He smiles. "Never mind, don't tell me, they go on this rectangle thing here, right?" Both women laugh, as he and everyone helps put the meal on the table.

After supper, Henry asks Anna, "Do you want to go for a walk, or go for ice cream?" He winks at her. "We do need to decide on a few details, without an audience." He nods at their families.

"Ma, we are going out for a drive and maybe some ice cream." Henry's arm is around her waist, leading her out. She suddenly remembers something. She dashes into the bedroom and comes out with a package.

"What's this?" He asks.

"I bought you a little something. A thank you gift for the beautiful cameo. It isn't much but . . . open it now, before we leave."

He takes it from her hands and unwraps it. "Anna, I've never had a fedora of this quality before. It's beautiful. Can I see it in a mirror?" He puts it on his head and Anna leads him into her bedroom. He stands at the doorway for a second. "I've never been in your bedroom before." She smiles.

"Well, come on in, here is the mirror." He sits on the chair to look in the mirror. She looks at his reflection. "Dapper, dashing, engaging, no engaged!"

He turns to face her, "I love it, Anna. I love you, Anna." He looks at the beds. "Which one is yours?" Anna points to the one on the right. "I thought so. I can see you sleeping, there."

"And how do you do that, are you one of those window peepers? She feigns being frightened.

"Of course not, I'd have to get a milk crate to peep in those high little windows. And what would I see? The ceiling?"

"Sounds as though, you've tried."

"Anna," he winks at her, "our ice cream is melting."

"Yes, of course, let's go." She takes his hand and leads him out of the room and out of the hut. As soon as they get outside, she stops and turns to him, "You've made me so happy."

"This is just the beginning, sweetheart." They walk hand in hand to his truck. He opens the door for her. As she puts her foot on the running board, she turns and kisses him, sweetly at first, then with more passion.

"Get in the truck, Anna, or I'm going to take you right here."

She does as he commands. He goes around to get in from his side. She slides over to lay her head on his shoulder, and she sighs. "This is the spot." She's nuzzling his neck, then kissing it.

"Anna, I need to drive, don't I?" She stops and he starts the truck and backs it up and pulls out of the camp. She's back nuzzling his neck and now she has her hand on his thigh. "Anna . . . " He pleads. She starts kissing his neck now, and her hand is moving up his thigh. "Anna, I'll go off the road if you continue . . . oh . . . stop, I won't be able to control myself, I'm warning you."

She stops and lifts her head from his shoulder. "Henry, I want you. We are going to be married in a few days, and I'm going to have you. Now pull over."

He looks for a good spot. It's dark out now, so, they're all good spots, if they're off the road. He pulls over and shuts off the engine. Before he turns to her he says, "Anna, if you have any doubts about what we are doing, just tell me and I'll pull back. I hope I'll be able, I want you so bad."

"I've no doubts, Henry, look at me." He turns his head. It's very dark in the truck but it looks as though he has tears in his eyes. "Henry, do you want to talk for a bit, first?"

"Yes, I want to talk. I've questions for you. We have decisions to make. I want you right this minute, but we need a plan."

She moves over to the passenger side of the truck. "So, ask me."
"I know how close you are to your family. I don't want to ever tear you from them. Da needs me also. I'll ask Mark at the Camp store if he has a Hut with two bedrooms, like you have and then we can stay close to your family but still stay with Da. Would you mind?"

"No, Henry, I wouldn't want you to stop helping your father. If we can be close to my family. You saw my mother tonight. She's devastated, already."

"If we can get married the day after tomorrow, is there somewhere you can buy a proper white dress? If there's nothing in town, we can get married next Sunday. Do you think you can get a day off to drive up to Wichita, to buy one? I've Three Hundred dollars saved up for a rainy day. That should be enough to cover moving into a new hut, buying a brand-new bed, getting you a proper wedding ring set and you having the dress of your dreams."

"Henry, I'm marrying the man of my dreams. Nothing else is important." She hesitates. "Okay, I do want a new dress, but it doesn't need to be a gown, just a very pretty dress. And if you cooperate, we won't have to worry about it being white."

He tries to see her face in the darkness. "Anna, we should spend two or three days in Wichita for a proper honeymoon. I mean, you don't want to be keeping Da awake with the sounds of us making love, do you?"

"There are sounds to making love? What kind of sounds?" He can barely see her face but he knows she's serious. She slowly smiles, "Teach me to make those sounds, Henry." She moves back to the middle of the seat. She starts to unbutton her blouse. He puts his hand on hers stopping her from undressing. "Henry, I'm sure, I want you. You are my husband-to-be and there's no reason why we shouldn't. Henry, you're awful quiet over there, what are you thinking?"

"I don't want to make you pregnant, if we . . . do it?

"If we?" She asks. "Henry, I'll be your wife next week. Don't you want kids?"

"I cannot imagine a life with you without baby Anna's and baby Matthew's, but I would like to have you to myself for a while." He starts the engine and turns on the headlights so that the dashboard glows. "There, now I see you. Smile so that my heart sings."

She smiles and returns to unbuttoning her blouse. She keeps eye contact. Henry reaches to pull the ribbon that's struggling to hold her curls on top of her head. The curls cascade down onto her shoulders. He runs his fingers through her hair, just like he imagined doing, weeks ago. Anna unzips her skirt and removes it. She has on just her slip. He reaches for her and slips the shoulder strap off on one side. She looks down at it, and says, "Oops, how did that happen?" He reaches for the other side.

"Anna Rose Masters, I love you so much, you are the most beautiful woman I know. I promise to love you and take care of you and do everything in my power to make you happy." He's over her now. He starts kissing her again. She's practically purring under him.
"I love you, Henry Francis Harrick, and I obviously, cannot wait until I'm your wife. I want to do everything in my power to make you happy." She arches up to kiss him as passionately as she knows how. Without hesitation, she gives herself to him. Henry was very loving and gentle but worried about hurting her.

Afterward she says, "I didn't expect it to feel like that." She says it with no emotion.

"Anna, I'm sorry, I couldn't stop. I wanted you so bad. I cannot wait until our marriage bed, so we can do this as often as we want, and not worry about getting with child.

"Henry, I wanted you, also. I didn't want you to stop. In fact, I want you to do that to me again." She smiles at him. "Can you?"
Henry takes a moment to answer. "Anna, let's get some mint chip, while

I recharge. I love you." He reaches for her and she kisses him with the continued passion of before. She isn't satisfied, but at least she isn't sorry. "I cannot wait until you feel your first explosion. You are going to be so surprised."

"Women explode?" She asks while she's dressing. "How?"

"It happens inside you, Anna, I'm pretty sure that didn't happen for you this time, but I'm willing to keep trying if it takes thirty or forty years." She's dressed and is putting her hair back into the ribbon.

"Should I bob my hair, like Susan's? Her hair looks like she stepped out of Hollywood. I wonder who did it for her?"

Henry is finished dressing. "Your heart shaped face would look good with that style. If you want to cut your hair, you should. You have beautiful hair. Just leave me enough to run my hands through it." He thought of something else but is hesitant to say it. "Anna, this might shock you, but I'll say it anyway. Leave enough hair that when we are making love and you are on top, your hair tickles my face."

Anna tries to imagine this in her mind and she feels a quiver run through her insides that reaches her toes.

"Oh, Henry, I think I know what you mean about the explosion thing. I just felt something like that and you weren't even touching me." He looks over to her. She looks as if she just stepped out of a salon.

He smiles at her, "How beautiful you are!! Are you ready for that ice cream?"

"I'm dying for some ice cream, and as you say, it's melting as we speak"

He pulls out into the road and continues to town. She's looking out the window smiling. "A penny for your thoughts?" He asks.

"I'm trying to think where to get a dress for my wedding. I don't think Ted will like giving me any time off. I just started. We might not get a two or a three-day honeymoon. I was thinking, since the Camp is nearly empty, couldn't we use the two-bedroom hut while Da lives in the one bedroom until we are ready for him to join us? We will have all the privacy we need, and I won't miss work."

"That's good, Anna. We might be able to do that for a week, maybe. I might be tired of doing that to you by then."

"You better not be! Remember, I'm in this for the long haul."

When they get to the Central Avenue Soda Shoppe they see Pa's truck. Anna says, "I don't want to see Matthew, right now. I feel like he'll know what we just did."

Henry says, "And plan on doing, again, right after the ice cream, might I add."

Anna blushes. "See, Matthew will know, look how I'm blushing."

"Your little brother might have lost his virginity tonight before you did, silly girl. He's too smooth to be minus some action."

"Don't say that, he's just a kid."

"Well, imagine that he has come here to cool off and recharge like we are doing. Then you won't feel guilty."

He gets out of the truck and goes to her side. Again, she steps onto the running board and has her mouth on his. Simply insatiable, he thinks.

He breaks loose, and gives her his arm and they walk in the shop. Anna doesn't look toward Matthew but keeps her eyes toward the front of the store as Henry orders.

"Anna, there you are! I told Susan that you'd be here. I told her about your engagement." Matthew is saying it so loud that everyone in the shop hears it. Anna walks over to them. Susan is once again, perfectly coiffured and elegant.

"Hello, Susan, I'm glad you are here. Do you know where I can buy a dress for my wedding? Is there anywhere in EL Dorado or nearby? And I think I'd like to get my hair cut like yours. Where do you go?"

"For a dress, there's Milady's on the outskirts of town that's where my sister bought her dress. I get my hair done in Wichita. The girl I go to is booked for weeks ahead of time. She trained in Hollywood, and worked on the set of the Gay Divorcee Movie. She's just fabulous. I could call her for you and see if she can get you in as an emergency. Matthew said that you are going to try to get married the Sunday after next? That's very quick."

"I'd marry him tonight if we could get a preacher! I don't think I want to pay a lot for my dress or hair. It's not like we are having a big wedding. It will be just words in the barn where the social was, I imagine."

Henry is delivering her mint chip and hears her say the last part. "Anna, I want us to be married in the church, not the barn. I want you to have a dress fit for a queen, and if you don't want to cut your hair, you should wear it up in lots of curls like you did on our first date. But if you want to get your hair cut, please don't let the money stop you. This is the most important day of your life and I want it perfect for you."

Before Anna could answer, Susan says, "Oh Anna, he's a keeper. It's a good thing, I didn't see him first. Sorry Matthew, but your brother is great."

Matthew answers with his ice cream spoon still in his mouth. "I know, I taught him everything he knows." They all laugh. Henry mock punches him in the jaw. "I did. He was nothing before I started with him."

Anna leans over to kiss Matthew. "I'm so grateful to you."

"As you should be, Anna. And if he forgets any of the lessons, I taught him, send him back, I'll give him a refresher course, he'll never forget." Henry just raises one eyebrow, while he busily eats his ice cream.

"Anna, I can take you to Milady's tomorrow, if you like. She does have dresses from last year that she marks down, considerably. You have a perfect figure so alterations won't be a problem."

"I work all day tomorrow. Sunday is my only day off. This is going to be hard to plan, if I cannot get some time off. Maybe Ted will let me work some evenings, so I can get what I need bought during the daytime. I'll ask him tomorrow. Is Milady open on Sunday, by any chance?"

"I don't think so but I can call them tomorrow and let you know. I know that there are wedding dresses at JC Penney's for the cost conscience, and they're open on Sundays. I used to go to Hazel Smith's Beauty Shop in town, before I changed to this style and Hazel is quite good. I'm sure she could do your hair like this, and it won't cost nearly as much and she is open evenings, too. I'll call her tomorrow, also."

"I wish we had a phone at the Camp. Can you call the diner tomorrow after you've called the other places?"

"I'll do you one better. I'll come for coffee and pie and a quick chat with you there, even if I've to stand next to you by the grill."

Anna laughs, "She isn't just some grill, she's Big Bertha and she's hot! I would love it if you could help me in this way. This is so kind of you Susan. I'm so grateful." They're finished with the ice cream, so Anna stands up. "We must go. Susan, can I ask . . . um, how old you are?"

"Of course, I just turned seventeen."

"You look and act much older, I mean you are so sophisticated." Anna blushes as she tries to compliment Susan.

"Thank you, that's so nice of you to say so. Matthew told me he isn't sixteen, yet. I like being the older woman, makes me feel so wanton. Matthew is more mature than so many men out there, and smart. That's why John likes working with him. He can think fast on his feet."

Matthew asks, "Have you seen or heard from John since last night? We are worried. He might try to do something stupid because of the punch yesterday."

"No, I haven't, I tried to call him today, but either he wasn't home or just didn't want to answer his phone. The rat should have inquired if I made it home from the games, even if he did get punched. I plan on giving him a piece of my mind when I see him, and try to talk him down from whatever ledge he's currently on."

Henry says, "Tell him that I feel bad about punching him, if you think that helps. I've always tried to get along with him, but he has put up walls, the whole time. I cannot figure him out." Henry is standing, also, to leave. "I'll meet with him if he likes. Matthew and I, if he prefers. I just want to patch this up, before it gets any worse. I'm sorry to say; I don't trust him. He was shouting that he'll make me pay. I believe he'll try, so whatever you can do to help will be appreciated." He puts out his hand for her to shake it. She laughs and takes it from him and shakes it.

"You have class that goes with your charm and good looks. That must be John's problem with you, Henry, you are perfect!" She turns to Matthew, "You did a really good job, Matthew."

They say good-bye and get out of there as fast as they can. "I thought we were going to be stuck there all night. I want Susan's help but she's a talker! I'm glad, that I saw you first. She's a bigger flirt than Melinda. And I wanted to pull Melinda's hair out every time she looked at you." He gives her a confused look. "Melinda and you, have more in common." She explains. "She's ten times sexier than me, with her ample curves. I'm still surprised that you didn't try to date her."

They get into the truck and she slides over to the center so that she can put her head on his shoulder, as he drives. He's so tempted to tell her about Melinda, have a clean slate with her, if she can forgive him. He's lost in his thoughts and Anna is very quiet also. He calls her name, but she doesn't answer. He finds an area, to pull over, she doesn't wake up when he pulls on the noisy gravel. He just sits there, watching her sleep. *Oh, God*, he thinks, *why do I love her so much? God, let me grow old with her.* He adjusts her so he can kiss her. She responds to his kisses with closed eyes.

"Henry? I'm so tired. There's nothing I want more than to make love to you and fall asleep in your arms."

"Your wish is my command, my love." He tenderly takes her again.

Afterward, she's trembling under him. He did it. He got her to feel the explosion. He didn't want her to wonder how it feels. She deserves all he can give her. "Anna, I couldn't love you more. Will you be mine?"

"Forever, my love, I'm forever yours." She says smiling. "Now, if I can just lay with you and sleep the night away. I'm so tired." She says.

"Soon, I'll have you home and getting a good night's sleep. I just can't think how to do that just yet. My brains, seems to have disappeared for a moment."

"My poor Henry, what have I done to you?" She asks.

"Not enough, yet, my sweetheart. Not enough, yet.

FORTY

The Fourth Saturday in September, 1935
In EL Dorado, Kansas

Anna is driving down the highway in her Pa's truck all by herself. It's her sixth day in a row working at the diner. It's been twelve hours since she got engaged and ten hours since she became a woman in all ways. She has eight days to get a dress, a new hairdo, a church, a preacher, and a home, so she can have her man forever.

There's so much to do. She's worried that Ted will tell her that she cannot work nights. If she can't get to the shops, she doesn't know what she'll do. Susan and Melinda will help, surely, but it's her wedding. She needs to pick out her dress, herself.

She's also worried about her mom. She has been crying since her engagement. Anna tried to comfort her as much as she could. "Ma, Henry and I are going to move into the hut just the other side of the outhouse. Frank is going to live with us. We are never going to be away from you. Henry promised. I promise. I would die before I stay away from you."

As she's driving and lost in thought, a car is on the side of the road and the driver is waving wildly in the middle of the road. *Oh, my God, is that John?* She thinks. She slows the truck down and lowers the window to ask what's the trouble.

John walks up to her window. "Hey Anna, I've got a problem. Can you help a guy out?" He has two black eyes and a huge bandage across his nose. *Oh, Henry was right. He did break John's nose.*

She looks at the car, she hasn't seen this one before. It looks like a newer Model A. "Is something wrong with your new car?"

"Yes, the radiator overheated. Do you have any water in the truck?" He's standing on the running board as he looks in the truck. "Melinda not with you, today?"

"No John, she doesn't work on Saturdays. And I'm going to be late for my job, I don't have any water for you. When I get to town I can call someone for you." She's getting nervous. She has seen overheating radiators. They usually smoke or steam quite a bit. This one isn't.

She's about to ask him if he'd get off her running boards when someone jumps into the truck from the passenger side. "Wait, who're you? Get out of my Pa's truck!" She yells at him. He just smiles. "What are you deaf? Get out of the truck!" She turns to John, "John please, ask him to get out."

"I cannot do that, sweetheart. He's here to help me get even with the nose breaking asshole. I was hoping that Melinda was with you."

195

The guy in the truck reaches past Anna and opens the driver door for John. He pulls Anna over so John can sit down behind the wheel. Then the stranger gets out of the truck but stays on the running board holding the door so she can't escape. John starts to drive away. Anna pleads some more. "John, Henry is very sorry about hitting you. Did you talk to Susan? She has a message from Henry saying that very thing.

"Like I give a shit, if that asshole is sorry! I want to hurt you and Melinda to make Henry pay. Oh, well, I'll settle on the fact that Henry isn't going to see his precious little Anna ever again."

Anna knows he's serious. She tries to grab the steering wheel and ram the truck into something so he cannot take her somewhere. *There are no trees when you need them in drought-weary Kansas.* As she's struggling for the wheel, he grabs her by her bun and slams her forehead into the dashboard. She screams from the exploding blinding pain. She can feel liquid trickling down the side of her nose. She reaches up to hold her head and realizes that its blood from a large cut across her forehead. "John, you must help me. I'm bleeding." She says just barely above a whisper. "If you've ever cared about me, please don't hurt me."

He glares at her, grabs her bun again, tilts her head back then slams her into the dash again. This time he holds onto her hair that was barely a bun, now. He pulls her back again and looks at her. Now her nose is broken, he can tell. She puts her arms in front of her to try to defend the next slam. He smiles and let's go of her hair. "You're not so pretty, now, Anna. How can Henry love you now? How will anyone love you? You are all cut up and your nose is broken. I'm going to make you unrecognizable, before I'm through." He suddenly grabs her hair, again and slams her into the dash. He pulls off the main road and onto a dirt road.

Anna has never felt so much pain. She's so frightened but feels herself losing consciousness. She fights to stay focused and awake. She hurts so bad that she becomes detached from it. It's as though, she's above herself, watching the pretty heart shaped face girl get mutilated. *I need to fight him, somehow. But how? I can hardly breath through this broken nose. The pain is too bad to fight him. Let him kill me. I don't want to be so ugly that Henry won't love me.*

John has been driving for a long long time. She knows that she was out of it through most of it. It was out of her control. He pulls off the dirt road into more dirt. *What is he going to do to me now?* "Please, John, kill me, now. It hurts so bad. You are right. Henry won't want me like this. No one will. Please kill me." She sobs but it hurts too much to continue.

"Anna, why didn't you want me? Why didn't Melinda want me? Henry, that's why. He had the two of you dangling for a month, and you never knew. He doesn't want Melinda anymore, so I get his sloppy seconds?" He looks at her, "Maybe I won't kill you. Maybe I'll take you right here in your Pa's truck and he can have my sloppy seconds! I like that idea. Even if he still wants you, he'll always think of the fact that I was there before him! That's sweet revenge."

He reaches over and grabs her by her neck, with one hand and rips the front of her blouse with the other hand. She doesn't fight him. She's in too much pain, already. She thinks, *Let him use my body. I know Henry will never look at me again and say I'm beautiful. I'm so glad, that I had last night. Nothing John can do to me now, will harm me because I know what true love is.* John is pulling down her pants and panties. She's totally naked and her clothing is torn. She's just lying there waiting for him to do it and get it over with. Somehow, she isn't even afraid. She'd smile but her mouth is too swollen.

John looks down at her, "Damn, Anna, I should have had you while you were still beautiful. You are disgusting now." He's pulling down his trouser as he's saying this. "Take your blouse off the floor and wipe up the blood on your face." She takes the blouse but her face hurts so bad, she doesn't want to touch herself. "If you don't do it, I'll punch you right in the broken nose. That'll hurt more, won't it?

She starts to wipe up. *There's so much blood!* She feels sick to her stomach. She tries to say, 'I need to vomit' but she couldn't. She just turns her head to the floor and let's go. She uses the blouse to wipe her swollen lips.

"Jesus, Anna, how am I going to have you with vomit on the floor stinking up the truck. Get out of the truck. NOW!" He opens the driver's door and roughly pulls her out. She can barely stand. She looks around. *Kansas flat land as far as the eye can see. And not a soul, house or car in sight.* She holds onto the truck door for support, completely naked. "Lay down, I can't have you standing up. Wait a minute." He goes back into the truck for her pants, and he hands them to her. "Lay down and put those over your face. I can't look at you like that." Tears fall from her once innocent brown eyes and she does what he tells her to do.

She's in the dirt on the ground, with the pants on her face. He spreads her legs, and enters her. She doesn't make a sound but tears continue to fall from her eyes.

"Oh, so someone has beaten me to it? I thought I was getting a virgin, here. Well, put your experience to use, don't just lay there." She starts to move. She thinks, *this isn't making love or even sex. This is a mad dog with a bitch in heat. An animal in rut.* Suddenly, he stops and she can feel him filling her. *Damn, and Henry was worried about getting me pregnant.*

John rolls off her and takes her pants with him to wipe himself. He throws them into the front of the truck. Anna struggles to stand up. Her hair is down, bloody, and now encrusted with dirt. His seed is leaking down her leg. She doesn't care. She stands there waiting for him to finish what he started out to do, to kill her. Without a word to her he gets in her Pa's truck and pulls away, leaving her naked and alone. She sits back down. She hurts too much to try to walk anywhere. *Why bother? I can die right here.* He's gone for a few minutes. Suddenly, she sees Pa's truck heading for her with immense speed. *He's going to run me over with the family truck! I can't let him do that. That's their only truck and they wouldn't be able to use it again, if they knew it killed ME.* She starts to run. *This is pointless,* she thinks. *I've nowhere to go, nothing to hide behind. I cannot outrun even Pa's old truck.* She can hear the truck is slowing down and it's getting closer.

She stops running, and turns around to face her killer, bent over and breathless from running. *I am going to die, now.*

Her last thoughts were, *'Thank You God, I Loved My life!'*

FORTY-ONE

The Fourth Saturday in September, 1935 cont'd
In EL Dorado, Kansas

Sally's Diner is having a very busy morning. Ted has been in front of Big Bertha since five-thirty a.m. and is watching the clock for Anna to arrive. He's so glad, his nephew, Mark recommended her. She isn't intimidated by the heat or the work. He needs a break. *Where is she?* He thinks, *I shouldn't hire pretty girls.* They fall in love and don't want to work. He's thinking more of his sister than Anna.

He remembered that she was so tired, yesterday, she could hardly keep up with the orders. Her boyfriend, Henry likes the late nights, his waitresses have told him. *He's a bad influence then, because she's late!*

The morning turns to afternoon, and Anna is a no-show. He never expected this from her, especially after only a week of work.

Around two o'clock, Susan comes into the diner and sits at the counter and orders a coffee and a slice of Apple pie. She says to Betsy, "Can you tell Anna, that Susan is here? She's expecting me. If she's too busy to come out, could I go back there and have a little chat with her?"

"Oh sweetie, she didn't show up today. Ted is fit to be tied!"

"I saw her just last night and she asked me to come in, today. I can't imagine why she's not here." She puts a dollar on the counter and starts to leave then decides to ask to use the phone. She explains, "My brother-in-law Mark works at the encampment, where Anna lives. He might be able to find out what is going on." Betsy hands her the phone and she makes the call.

"Mark, I'm telling you, something isn't right. She was so happy, last night about getting married and asking me to help her. Can you go to the Masters' place or Harrick' place and see if either know why she's not here? Your uncle Ted is ready to fire her! I'll wait here at the Diner. You have the number? Great, talk to you soon." She puts down the receiver and goes straight into the kitchen.

Everyone's back is to her. "Ted?" She says to Bruce, who turns and nods to the grill cook. Susan steps forward and repeats, "Ted?"

He turns around, "What the hell are you doing in my kitchen?"

"You might not remember me but I am . . . I was your nephew Mark's, sister-in-law. I have Mark going to look for Anna. Last night, she said that she had to work at nine a.m. so something is wrong. Mark is going to call me here with news. I thought I should tell you." She turns around and goes back to the counter. She's too nervous to eat her pie or drink her coffee.

The phone finally rings, and when Betsy hands it to Susan, Mark says, "Mr. and Mrs. Masters were very upset when I told them that Anna didn't arrive at work. She left for work at eight this morning!! Henry and Matthew are both out at the tomato field, today"

"Oh, Mark, this is bad. She was driving her Pa's truck, right?"

"I guess so."

"I'm going to drive out to the Camp and see if the truck got into an accident on the way to work. Can you call Miller at the field and get a message to Henry and Matthew?"

"Yes, I'm on it. I hope Anna is okay. I really like the Masters family, especially that beautiful Melinda."

"I hope so, too, and I especially like that cutie Matthew. I'm on my way. I'll come see you if I don't find the truck." She looks to Betsy. "Anna left to come to work at eight a.m.! Let Ted know, I'm going to look for her."

She's in her car and on the road driving slowly and looking down all the side streets. She makes it to the Camp, hardly passing a single vehicle. She goes to the store and asks Mark where Anna lives so she can get Anna's Pa to come with and keep searching.

Mark is very concerned and says, "Let me know if I can help. I've a bad feeling about this, too."

Anna's mother is crying and wringing her hands, when Susan introduces herself and says, "I was going to help Anna buy a wedding dress. She was so happy about marrying Henry. Can I take you to get Henry and Matthew or something?

Judd says, "No need. Melinda ran down and told Henry's Da. They're going to get them. I would like to retrace Anna's route with you again. If you don't mind?"

"I'm here to help in any way I can." She and Judd are almost to her car, when Frank Harrick pulled into the lot with Henry, Melinda, and Matthew.

When Henry sees Susan, he jumps out of the truck. "Susan, do you know where John is? I bet he has something to do with this! I know it. I'll kill him!"

"Oh Henry, John wouldn't do anything to Anna. I don't think." She starts to tremble. She never gave it a thought. She just assumed that Anna had an accident due to the lack of time behind the wheel. She suddenly, can picture John, with his broken nose, kicking the defenseless Anna. "Oh God, Henry, I pray you are wrong! Now, I'm really scared!"

Matthew speaks up. "Susan, can you do us a big favor? Let's go to the store and you call your cousin up and just ask him, how his day is going. Very casual." She nods and turns to walk to the camp store. They all follow her.

Melinda catches up with Susan, "You looked around for the truck on the way here, right?"

"Yes, of course, I looked down the side streets, too. Oh, Melinda, what if it's John? I'm beside myself with worry."

When they reach the store, Mark hands them the phone. He looks to Melinda, "I can't believe this is happening. I'm so sorry."

"Me too." She says. "My Ma is so very upset. She's been crying since Anna got engaged but now she's on the brink of hysteria. I'm going to stay with her, as soon as Susan talks to John."

They all watch as Susan waits on the line for John to pick up the phone. It just keeps ringing.

"Now what do we do?" Asks Melinda.

"Call the Sherriff's Department and have them question John." Susan answers. "The longer we wait, the worse it can be."

"I think Judd needs to go there and file an official missing report and then I'll go question John myself." Henry says this, as he runs his hand nervously through his already grown out hair.

"We will go question John together, brother. He's not going to get away with this." Matthew's anger is growing the longer his sister is out there, possibly in danger.

Frank holds up his arms. "Let's have a plan here, without violence. John might be innocent of this and you'll be wasting time on him, with no proof he's involved. I'll take Judd to the Sherriff's department." He pauses and looks around. "We only have my truck. We can't look and report at the same time."

Susan replies, "Take my car. I'll stay with Mrs. Masters."

Matthew kisses her cheek, "That helps, thank you. Susan.

"You can have my car, too. I'll close the store and help you look for her." Mark offers. Melinda kisses him on the cheek and he turns bright red. "Don't make a big deal out of it." He smiles at her nervously.

Henry takes charge, "Matthew take Susan's car and go with your father to the Butler County Courthouse on Central Avenue. You'll find the Sherriff's Department in there and file that missing person's report and tell them about John. Da, you and I'll go to town and ask around. Mark, you and Melinda, drive the path that she'd have taken, if you see anyone outside, ask if they remember seeing Anna, the truck or anything else suspicious this morning. Then take any back roads you can think of that Anna might mistakenly have gone down. She might just be lost, you know. Let's meet up at the diner in say three hours, gosh that's a long time, and let's regroup. Maybe we will concentrate on John at that point. Agreed?" They all nod.

Susan looks to Mark, "I'll stay with Mrs. Master, but can I have the keys to the store, so I can use the phone? If Anna shows up, I'll call the sheriff and the diner and get a message to you. If you don't have a message from me, when you go to the diner in three hours, call me here and tell me what the next plan of attack will be, please. I'll be with Anna's mom.

Matthew looks to her, "That's a great idea. I know we wouldn't even know that she's missing, this soon, if it wasn't for you. Thank you for everything." He bends down and kisses her on the lips. "I sure hope that you'll be calling and we are just wasting gas. Tell Ma, not to worry. We are handling this."

They all walk out of the store, Mark locks up. Before he tosses the keys to Susan, and says, "Here you go, sis."

She smiles, "You haven't called me sis, since . . ." She doesn't finish her sentence. *This is no time to think about my dead sister.*

She turns and goes to Anna's hut to stay with Judy. When she knocks on the door, Mrs. Master opens it up in a hurry. She's disappointed that it's Susan. "Sorry, dear, I was hoping that it was . . . good news."

"Well, Matthew and your husband are going down to the sheriff's office in my car. Henry and his dad are going to town to ask around. Melinda is going with Mark, my brother-in-law, to drive around to see if Anna is just lost or something."

Judy smiles a half a smile. "That's a good plan. Can I offer you a cup of coffee, Susan? This might be a long afternoon." She goes into the kitchen. Susan follows. The pot is already on the stove. She lights a match to catch the burner and turns to Susan. "Would you like to sit down?"

"Thank you, Mrs. Masters, but you don't need to entertain me. I'm just here to keep you company." Susan takes a seat at the table and Judy goes to a cupboard for a coffee cup. As she grabs one she hesitates, and Susan can hear her silently sob.

She gets control of her tears and says, "We are a funny family. One of the odd things we do is have our own coffee cups. We've all picked out our special one and no one else uses it." She reaches up for a flowered mug. "This one is for Anna Rose." She puts it on the counter and sniffles. She heads to the coffee on the stove, shuts off the burner, then pours Susan a piping hot cup. "Do you take cream and sugar, dear?"

"Yes, please. Mrs. Masters, she has only been gone a few hours. She might have gotten the idea to go to Wichita, wedding dress shopping. Or decided to get her hair bobbed like mine. She was asking me where I got mine done, last night. We might all be worrying for nothing."

Judy gets cream from the ice box and a sugar bowl before she sits down next to Susan. "It's not for nothing. Something terrible has happened. I've been feeling it for a couple of days. I keep having the feeling of NEVER-EVER seeing my Anna again." She starts to cry hard. Susan stands and hugs the sitting woman, from behind. Judy calms down enough to continue. "She kept saying that her getting engaged and married wouldn't separate us but I couldn't shake it off." Susan sits as Judy takes a sip of her own cold coffee. She puts her hand down on Susan's. "Thank you for being here. I needed to tell that to someone. I couldn't say it out loud to my husband or the children. It's just an awful thing to say, but it's what I've been feeling and it's been eating me up alive."

Susan is at a loss for words. What could she possibly say to this woman that looks just like her missing daughter? She just gives her a weak smile and sips her coffee.

"Mrs. Masters, we will see her again. I know it. Your Matthew and Henry won't leave a stone unturned, looking for her. They're very smart and very determined." She takes another sip. "I really like Matthew, I must confess. Those blue eyes make me weak in the knees." She blushes.

Judy laughs at that. "He has Judd's eyes. I've known that man for over thirty years, and those eyes haven't lost their effect on me. It's like he's looking through me, into my heart, mind and soul. If you're like me, it'll be something that you can't live without."

"Now, I see where Matthew gets his gift for turning a phrase! I'm older than him. I hope that doesn't bother you. I just turned seventeen, but he's so much more mature than men with years on him, that I've met."

"Well, all my children have had to take on a lot of responsibility since we lost our farm. It hasn't been easy on any of them."

"I don't get that sense from any of them. They all love this family, ferociously. Henry does, too."

"Well, he's been part of the family his whole life. Our farms were next to each other in Hope. Have you ever been up there?" Susan shakes her head. "No, well, it's heaven on earth, up there. Judd hopes to buy back our farm, someday. We'd like to get Matthew back in school too. He's very smart just not educated smart. His mind should be in business." She looks at her wristwatch and sees that hardly any time has passed. "Tell me about yourself, my dear. Have you lived here your whole life?"

"Yes Ma-am, born and raised. My daddy, got rest his soul, was a doctor. He was partners with Doc Johnson, and they started the EL Dorado clinic, together. This was before the Allen Memorial Hospital opened. My mom was their head nurse. Daddy volunteered in the army during the big war. They made him a Lieutenant, and he was in an Army hospital when it was bombed. My mom found out that she was with child, me, after his death. I was raised by my mom and her parents. She never married again. She still is at the clinic, volunteering a day or two a week."

"Well, that was your parents, now tell me about you." Judy smiles. "Are you still in school?

"No, Ma-am, I was in the last graduating class from the old Central

High School, before it was torn down and rebuilt. I was . . . I am a bookworm. I had tutors and I jumped a grade or two, and graduated two years early. Now, I work at the main Library downtown."

"You don't look anything like a librarian! I must admit, you look too sophisticated and pretty to be smart, too."

"Oh, thank you, Ma-am, but I never claimed to be smart." She blushes.

"You didn't have to." Judy replies with a smile.

The next two hours drag on, even though the women talk endlessly. Susan avoids mentioning her sister who died in childbirth, trying to keep things light.

Meanwhile, Matthew and Judd are at the Sheriff's Department at the Butler County Courthouse. They explain that Anna is missing and that John Walker threatened to get even with her fiancée. They're told that not enough time has passed for an official missing person's report. Matthew is ready to scream. "You don't understand. My sister would never go anywhere by herself." He slowly pounds the desk as he emphasizes each word to get the Deputy to understand. "She . . . has . . . never . . . gone . . . anywhere . . . by herself."

The sheriff's deputy quickly responds, "There's a first time for everything, kid. Now, the missing truck is another story. You can claim that your truck was stolen. If we find Anna or this Walker guy behind the wheel, we will bring them in for questioning as a suspect. That's the best we can do. Is that what you want?" The deputy was looking from father to son.

"Yes!" They both say at the same time. Judd continues, "My daughter had my permission to take the truck to the diner for work, but she isn't there so she has taken it without my permission. Arrest her, if you must, but find my truck, find my daughter. Please!"

Henry and his father are downtown going into all the shops on Main Street and Central Avenue. Anna had time to do a little shopping before work, but no one has seen her. They all promise to call the Sheriff if they saw Anna or the truck. Then Henry remembered about Milady's Bridal shop across from the Susan B. Allen Hospital. No one fitting Anna's description has shopped today.

Mark and Melinda drive the route to town several times, both getting out and asking people if they had seen Anna or the truck this morning. One old man told Mark that he saw two men, one short and one tall, parked on the side of the road at a little after eight a.m. this morning, but no truck or girl. Mark asked what the vehicle was that they drove and he said it was a newer Model A. Mark gasped, this is the kind of car that was seen the night of the robbery. They still had an hour left so they took all the wrong turns, that Anna could have possibly taken. Melinda didn't know EL Dorado was so big! Mark was going out of his way to help, and Melinda thanked him again. "It's nothing, I know what it's like to lose someone. But to never know how or why would be a hell all by itself. We must find her."

Each of the pairs, having exhausted every option, meet up at Sally's Diner to regroup. They discuss what to do next since everything so far has been futile, until Mark mentions the Model A sighting. Matthew and Henry both jump up! Melinda says, "It doesn't mean it's the same one."

Matthew says heatedly. "It doesn't mean – it isn't, either. One short man and one tall man? That describes John and his friend Pete." He explains to Mark, Judd and Frank that John has a secret '31 Model A that he uses, when he wants to go around unrecognized.

Mark says, convinced. "Then that's the missing proof we need, to question him!"

Then the diner phone rings and its Susan with Judy at the Camp Store. Henry gives them an update. Then adds, "We want to come get you, Susan, and go to John's house to see what he knows. Mr. Masters and my Da will get the store key and stay with Mrs. Masters. It's getting too dark out to do any other looking. So, we will see you in a little while." Henry sighs. He looks at his watch. It's been twenty-four hours since his engagement and their initial lovemaking. It's been twelve hours since Anna has been away from all those who love her. *What will he do if he can't find her? He must find her. He cannot live without her.*

FORTY-TWO

The Fourth Saturday in September 1935 cont'd
In EL Dorado, Kansas

Judd and Frank are with Judy. Everyone else, including Mark and Melinda are on the way to find John. Susan's car is in the lead. The plan is for Susan to drive up to John's front door, get out of the car and ring his front doorbell. They're going to be at all the exits in case he tries to get away. Henry and Matthew are ready to do anything to John to get him to confess. They're bringing Susan and Melinda to be the 'good' cops and try to get the information, in a nice way. Mark is there to help, however necessary. He assures them.

John lives on Locust Ave at the corner of Emporia. Susan let Matthew out of the car, two houses down from John's house. Everyone parks there and gets into place before Susan pulls into John's driveway. She walks onto the front porch and rings the bell.

John's house lights are all on, but it took multiple rings for him to answer. When he finally opens the door, Susan says, "John, I was worried about you. I heard about your broken nose and I've tried to call you, yesterday and today. Are you okay?" John takes one step over the threshold and looks to the right and left side of the porch. Susan can smell that he has been drinking. "What are you looking for, John?" She asks. He stares at her. "John, are you going to talk to me?" He holds out his hand to take hers. She instinctively pulls away.

"That's what I thought. Where are your friends, Susan? I know you are tight with that sucker-punch asshole and his adopted kid brother, Matthew. What do you want?"

"I was worried about you. Did you let Doc Johnson see your nose?" She pauses and waits for him to respond. When he doesn't, she tries a more direct approach. "Have you've seen Anna? She and I were going to go dress shopping but no one has seen her. Do you know anything about that?"

"Why would I know anything about your dress shopping with Anna? Is there anything else?"

"You didn't tell me how you are? That's what I asked you first. Is it natural for both eyes to turn black, like that?"

"Look at you, showing all this concern. You've hardly paid this much attention to me in the last two years. What gives?"

"She forces a smile. "Big fat liar! I've gone with you to lots of crap games and socials. I thought we were more than cousins. I thought we were friends." Susan sees that Matthew has gotten inside John's house, most likely through the kitchen door.

John turns to see what she's looking at. "I knew it! Look here . . . " He reaches forward and grabs her by her beautiful finger-waved curls. "You brought them here? What for?"

"Ow, John you're hurting me! Let go of me!" Matthew rushes toward him, but Susan takes her own action and uses the spike heel of her shoe to smash down on his bare foot. He lets go, yowls in pain and Matthew tackles him down just as Henry, Melinda and Mark rush in.

Mark thought to bring rope from the store so he ties up the wiggling John with Matthew sitting on him. Melinda is giving aid to Susan, who is very angry, but unhurt.

Henry begins, "John, we know that you had something to do with Anna's disappearance. Tell us where she is, and you won't get hurt here." He says this very calmly though he's trembling inside with anger and worry.

"I've nothing to say to anyone, and don't think that I won't press any charges against you. There are witnesses who saw you sucker punch me and now you are in my home to assault me further! You are looking at jail time, asshole."

Matthew says looking down. "Really John? You are going to the sheriff on us when we all know that you pulled the robbery at the paymaster's office?" Susan's eyes widen, as do Mark's, who now understands the importance of the "A" sighting. They can see that Henry and Melinda accept this as fact.

"That's bullshit, Matthew, I'm as innocent of that as you are!" John looks at his cousin. "You thought Matthew was cute and innocent, didn't you Susan? They have you brainwashed!"

Susan walks over to him. She looks at Matthew still sitting on him, then back down at John. "I haven't heard you tell us where Anna is."

"I'm not telling you anything, Bitch!" Susan gives him a swift kick right in the broken nose with the pointed toe of her shoes. John screams in horrific pain. Henry grabs her before she can kick him again.

"He knows where she is. He has done something to her! When he says, 'I'm not telling', it means he has something to tell." Henry looks at Susan. She's trembling and near tears.

"Mark, can you take Susan? She needs to step away for a minute. And I think it's time to get sheriff here. Do you know where his phone is?" Henry still sounds very calm. Susan points to the kitchen and Mark takes her by the hand and takes her to make the call.

Now it's just Melinda, Matthew and Henry with John. John is whimpering in pain from his re-broken nose. Henry smiles as he squats down to look John in the eye. "Your cousin, apparently isn't the type of lady, you should piss off, John. You should have known that about her. You've known her, for what seventeen years? She was supposed to be the 'good' cop, but I guess she cannot stand the thought of what you've done to Anna. Now, why don't you make it easy on yourself. Tell me where my Anna is or I'll bring Susan back."

"Go 'f' yourself." John writhed underneath Matthew. "And get him off me!!!"

Matthew looks down, "That's not happening. You need to tell us what you know about my sister Anna, or you won't be seeing the morning's light, my friend. I know you know. We know that you had the Model A out this morning. Did you stop her in the street, then take her somewhere?"

"Good guess, Matthew. Tell me another theory." Matthew grabs John's head by his curly hair so hard that his face is off the floor. Blood is dripping from his nose.

"Don't be an asshole your whole life, John. Where is she?" John is just able to grunt with Matthew holding his head in that position. "Wrong answer." Matthew slams John's face into the floor. He doesn't let go of him. He has his head pulled back, again, as far as it will go. "God, John, you're making a mess all over your own living room floor. Who's going to clean this up? If you tell us where Anna is, we will leave you alone. Until the sheriffs arrest you, that is. The sheriffs won't hurt you, though. You'll be safe in a little ten by ten jail cell. Doesn't that sound nice right about now? No 'Matthew on your back' and your nose healing from . . . how many breaks is this, Henry, I've lost track . . . maybe the state will take you to a hospital where they can put all the pieces of your nose back together again. Would you like that John?" John nods as best he can. "Good, I'm going to let go of your hair and you are going to give us the location of our Anna. That's the only thing I want to hear. If you cuss or give us any other kind of answer, your nose will no long be attached." Matthew turns John's head toward Henry who is squatting down and twirling a knife, point side down, on the floor in front of them. "See that man? He'd rather die than live without his Anna, and that isn't someone you play with, John. Are you ready to talk?" John nods a second time. Matthew lets go of his hair.

"She's where --- you'll never find her. I don't think I can find her, now, if I tried. You wouldn't want her now, anyway. Thanks to me, she'll never look the same. Your beautiful Anna, is dead and gone!"

"NOOOOOOO!" Melinda screams as Henry reaches over to cut John's throat. She pulls him away before the cut is too deep. "What if he's lying? She might be hurt and he's hidden her. We will never know with him dead!" She pleads.

Melinda gets down on the floor and gets very close to John. "John please, if she's gone, then tell us what direction to go to find her. We need to give her a proper Christian burial. Let my Ma and my Pa kiss their Anna good-bye before putting her in the ground. Please John, I beg of you!" Melinda is crying very hard. "Let us bury her, John, please." Henry is on his feet and pacing. He wants to kill him but Melinda is right. She might be hurt somewhere and they need John to tell them.

Mark and Susan are back from the kitchen. Everyone can hear sirens from police vehicles getting louder. Melinda is panicking, "John, there isn't much time. Did you drive toward Wichita? Did you go up North, down South, to the East or West? Give us a something to go on?" She sobs, hysterically.

John just grunts again. He loses consciousness as Susan is at the front door. She opens it for Sheriff Larkin Bailey and his deputies. Matthew is off John, since he's unconscious and not moving.

Mark goes to the sobbing Melinda and gently lifts her off the floor and takes her to the couch. He's cradling her as she continues to hysterically cry onto his shoulder, as his own silent tears fall to her hair. He knows that he cannot take her pain away and it's killing him. Susan is explaining to the officers that her cousin on the floor just admitted to beating and killing Anna, without telling them where her body is. Then she breaks down in tears, also.

***

The sheriffs have taken John's still unconscious body out of the house and into an ambulance. The sheriffs have everyone sitting in the living room for questioning. Matthew and Henry try to be cooperative but they want to go find Anna or her body.

Melinda says to Matthew, "What are we going to tell Ma?"

It's Henry that answers, "The God-awful truth. I couldn't protect her. She's gone because of me. If I hadn't hit him, she'd be alive now." Henry is sitting on John's couch with Matthew and Melinda. Mark and Susan are in the chairs across to them.

Susan says, "That's the most asinine thing I've ever heard you say, Henry! John was so rude and mean Thursday night that I was ready to punch him. He deserved what he got then and what he'll get now. And the worst part of the whole evening is that I've ruined my favorite pair of shoes." She holds out the right foot for all to see. "I'll never get John's blood off them. Totally ruined."

Mark knows her best and understands her nervous humor. Melinda sees that she's smiling. Matthew looks up and sees it, also. Melinda and Matthew look at each other and start to laugh. Mark joins them, then finally Henry.

Henry says, "Anna would have loved that joke!" For the first time since she has disappeared, Henry starts to cry. Matthew is next to him and holds him, and starts to cry, also. Melinda joins in and Mark and Susan reach to each other to hold hands, with tears in their eyes, also. They both know this pain of losing a sister and a love. They lost Sharon together.

The sheriff has John in an ambulance with an armed guard. He'll get immediate medical attention then to jail to be arraigned in the morning for the kidnapping and attempted murder of Anna. Without a body, they cannot get him on murder. They tell everyone to go home. "Maybe once this Walker is in front of the Judge, he might have a better memory of where he left Anna." One of the Deputies tells them. It's of little comfort.

As they were walking out, Melinda thinks of something and goes to Sheriff Bailey. "When he's awake, ask him where Pa's truck is. He might have driven it back from where Anna is."

Susan stops walking and says, "What if it's in his garage?" They all run to the back of the house to the garage. The sheriff is right behind them. He has his flashlight out and shines it into the garage's side window.

"Pa's truck!" Matthew and Melinda scream. The doors are locked. Matthew picks up a large rock and throws it against the window and glass shatters all over the floor in the garage. Henry helps him over the window ledge and Matthew uses Sheriff Bailey's flashlight to go unlock the big doors from the inside.

By the time the doors are open, more officers are there with their flashlights shining on the front of the truck. Melinda and Susan both start screaming. The driver's side headlamp is shattered and has blood and long hairs stuck onto it. Anna's long beautiful hair.

Henry feels as though someone punched him in the stomach and the air is out of him. His knees collapse under him. He's on the ground. He hears this awful, awful sound in the night. The sheriffs are searching the truck for Anna, but they're moving in terrible slow motion. He looks over to Melinda and Matthew. They were standing crying into each other. *Why won't that sound stop?* He looks to the headlamp again. His Anna, it can't be, he struggles to rise. He feels someone's hands under his arms trying to help him to his feet, from behind. He turned to see it was Mark. His mouth is moving, but it's in slow motion and soundless. Susan comes into view. She's slowly reaching for his face, and, her lips are moving without words too. *That awful sound is drowning out everyone's words.* He suddenly felt a sharp pain to his cheekbone and jaw. He blinks from the pain and the gut-wrenching sound stops. He looks at Susan.

"Sorry, Henry, you wouldn't stop screaming – 'NO." She rubs her reddened hand. She isn't moving in slow motion, anymore.

Mark is still holding him up. Henry manages to say, "I can stand now." His eyes go back to the headlamp. He wanted to go get his Anna's precious hair. *She wanted to cut it for the wedding but there it was: still long but soaked with her blood!*

FORTY-THREE

Friday, September 25th 1936
Kansas

Rosanne is so tired of just of being in the bed in traction. The morning was spent in water therapy, which would have been great if they didn't put a waterproof collar on her neck. She was still in great pain. Dr. Mason suggested that she stay another day or two. Rosanne didn't want any part of it.

Carolyn called and left a message for Rosanne that she isn't coming for a visit today. Carolyn never missed visiting. Something big must have come up. Dr. Mason swore to her that the Colonel was doing better, not out of the woods yet, but better. So, what could be keeping Carolyn?

Carolyn had called Dr. Mason in the morning and since he said that both patients were doing fine, she decided to accompany Eddie to EL Dorado to confer with the other Professor.

Professor Lark Bailey is very serious about starting a classroom project around a cold case. After all his years as Sheriff, he'd seen far too many cases go cold. He can't wait to hear the details of this case. All he knows about it's that it involves a found person who has amnesia. He isn't surprised when Professor James introduces him to Carolyn, he'd mentioned bringing her and possibly the 'found' girl also. He's told that Rosanne is in the hospital, due to a relapse of her neck injury.

Carolyn tells her story of finding Rosanne on the property. Eddie gives him the official Sheriff's findings as well as the extent of Rosanne's injuries. He mentions that he had a sketch drawn as Rosanne looked at the time she went missing, and hands him a copy. The last thing that he mentions is the headlamp damage on the old Ford truck and the possibility of her being presumed dead.

Retired Sheriff Bailey, sits back in his chair, the sketch in his right hand, and his left hand rubbing his chin in thought. He looks at Carolyn and asks her to repeat the date she found Rosanne.

"I found her on Sunday, September 29th of last year."

Professor Bailey, still rubbing his chin, puts down the sketch. He says, "Well, I'm very disappointed that my classes won't be able to participate in this case."

Carolyn and Eddie just look at each other in total despair. Eddie is about to object when Professor Bailey gets up and walks to the doorway and calls to his secretary, "Helen, get me Sheriff Sam Johnson on the phone. Tell him that I found Anna Rose Masters. She's alive. Get him over here right away."

The two sitting in the office, are dumbfounded. "You know who Rosanne is?" is Carolyn's first question but she doesn't wait for an answer. "Who is she? What happened to her? Why is no one looking for her?"

"We have a confession from Anna's killer, we had the murder weapon, the 1926 Ford Model T Truck covered in her blood and long hair. He said he didn't know where he dumped the <u>dead</u> body. We had search parties out in a sixty-mile radius, for weeks. Her fiancé, I'm told, still drives into deserted territories looking for her body."

"Her fiancé? She was engaged?" Carolyn knows her brother will be crushed. "Rosanne, I mean, Anna was right, she did have a long-lost love. She always knew it."

"Yes, he asked her to marry him, just the night before she disappeared. I've seen many a husband face the death of their love but Henry took it the hardest, I've ever seen. He refused to believe she was dead, even after he and her brother beat the confession out of her killer!"

"She has a brother, too?"

"She has a brother, a sister and parents. All wonderful people. They were roaming the harvests and were here for Grant Johnson's tomatoes. After the tragedy, they didn't want to leave EL Dorado, so Grant let them stay in his encampment, rent free. The community reached out to them, too. Since their only vehicle was used to kill her, the town held a charity event and raised $250 to buy them a good used truck to replace the one that killed Anna."

He goes back to the doorway, "Helen, did you talk with Sam?"

"Yes, Professor, he said he'll be here in a jiff. He was going to swing by Anna's place and see if anyone is home."

Carolyn looks at Eddie. "Could this be happening? Did we find Rosanne's family?" She kisses Eddie before the retired Sheriff turns back to them.

"Aw, Carolyn, I really didn't do anything. We just got extremely lucky." Eddie says, embarrassed.

"Looks like the family might be on the way. I'm going to see if I can find and open an empty classroom. Too bad your Rosanne couldn't be here." The Professor leaves the room.

"Eddie, this is going to be too much information for Rosanne. We must break this to her gently. She gets a head-ache when she gets overwhelmed and with her new neck injury . . . I don't know the best way to . . . tell her."

"Well, let's start with us, meeting her family. Take it one step at a time." Eddie advises.

In a few moments Professor Bailey comes back in the room. "I've a small classroom, available. Gather up your things, I'll bring you there."

As they're walking down the corridor, Eddie asks, "You said you have a confession from her killer? Was he convicted?"

"Oh, yea. Easiest case the county ever prosecuted. He got life in prison. I guess we must do something about that since she's alive. Or, maybe he won't find out. He's over in Leavenworth Prison."

Carolyn is getting very nervous. A part of her didn't want to believe that Rosanne was this Anna. *I want to keep her, take care of her, have her take care of the Colonel, maybe marry Joshua. All of that's over. As much as I wanted to help Rosanne, it feels like Rosanne will no longer be. She'll be Anna now, Anna Rose Masters, with parents, a brother, a sister, a fiancé and many friends in this town.*

"Professor?" Both Eddie and Sheriff Bailey turn to answer her. "Did Anna cook in a restaurant, by any chance?"

"Yup, she worked about a week as a short order cook at Sally's Diner. Best meatloaf in town." Professor Bailey answers. He can hear a commotion back by his office. "Wait a minute, I think someone is here." He leaves the room and comes back with six very anxious people plus the current Sheriff and his Deputy.

Professor Bailey begins. "Sam, did you tell them?"

"I just said that we have a strong lead on Anna. I didn't know anything else."

"Please everyone be seated." They move the chairs around so that everyone is facing each other in a big circle. "Let me start with introductions." Sheriff Johnson and Deputy Willard take a seat also. "This is Judd and Judy Masters, their second daughter Melinda and their son, Matthew. This is Frank Harrick and his son Henry, who is Anna's fiancé. This is Miss Carolyn Lewis from Lawrence, Kansas, and Professor Edward James from Washburn University in Topeka. And of course, our current Sheriff Sam Johnson and his Deputy James Willard.

"Anna was found by Carolyn on September 29th, last year. She was barely alive but is now living with Carolyn in Lawrence. She goes by the name of Rosanne. Because of severe head injuries, she has no knowledge of who she is, but she's alive!"

They all talk at once. Henry stands up, looking around, "Where is she, is she here, now?"

Carolyn speaks, "No, Henry, she's in a clinic in Lawrence. She had a relapse of the neck injury from . . . we refer to it as 'the accident'. I just want to say, I'm very, very fond of Rosanne, I mean Anna. She was found on my land and she has been with me since she was released from the hospital. She was in a coma for months. None of the medical staff understood how she survived. Her nose was broken, her neck had two fractures, both her shoulders were broken, cracked ribs punctured her lung and her skull was cracked and her brain swelled. That's why she was in a coma."

Judy Masters starts crying. "Oh my poor little girl." Carolyn looks at her, closer now. Rosanne resembles her. The 'before' sketch resembles her even more but still Carolyn can still see the likeness. *The sketch, oh, she forgot about the 'now' sketch.* She reaches for the folder that they brought. Carolyn found both sketches attached to the mirror, in Rosanne's bathroom and brought them with her. She finds it and holds it up.

"This is my Rosanne, your Anna. This was done a week ago. I know she doesn't look like before but . . ." She doesn't finish her sentence.

They all pass the sketch around. When Henry gets it, he says, "It's her, it's my Anna. Look at her eyes. I'd know those eyes anywhere." They all agreed. "How far is Lawrence. Can we see her tonight?"

Carolyn braces herself. They aren't going to like what she's going to say. "Rosanne, I mean, Anna, is the strongest person I know. But the many months of traction, then the . . . I'm sorry, you don't know, but she was also raped by her attacker. She was so sick, and thin and frail. She guessed but didn't tell us that she was pregnant then she miscarried. The doctors said the baby was about five months, along, so it was assumed the rapist's. She fell apart after losing the baby. What didn't kill her physically almost killed her emotionally. She's still in a very fragile condition. I'm worried how much to tell her. How soon to tell her?"

She stops because Henry is on his feet again. He walks to the doorway, crying. "My Anna, my poor Anna. What have I done to my poor Anna?" Matthew goes to him and is holding him, letting him get it all out. Carolyn can tell that this isn't the first time for them. "My beautiful Anna, it's all my fault. How can she ever forgive me?"

Carolyn looks around for an explanation. *They've a confession from her assailant. So, what does Henry mean?*

Matthew brings him back to the group. Henry is rocking, "I asked her to marry me, the night before. We were so much in love. We were going to be married the following week. We couldn't help ourselves. My poor Anna, it might have been my child that she lost. How can she forgive me?" Henry's head is in his hands.

Matthew explains further. "Henry blames himself because he punched John, her attacker, a couple of nights prior to her disappearance. Henry feels he caused the whole chain of events."

Carolyn understands. "Henry, I don't think you need to worry about her forgiveness. You see, she has always felt that she was married or had a great love but with no actual memories of it. Just a sense of the greatest thing that could happen to two people. She has been longing for you, this whole time. I just don't know if she'll remember any of you."

"What makes you think she won't?" Melinda speaks for the first time.

"Well, the artist that drew that sketch, drew a 'before' sketch erasing all the imperfections caused by the accident. Rosanne just stared at it. She didn't recognize herself." Carolyn finds that sketch and holds it out to them." They all gasp and say that is an exact likeness of her.

"She didn't recognize herself? This is exactly what she looked like." Melinda says. "Oh, but Anna wouldn't think so. This girl is too pretty. Anna would never recognize that in herself. That was her one fault. She didn't see herself as the world sees her."

"That hasn't changed." Carolyn said. "Okay, why don't you all come home with me. In the morning, I'll take you to Rosanne. I mean Anna. I'll just bring you into her hospital room and introduce you by name only, and then see what she says. If she doesn't catch on, then out you'll go. I'll have the hospital psychiatrist give us advice from there. It's not a great plan but I'm not willing to hurt her in any way.

Judy rushes to Carolyn. "Thank God, she has you!" She bends to kiss her on the cheek and hugs her very hard. "You want us all to come home with you? My dear, where will we all sleep? Is there a motel nearby?

Carolyn chuckles. "No, Mrs. Masters. I've a large home. I think if we double up, we can manage. Come, we'll follow you home so you can grab a few things for the road?

Matthew interrupts, "Sheriff? I mean Professor Bailey. Can I use your phone? I need to tell Susan Walker the good news."

The Professor leads him to the office, shows him the phone then returns to the group. Professor James is saying, "Carolyn's brother contacted me about recommending a private detective but I thought it would be a great class project. Professor Bailey heard about the project and called me to ask if he could share it with his class. He didn't know our Rosanne was your Anna Rose, until we gave him details on the Ford truck headlamp."

After a few minutes, Matthew rejoins the group. He goes to Carolyn. "Miss Lewis, I know that you are putting us all up and everything, but would it be too much trouble to add one more? My fiancé, Susan, was the one who was first to know Anna was missing and she was there when her cousin confessed to killing her. I'd sure like it, if she was there to see Anna again with us. She can meet us at home, and she has her own car so I'd go with her."

"Of course, Matthew. I don't see why not?"

Melinda hears this. "If you have your fiancé, can I have mine?"

Matthew says, "So does that mean Mark has finally asked you to marry him?"

"Yes. He did six months ago. It was too soon to say anything. I was just kidding. I'll need to tell him I'm going on a road trip, though."

FORTY-FOUR

Saturday, September 26th, 1936
Lawrence, Kansas

Rosanne cannot wait for Carolyn to come. Even when she was in the hospital the first time, a year ago, Carolyn hardly missed a day. What could have been so important?

Dr. Mason said that Rosanne could sit up and be wheeled to the Colonel's room. He was well enough to receive visitors. Rosanne isn't sure, if he'll want to see her. He hated her in his delusions. Will he remember that? She prays that he doesn't.

The nurse wheels her into his room, right after the breakfast. He's sitting up in bed. He has a meal tray next to him but Rosanne can tell he hasn't touched it.

When he sees her, he smiles. "Rosanne, where have you been? I wanted you to meet my Julia, she was just here. She told me I was mean to you and she told me to apologize. I'm very sorry, Rosanne. I didn't know what I was doing, honest."

"I know you didn't mean it, Colonel. Now why is your food tray untouched? Do you want to get out of here and come home? You must eat, now."

"Rosanne, why are you wearing that collar? I hurt you, didn't I? I'm sorry, for doing that, if I did. Julia said I was a very bad person to you. I don't know why I did it. I love you Rosanne, please, don't be mad at me."

"Now, Colonel, I'll be mad if you don't try to eat something off this tray. Shall I get an aide to come feed you? I'd do it myself, but my neck . . ." She goes to wheel herself around when Carolyn walks into the room with someone. "Carolyn, I'm so glad to see you. The Colonel hasn't eaten. I was just going to call someone to feed him." Carolyn goes to her grandfather, leaving a tall man behind her. Rosanne needs to look up, from her wheelchair to see his face. She hesitates for a second, and smiles. "Do I know you?" She says at last.

Henry doesn't think he can hold it in. "Yes, I think you do. Do you remember me? I'm Henry."

"Yes, Henry, I do remember you. Did you work here at the hospital, the last time I was here?"

"No that isn't it." He smiles a very nervous smile. Rosanne smiles back at him. She knows that smile, that silky voice, those eyes, why can't she put her finger on it.

Rosanne looks at Carolyn, who is fussing with her grandfather's tray. "Carolyn, I'm not feeling very well. Can you call someone for me? I

216

feel a little faint."

Henry runs out to the nurse's station to tell them.

He takes her back to her room, but the nurses get her into her bed. Rosanne says to Henry that she just needs to lay her head down for a moment or two, her head is spinning. The nurse leads Henry out of the room.

A few moments later, there's a faint tap on the door and a small voice says, "May I come in?" Says Judy, "How are you feeling, does your head hurt?" Judy's eyes are near tears. She crosses to Rosanne and puts her hand to her forehead to check for a fever. Rosanne is transfixed. She knows this woman like she knows the back of her hand, but who is she? "My dear, can I get you a glass of water or something?"

"Whhooo are you?" Rosanne is trembling. "I know you. Do you know me?" Judy sheds one tear. "From before . . . my accident?" Judy nods her head.

"My poor sweet child, my name is Judy Masters, but you always called me . . ."

"Ma? Oh, Ma? Is it you, Ma? You are my mother, aren't you?"

Judy can only nod. "Anna, my beautiful girl, I've missed you so much."

"Anna? My name is Anna? Oh, Ma . . . I know you but I don't remember. My head hurts, Ma. Can you call someone?"

"Yes, Anna dear, I don't want to leave you, but I'll get someone. I'll hurry."

Anna is trying to think what is happening. How does she know that woman is her mother without remembering her? Is it like cooking, without remembering ever having cooked? "Oh, my head hurts!" She says out loud.

Dr. Mason comes into the room. "Anna, how are you feeling?"

"My head is killing me. I think I'm daydreaming. I think I just saw my mother and you . . . you, just called me 'Anna'. What is happening?"

"From what I understand, Carolyn has found your family. Your name is Anna Rose Masters and they're all here and want to see you, but . . . not until your head is better and you feel up to it. Okay?"

"Is there something you can give me for my headache? I'd kill for a Bayer Aspirin right now."

"Let's not take it to that extreme. I'll go get you an aspirin. We will give you twenty minutes of rest and we will bring your mother back in. Does that sound, acceptable?"

"Doc, do you know who that man is, I think he said his name is Henry?"

"Yes, Anna, he was very important to you. Do you want to see him again?"

"After my aspirin and rest . . . but before my mother, please."

"You are calling the shots. I'll be right back." He leaves.

Anna closes her eyes. *My name is Anna. My name is Anna. I'm Anna. I'm Anna Rose Masters.* She thinks over, and over, again. The doctor is back with her medicine, and a glass of water. She takes the pills, gladly. "You said my family is here, how many of them are there?"

"I don't know, Anna, I didn't count them but it's quite a few. I'll tell Henry that he has twenty minutes before he can come in. He's waited a year to see you. So, twenty minutes won't kill him." With that, the doctor leaves.

Anna closes her eyes, again. *I have family. My name is Anna. My mother is Judy. Henry has waited a year for me. My name is Anna. What if I don't remember them? Does that stop me from cooking? My head isn't going to get any better, trying to piece this together.*

She lays with her eyes closed and soon dozes off. When twenty minutes have passed, Henry makes the smallest knock on her door then comes in. She doesn't awaken. He goes to her and lowers himself to whisper in her ear. "Smile for me so that my heart will burst with joy, my darling Anna." Without opening her eyes, she smiles. He continues, "I missed you so much, please remember me, my beautiful Anna."

That deep soft sexy voice that she's heard so many times in her dreams is calling her 'Anna'. *If only, when I open my eyes the dream would become real!* She opens her eyes and Henry is next to her. "Henry?"

"Yes my love?"

"I've dreamt of your voice, but every time I woke up, you were gone."

"I'll never leave you again. Do you remember me, darling?"

"I know you, but I've no memories. I've dreamt of you without seeing you. I don't remember Ma, but I knew her. My mind works that way now. I don't remember ever sewing but I can. Some things, you just know, you know. You know?"

"Do you know that you loved me? We were going to be married."

Anna looks down at his hands holding hers, "Henry, my 'accident', do you know what happened to me?"

"Yes. A man named John Walker confessed to killing you. He's in prison for it."

"He . . . also raped me." She says simply. She turns away which hurt her neck, terribly, but she cannot let him see her face. She's so ashamed.

"Anna, look at me, no, look at me." She moves painfully to turn back and look up. "It breaks my heart, what he did to you, but it doesn't change anything I feel for you. Carolyn told me about you losing the baby. Had I known, it would have been ours, Anna. I would have raised that child, whether mine or not, because it was yours. I would love anything that was a part of you, even if the other part was his."

"Oh, Henry, I was so upset when she died! She looked up at me and took one little breath, the poor little thing. She had gray eyes, Henry." She looks at his eyes and realizes, "and so do you! She was ours, yours and mine." She says with such sadness. He starts to cry with his head in his hands. She strokes his hair saying, "It'll be okay." It's all that she can say. She knows his grief, well. She has carried it for seven months now.

He gains control of himself. "Anna, we will have a family still. If we cannot have any other children, we will adopt one or twelve, if you want." She lifts his hand to her lips, and kisses the back of it.

"My Henry, you always knew just what to say." She smiles at him.

He pulls himself together and wipes his eyes with the back of his hand. "I'm being very selfish. There are others waiting to see you. Is your head better? Shall I bring in the next person to see if you know them?"

"Yes, please." She's getting very nervous, like just before a test.

Henry goes to the door and waves to someone. An older man with light blue eyes comes in. He's shy and very hesitant. Anna looks at him. "Come closer, please." He goes to her. "Who are you, sir?"

"My Anna, I'm your ole Pa!"

She smiles at him. "I'd know you anywhere! I swear, I would!"

You remember your ole Pa, Anna?" He's holding her hands, with a look of desperation on his face.

"Pa, I've no specific memories, yet, but I know you." Tears are coming down her face. He kisses her carefully, because of her neck. "Pa, would you have known me? I had so many cuts to my face and breaks to my nose. I was so swollen for so long that I know I'm not the same."

"My Anna, my girl, you are so beautiful, just like before. But I'm seeing you with my heart and not my eyes." He kisses her on the cheek, even more softly this time.

Carolyn has slipped into the room and heard the phrase that *Rosanne had just used, last week, when Joshua was looking at her sketch. She's absolutely a product of this wonderful family.* Carolyn goes to the window to sit on the sill out of the way.

He looks at Carolyn, but says to Anna, "I'll go and let your sister and brother come in." He exits.

Anna looks to Carolyn, "This is too much to take in, Carolyn."

"Do you want to take another break? Does your head still hurt?" Anna starts to shake her head but the pain reminds her to lay still.

"I've waited too long. I want all the holes filled in. I've missed these people, so much. My heart has been sick without them, for so long." She's tearing up again.

Henry has been standing guard at the door. Anna looks to him and smiles, through her tears. He says, simply, "Keep smiling like that, my

Anna, my heart hasn't felt this happy in a whole year."

She holds out her hand to him. He crosses the room in two steps and takes it and kisses it. Carolyn can see the look on Anna's face. She hasn't seen her so happy, EVER! This is what she has wanted, for this beautiful person that's taken her heart as well as her grandfather's and brother's.

Oh, Joshua! She thinks. *I must call him.* She knows that Eddie was on the phone with him last night. He took it with mixed emotions. Of course, he was happy for Rosanne but as he predicted, now he's lost his chance with her forever. Joshua told Eddie that he knew it was a lost cause, the minute the class was on the case. Unfortunately, on Thursday night, Joshua had to go back to the college for his Friday classes and he was on the dance committee so he must to attend it. *Oh, my, it's tonight! I'll miss the event. Eddie will understand.*

Melinda slips into the room. She watches Henry with his Anna. The last words from Romeo and Juliet came to mind.

'For never was a story of more Woe,
Than this of Juliet and her Romeo'

Anna looks different but she'd know her anywhere. "Anna?" she says quietly, not really, wanting to interrupt.

Anna looks up. She ponders the beautiful dark haired short woman in front of her. She has the same bright blue eyes as her father. "Sister? I know you. What is your name?"

She rushes to her side, "I'm Melinda, your <u>little</u> sister. Oh, Anna, this is the happiest day of my life, to see you alive and that happy look on your face. I just want to stand back and look at you. It really is you, isn't it?"

"You tell me, I hardly know. Melinda, I'd like you to meet my other sister, Carolyn. I'm alive today because of her. She found me, paid for all of my medical expenses and has taken me in, when I had nowhere to go."

Carolyn blushes from the attention. "I've met everyone, Rosanne. I mean Anna. This is will be an adjustment for everyone."

Anna suddenly realizes that Carolyn's Rosanne is gone. Now that she's Anna, that she <u>knows</u> that she's Anna, her place in the main house, is no longer an option. "Oh, the Colonel!" She says out loud. Tears fill her eyes, yet, again.

Carolyn is shaking her head. "We will be fine, Anna. It will be okay." Using Rosanne's words, no, Anna's words to ease the pain of others.

Melinda is watching this interchange. *We all owe Carolyn, everything.* "Anna, Matthew wants to come in, are you ready?"

Anna nods, waiting for this next stranger to tug at her heart. A six-foot-two young man walks into the room with Pa's eyes, he goes straight to her and takes the hand that Henry isn't holding.

Anna says, "I know you, but . . . you've changed."

Melinda laughs. "He's grown three inches since you've seen him, Anna. I barely recognize him myself and I live with the guy."

As she says that, Anna can picture Melinda on the couch with a much shorter version of Matthew and ruffing up his hair. "Oh, we were so happy, together, weren't we? I remember you teasing him, messing his hair. He hated when we messed his hair."

Everyone in the room says a different version of: "You remember?"

"Yes, I do. Oh, my god, I remember!" She slightly turns to Carolyn, "And my head doesn't hurt!"

The room is full now, but the Doctor comes in, and makes his way to the bed. "Rosanne . . . I mean Anna Rose, are you doing all right?" He crosses to her and takes her pulse. "This seems very fast for you, young lady. Do you want to take a break?"

"Doc, that's the pulse of someone whose heart isn't just singing but dancing. Can my Ma and Pa, come in? I know we are crowded."

"Anna, if you want, we will pack them in like sardines. There are others here besides them." He walks to the door and motions to her parents and leaves. Henry and Matthew step away and move to the side. Melinda takes Matthew's hand and squeezes it.

Judd and Judy come in together. They each go to a different side, and each take a hand. "We are so happy to have you back. Are you still okay?" Judy asks. "Frank is dying to see you, Anna. Do you have strength left?" She nods slightly. Henry crosses to the door and goes out to get him. As they walk in together, Anna is amazed how much the son resembles the father.

"Anna, my prayers have been answered. I can die a happy man. My Henry has his Anna, back." He says crying unashamed.

Anna turns to him and says, "Don't you dare, Da, you still must bounce your grandchild on your knee." She was quoting her father from the night they engaged her to Henry. They all look around, amazed at what she's remembering.

Matthew speaks up for the first time. His voice has gotten lower than she remembered it. "Anna, do you want to meet my fiancé?"

"Oh, Matthew. Aren't you too young?" They all laugh.

"Anna, I feel that I've lived three lifetimes this year alone."

"Well, bring her in. We aren't sardine level quite yet."

Matthew goes out and brings in a beautiful girl with perfectly coiffured blonde curly hair. Her beauty takes Anna's breath away. "Anna, this is Susan. You met her a week before your 'accident'." Susan nods to Anna. She was clinging to Matthew, at a loss for what to say.

"Susan, it's very nice to see you again. Are we still on for that wedding dress shopping trip? That's if my Henry still wants me?"

All eyes look to Henry in the crowded room. He goes to her side. "Must you ask? My heart died with you and it's come back alive. I want to wait, though. No rushing this wedding. I want it to be the biggest celebration that both EL Dorado and Lawrence have ever seen."

"Then you'll have it on Legacy Plantation. It will be my wedding gift to you both." Carolyn offers. Anna just gasps. Henry bends and gives Anna her first kiss. Very gentle; pain is the last thing he wants to cause her. When they look up, there isn't a dry eye in the room.

"Henry, there's so much to decide. I think I'm getting another headache."

Carolyn jumps down from the window sill. "Okay, wonderful people, that's your cue. Your time is up. She needs to rest. Everyone out. We can come back later. Why don't we go have a long lunch downtown? My treat." She is waving her arms like her ranch hands wrangling her cattle. "Come on, she isn't going anywhere. And when she does, it will be back to the Plantation where you are all staying."

Henry is the last to be pushed out. "Rest up, my darling." He blows a kiss to her, which she pretends to catch and apply to her cheek. He just smiles and shakes his head in disbelief. Carolyn is closing the door.

"Shall I shut the light, Rosanne . . . um, Anna?"

"Can you come here first?" Carolyn goes to her. "I don't want to leave the Colonel. Can I still work for you after I'm married?"

"Sweetheart, you can do anything you want. I was praying that you wouldn't leave me, but you have your whole family in EL Dorado? You can't leave them as you are just getting them back. We will figure something out. I could always use more hands. None of this needs to be decided, anytime soon. You need to be released from here, first. By the way, you learned to cook from your mother. When she got to Legacy Plantation and saw the kitchen, she said she just had to cook. So, she made a huge dinner. It was delicious! Then she and your Pa made us a great big breakfast, this morning."

"My Pa made the coffee and the toast?" Anna asks. Carolyn just nods. "Aren't they just the cutest together? I don't know a more perfect couple."

"I can think of just one other. Sweet dreams, Anna." Carolyn shuts off the lights and closes the door behind her.

FORTY-FIVE

Sunday, September 27th, 1936
In Lawrence, Kansas

Anna woke up feeling wonderful. Yesterday was not a dream. She has her family back. She has her Henry back. Now, if she can just get out of the Hospital. Dr. Mason comes in her room at seven in the morning. He takes her pulse and smiles. "That's more like it. Move your head left; good. Move your head right; good. How does that feel?"

Anna is smiling. "What is the answer that will get me released?"

"The truth will set you free, my girl."

"Have I ever told you that you work too much, Doc? I think you need some time off. Would you like to go to a great party and have a wonderful time?"

"What did you have in mind?" He asks with a raised eyebrow.

"I hear that there's going to be the wedding of the century at Legacy Plantation. Guaranteed good time to be had by all."

"When is this party of all parties?" He's behind her, manually moving her head from left to right. She isn't crying those silent tears of pain.

"I don't know, a girl has to get out of the hospital to plan it. Can you help with that?" She's facing him now and smiling.

"I think that I can, but I must ask two questions first." He's smiling back at her.

"Ask away. I'll answer anything for you."

"Your memory is back?"

"A little, but I knew each and every one of my family, yesterday. Next question?

"Just one more, are you happy?"

"I'm so VERY happy, doc, I didn't think I could ever be this happy."

"Okay, pack your bags, and get out of here. But try to take it easy. I don't want you back here with another relapse."

Anna puts her arms around his neck and gives him a big kiss on the cheek.

"I've to do some things first. I've to go wake the Colonel and tell him that I love him and that he'd better eat the food on his tray, or he's not coming home for the wedding. And, then I must call the main house, for a ride."

A little more than an hour later, she's dressed and ready to leave. Henry and her Ma are there to pick her up. The staff wheels her out to Henry's truck. She climbs in and slides over to the middle seat. Judy gets in next to her. Henry, always the gentleman, assists them both then closes the passenger door. He gets behind the wheel and they're off toward Legacy Plantation.

Judy is holding her hand. She's so happy to have her look-alike daughter back. She's telling her how much she loves Carolyn and Carolyn's house. She goes on and on about each room and she especially loves the spacious kitchen. Anna doesn't have a chance to get a word in, but she loves listening to her happy mother. She closes her eyes and puts her head, on Henry's shoulder and sighs.

Henry looks down at her and says, "That's your happy sigh." Then he reaches for her left hand, squeezes it, then raises it to his lips and kisses the back of it.

"Yes, it is." She turns to her mother and says, "Ma, what has Pa been doing for work this whole time?"

"Mr. Johnson, who owned the Farm, has been wonderful to us. He felt so bad about our loss and so grateful to Matthew for testifying against John Walker and the other two guys that robbed the paymaster's office that he has let us live there rent free. Thanks to Matthew, who returned the two hundred dollars he got for driving at the robbery, they got John's cut of the money and quite a bit from the other guys that were too stupid to move on. I'm very proud of Matthew. He took your disappearance hard but used it to make bad men pay for taking something that didn't belong to them."

"Oh, that's what he meant by living three lifetimes, then? He testified at their trials! But you still didn't answer my question. Has Pa been working?"

"Oh! Yes, sorry, my dear, Mr. Johnson made him a foreman. So, your Pa has been very busy with the different crops. It's not quite like your own farm, but he works it just as hard. Mr. Johnson relies on him for much of the scheduling of plantings, maintenance and harvesting."

"So, what about you and Matthew, Henry? What have you been doing for work now?"

"I've been working under your father. I've taken lots of time off, so your father has me down as a day laborer. Matthew is his assistant. Matthew still plays poker, regularly. The word is out that he's the one to beat. His games are the high-stake games but no one stands a chance against him. Are you keeping up with all that we are telling you? Do you remember everything now?"

"I'm following, so far. Henry, you said that have taken lots of time off, have you been sick?"

Judy answers, "Henry refused to believe you were dead unless he saw your body. He'd leave Frank with us and go for days on end, looking for your body in all the deserted areas, within sixty miles."

"Oh, Henry, when did you stop?" She's squeezing his hand with hers.

"The last time I went out was . . . um." He stops to think.

Judy answers for him. "It was Wednesday morning. Mark Collins went with him. Henry came to pick up Frank on Thursday night."

"So you never stopped looking for me, then?"

"How could I? John insisted that he drove for about an hour and left you for dead, then got lost finding his way back to EL Dorado. He made a deal to lead us to you, in exchange for not going to death row. I was with Sheriff Bailey's detail. He led us in circles, then cried when the sheriff tried to put death row back on the table. I believed him that he didn't know where he took you."

Judy interrupts, "Oh, look, we are back. This is such a beautiful place. Those lovely columns out in front are just gorgeous. Did you know she has a side garden just like we had in Hope? It's all my favorite herbs."

"Ma, that's my garden. Carolyn, had it plowed for me last spring and I planted it all, myself. Do you really like it?"

"I love it, Anna, the flowers are beautiful, too. You did this all by yourself, so soon after your injuries?"

"Yes, ma-am."

Henry parks by the front door. Carolyn rushes out of the house, and takes her by the arm and leads her in and yells, "Surprise!!!" There are about thirty people in the formal Parlor, all, so happy to see her. Melinda is the first one to come to her.

"Anna, I want to introduce my fiancé, Mark Collins. He works at the Camp store."

"I remember you, Mark. I worked for your Uncle at Sally's."

"He's here too, Anna. We are all so happy that you're alive."

Anna leans in to Melinda, "Will you stick with me, in case I blank out on someone? I don't want to embarrass someone if I don't remember them."

Melinda laughs, "Matthew has a pool going with people's names on it that you might forget. He's charging four dollars per square!"

"He's betting that I don't remember someone? He has that little confidence in me?" She loses her smile and looks down at her hands.

Melinda follows her eyes downward, takes her hand, and lifts her chin up, "Your baby brother doesn't take foolish bets. He's 'all in' that you'll know everyone, Anna. We are all amazed at how far you've come." Anna smile returns.

"So when did you and Mark, start . . . um seeing each other? I love the way he looks at you, like you're a queen . . . His Queen! He's in love, you know."

"When you went missing, Susan was the first to call the alarm. She called Mark, who dropped everything and helped us. He was at our side through it all. He was a great comfort to our family. He and Susan organized a fund raiser to get us a different truck. They raised $250 to buy a 1930 GMC truck from McClure's Auto. I think he talked his cousin,

Grant Johnson, to offer Pa work AND free rent. He spent days with Henry and Matthew looking for you, and even more time helping me enjoy living again. I felt so guilty every time I smiled or laughed, without you. He understood, having lost his wife. I felt that God took the best of us because of our wicked ways and I promised that I would be as good a girl as you were. If only God would just bring you back. I would never sin again. Mark helped me figure this all out. He never judged my past or pushed me to give in to temptation. He wanted our Love to be pure. I've never felt anything like this before."

"Oh, sister, we are sharing my room tonight and we are going to talk all night!"

"I'd thought you'd be sharing it with Henry?"

"Spend the night with him, under the same roof as everyone, without being married? How could I do such a thing?"

Melinda leans over to whisper in her ear, "We all know, Anna, that the baby could have been Henry's. When Carolyn told us about the miscarriage Henry broke down and said the baby might be his. Ma and Pa love him so much and saw how he was beside himself with guilt. They love him like a son, Anna, so they comforted him in his grief".

"They all know?" Anna was going to say but she suddenly feels faint. The room starts to disappear before her eyes. She tries to reach for Melinda but cannot see her. The last thing she hears is her sister screaming her name.

Henry is just coming in from parking and he sees Anna start to fall. He rushes to her side just in time to catch her in a dead faint. The whole room goes quiet as he carries her over to the couch. Carolyn runs to get a glass of water and a cool towel, passing Joshua, entering the room with Eddie. Joshua runs to Anna's side. He hasn't met Henry yet, and thinks Henry has done something to her.

"Step away from Rosanne, sir. I'll carry her upstairs." Henry doesn't move. Joshua puts his hand on Henry's shoulder when Henry ignores this ridiculous order.

"Sir! I said back away from Rosanne. Let me take care of her!"

Henry stands up and is taller than Joshua. He looks down at him and says, "If you haven't heard, SIR, her name is Anna and she's to be my wife. I AM taking care of her." With that statement of fact, he's back kneeling at her side. "I think I'll carry her to her room, though, if you can show me the way." He very carefully puts his arm under her neck and under her legs and lifts her. Carolyn is back in the room and missed their whole conversation. Henry looks to her, "I'm taking her to her room. Where is it?"

"This way, Henry, excuse me, Joshua." Carolyn brushes past him to get ahead of Henry. "I thought that this party was a little premature. She hasn't gotten used to being Anna, yet, and she's thrown into a room of full of people from her past. I blame myself. What were we thinking?" Joshua is following them up the stairs.

Joshua asks, "Carolyn, is this her fiancé?" They're at the top of the stairs now.

"Yes, Joshua. This is Henry. Henry, this is my brother, Joshua." She's opening the door to Anna's room, and rushes to turn down the bed, and fluff the pillow. Henry lowers her to the bed, very slowly, again, taking every precaution to protect her neck.

Melinda has followed them up the stairs, and into the room, also. She crosses to Joshua and holds out her hand. "Joshua, I'm Anna's sister, Melinda. We are so grateful to you for calling Professor James. We are so lucky that my poor sister was left on your property, of all places. Joshua, do you think we should call Dr. Mason?"

He looks down at Melinda. "I'm sorry, I just got here and all these strangers are in my home, and Rosanne, I mean Anna, is sick. I just didn't know what was going on." He says that last line to Henry, more than Melinda.

Carolyn says, "Yeah, yeah. All men leave and let us girls get her undressed and comfortable. Joshua, call the clinic and talk with Dr. Mason. I'm sure that the last thing Anna wants is to go back there, so, see if he'll come here, please. Go . . . Go!"

Melinda is leading Henry to the door as Carolyn is pushing out Joshua. As Melinda, closes the door behind them, Carolyn is already at Anna's side. She starts to undress her as Melinda makes sure that her neck is supported. Carolyn looks at Melinda and sees she's silently crying. She puts her hand out to her. "It's going to be okay. That's what Anna always says."

"I know why she fainted. It's my fault." Melinda says with deep guilt.

"Explain." Says Carolyn.

"She didn't know, we all knew that the baby could have been Henry's. She's mortified that we know."

"Rosanne, I mean Anna is much stronger than that. She always talked openly that the baby might not be the rapist's."

"Carolyn, feelings and unknowns aren't absolutes, in front of her parents. Last year, in the beginning of September, she'd never kissed a boy and by the end of September, she was engaged, not a virgin, kidnapped, raped and left for dead with amnesia. My sister, Anna, could barely kiss Henry in public, until the engagement."

"I still don't think that would make her faint, so don't worry yourself." The girls have her in a gown and robe and are putting a cool towel on her forehead when there's a knock on the door.

"It's Judy, can I come in?" She doesn't wait for permission but rushes to Anna's side. Both women step back for her mother to attend to her. The women look at each other and reach out for each other's hands, watching Judy baby her daughter. She's talking very quietly to

Anna, wiping her brow and telling her "It'll be okay."

So, she got that phrase from Judy, Carolyn thinks. Anna starts to come around. "Ma, what's . . . What's going on?" She looks to Melinda. Then looks down and starts to tear up.

Judy lifts her chin, "Anna, we are all here for you, what is wrong, child?"

"Mama, I wasn't . . . I'm so ashamed." She looks down again.

Judy looks at the girls behind her, "Ladies, can I have a moment with my lovely confused daughter?" Carolyn and Melinda walk out of the room and close the door.

"Now, tell your Ma everything." She's caressing Anna's cheek with the back of her hand.

"I can't Mama. I'm too ashamed."

"Then let me tell you, what I know. You were a good girl, Anna. You fell in love hard, with a good man. That kind of love consumes you, I know. But before you can legitimize your love, you are taken from the bosom of ALL who love you. I thank God John Walker was not your first, Anna. You knew the love of your soulmate, first. If the rapist was the first, you would always have a hard time in the marriage bed. Even if you don't remember, I'm sure at the time you thought to yourself that what he was doing wasn't lovemaking. It was an animal in rut. Having Henry first has saved you from always thinking when a man comes to you, he's an animal."

"Ma, how do you know these things? I do remember thinking that, exactly. I did think to myself that he couldn't reach that part of me, where Henry's love went. But, how do <u>you</u> know this?"

"Your father and I were newly engaged when I was raped. That's how I felt. If I hadn't 'known' your father intimately first, I don't think I could have let him touch me, afterward."

"Oh, Ma, I'm afraid. I remember very little of the rape, but I'm afraid it will feel like that again. Henry deserves better than having a terrified wife on her wedding night."

"So, don't wait until your wedding night." Anna cannot believe her ears. Her Ma is telling her to . . . "Anna, I've lived through this, already. I didn't have amnesia for a year, but it was an animal that raped me. I cried myself to sleep many nights reliving it. My Ma told Judd that I wouldn't go through with the wedding because of it. He came to me and . . . made me relive a different memory. I haven't cried about that rapist since."

"Ma, about your attacker, did you know the man? Was he caught?"

"No, Anna. I didn't know him. I was alone in the barn on my father's farm and he wandered in looking for food. I said that I would make him something, but he decided that he wanted something else, first. He was never found again."

"I'm so sorry, Ma. How long afterward did you and Pa get married?"

"Well, we got married a month later and you were born about eight months after that. Your Pa never questioned if you were his or not. He just loved you from the very start."

"So I might be the rapist's?" Judy nods. Anna is quiet for a moment. "I always thought that Pa loved me best, though."

"Well, my little one, who do you look like?" Judy smiles and Anna remembers what Henry said. He'd love anything that was a part of her.

"Ma, my little girl had Henry's gray eyes. She lived long enough to take one breath. I just knew she wasn't the rapist's. How I knew, I don't know. She's in Carolyn's family plot. I'd like to take you and Henry to meet her."

"I'd love to meet my granddaughter. Did you name her?"

"No, Ma. I couldn't. That would have made her too real and I hurt so bad as it was. I would like to name her, though. Is it too late?"

"Of course not, my dear, it's never too late." They embrace and cry on each other's shoulder for comfort for a few moments.

As they pull apart and dry their tears, there's a knock on the door. Henry announces, "Dr. Mason is here." And he opens the door for the doctor to come in.

Anna looks at him, and gives him a timid smile. "False alarm, doc, I'm fine. I just moved too fast after bending over." She swings her legs over the side of the bed and goes to stand up. She's slightly light headed but makes it to her feet. "I'm sorry that they got you all the way out here for nothing. As long, as you are here, though, you should join the 'Anna's Alive' party, downstairs. I was just going down, myself." She takes a step forward but Henry blocks her path.

"Henry, I'm fine, please get out of my way."

"Anna, I just thought that you'd like to get dressed first, darling." Henry smiles at her.

She looks down and for the first time sees that she was put into a nightgown and robe. "Who undressed me?" She looks around.

Henry says, "Don't look at me! Please examine my Anna, Doc. She still seems a little off, if you know what I mean."

Judy says, "Anna Rose, let the Doctor look at you, please, to be on the safe side. Henry and I'll be right outside the door." She takes Henry's hand and pulls him out and closes the door behind her.

Anna smiles at Dr. Mason. "Did I fool you, even a little?" He smiles back and slowly shakes his head no.

On the other side of the door, Judy is still holding Henry's hand. She whispers, "Henry, I just had a serious talk with Anna and you need to help her through this."

He was about to object but she put her hand up to silence him. "She's worried that she'll be terrified of you on your wedding night. My advice to her was 'don't wait until the wedding night'. I don't believe I said it either but it's what I had to do to get over my rape. I'll let Anna tell you the rest of the details, if she wants. But what I'm saying is love her Henry, make love to her like you did on the night of the engagement." She lets go of his hand, and shakes her head. "I've just said more than I ever thought possible! We will never speak of this conversation. I won't look at you and STOP looking at me. I'm going downstairs." With that, she smooths her hair back into her bun and rushes down the stairs.

Henry just shook his head after her, and says aloud. "What a woman!" He leans up against the hallway wall, thinking. Did I just hear her, right? She said that I need to make love to her like it was our engagement night. Wow! I thought that it would be best to wait until after the wedding. Maybe, long after, if Anna isn't ready. What do I know?"

The door opens and the Doctor walks out. "She's fine, I think the excitement of the surprise party just got to her. I'm going to make myself a plate and talk with Carolyn. I'll examine her again, in an hour or two. She wants to go downstairs. She's dressing now." He goes to the landing and heads down.

"Thank you, doc." Henry calls as he resumes his leaning on the wall of the long hallway that divides the upstairs.

A few moments go by and Anna opens the door. "Good. Henry, can you do my zipper? I'm having the dickens of a time." She's wearing the royal blue dress that she just bought with Carolyn that looks perfect with her fair complexion. She turns around to show him the zipper is undone to her waist.

He starts to zip it up, slowly and leans in to whisper in her ear. "This is a gorgeous color on you. Promise that you'll let me unzip it, also." He stops zipping and is kissing the back of her neck and his hand is inside the back of her dress touching her warm smooth skin. She steps back into the room and Henry follows and shuts the door. She turns to him and their lips meet hesitantly. This is their first passionate, no-neck-collar, no-family-members-watching kiss, in almost a year. She leans into him.

"Henry, I don't . . . ," before she can finish her sentence he pulls away, but stays in place.

"Anna, I'm sorry, forgive me. I just miss you so much." His hands are caressing her face while he searches her eyes. "I never want to hurt you."

She puts her arms around him and pulls him closer. "Henry, you didn't let me finish my sentence. I don't want to stop. I don't want to mingle with those people downstairs, as much as I love them and miss them. I just want you!" He's covering her face with kisses, so happy to hear these words from her.

"We must go downstairs, my darling. We will get our chance, and soon. Let me come to you, here, tonight. I can sneak in and I can just hold you in my arms like I've dreamt, so many times."

"Tell me, about this dream, Henry." She still has her arms around him.

"One year ago today, we got engaged and I told you that my dream was to make love to you, every night, then fall asleep with you in my arms and wake to find you still in them."

"Then why are we waiting to get married? We have our family and friends here now. Let's call a preacher and have him say the words. I don't want or need a fancy wedding. I need my Henry, because your dream is my dream, too."

"Anna, this isn't something that you should joke about."

She turns around, "Henry, zip up my zipper, now, please." He does as he's told. She reaches for the door and opens it. "Come, Henry, we must call and find us a Preacher!!" She doesn't wait for him but practically runs down the stairs.

"Carolyn, where is Carolyn?" She goes from room to room. She finds her in the sitting room with Joan and Petro from the grocery store. Anna nods to them. "Oh, there you are, do me a huge, huge, favor?" Anna says as she pulls Carolyn to her feet. Carolyn nods, hesitantly.

"Call Pastor Jonas and see if he'll come to the party and marry Henry and me? Offer to give him a big donation if he comes right away, I beg you."

Carolyn is staring at Anna. *Is this the girl always asking her not to spend money? She looks so excited and glowing.* "Anna, you were just faint, and you just found Henry, are you sure?

"As sure as my name is Anna Rose Masters, soon to be Anna Rose Harrick! Please Carolyn, look, I'm saving you on that big wedding you offered."

Henry has finally caught up with Anna. "Anna, what are you doing?" She looks up at him, smiles and blows him a kiss. He catches it and puts it to his cheek. "That doesn't answer my question?"

Carolyn answers it. "She wants Pastor Jonas here to marry you both, today!" Carolyn cannot believe that in two days, her Rosanne is changed to Anna Rose Masters and now she wants to change her name to Anna Rose Harrick, just like that. Carolyn says, "Is that what you want, Henry?"

Henry smiles at his Anna. "I asked her to marry me one year ago today and I don't want to wait another minute. Call the Pastor, and make me the happiest man alive."

Anna rushes to him and kisses him, then turns back to Carolyn, "What are you waiting for, Carolyn?"

"I don't know, Anna. Are you sure?" Anna goes back to Carolyn.

"I love him, so bad that it hurts not to be with him. Carolyn, all that you have done for me, I can never repay you, but . . . I've never asked you for anything, have I?"

"Never."

"I'm begging you, please. Pastor Jonas will only come if you call him. Pretty please?"

Carolyn puts down the plate she was holding and walks the dining room. She lifts the receiver and asks to be connected to Pastor David Jonas. She smiles as she waits on the line. "This is the most absurd thing I've ever done, Anna."

Her attention is back on the line as she hears the call ringing on his end. He answers, "Pastor Jonas, this is Carolyn Lewis. Oh, I'm very good, Pastor. My grandfather has been ill and, well, he'd like to make a good faith donation to help him with a speedy recovery. The only thing is, Pastor, you need to come to Legacy Plantation today, to receive it. It's a very large check. Oh, you can come out, at two p.m.?" She looks at her watch. "Great, thank you Pastor. Oh, Pastor, there's one other thing. The Colonel would like for you to do one small favor for the donation. A simple service. What kind? Well, a marriage, for Rosanne. No, it's not to Joshua. It's a long story. She knows who she is now. I'll explain it all when you get here. See you at two, Pastor? Okay, see you then." She hangs up the phone and smiles.

Henry has new respect for Carolyn's commanding nature. "Very impressive, Carolyn. Okay, my Anna, I love that dress, is it wedding appropriate?" He leans in to whisper. "It's something blue, and I think you made a promise to me about that zipper."

Anna looks down at her dress. It's the very best dress that she's ever had and she feels beautiful in it. "It's a good wedding dress, but I'd like to do a little more with my hair. Where is Susan? Wait! I think we need to make an announcement to our guests!"

She takes Henry by the hand and hurries to the Front Parlor, where almost everyone is gathered. She walks to the center of the room, and claps her hands loudly so everyone stops chatting, and looks to her.

"Everyone, can I have your attention, please? You have come such a long way, and then had to watch me faint and disappear for almost an hour. I think we owe you something for being so patient. Ma? Where is Ma? Good." She looks around the room. "Pa, where are you? There you are, good. Everyone, I'm so very happy to announce that at two o'clock this afternoon, you'll all be Witnesses to Henry and me getting married!" Everyone screams, shouts or runs up to congratulate them.

Henry looks down at his clothing, and thinks, *I can't get married in these!* He looks at his wristwatch. It's a little past noon. He sees Joshua in the crowd and goes to him. As he about to tap him on the shoulder to get his attention, he remembers Carolyn saying, 'No, it's not Joshua'. *Did he have designs on Anna? That would explain the business when she fainted. Okay, that might complicate things.*

"Joshua?" Joshua turns around, "I've a big favor to ask. I didn't bring any good clothes. Do you have anything, I can borrow? I'm a little taller but there isn't time to go shopping. You'd be doing your Rosanne a huge favor. She doesn't deserve to be married to a guy in a poor man's outfit."

Joshua just looks at him for a minute. *Rosanne – no, Anna wants this. She told me that she had someone out there that loves her deeply. This is that someone.* He looks at Anna and sees how happy she is, this is what she has been waiting for. *I can't be a sore loser and deny her groom a decent attire.* Not when he has a closet filled with clothing appropriate for the Groom. "Okay, Henry, let's go see what we can do for you."

FORTY-SIX

Sunday, September 27, 1936 cont'd
In Lawrence, Kansas

There's a whirlwind of activity to get ready in a less than two hours for the wedding ceremony. Joshua is outfitting the Groom, Matthew the best man and the father of the Bride. Henry and Judd are three inches taller than Joshua and Matthew is four. Luckily, Joshua's tailor leaves a large hem when he hems his pants and Judy and Anna quickly let down the seam and baste stitch re-hem them. Melinda irons the seam in place. While Anna is quickly sewing, Susan is taking a curling iron on and off the stove to give Anna the look like the one she wanted a year ago. Thank God, her hair has grown out, Anna thought.

Judy fits in a dress from Carolyn's closet, as well. On Carolyn, it was below the knee, but Judy being six inches shorter, it is nearly formal. Judy feels like a queen! Carolyn also lends Anna a tiny royal blue cap that had a large blue veil in the front. It's beautiful, but most important, it allows her beautiful new curls to show.

Melinda comes into Anna's bedroom wearing a large smile and a beautiful heart-shaped cameo necklace. Anna stares at Melinda's neck. Melinda nods, waiting for Anna to put the memory together.

"That's Henry's grandmother's. Why do you have it?"

Melinda smiles. "You left it on the dresser the day you disappeared. I held it, night after night crying and praying that you would come home to wear it again. Thank God, I thought to grab it before we came here. Here, it's your something 'old.' So, the dress is 'new', the hat is both 'borrowed' and 'blue', so we got it all covered." Melinda takes off the cameo and puts it around Anna's neck, and kisses her cheek. "and my prayer is answered."

Carolyn looks at the time. "You are radiant! I'll go and wait for the Pastor. I think we have everything set up down there. I'll come and get you when it's time." She kisses Anna and heads downstairs.

"Melinda, can you go check on the men and see if they're set?"

"I did on my way here. I didn't show Henry the cameo. I wanted you to surprise him by wearing it. He never knew that it was home on your dresser and I did want not add to his pain by giving it back. The men are ready and looking wonderful."

Judy turns to her daughter and sighs, hesitant about telling her daughter something. "Anna, Carolyn offered all the men jobs here on the Plantation, so that you can stay with the Colonel, and we can be with you. It was a very generous offer. I don't know if your Pa is going to accept it or not. He loves working for Grant Johnson. Matthew doesn't want to leave EL Dorado and his Susan." She clears her throat and continues. "Melinda and Mark will be getting married there, also. I think we will stay the winter, here with you, at least, if Pa doesn't accept the offer." Anna was looking at the cameo, in the mirror but turns to face her Ma.

"Ma, I don't want the family separated." She starts to tear. Judy and Melinda rush to her side.

Melinda starts, "Anna, Mark has his own home and he offered for Ma and Pa to move in with us, as my wedding present. Susan's family want to give Matthew and Susan their own home, in EL Dorado, when they're married. Matthew will attend the University, next fall. Over the winter he's going to study and take the entrance exams. We all continued with our lives. We didn't want to, without you, but it happened."

Judy continues, "Anna, in case you didn't know it, EL Dorado is only about an hour and a half drive from here. That's not far. Mark has a phone in his house and we can talk whenever you want. But, I repeat, we will spend the winter here at Legacy, if we don't take the job offer."

"That's good, Ma. I didn't realize EL Dorado was that close, I guess. I cannot believe her generosity. Carolyn is my Guardian Angel put here on earth. I've never understood why she has been so good to me. I was so desperate and in pain when I woke up in the hospital. The physical pain wasn't the all of it. I felt wrenched from all that I loved with the bonus of not being able to grasp who I was. Carolyn's loving presence was what saved me when I was at that low point. Then after I lost my sweet baby, the Colonel sat with me and saved me from total despair. I owe my life to this family, many times. They've never asked anything from me. I started taking care of the Colonel just because he responded to me."

There was a small knock on the door. It was Carolyn. Anna rushed to her and kissed her. "I'll say for the millionth time, 'what have it done to deserve you' !!" Carolyn was taken aback by this new show of sudden gratitude.

"Anna, I've a visitor for you. He wanted to see you before you walked down the aisle." She opens wide the door. The Colonel is standing in the threshold, smiling.

"Colonel, you are out of the hospital? I'm so glad that you are here! Are you well enough to be here?" She looks at Carolyn for the answer.

"When Doc heard that the wedding was at two, he called the clinic and arranged the Colonel's release. He has to go back tonight."

"Rosanne, Carolyn told me the good news. I'm so happy you've found the love you always knew was out there." Anna rushes to him and kisses both cheeks. The Colonel blushes.

Anna turns to her mother, "Ma, do you think Pa would mind, if BOTH he and the Colonel walk me down the aisle?"

Judy smiles, "I think he'd be honored. Let me go ask him."

Carolyn beams with tears in her eyes, "Either way, Colonel, we must get you into wedding attire. Come with me. Joshua is picking out a proper outfit from your closet, as we speak."

As they leave, Anna goes to her bed and sits, down. "Too much is going on." Melinda goes to her side. "Are you well, Anna? Did you want to lay down for a few minutes?"

"And mess my hair? Not on your life, sister, not on my life, either!" They both laugh. Another knock on the door and Judy re-enters.

"I was right. Your father is honored to have the Colonel assist him in giving you away. He said that he's very proud of you to have offered this to the patriarch of this wonderful family."

"I knew Pa would be fine with it. It's past two, isn't it? Is the Pastor here yet? I'm getting nervous." She sighs, "The worst part is that it's been too long since I've seen Henry!"

Her mother laughs. "Anna, may you feel this way as I do, when you are my age and beyond." Then she adds, "You, too, Melinda. This is every happily married mother's prayer for her children."

Another knock on the door, happens. Anna says, "My door has never had this much wear! Come in."

Carolyn is back. "Anna, it's time. The Pastor is here. I've explained the situation to him. All the men are downstairs. Are you ready?"

"I've never been more ready!" She stands up. "Time to marry my Henry!"

Carolyn, Judy, Melinda and Anna go down the stairs and in the front entryway meet up with the Colonel and Judd and Matthew. Judy and Carolyn both kiss Anna then go into the Front Parlor and take their seats in the front row. Henry is waiting with the Pastor in front of everyone.

Suddenly, music starts and Anna raises an eyebrow. Matthew explains, "Susan is classically trained on the piano. This is our cue, Melinda. Anna, I love you." He, too, kisses her cheek as Melinda hands her a large lovely bouquet of flowers, from Anna's own garden, and then takes a similar but smaller one for herself. She links arms with Matthew. They slowly walk down the aisle, to the beat of the music. When they get to the aisle's end, Matthew lets go of her arm, and they separate and stand on opposite sides.

The music of the Wedding March begins. Judd offers Anna his arm and then she offers the Colonel, hers. She's still able to hold her flowers in the middle and they start their descent down the aisle. Anna thinks her face will break from smiling so wide, but she couldn't stop it if she wanted to. When they reach Henry, the music stops and the Pastor asks, "Who gives the bride to her groom?"

The Colonel and Judd both answer, "We do." And both kiss her cheek at the same time. They step back and take their seats. Henry holds out his left hand and Anna steps forward to take it with her right. Henry is wearing a nervous smile until he notices the cameo around Anna's neck. His eyes go wide and a true smile takes its rightful place. He'd forgotten all about his Grandmother's cameo. Anna is beaming and her eyes are brimming with happy tears.

The rest of the ceremony is lost on Anna. She's smiling, and talking in a dream-like state. Her gaze almost never leaves the gaze of Henry's. It's as if no one else is in the room. Finally, the Pastor says, "Henry, you may kiss your bride." As they do so, the room explodes with applause and Susan is playing music again. They turn to their friends and family.

Joshua is in the aisle behind them. He can only take a few quick pictures with his new Eastman Kodak Bantam camera, because Anna and Henry are suddenly surrounded by all the guests. She's holding Henry's hand and doesn't want to let go, but they're being hugged and tugged in all directions. It takes a few minutes for everyone to settle down before Henry is at her side, again.

Sparkling Grape juice is being served, all around, since Kansas is still officially a 'dry' state. Henry and Anna link arms to drink. He kisses her after they swallow. He cannot believe this, and, like Anna, feels that he's dreaming it all. He prays that he doesn't ever wake up!

Matthew approaches Anna and Henry and says, "Susan and I've a little surprise for you. Can you come with me?" They follow Matthew to the Front Parlor where Susan is sitting at the piano, again. Matthew turns to his sister, "I hope you remember this." Matthew looks to Susan and asks, "Ready?" Susan nods and starts to play the Cole Porter song made famous in the movie 'The Gay Divorcee'. Matthew smiles and starts singing *Day and Night*. Melinda is holding Mark's hand while watching. She lets go of his hand and sits next to Susan and joins Matthew in the last verses just like she did just a few days before Anna's engagement.

Anna is crying very happy tears as her Henry takes her in his arms for their first dance as man and wife. Everyone is surrounding the happy couple who're unaware of anyone else in the room.

Carolyn and Joshua recognize the song as the one Anna remembered in her dream. Joshua takes a few more pictures of Anna and Henry, who are gazing in each other's eyes. Joshua understands now that he didn't stand a chance. His Rosanne, now Anna, is so very happy in her husband's arms.

The rest of the afternoon flies by. Henry tries to stay at his beaming Bride's side. As evening approaches, most of the EL Dorado guests leave for home, but wish the couple all their best. The Colonel is taken back to the hospital knowing that his beloved Rosanne is happy. Anna doubts that he'll ever remember to call her Anna.

Anna is beginning to get nervous, again. Her wedding night is soon approaching. She's trying to recall her mother's words. 'He made me relive a different memory.' She knows Henry can do that for her.

Carolyn approaches Anna and holds out her hand for her to take it. As Anna, does, Carolyn puts a set of keys in her hands. "What are these for?" Anna asks.

"These are the keys to the first little two-bedroom house that the Colonel built for his Julia. It's been abandoned for years but I had Joseph, Jose, and their wives clean it out and put fresh sheets on the bed. It's your Honeymoon Suite, my darling." Carolyn smiles. "Did you think I was going to let you honeymoon in a bedroom next to mine? How would I get any sleep? You know how I love my sleep, Anna. If you are comfortable there, you can stay in it as long as you'd like. Henry has accepted my offer of work, so you'll need place of your own. I'm being very selfish here, Anna. This way, you aren't far from my every beck and call just like before." She winks at Anna.

"Carolyn, I'm beyond words, right now."

"Well, then 'wordlessly' go upstairs and pack yourself a little bag, and go on your honeymoon. We will all be down here to give you two a proper send off. Go on. Melinda, maybe you'd better help your sister. She looks flummoxed."

Melinda takes her up the stairs and they manage to get a bag packed in a short time. Henry has his little packed bag and is waiting for her at the front door. His truck is outside to take them. She goes straight to him and takes his hand. They turn to the loved ones surrounding them. Anna is blushing. She knows, they know, what they're going to do. She cannot look any of them in the eye. Henry sees her discomfort and says, "My Anna is blushing, so I think this is Good-night."

He opens the door and he pushes Anna through it gently. Everyone behind them is yelling well-wishes. Matthew and Melinda are whistling and yelling "Woo Hoo! Go Henry, Go Anna!"

Once in the truck Anna turns to Henry, "If they're this bad now, what are they going to be like in the morning?"

Anna knows where the cabin is located, and leads him to it. Once there, Henry unlocks the door and swoops down to carefully carry her over the threshold.

He goes back to the truck for their bags. Anna is surveying the place. She notices that the bedrooms are on opposite sides of each other in this home. She remembers that when Henry wanted Da with them in the two-bedroom hut, he was concerned about the sounds of their lovemaking waking him up with the rooms sharing a thin wall. She smiles. This layout will work quite nicely. "They did a nice job on the place." She runs her finger over several surfaces, finding everything clean. "I think this will do very well, for our first home, don't you? I love that the Colonel built it for the love of his life, his Julia. You should hear how he talks about her, Henry. I think he's as in love as we are. I say 'is' because most of the time, the Colonel thinks she's still alive."

"I know that feeling!" He's right behind her and as she turns to face him, his lips were on hers. She responds with passion, but Henry breaks away. "Anna, we have the rest of our lives together. I promise you, I'll do only what you tell me to do."

Anna takes a step back, and smiles. "I'm in charge?" He nods. "This day just keeps getting better!" Then she blushes at the possibilities.

Henry's expression now changes. "Now, I'm scared. You'd better be easy on me. I, too, have been through a lot this last year, and the last couple of days!"

"Oh, Henry, I'm confident that we will both survive quite nicely. Do you trust me?" Anna walks back to his arms but he holds her at arm's length.

"Completely! Do you trust me?"

"I'm not so sure, Henry. I didn't even know you, two days ago. This is happening so fast." They're both laughing at her joke. Her brown eyes are twinkling.

His love for her is overwhelming. He swoops down, picks her up and gently carries her to the bed. She starts to undress him and he's kissing her. Henry looks in her eyes and a smile slowly spreads across his face. Anna smiles back. Anna says "I've been waiting to feel your smile in my heart for so long! I knew you were out there, my one true love. Tell me you love me, too."

"Oh, Anna. I do love you, so very much!" They each know what to do and how to do it, even though they only had one night together and it was a year ago. Henry can tell that she has no more need of words, no need of reassurances, other than his constant, 'I love you so very much,' which he cannot help but repeat. They're as one, and both reach their highest point at the same time.

After they're both spent, they fall asleep, unclothed, and wrapped in each other's arms. At first light, Henry stirs. He turns to his Bride and sighs his 'happy sigh'. They did it, she's still in his arms! He kisses her cheek to wake her. As the new Mrs. Henry Harrick opens her eyes, Henry says, "Good morning, Anna darling. You are finally mine, forever. You are my Anna At Last!"

THE END

ABOUT THE AUTHOR

Cherisse Marie Havlicek lives and writes in the beautiful town of Bridgman, Michigan halfway between Grand Rapids, MI and Chicago, IL. Raised in the suburbs of Chicago, she fell in love and married an Chicago Police Officer in 1985 and when he retired with thirty-three years on the Force in 1999, they had a seven-year-old boy, Arthur, and a two-year-old girl, Alisse and it was off to Michigan, where they had been coming up on weekends for decades! She has worked in many different fields: Hairdressing, Interior Landscaping, Juvenile Court, and in Michigan she worked at a daily Newspaper where she went from a Route manager to Single Copy manager to the top producer in the Advertising Dept. while raising her children, attending their sports activities while also taking care of her husband's elderly mother and disabled cousin.

After her husband was diagnosed with Lewy Body Dementia with Parkinson's, she realized that she could no longer work full time out side of the home. She sold antiques at a local store but even that took her away from home too much. In September of 2016, her grown son, Arthur, found Chapter One of a book she started in high school and gave her grief about not finishing it. She wrote the next forty-five chapters in eight months and her first novel *ANNA AT LAST* was complete. She didn't stop there, though. She has written two more installments in the A Present / Past Saga series - *THE LEWIS LEGACY* and *JUSTICE FOR JOSHUA* and has written a Children's Christmas story called *A SILENT NIGHT*. These works will soon be available for purchase. She, obviously, is making up for lost time.

You can connect with her on her Facebook page:
Author – Cherisse M Havlicek